MW00529602

RECKONING

RECKONING

A TY DAWSON MYSTERY

BARON BIRTCHER

OPEN ROAD

INTEGRATED MEDIA
NEW YORK

ISBN: 978-1-5040-8651-6

Published in 2023 by Open Road Integrated Media, Inc.
180 Maiden Lane
New York, NY 10038
www.openroadmedia.com

This one's for
my Mom

RECKONING

"The wheel is turning and you can't slow down
You can't let go and you can't hold on
You can't go back and you can't stand still
If the thunder don't get you then the lightning will."

—The Wheel
(Lyrics by R. Hunter; Music by Garcia/Kreutzmann)

"What loneliness is more lonely than distrust?"

—George Eliot

PRELUDE

A TRANSITIVE NIGHTFALL

NO CHILD IS brought into this world with any knowledge of true evil. This they learn over the passage of time. In my experience as a sheriff, and as a rancher, I have found this precept to be true.

Time passes nevertheless, even if it passes slowly. Here in rural southern Oregon, sometimes it seemed as if it hadn't moved at all, advancing without touching Meriwether County, except with glancing blows.

That is, until the day it caught up with us all and came down like a goddamn hammer.

PART ONE

DEAL

CHAPTER ONE

ORDINARILY, AUTUMN IN Meriwether County would come in hard and sudden, like a stone hurled through a window. But this year it snuck in slow and mild, lingered there deceitfully while we waited for the axe to come down.

The sky that morning was turquoise, empty of clouds, the altitude strung with elongated Vs of migrating geese and a single contrail that resembled a surgical scar, the narrows between the high valley walls opening onto a broad vista of rangeland some distance below. I had expected ice patches to have formed on the pavement overnight, but the weather had remained stubbornly dry, even as temperatures closed in on the low thirties. I tipped open the wind-wing and let the chill air blow through the cab of my pickup as I stretched and drank off the last dregs of coffee I had brought for the long southward drive from the town of Meridian.

I had received a phone call at home the night before from an unusually distressed KC Sheridan. I had known KC for as long as I could remember, a pragmatic and taciturn cattleman whose family history in the area dated back to the late 1800s, much like that of my own. Three generations of Sheridans had stretched fence wire, planted feed-grass, and run rough stock across deeded ranchland that measured its acreage in the tens of thousands, and whose boundaries straddled two separate counties, one of which was my jurisdiction.

But the decade of the '70s thus far had not been any kinder or gentler to cowboys than to anyone else, and KC and his wife, Irene, had found themselves increasingly subject to the fulminations and intimidation of both local and federal government. While the Sheridan ranch had once numbered itself among a dozen privately held agricultural properties in the region, KC now found himself surrounded on three sides by a federally designated wildlife refuge that had swollen to encompass well over three hundred square *miles*, a bird sanctuary originally conceived under the auspices of President Theodore Roosevelt's White House. All of which would have been perfectly fine and acceptable to the Sheridan family, given the understanding that the scarce water supply that ultimately fed into the bird sanctuary belonged to the Sheridans by legal covenant, as it had for nearly a century.

I turned off the paved two-lane and onto a gravel service road, headed in the direction of the ridgeline where KC sat silhouetted against the bright backdrop of clear sky, mounted astride his chestnut roping horse. KC climbed out of the saddle as I parked a short distance away, switched off the ignition, and stepped down from my truck. KC trailed the horse behind him as he moved in my direction, took off his hat, and ran a forearm across his brow, then pressed it back onto his head. His hair and his eyes shared a similar shade of gunmetal gray, and the hardscrabble nature of his existence as a rancher had been recorded in the deep lines of his face.

"What the hell am I supposed to do about these goings-on, Sheriff?" KC asked and cocked his brim in the general direction of a reservoir that was the size of a small mountain lake. Two men wearing construction hardhats were surveying a line on the near shore where a third man studied a roll of blueprints he had unfurled across the hood of his work truck.

"Is that who I think it is?" I asked.

"They aim to fence off my water. My cows won't last a week in this weather."

"Have you talked to them, KC?"

He nodded.

"'Bout as useful as standing in a bucket and trying to lift yourself up by the handle. It's the reason I finally called you, Ty. I didn't know what else to do."

The vein on KC's temple palpitated as he cut his eyes toward the foothills and spat.

"I'll have a word with them," I said. "You wait here."

A wintry wind had begun to blow down from the pass, pushing channels through the dry grass and the sweet scents of juniper and scrub pine. A harrier swept down out of a cluster of black oaks and made a series of low passes across the flats.

I averted my eyes as the sun glinted off the US Fish and Wildlife shield affixed to the driver-side door of a government-issue Chevy Suburban. The man studying the blueprints didn't bother to lift his head or look at me as I stepped up beside him.

"Care to tell me why you and your men are trespassing on private ranch land?" I asked.

The man sighed, scrutinizing me over the frames of a pair of steel-rimmed reading glasses. He had a face that put me in mind of an apple carving, and a physique that resembled a burlap sack filled with claw hammers.

"Who the hell are you now?" he asked.

"Ty Dawson, Sheriff of Meriwether County. That's the name of the county you're standing in."

He took off his reading glasses and slipped them into his shirt pocket, hitched a work boot onto the Suburban's bumper and offered me an approximation of a smile.

"Well, Sheriff, I'm with Fish and Wildlife—that's an agency of the federal government, as I'm sure you're aware—and I have a work order that says I'm supposed to put up a fence. And that's exactly what me and my crew are doing here."

I gestured upslope, where KC Sheridan stood watching us, his arms crossed in front of his chest.

"You're on that man's private property," I said.

The government man made no move to acknowledge KC.

"I don't split hairs over those types of details, Sheriff. The work order I've got lays out the metes and bounds of the line, and me and my crew just install the fence where it says to. It ain't brain surgery."

"Scoot over and let me have a look at that site map."

"I oughtta radio this in."

"You do whatever you think you need to," I said. "But do it while I'm looking at your map."

He lifted his chin and looked as though he was conducting a dialogue with himself, then finally stepped to one side. I studied the blueprint for a few moments, looked out across the rock-studded range and got my bearings.

"Looks to me like the boundary line for the bird refuge is at least a hundred yards to the other side of this reservoir," I said. "Your map is mismarked."

"The agency doesn't mismark maps, Sheriff."

"They sure as hell mismarked this one. You need to stop your work until this gets sorted out."

"That's not going to happen."

"Care to repeat that? There's clearly been a mistake."

"No mistake. You need to step away, Sheriff."

"Let me explain something to you," I said, removing my sunglasses. "It's the law in the State of Oregon that the water that comes up on Mr. Sheridan's property belongs to Mr. Sheridan. *Period*. If you fence off his reservoir—especially this late in the season—you're not only stealing his water, you're murdering his herd."

The agency man lifted his foot off the bumper, set his feet wide and faced off with me. He slid both hands into the back pockets of his canvas overalls and rocked back on his heels.

"Now it's my turn to try to explain something to you, Sheriff: I been given a job to do, and I intend to do it. If you don't walk away right this minute and leave me to it, I will be forced to radio this in. Long and the short of it is, the guys who will come out here after me will have badges, too. And their badges are bigger than yours."

"I won't allow you to trespass onto private property, steal this man's water, and kill his livestock."

He glanced at his two crewmen staking the line then turned his attention back to me.

"You going to arrest us?" he asked.

"What is it with you agency people? Why is it that your first inclination is to slam the pedal all the way to the floor?"

"When me and the boys come back out here, it won't just be the three of us no more."

"I'm finished talking about this," I said. "Pack up your gear and go."

I could feel his eyes boring holes into the back of my head as I picked my way back up the incline where Sheridan stood waiting for me.

"I can tell by your stride that you had the same kind of dialogue experience I had with that fella," KC said.

"Bureaucrats with hardhats."

"I ain't no cupcake, Dawson. But you know that those sonsabitches have been tweaking my nose for years."

"Those men are part of a federal agency, KC, make no mistake. If you're not careful, they'll try to roll right over the top of you."

"What do you call what they're doing right now? I don't intend to lay down for it."

"I'm not saying you should."

"What, then?"

"Get on the phone and call Judge Yates up in Salem," I said. "Ask him if he can slap an injunction on these clowns until we get it sorted out."

Sheridan's horse pinned back his ears and began to shuffle his forelegs, responding to the tone our conversation had taken. KC calmed the animal with a caress of its neck, dipped into the pocket of his wool coat, snapped off a few pieces of carrot, and fed it to the gelding from the flat of his palm.

"I'll do it, Ty, but I swear to god—"

"KC, you call me before you do anything else, you understand?"

CHAPTER TWO

YOU STILL PISSED off at me?

What do you think?

You're turning into a real pussy, then, dude.

Says the fool who couldn't find his own dick if it had a bell tied to it.

Screw you.

You better pray that guy you were beatin' on isn't hurt too bad.

He came at me.

What'd you expect the guy to do? You damn near busted his girl's finger trying to get her ring off.

That's what we went in there for. To steal stuff. Get off my butt.

We went in there for the register, asshole. Those people weren't even supposed to be there. I told you to keep 'em boxed up in the corner. That's all. Just keep 'em out of the way for two freaking minutes.

Well, the guy came at me.

You already said that.

Plus, the dude was a cop. I'm just supposed to let him shoot us?

He wasn't a cop. He was a security guard. He didn't even have a gun.

Hell he didn't. What do you call this?

Where'd you get that thing?

I told you. Offa the cop. Security guard. Whatever. I'm not getting rid of it, either, if that's what you're thinking.

You *better* get the hell rid of it. I'm not stacking hard time just 'cause you've got a gun on you now.

Stop being such a whiner . . . It's goddamned dark out here.

You understand the whole back-roads thing, right?

I think my ribs are busted. Front tooth feels loose, too.

It's your own damn fault.

What was I supposed to do?

How about *not* beat the sorry bastard half to death? I keep telling you over and over, all we gotta do is go in easy. Nobody gets hurt, nobody does time.

I heard you already. Shut up about it.

Right there, Shannon. I swear to Christ, that's the kind of attitude that keeps us on the run, you know that? If you wouldn't pull stupid shit like this, we could sleep on real bedsheets once in a while.

You're getting to sound like an old lady.

You think I enjoy driving all night long?

You sure as hell seem to enjoy complaining about it. Seriously, man, that dude landed a couple good ones before I put him down. I think he might've broke something inside me. It hurts when I breathe real deep.

Then don't breathe real deep. What are you smiling about?
Just found something in my pocket. You want a hit of this?
What is it?
Purple acid. Looks like I got a few tabs left.
I thought we already did it all.
We did all of *yours*.
Asshole.
How long you plan on staying mad at me, man?
I don't know. It's hard to tell.
I told you, the goddamn guy came at me. What was I supposed to do?

STOP MAKING that noise, man. You sound like hell, Shannon.
I don't think I can go any further. I gotta lie down. In a real bed.
You're sweating like a pig.
I swear it feels like my rib's gonna bust through my shirt.
Map says there's a town a couple hours up the road. I guess we could probably take a chance with a small-town doctor. At least we're not in Montana anymore.
You gotta stop the car, dude. Seriously. I gotta get some rest, something to eat.
Okay. Jesus. Stop bitching.
I mean it.
Give me a minute to think, goddamnit.

WHAT IS this place?
Hell if I know. Fishing cabins, maybe. I can hear a river running beyond those big trees.
I don't see any lights anywhere. Think anybody's out here?
It's two o'clock in the damn morning in the middle of the damn forest. Who's gonna have lights on?
Why do you have to be like that, man? I was just saying that it doesn't look like anybody's around, that's all. Shit.
You think normal folks do a lot of fly fishing at this time of night?
How the hell would I know? Just pick a cabin, man. I think I'm gonna pass out. I'm not screwing around.

SHANNON. Wake up!
Ow. Goddamn it, stop shaking me. That hurts.
I can't tape up your ribs any tighter'n I already did. And keep your voice down.
I am keeping it down.
Did you see that?
See what?
Car lights, I think.
I was asleep. How could I have seen any car lights? Go back to bed.
Did you at least hear that noise? You had to have heard it.

I told you I was sleeping. Shit.

I swear, I think it was a car. Somebody drove in and parked a goddamned car behind that woodshed over there.

Let me have a look.

Keep back from the window.

Then how the hell am I gonna have a look outside? It's as dark in here as it is out there, man. Nobody's gonna see me through the glass.

There it is again! You see that?

I saw it that time. Looked like a light went on inside that place.

Get the hell down.

What're we gonna do?

We're gonna shut the hell up and wait.

What if they come over here?

They're not gonna come over here.

How the hell do you know that?

'Cause if they wanted to come here, they would've parked right in front of this cabin, not fifty yards away.

Light just went out again.

Where'd they go?

I don't know.

Get down outta that window.

Shhh.

Don't shush me, goddamn it.

You're the one who woke me up.

Just get down outta that window.

I wanna see if—Shit.

What the hell was *that*?

Sounded like a gun.

I know it sounded like a—

There it is again. That's definitely a gun.

Where the hell's it coming from?

That goddamn cabin, I think. I saw the flashes in the window.

Shit, shit, shit.

We gotta get out of here.

Now? Are you out of your mind? What if they spot us?

I'm just saying.

We can't go anywhere until we're sure nobody'll see us.

When's that gonna be?

How the hell would I know that?

Let's just wait 'til we hear the guy leave.

Fine.

Fine.

Go back to sleep.

How'm I supposed to go back to sleep after all that?
Just shut up, okay?
I'm thirsty.
You gotta be kidding me.
What? I'm not allowed to be thirsty now, either?

CHAPTER THREE

I HELPED MY ranch foreman, Caleb Wheeler, buck a load of hay into the loft while we waited for the veterinarian to arrive. One of my breed cows had stopped eating, and we'd tried every remedy we knew, but nothing had worked. I didn't want to risk losing her.

As a result, I was late getting into the station that morning, a little past ten by the time I arrived. Sam Griffin, one of my deputies, sat alone at his desk near the front door, sipping coffee from a Styrofoam cup.

"Where's Powell?" I asked as I pulled the door shut against the brisk wind.

"Answering a call out at the Kinnet place."

"What is it this time?"

"Water company called. Looks like the old coot pried up the cover off his meter box and filled it with concrete again."

The office was still cold inside, in spite of the burnt smell of singed dust blowing out through the furnace vents. I peeled off my gloves, but left on my hat, coat, and muffler as I sat down to thumb through the pile of mail on my desk. I was about to say something about replacing the furnace filter when the phone rang.

Griffin answered it before it had time to ring a second time, and I watched his expression turn grim as he pressed the handset to his ear.

GRIFFIN RODE in my truck with me, and a half hour later, we pulled off the road and onto the single lane dirt track that led to the Catonquin River Resort. The word *Resort* was such a stretch that it nearly constituted fraud, though the river itself was magnificent and home to some of the finest fly fishing in this corner of the state.

I parked at a diagonal outside the swing gate to block the entry to any further traffic until we completed our work inside. Griffin strung crime scene tape between the gateposts while I picked my way through the hip-deep growth of bitterbrush, snowberry, and fern in an effort not to disturb any evidence that might still remain on the roadbed. A cone of pale sunlight shone through a gap in the pine canopy, and the air smelled of humus and loam. The soil beneath my boot soles was spongy from yesterday's rain and gave way under my weight. Any usable evidence that had existed prior to last night had likely been washed away, but anything more recent might still have a chance at preservation.

"Is that you, Sheriff?"

A man's voice called out from inside the seclusion of the old growth, and I climbed up on a stump of deadfall to scan beyond the foliage. I caught a brief glimpse of red plaid moving among the shrubs and waited as the scrape of footfalls on the gravel grew nearer.

"Step off the road," I called out.

I motioned for Sam Griffin to follow me, and we pressed our way together through the boscage. We entered a clearing a short distance further on, where a middle-aged man wearing a red lumberjack coat and a crumpled, moth-eaten cowboy hat stood by himself, packing a wad of tobacco snuff into his jaw. He was of medium height, beardless but for two or three days without a razor, and thick around the middle, like a man who might once have been an athlete. A sheen of perspiration glazed the rounded contours of his face.

"Doug May," he said and slid the tobacco tin into his shirt pocket. "I'm the one who called you."

I introduced myself and Deputy Griffin and asked Doug May to repeat what he'd previously told my deputy on the phone.

"I guess you could say I'm the caretaker around here, but mostly I'm a fly fishing guide," he said. "I was supposed to meet up with Mr. Wehr and take him out on the river this morning."

"You live in one of these cabins?"

"Aw hell no," he said, and spat a stream of brown tobacco juice onto the trunk of a hemlock. "I live in a trailer up there a ways, beside the oxbow. There's only six or seven of the old cabins left standing anymore. Nobody lives out here full-time. Except for me, I guess."

"How did you come to know Mr. Wehr?"

May glanced at his wristwatch, then buried his hands deep into the pockets of his coat. The wind shifted direction and the odor of stale spirits drifted from his pores.

"He's been fishing with me a couple of times," he said.

"Mr. Wehr is one of the cabin owners?"

"No, sir," he said, and I watched the man's posture change. "He's a guest of Mr. Stricklyn's."

"Can you spell that for me?" Sam asked.

I waited as Griffin scratched the name in his notepad. I followed the direction of the fishing guide's eyes as they drifted away from me, toward the river.

"Are you okay, Mr. May?" I asked. "You're looking a little green around the gills."

"Can I just show you where I found the body, Sheriff?"

JORDAN POWELL, my other deputy, pulled in and parked behind my truck about fifteen minutes later. He was trailed by three forensic techs from the Criminal Investigation Division of the Oregon State Police, each wearing coveralls and carrying black canvas bags.

"You got here in a hell of a hurry," I said to the lead CID technician as he followed me to a small cabin where the body had been found.

"Captain always says that Sheriff Dawson don't ask for help unless he means that he wants it *right now.*"

"When you get back to your office, tell Captain Rose he just moved up a few notches on my Christmas card list."

Powell ducked under the yellow tape Sam Griffin had strung across the porch landing and held it for the techs as they passed inside.

"What's the deal, sir?" Powell asked me. "Suicide?"

"Maybe," I said. "Thing is, there's a second bullet hole in the wall behind the couch."

"Sometimes they lose their nerve."

"Sometimes they get murdered by somebody else," I said.

Powell leaned in for a closer look.

"Do you know who the victim is?"

"Clark Wehr," I said, and showed my deputy the Portland Police Bureau ID and badge holder I had already sealed inside a plastic evidence bag.

"The dead guy is a city cop?"

"Detective."

Powell bit his lip and his eyes dropped to the floorboards.

"Shit."

"My thought exactly," I said.

"What do you want me to do, boss?"

I hooked a thumb in the direction of the clearing where Doug May had been pacing circles around the victim's parked car, checking his watch every few seconds, and spraying brown spittle into the woods.

"The caretaker told us that nobody else has been out here for the past several days," I said to Powell. "Why don't you poke around these other cabins anyway, see what you find."

I knelt down for another inspection of the Smith & Wesson .38 that lay on the plank floor beside the sofa, taking care not to disturb it until the techs had shot photos and lifted prints.

From behind me, I heard the front door hinges squeal and got to my feet in time to see the shadow of a tall, broad-shouldered man outlined inside the doorframe. Sunlight streamed through the kitchen window and illuminated his features as he stepped further inside. He was dressed in street clothes, bell-bottom slacks and a wide-collared shirt he had left open at the neck where an ornament that looked like an animal horn dangled from a narrow gold chain. His long hair and mustache were the same shade as his leather jacket, his sideburns meticulously groomed, angled and sculpted all the way to his jawline, more Los Angeles than rural Oregon.

"Did my deputy sign you in?" I asked. "This is an active crime scene."

"The black one told me—"

"Deputy Griffin," I corrected.

"*Deputy Griffin* suggested that you wouldn't mind if I joined you."

"Why would he suggest something like that?"

"Because I'm a cop."

"I was about to turn the scene over to the crims and the coroner," I said. "Why don't you and I move this conversation outside."

Instead of moving toward the door, he sauntered up next to me, cocked his head and stared into Clark Wehr's empty eyes.

"This man is PPB," he said.

"I'm aware of that," I said. "I found his ID in his pocket. Question is, what are *you* doing here, and how did you get here so quickly?"

"Lights and sirens," he said. "You have lights and sirens out here in the boonies, don't you, Sheriff?"

I took hold of his elbow and spun him around.

"Like I said before," I said, "let's take a walk."

Doug May stopped dead in his tracks as we moved out of the cabin and down the porch steps, into the afternoon glare. The movie star cop shielded his eyes with the flat of his hand, and the brief look the two men exchanged made it clear that they were acquainted.

I nudged the cop toward a footpath that led to the river, shot a glance over my shoulder as the caretaker attempted to disappear into the depths of his lumber-jack coat.

"I don't believe I caught your name," I said when we came to a halt a short distance away. "In fact, I don't believe you offered it."

The translucent water of the Catonquin moved swiftly along the scree, and the air smelled of lichen and rusted leaves. A water bird dipped low across the smooth surface where the current was creased by a snag in the flats.

"Detective Dan Halloran," he answered finally. "Portland Police. SID."

"SID," I said. "That's vice and narcotics. You've grazed a good distance off your pasture, Detective."

He began to reply but stopped himself short. I waited in silence, watched his eyes follow the course of the water bird as it plucked something out of the river.

"Mr. Stricklyn phoned me this morning," the detective offered. "He asked me to look in on things."

"Dean Stricklyn is the owner of the cabin where the victim was found, is that correct?"

"That's right."

"Who is Mr. Stricklyn to you, detective?"

"He's an attorney in town."

"What kind of attorney?"

"The important kind."

"How are you acquainted?"

"He shared his toys with friends from time to time," he said and winked as though we were communicating in some sort of code.

"You're saying that you and the deceased are among Mr. Stricklyn's friends."

"He can be a very generous man."

I didn't exactly believe Halloran, but it didn't mean that what he was telling me wasn't true.

"And Detective Wehr? What's his story?"

Halloran looked away from me for a long moment, stared at the steep cliff on the far side of the river.

"Clark Wehr was my partner."

I WAS escorting Detective Halloran back to the entrance of the resort where he'd parked his unmarked police-issue sedan when Jordan Powell called out to me from somewhere deep inside the fern overgrowth.

"Looks like one of the cabins has been burglarized," Powell said as he caught up with us.

"Not now, Jordan," I said. "I'll be with you in a minute."

"There's a fresh pair of tire tracks out behind the place," Powell added.

"Good," I said. "Get a plaster cast of them before the rain starts again."

"Nice work, deputy," Halloran said, and dipped into the breast pocket of his leather jacket, withdrew a business card, and tried to pass it to Powell. "Keep me posted."

I snatched Halloran's card from his fingers.

"Do you think it's going to be useful to you to be a deliberate pain in my ass?" I said. "You are way out of line here, detective."

"Pump the brakes, sunshine," Halloran said. "I'm trying to help you. My partner just committed suicide."

"That hasn't been determined yet."

"Excuse me? Did you see the same scene that I did?"

"How many suicides shoot themselves in the center of the forehead?"

"I've seen it before."

"And fire two shots in the process?"

"Plenty of suicides lose their nerve on the first try," he said. "This isn't your first investigation is it, Sheriff?"

"You just used up your free pass, Halloran," I said. "Have a pleasant drive back to Portland."

A MESSAGE awaited me when Sam Griffin and I returned to the office that evening. Outside, the lights along Meridian's main street glowed muted yellow in the fog that had rolled in from the gorge.

I studied the phone number that had been scrawled on the pink message slip. It wasn't one I recognized, but the exchange was for Portland metro. I dialed half expecting my call to go unanswered at this hour.

"Deputy Chief Overton," came the voice on the other end of the line.

I hadn't ever met Overton but knew him to be the PPB's number two man. His tone was like a crosscut saw, freighted with impatience and fatigue.

"Sheriff Tyler Dawson, Meriwether County," I said. "Returning your call."

"I appreciate your getting back to me," Overton said. "I understand you met with one of our detectives earlier today. Dan Halloran."

"I didn't exactly meet with him. He appeared at my crime scene unannounced and uninvited."

"We're all understandably shaken by Detective Wehr's suicide."

"Apparent suicide."

He brushed past my comment as though he had not heard it.

"I would appreciate it—would consider it a professional courtesy, in fact—if you could clear the case as expeditiously as possible, Sheriff. I would be in your debt. The entire department would be."

"I make it a point to clear all of our cases as expeditiously as possible," I said.

"That's good to know. But just in case, Detective Halloran will be staying at The Portman in Meridian. To make himself available to you if you need him."

"I strongly suggest that you order your detective to go home, Deputy Chief."

A brittle silence hung on the line before Overton gathered himself to reply to me, and when he finally did, he made no attempt to disguise either his contempt or condescension.

"You're familiar with the Police Bureau's past troubles, Sheriff Dawson?"

"Hard not to be," I said.

For several well-publicized weeks about a decade ago, a virtual pageant of law enforcement officers and elected public officials had been paraded in front of the Senate Rackets Committee in Washington, D.C., to testify as to a roster of unflattering allegations of corruption. Much more recently, certain members of the police force had been found to be deeply involved in a sophisticated network of narcotics, prostitution, and illegal gambling operations. It had all been very ugly, protracted, and embarrassing for the city, and the voting public's collective memory was proving to be far longer than anyone had anticipated.

"PPB still walks on eggshells, as you might imagine, Sheriff," he said. "We don't need another scandal here. I'm sure you understand."

There it was. This conversation had nothing whatsoever to do with remorse, morality, or redemption.

"Your district attorney hid behind the Fifth Amendment," I said. "And your mayor refused to answer the committee's questions about payoffs. With due respect, Deputy Chief, your PR problems couldn't register any lower on my list of things I give a damn about."

My remarks were met with a silence so complete I thought he had hung up on me.

"Nevertheless," he said with exaggerated patience, "I would appreciate it if you would keep us in the loop."

"I will let you know when I've completed my investigation," I said. "In the meantime, please order Detective Halloran back to work. In Portland."

* * *

I SLEPT that night inside a tangle of sweat-dampened sheets and nightmares of a far-off war; not the war from which we had so recently been extricated, but the one that had already been forgotten.

CHAPTER FOUR

THAT SUNDAY AFTER church, Jesse and I ate breakfast at Rowan Boyle's diner in Meridian. Sam Griffin joined us, as he sometimes did, and I dropped him off at the station house before Jesse and I returned home. I could hear the jangle of the telephone inside the house as we climbed out of the Bronco. I sprinted for the door but missed the call.

A few minutes later, I was standing at the sink watching Jesse refill the bird feeder outside the window when the phone began to ring again. I smiled as my wife returned the feeder to its place, reacting with surprise as a flock of junco swarmed the loose seed that had spilled at her feet. That smile fell away as I picked up the phone and recognized the distress in the voice of Irene Sheridan.

Short minutes later, Jesse stepped into the mudroom as I strapped on my holster. I grabbed my coat and hat from the rack beside the door, kissed her, and told her that I didn't know when I'd be back.

It took nearly two hours to drive from my ranch to the Sheridan place, the time it took not being prescribed by distance so much as the nature of the winding two-lane county road that weaved inside of narrow mountain passes and over spans of ancient trestle bridges that had been constructed long before the turn of the century.

IRENE SHERIDAN was nearly shouting into her phone as I rapped on the glass inset of the back door of their house. She waved me inside but did not interrupt her conversation as I stepped across the threshold.

"—this morning," she said into the receiver. "Three o'clock. Yes, at least six of them."

She gestured toward a percolator on her kitchen counter, but I declined with a shake of my head and removed my hat. The loose skin beneath her blue eyes was discolored, and the whites were shot through with a webbing of red veins. As she spoke, she ran her splayed fingers through closely-cropped hair that was the color of a dull metal, smoothed the wrinkles out of a print blouse that hung loosely over a pair of faded jeans. Even as I stood watching, her posture appeared to sag beneath the accumulated weight of each day, each year and decade she had labored beside her husband, KC Sheridan.

I turned away, left Irene alone with her phone call, and moved into the living room to wait. A man I had never met before was standing at the bay window, the skin of his face drawn tight and pale in the weak light.

"You wondering why I'm drinking beer at this hour of the morning?" he asked without turning to look at me.

"I don't generally offer judgments regarding a man's choice of morning beverages. Unless he draws a paycheck bearing my signature."

"Name's Jarvis Lynch," he said as he turned to address me, but didn't offer a hand to shake. "I'm Irene's brother. Drove out here from Nevada. Nye County."

"Ty Dawson," I said. "How long you been here, Mr. Lynch?"

"Not long. My sister called me first thing after the feds rolled up this morning. I got in my truck as soon as we hung up and drove straight through."

I noticed the resemblance between Jarvis Lynch and Irene Sheridan then, though I pegged him to be a handful of years younger than she, mid-sixties or thereabouts.

"Have any idea who she's speaking with?" I asked.

"Can't be sure, but I'd guess it's someone from the press."

"Why would you guess that?"

Lynch cleared his throat and cast a long glance beyond the ridgeline before answering me.

"Because I've seen this kind of shitshow before."

I waited for more, but nothing came.

"I don't believe I follow your inference."

"Were you aware that the federal government controls eighty-five percent of all the land in the state of Nevada?" Lynch asked.

"More than half of the land in Oregon, as well," I said.

Lynch nodded and his features took on a cadaverous appearance as the low autumn sun lost itself inside a cloudbank.

"No man is good enough to govern another man without the other's consent," he said.

"Abraham Lincoln?"

"At least somebody around here hasn't spared himself the burden of an education."

"I'd advise you to curb your hostility until you know who you're speaking with if you're planning on sticking around here."

"I know exactly who I'm speaking with. You're the sheriff of Meriwether County. It was the sheriff of *Hemmings* County who helped federal agents drag my brother-in-law away in handcuffs at three o'clock this morning. You'll understand if I don't genuflect."

"Porter Brayfield was here?"

"If that's his name. My sister gave me the impression that KC was well acquainted with him. Goddamned Judas if you ask me. Far as I'm concerned, you're all cut from the same cloth."

"I work for the people of my county, Mr. Lynch, and they're free to relieve me of that responsibility any time they choose."

He made no effort to conceal his antipathy—whether for me or for my office, I was uncertain—then he placed his nearly empty beer bottle on an end table with exaggerated care. He stepped outside without a word, into the dry, frigid wind that swept across the work yard.

Irene was still occupied with her phone conversation, one that had begun to sound more like an interview than it had when I'd first come in. I walked out to my truck and tried to raise Sam Griffin on the radio. The terrain in the valley rendered it ineffective half the time, but I thought I'd give it a try since the Sheridan place was out here in the flats.

"Unit one to base," I said into the microphone.

The speaker hissed with static, so I made an adjustment to the squelch and tried again. A few seconds later, Griffin's voice responded through the noise.

"I need you to run down a Jarvis Lynch," I said and spelled out his name. "Male. Age approximately sixty-five. Resident of Nevada. Nye County."

"Roger that," he said and repeated my order. "But I believe I'm familiar with the name, Sheriff. I suspect you are as well, sir."

I FOUND Lynch pacing the gravel path that cut between the Sheridans' main house and their barn, his cheeks gone ruddy with the cold.

"Why don't we step back inside?" I said. "I believe you have something to tell me."

He turned on me, startled, and followed me into the house without a word, his hands buried deep in the pockets of his sheepskin coat.

"Seven years ago," he began, "the Bureau of Land Management canceled the lease on land my family has been grazing on since before the Civil War. Those sons of bitches hadn't even invented the BLM until eighty years later—"

I remembered his story, but I let him tell it. Lynch's eyes were moist with a rage whose origins were more than half a decade old.

"—I told them they could do whatever the hell they wanted with their lease," he said, "but I wasn't about to move my cattle. If anybody had a right to graze that land it was me."

He was describing every rancher's nightmare, a story that had been widely broadcast as it unfolded in real time those few years ago.

"They came after me for trespassing and nonpayment," Lynch continued. "Over half a million dollars they said I owed them. I told them they could shove that the same place they could shove their so-called lease. So, they sent a small army of federal agents, plus three dozen hired cowhands, a couple helicopters, and a fleet of transport trucks and set about rounding up *my* cows for seizure."

"I don't recall that working out too well for the feds," I said.

A smile touched the corner of his mouth, then disappeared.

"The media couldn't get enough of it," he said.

"How many folks came out to block that highway, Mr. Lynch?"

"I don't remember exactly."

"I do," I said. "Over a thousand. Some of those folks were well-armed."

"Most of them were," he admitted.

The only sound inside the room was the ticking of a longcase clock, and it dawned on me that Irene was no longer on the phone.

"You tipped off the press about what happened to KC this morning, didn't you?" I asked.

"You bet your ass I did."

"SHERIFF BRAYFIELD was with them," Irene told me. "Led them right up to our front door. It was three o'clock in the morning, Ty. They shined their floodlights through the windows of our home and spoke to us through a bullhorn."

She was quaking with anger and dread, unable or unwilling to allow either me or her own brother witness the tears welling behind her eyes.

"KC threw on some clothes and stepped out on the porch," she said. "He thought he might be able to reason with Sheriff Brayfield. But KC couldn't even see them. He was blinded by their spotlights."

Jarvis Lynch poured a glass of water for his sister from the kitchen tap. He delivered it, then stood behind her armchair and rested one hand on her shoulder as she spoke to me.

"They forced him to get down on his knees, Ty. Like a criminal. With his hands on his head. All I can think of is how he was shivering out there in the cold, blinking against those bright lights, kneeling on the front porch of his own house—"

"They cuffed him and drove him all the way to Portland to the federal lockup," Lynch finished for her.

"What were the charges?" I asked.

"Interfering with federal officers and the destruction of federal property," Irene said.

"They fenced off his goddamned water," Lynch said. "Not to mention about three hundred acres of his land. What did they expect him to do?"

"I understand," I said. "Do you know if KC ever spoke with Judge Yates?"

"Three hundred goddamned acres," Lynch repeated.

Irene's silence felt like a living thing. Her expression reflected an emptiness that seemed to have no end.

"What did the judge say to KC?" I asked again. "What did he tell him?"

"The judge said there was nothing he could do," she said. She spoke softly, but her tone carried serrated edges honed by decades of hard labor and adversity. "He said he could try to enjoin the agency to stop their work, even subpoena the Fish and Wildlife Service, but they'd never be compelled to comply with his order. They'd simply ignore him, even though he's a judge."

"Have you got a lawyer, Miss Irene?"

"KC used somebody over in Roseburg."

"I'm talking about a criminal defense lawyer."

My words appeared to startle her.

"My husband isn't a criminal."

"I'll make sure to get you a phone number, someone you can call before I leave here," I said.

"But KC isn't guilty of anything, Ty."

I glanced at Jarvis Lynch and watched him gently squeeze his sister's shoulder.

"It's innocent people who need lawyers, ma'am. They need 'em a lot more than guilty folks do."

A SPECTRAL silver trail was drifting from the chimney when I returned home that night. Warm light glowed behind the windowpanes, and the air was sweet with cedar smoke and the distant scents of ozone and moisture that carried on the wind.

Jesse was stacking dishes in the rack as I stepped up behind her, encircled her narrow waist with my arms, and pulled her close.

"Everything okay?" she asked and leaned into my kiss. "You're late."

"Everything's fine," I deferred.

"I saved some dinner for you," she said. "Caleb's in the living room. He refilled the wood box for me."

I found my ranch foreman kneeling on the stone hearth, feeding kindling to the flames that cradled the logs in the fireplace. He turned and studied me as I crossed the room, his weathered face, silver hair, and mustache marbled by the flickering light.

"Well, ain't you a dewy little blossom," he said.

"Long day."

I heard his joints crack as he stood and gestured toward the distant peaks outside the window.

"Weather's coming," he said.

"I know. I can smell it."

"I could be wrong, but you look as though you might welcome a drop or two from old Jimmy B's barrels. I sure as hell would."

I took a pair of tumblers from the bar cart and poured three fingers of Jim Beam into each of them. I handed one to Caleb and took a seat on the hearth. The fire warmed my back as I told the old man about KC Sheridan. He listened without interruption until I had finished the entire story.

"Arrogance and ignorance spring from the same well," Caleb said as he warmed his whisky glass between his palms.

"Are you referring to the Sheridans or Jarvis Lynch?"

"Neither," Caleb said.

"Lynch is carrying a monument-sized chip on his shoulder."

"I suspect he's earned the right." I stood and collected Caleb's empty glass, carried it to the bar, and refilled both mine and his.

"You know how this works, Ty. Same clowns, different rodeo. If they want what you've got, they'll up and take it from you. If you don't have the means to fight back, they win. And quick as a hiccup, you lose your ranch, your livelihood, and everything you spent your life working for."

"I don't want to believe that, Caleb."
"Nobody does, but the change is coming."
"Looks to me like it already got here."

PART TWO

BROKEDOWN PALACE

CHAPTER FIVE

SHOULDN'T WE BE there by now?

How the hell should I know? I've never been here before.

You told me the hippies would help us.

They will. First, we gotta find the goddamn place.

Well, hurry it up. My chest hurts like hell.

Settle down, man. You're panting like a frickin' dog.

It feels like busted glass in my lungs.

It's your own goddamn fault.

Saying that over and over doesn't help.

It's been one goddamn thing after another since we split Montana.

That's *my* fault now?

Hell yeah, it's your fault. We're on the run 'caus'a you, Shannon. You're bad goddamn luck is what you are.

Don't say that, man.

There. See that sign?

I don't see anything, man. The sun's in my eyes.

You whine 'cause we gotta drive in the dark, then you whine 'cause the sun's coming up.

That's not a road sign, it's a goddamn oil drum, man.

You don't see those words spray painted on it?

Rainbow Ranch.

What'd I tell you. It's right up ahead.

Just get us offa this dirt road. I feel like I'm bleeding internally.

You're not frickin' bleeding internally.

You a doctor, now?

I wish I was a damn veterinarian. I'd put you to sleep like my stepfather's dog.

WHERE THE hell is everybody?

Why do you ask me stupid questions like that?

Looks like a movie set from one of those western deals or the Twilight Zone. You said there'd be hippie chicks and free dope and shit.

My buddy said they'd be here.

Well, they're not. Looks to me like they bugged out. Some goddamn commune this turned out to be.

Get off my back, Shannon.

Commune for squirrels, maybe.

I'm serious. Get off my goddamn back.

Lighten up. I'm in pain here.

You want I should take that pistol you stole and put you out of your misery? Maybe bury you out here? It's not like anybody would know about it if I did.

That isn't funny, man.

Then shut the hell up, and let me figure out what we're gonna do now.

CHAPTER SIX

A THIN BLANKET of cloud cover moved through the early morning light behind the mountain peaks and cast complex geometries along the valley floor. I left my pickup in the lot at the substation and rode shotgun while Jordan Powell drove his Blazer up the interstate toward Portland. KC Sheridan was expected to be arraigned in federal court later that morning, so we'd departed before daybreak in order to allow me enough time to make arrangements for KC's bail beforehand.

Powell used the long drive to catch me up on the forensic results of the Clark Wehr case, including the potentially interesting fact that the plaster casts of the tire treads my deputy had discovered outside the burglarized cabin indicated a vehicle with two separate types of tires on its rear axle. The team had narrowed down the likely model to a light-duty truck or van and concluded that the tracks had most probably been made around the same time as the victim's time of death, based on the absence of damage from weather. This meant we *might* have a witness, though both Powell and I knew that identifying and locating such a witness was another matter altogether. The coroner had not yet completed the autopsy on Clark Wehr, and there was no usable evidence with respect to the break-in of the second cabin, so the tire impressions were all that we had. Which is to say we didn't have very damned much at all.

It was nearly ten o'clock in the morning by the time we located a parking space a short distance from the courthouse. I sent Powell inside to wait for KC Sheridan's case to be called while I walked a few blocks down Yamhill to make arrangements with a bail bondsman I knew.

They called the last case on the docket at two thirty that afternoon, and KC's had not been among them. As the courtroom emptied out, I identified myself to the bailiff, and a short time later, I was escorted through a doorway posted with an engraved sign made of brass bearing the name of Judge Gerald Bonner and was led into the judge's chambers.

"Your honor," I said. "I've been waiting all day for the KC Sheridan arraignment. Mr. Sheridan is the rancher from Meriwether County. His case was never called."

The judge studied me for a moment, his face impassive, before he turned toward the window so I could not see his eyes.

"That case has been rescheduled until tomorrow," he said.

"Is there a reason for that?"

"I haven't the faintest idea, Sheriff. Check with his lawyer."

I looked past the judge's shoulder, outside the window that overlooked the street. Pedestrians bundled in long coats and wool caps and scarves elbowed past one another along crowded sidewalks where storefronts were already ornamented with holiday decorations, though Thanksgiving was still weeks away.

"Can you direct me to federal holding, then, please?"

"Unless you're his attorney, I'm afraid I can't allow that."

"Excuse me?"

"Are we having a communication problem, Sheriff Dawson?"

I was reminded of my years in the military and the futility of pushing against an entrenched bureaucracy. It was not only unproductive but was likely to aggravate KC's situation. This was Judge Bonner's world, and I was just passing through.

"No problem here, Your Honor."

"Good," he said and dismissed me by shifting the focus of his concentration to the packing of tobacco into a briar pipe, thereby rendering me invisible.

"THAT SHOOTS a hole in the day," Powell said as we walked back to the lot where he'd parked the Blazer.

"Two days," I said. "Makes no sense to drive all the way home just so we can turn around and come back here tomorrow."

"An old girlfriend of mine works at the Benson Hotel. It's only a couple blocks from here. I imagine I could pull a string or two and get us a decent rate."

I wasn't completely surprised. Powell probably had former girlfriends all over the state. He was a ruggedly handsome young cowboy who'd seen combat in Vietnam and returned home to a brief stint with the rodeo before becoming one hell of a ranch hand. There was one complication.

"You don't think Shasta's going to have an opinion on that subject?" I asked. "Canoodling with an old flame?"

"I don't plan on doing no canoodling, boss. Besides, you ain't of a mind to be tellin' Shasta something like that are you?"

"You're the one that's engaged to be married to her, son," I said. "I suppose you'll handle those details as you see fit and proper."

The wind that swept up from the Willamette River cut me straight to the bone. "I'll drive," I said, and climbed behind the wheel of Powell's Blazer.

A few minutes later, I pulled to the curb in front of the Benson and a uniformed doorman opened Powell's side. I slid a charge card from my billfold and handed it to Powell.

"Go ahead and get both of us checked in," I said. "I need to borrow your truck for a while."

"Where are you going?"

"There's somebody I want to speak with now that we're stuck here in the city. Might as well make use of the time. And one other thing."

"What?"

"Call Griffin at the office," I said. "Have him issue a BOLO for the vehicle from the Wehr scene."

"No disrespect, but isn't it maybe a little premature? We don't exactly know what kind of vehicle to be-on-the-lookout for."

"We know enough to keep an eye peeled. Make sure he includes the thing about the rear tires."

"Roger that," Powell said.

"Tell him to follow up with the neighboring counties to confirm."

I DROVE to the PPB headquarters building on SW Second Street and parked on the street about three blocks away. Pungent fumes of exhaust from the TriMet bus rolled through the intersection as I waited for the walking green. Across the street, a line of patrons snaked nearly halfway down the block from the Paris Theatre box office, waiting for a matinee of *Deep Throat*.

The lobby of the Portland Police Bureau was ripe with the funk of stale tobacco, body odor, and expectorated bile. A man wearing a topcoat with one sleeve torn away at the shoulder sat groaning beside the entry, bleeding from a deep gash in his head. He lolled his head in a state of semi-consciousness, one wrist handcuffed to a D-ring on a bench that was bolted to the floor, a viscous string of pink spittle oozing from the corner of his mouth.

I received directions to the Special Investigations Division from the desk sergeant and climbed three flights up the stairwell, elbowing my way through landings crowded with clusters of uniformed cops spending their breaks engaging in crude humor and smoking cigarettes.

A door marked with the letters SID stood at the end of a long, poorly illuminated hallway that appeared to vibrate with the jittering flicker of neon tube lighting. Inside, a dozen or so gray metal desks had been pushed together into groupings of four and arranged around banks of mismatched file cabinets. A heavyset cop wearing a rust-colored houndstooth jacket gave me the eye as he pressed his phone receiver to his ear.

"Help you with something?" houndstooth asked me, covering the mouthpiece with his palm.

"Who's in charge?"

"Lieutenant's office is back there."

He waved an unlit cigar in the general direction of a small room tucked into the corner of the bullpen, then turned from me to resume his phone conversation as I walked away.

The door to the office had been left partway open, so I rapped on the door frame and announced myself.

"Yeah," a voice called from inside. "Come on in."

The office was more spacious than I had expected, the desk tidy and organized, and the man who occupied it clean-shaven, lean, and well dressed. His posture and bearing suggested a military background, his hair cut high-and-tight, his complexion ruddy with outdoors.

"Benjamin Morgan," he said as he stood and shook my hand. "I run the asylum."

I introduced myself again and took the seat he offered.

"I'm here about one of your detectives," I said. "Dan Halloran."

"I respect a man who gets straight to the point, Sheriff." A brief smile lit behind his eyes, then disappeared. "Around here we call him 'Hollywood Dan.'"

"I suspect he appreciates that."

"Perceptive."

Experience had taught me to be wary of first impressions, but Lieutenant Morgan struck me as decent police.

"What kind of cop is Halloran?" I asked.

"I'm going to level with you, Sheriff Dawson. I'm fairly new with SID."

"That does not exactly answer my question."

Morgan leaned back in his rolling chair, crossed his legs, and took my inventory. The soles of his black oxfords were well worn, but the uppers held a shine that reflected the overhead fluorescents like a mirror.

"This unit has found itself to be among the sources of some"—he pulled his eyes away from me, seemed to study the photos on the wall as he searched for the proper word—"*disquiet* in the public eye."

"I'm guessing that's the reason you're the new guy on this desk."

Morgan's eyes narrowed, his expression pinched.

"Navy man?" I asked, referring to the photos on his wall.

"You strike me as a straight-shooter, Sheriff," he said. "Let's take a walk."

SEAGULLS FOUGHT for scraps along the river shoreline as Lieutenant Morgan pulled his wool scarf tight and popped the collar of his overcoat against the wind. I rested an elbow on the handrail that ran the length of the west bank, turned my face toward a fragile afternoon gloaming that tinted the cityscape in bronze-colored light.

"How long have you lived here, Sheriff?" Morgan asked.

"I was born and raised in Meriwether County. Lived in this state all my life, with the exception the stretch I spent in Korea."

A short distance down the walkway, a vendor was selling hot pretzels from a pushcart.

"Want one?" Morgan asked.

I declined and waited while the lieutenant stepped away. The water moved swiftly beyond the rip rock, and I watched a long-legged shorebird as it hunted the mudflats. I felt the handrail tremble as Morgan returned and leaned his weight on it.

"Plover," he said.

"Excuse me?"

"The bird you're looking at. It's a plover. You spend much time here in the city?"

"A little, when I was younger."

"I grew up on the North End."

"Rough."

He stared out at the whitecaps on the river and unfolded his pretzel from the square of waxed paper in his hand. He peeled off a chunk and chewed it slowly.

"I've been with PPB since 1950," he said. "Never been part of the inner circle; probably because I've never been a 'businessman.' Most I've ever taken from this job is a free cup of coffee now and then when I was a patrolman."

His tone seemed wistful, nearly lost in the ambient sounds of wind and current, as though he was talking to himself.

"I'm not bragging," he said, and turned his attention back on me.

"Cowboys have a saying, Lieutenant," I said. "'It ain't bragging if you actually done it.'"

He nodded and looked northward, followed the line of headlights on the Morrison Bridge.

"Portland has a history of corruption, Sheriff, going all the way back to the Civil War," he said, and took another bite. "Back then, the town marshal himself owned at least one saloon, a whorehouse, and a gambling joint. Ten years later, it was all about the port, and kidnapping inebriated sailors so they could be pressed into service on passing merchant vessels. It got so bad that foreign countries threatened to redline the whole town and render it off-limits to their fleets."

"There's a reason some folks don't care to live in the city," I said.

Morgan ignored my remark and clapped the crystals of rock salt off his hands, wadded the spent wax paper into a ball.

"Back in the Roaring Twenties, there were already five hundred hotels here in the city," he said. "More than four hundred of them were dedicated exclusively to prostitution. How about that shit, Sheriff?"

He turned his back to the water, sighed heavily, and tossed his trash into a rubbish bin.

"During Prohibition, every single speakeasy in town made regular cash drops to the police *and* city hall."

I shook a cigarette out of the pack in my coat pocket and watched the last remnants of a russet sunset leech out of the clouds. Dim snippets of music drifted across from a tourist-attraction sternwheeler as it passed beneath a bascule bridge.

"I remember when I was in my twenties," I said. "Some of the bars still had slot machines lined up along the walls. I never really gave it any thought at the time."

"Do you remember what happened after that, Sheriff?"

I shook my head.

"I had enlisted in the service by that time," I said. "Can't say I was keeping track."

Morgan gazed off in the direction of the old riverboat, the music and the laughter from onboard growing more distinct. The evening was heavy with the riparian smells of minerals and algae and the carcasses of fish, and his shoulders seemed to sag under its weight.

"What happened is that a reformist mayor got herself elected," Morgan said. "She hired a new police chief from outside the system, tasked him to clean up the card games and the slot machines and all the rest of it. Poor bastard didn't make it through half of her first term. When he resigned, he held a press conference and openly admitted that his officers refused to tell him where the gambling operations were even taking place."

I tipped the dead ash off my cigarette and watched the wind carry it away.

"I'm not sure I understand why you're telling me this, Lieutenant."

The windowpanes of high-rise buildings sparkled like jewels inside the brittle nightfall, the river lapped the shoreline, and beacon lights from passing aircraft winked high overhead, but I felt as though nothing I was looking at should be trusted.

"I'm telling you this because you came into my office and inquired about one of my detectives," Morgan said. "Because the kind of shit I just told you about has continued unabated to this day. You need to appreciate the dynamics at play here in town, Sheriff Dawson."

"This is why you're the *new* SID guy? To clean house on Narcotics and Vice?"

He shrugged and cupped his hands to his lips and warmed them with his breath.

"I understand that you're skeptical," he said.

I could have told him that I wasn't sure if I was being played; that it was growing more difficult to distinguish the liars from the lie, even though I had come to regard Lieutenant Morgan as a decent man who had been handed an impossible task. Whether he'd been cast as Diogenes or Sisyphus, I doubted that he was familiar with the fate of either one.

"I don't have a response for that comment, Lieutenant."

"You asked me why they gave me SID," he said. "In short, the chief assigned me there before anybody else could stop him. Are you familiar with the Oxford Theatre?"

"Peep shows and stag films."

"And live nude dancers who circulate among the audience for lap dances and other services. We busted five girls and a dozen of their johns less than a month ago, but the DA refused to prosecute. Flat out *refused*.

"A week later, we raided Golden VIP Club, a male house of prostitution. DA couldn't refuse to prosecute that one—we had too much evidence that time. What he *did* do was to arrange for the owner to appear *after* official courthouse hours had ended. The judge fined the guy two hundred dollars, and the case was expunged from the court record. Ask the courthouse clerk and he'll tell you that the file doesn't exist."

I fieldstripped my cigarette and tucked the spent filter into my shirt pocket.

"Listen," Morgan sighed. "I'm no moral crusader. Hell, as far as I'm concerned, if it doesn't involve kids or innocents, I'd just as soon leave it alone. But I know they're using these places to move dope, and not just a little bit of it, either. I'm talking about weight."

"The money's still running uphill," I said.

"The way it always has. I've got narcotics detectives wearing clothes and jewelry that cost more than what I take home in a month. Dan Halloran drives a brand-new Corvette."

"I assume you've passed your observations up the chain."

"I discussed my concerns with Deputy Chief Overton."

I debated whether to mention my earlier phone conversation with the Deputy Chief, and decided against that, too. I didn't like anything I was hearing from Morgan, nor could I claim I had any idea who the good guys were, or whether there were any left in this city at all.

"How did the Deputy Chief address your concerns?" I asked.

"He thanked me and said he'd look into it and get back to me. But so far, nothing but crickets."

He seemed genuinely troubled, a lone warrior. My experiences in wartime, and those as a cowboy and a cop, had rendered me much slower to bestow trust than most. It's not all maps, strings, and push-pins. Call it gut or intuition, sometimes it's the only tool left in the box.

"What do you know about a man named Stricklyn?" I asked.

"Dean Stricklyn?" he said. "Why do you ask?"

"His name came up in the Clark Wehr case."

Morgan shook his head, ran a palm across his scalp.

"Let me borrow one of your cigarettes, Dawson. I've got one more story for you. Have you ever heard of a woman they call 'the Countess'?"

"YOU LOOK like you've been breaking in a brand-new pair of boots, boss," Jordan Powell said. "Are you okay?"

"I just finished listening to a discourse on the history of corruption and malfeasance in the Rose City," I said. "I believe I could make use of a drink or two to wash it down with."

Powell had settled himself at a fireside table in the bar of the Benson Hotel. He was eating peanuts by the fistful from a bowl made of hand-cut crystal, his eyes alight with whisky shine. I warmed my hands in the heat of the fireplace, and I took in the décor as I waited for the bartender to fill my order. The lobby was locally famous for its rare Circassian walnut woodwork, Italian marble floors, and chandeliers that had been crafted in Austria, all arriving by sailing ship nearly a century ago.

"Sounds like a lot of laughs," Powell said as the bartender delivered my double Jim Beam.

"It'd be more amusing if I didn't feel like all this big-city crap was about to get tracked across our sidewalks."

"What's that supposed to mean?"

I took a swallow and looked Powell in the eyes.

"Don't share one shred of information on the Wehr case with anyone," I said. "Not to anybody other than me or Sam Griffin from now on."

I tossed back the remainder of my drink and signaled for another.

"You had anything to eat yet?" I asked.

Powell's eyes slid toward the reception desk as he began to fidget with his cocktail napkin.

"I didn't reckon you'd mind too much if I made other plans," he said.

"Is that your former lady friend batting her eyelashes at you over there?"

"She ain't battin' nothin'."

My new drink arrived, and I waited for a long moment before I replied.

"I'm not your confessor, Jordan, and I sure as hell ain't your daddy," I said. "But Shasta Blaylock is a good girl, and I strongly suspect she believes you don't dally with other women anymore, seeing as you're fixing to marry her and all."

"Are you sayin' that to me 'cause I don't follow you to church every Sunday like Griffin does?"

I felt the sweet burn of Jim Beam slide all the way down to my gut. I leaned in and rested my elbows on the table.

"Going to church don't make you a good man any more than standing in a barn makes you a horse," I said.

"Okay. Go on."

"All I'm saying is that you know what that girl's been through, and she's putting her stock in you now. That takes a damn sight of courage on her part. She trusts you."

"It's only dinner, Sheriff," he said and slid an embossed keychain across the table at me. "This here's the key to your room. I'm across the hall."

"Don't wear out your boot soles on that brass rail, son," I said, stood, and moved off toward the steakhouse next door to the hotel. "We've got things to do tomorrow."

CHAPTER SEVEN

I AWAKENED JUST after five o'clock the next morning, peeled back the drapes and looked out at the lights of the city. Sunup was still hours away, and a bank of stars shimmered and vanished in their turn, eclipsed by the curtain of mist that drifted above the rivercourse.

I showered and dressed and stepped into the hall. Adjacent to Jordan Powell's door sat a room service cart awaiting pickup. It was piled high with used glassware and linens, a pair of empty wine bottles, and place settings for two.

I ate breakfast alone in the hotel restaurant, drank coffee, and read the newspaper. The headline feature story covered an Arizona logger named Travis Walton who had been missing for five days, claiming he'd been abducted by aliens from outer space. On page seventeen, a photo of KC Sheridan the size of a postage stamp had been printed below the fold. The caption read: *Oregon Rancher Arrested by Feds*. I paid my breakfast tab with cash and left it on the table beside the used newspaper, made my way to the lobby, and dialed Powell's room from the house phone.

A BRISK ten-minute walk brought us to the front steps of the courthouse, an Italianate architectural beauty that dated back to 1869 and was said to be one of the oldest structures of its kind this side of the Big Muddy. The air was leaden with low overcast, the streets and sidewalks washed clean by morning showers.

"Go ahead and say what you're thinking," Jordan said as we stepped into the empty courtroom.

"Lying is for cowards, son."

"You ain't going to give me the benefit of the doubt?"

"This isn't a benefit-of-the-doubt sort of thing," I said.

"Never mind. Where do you want to sit?"

The warm air from the central furnace hadn't reached this floor yet, and the windows were opaque with a thin layer of frost.

"I'm taking the aisle," I said. "You sit wherever you want. I want to be able to get out of here soon as KC's bail has been determined."

The gallery was empty except for Powell and me and one rumpled man balancing a notepad and a pencil on his lap who had positioned himself in the back row. KC Sheridan's case came up third this time, and five minutes after that, the judge declared that he was suspending sentence on the charges levied against the rancher, and that KC was to be released forthwith. No reason was given, nor was one requested, but I knew deep down that both KC and I harbored suspicions that this was unlikely to be the end of it.

KC was ushered downstairs to the detention area where he could reclaim his belongings, and Powell walked back to the hotel to check us out and retrieve the

Blazer. KC's attorney was a man that I hadn't met before but had been recommended to me by someone I thought I trusted. I approached and introduced myself to the lawyer as he snapped the toggles on his briefcase and prepared to leave.

"Quentin Bahle," he said, and spelled it out. "But it's pronounced like 'Bailey.'"

"Can you explain to me what just happened here, Mr. Bahle?" I asked.

"In short, I think they're embarrassed."

"A federal agency? Embarrassed? You can't actually believe that."

"Can you think of another reason?"

I could think of a dozen other reasons, but I kept them to myself. Instead, I shook the lawyer's hand, expressed my gratitude, and withdrew to the lobby to await KC's release.

The old rancher looked as though he'd aged a decade in two days, but I could see that his resolve hadn't been diminished. His eyes were alert, but vacant in the manner of a man who had been hollowed out from the inside. I held the door for him as he climbed into the backseat of Powell's Blazer and buckled himself in. The man was so quiet for the first twenty minutes of our drive that Powell switched on the radio and tuned it to a country music station being broadcast from somewhere out on the coast.

As we passed across the Abernethy Bridge, I could see KC contemplating the roiling current of a waterfall in the near distance. He narrowed his eyes and made a gesture in the general direction of the valley that opened up behind it, beyond the outskirts of Oregon City.

"Bob Wills used to play at a little roadhouse down that way," KC said. "A friend of mine used to sneak me through the back door, and we'd drink beer behind the stage. My momma wouldn't have approved of me bein' there, and I'd have to change clothes before I went home so I wouldn't smell like cigarettes and booze."

He lost himself again for long seconds that expanded into minutes, his focus folding in upon itself again. We had made it nearly all the way to Tualatin before the radio station took a break for the news. The lead story was the release of KC Sheridan.

KC broke his silence with a string of top-shelf cussing that ended only when Powell switched off the radio.

"If they're going to bother to tell the goddamned story, they should by-god tell it right," KC snapped. "I knew old man Rafferty. He'd soil his drawers if he could see what they've done to his name."

He was referring to the Rafferty Wildlife Refuge, named after one of the handful of original ranch families that had settled the entire Jericho Basin.

"I was born in '05," KC said, "and Rafferty was already an old man when Teddy Roosevelt turned the salt pond into a 'refuge.' Hell, I was just a snot-nosed kid, not even four years old at the time, but I could set a horse good as any man."

I turned sideways in my seat, extended an arm across the seat back, and nodded at KC. It was easy to see that this retelling was getting his blood up, and he caught Powell looking at him in the rearview.

"What are you staring at, boy?" KC said. "Am I boring you?"

"No, sir."

"Well, your goddamned leg's pumping like a piston. Fingers are all twitchy on that steering wheel, too."

"It's just what I do when I drive."

"Folks your age ain't earned the right to tell lengthy stories, so don't be getting impatient with me. You listen up, youngblood, you're gonna be sittin' in this back seat one of these days."

"I understand, sir."

KC harrumphed and went silent. I thought he might have nodded off to sleep, but in the reflection of the window I could see his eyes roving the crest of the Cascades, then eastward toward the summit of Mount Hood.

"At one time," KC said as though from a great distance—he seemed to be speaking as much, now, to himself as he was to Powell and me—"there were a quarter million head of cattle ranging on the flats up near my place. There wasn't no water but for that little swamp. Folks call the damn thing 'Lake Rafferty' now."

I could see that Powell was about to interject, but when he saw me shake my head at him, he held his tongue.

"If it weren't for the old ranchers and the irrigation system we devised to water the herds way back then, why, there wouldn't be no Lake Rafferty a'tall; wouldn't be no meadows or no wildlife up there neither. Likely wouldn't be nothing there except fox's brush and rocks."

Anyone who grew up in this part of the state was familiar with the story, how that first generation transformed useless swampland into a meadow that eventually became a favorite waypoint for migratory birds. Then the passage of the Thompson Act in 1913 paved the way for anyone to "reclaim" a lake by draining it. All they had to do was seek approval from the Land Board for permission, and afterward, the "reclaimed" land could be sold off to developers. In the first year alone, there had been more than a half dozen separate attempts to drain Lake Rafferty, but the ranchers fought like hell to hold on to their water rights and succeeded in beating back the development efforts. As a result, Lake Rafferty survived.

It was easy to understand KC's bitterness at the irony: If not for the stubbornness of the ranchers, the Wildlife Refuge would have been lost right then and there, stillborn before its conception.

We pulled off the highway for a late lunch at a barbecue joint outside of Black Butte. I wasn't hungry, so I ate the salad that came with Powell's rack of pork ribs. In the time it took for Powell and me to clean our plates, KC devoured a half basket of bread rolls, a Porterhouse, and an Idaho potato wrapped in tinfoil that he had smothered in sour cream and butter.

We stepped outside into an afternoon whose sunlight had grown dim and cold behind a bank of storm clouds that had descended from the peaks of the divide.

"Nobody seems to remember it no more," KC said once we got back on the road. "But it wasn't long after all that reclamation foolishness had ended that the feds began to cancel grazing permits out of the blue. With nowhere for the cows to graze, Fish and Wildlife was able to acquire those family ranches up there on the plain for next to nothing. And once they did, they diverted all the water rights that came with them ranches into Rafferty Lake and—what do you think happened next, youngblood?"

Powell's expression registered surprise at having been included in KC's monologue, and it took him so long to reply that I had to nudge him with the toe of my boot.

"The water level rose?"

"Hell yes, the water level rose," KC said. "Rose up until a couple dozen more private spreads in the lowlands got flooded out, lock, stock, and barrel. It broke those poor folks to their last nickel, and they damn near gave their land away. My old daddy died that very same year, but my wife and me held on by our fingernails."

The landscape outside the window had transcended from dense forest to rock strewn flatland as we pressed deeper into the southeastern quarter of the county. Stands of dwarf juniper and wild grass grew inside the folds of low, rolling hills dotted with reefs of igneous stones and boulders that had been deposited over eons of volcanic eruptions and the ebb and flow of floodwaters. A brace of scavenging blacktail foraged in the shadows where thick bunches of nopal had taken root amid the deadfall and the rubble.

KC had gone silent again, and I turned to find him resting his head between the seatback and the glass, where he had drifted off to sleep.

I SHOOK KC's shoulder as we pulled into the driveway at his ranch.

"I guess I didn't get much shuteye over the past couple days," he said, yawning.

Powell left the engine running, touched the brim of his hat as the old man and I unfolded ourselves from the Blazer and climbed down.

"Come on inside, youngblood," KC said. "There's something I want you to see."

Irene met us at the back door, practically threw herself into her husband's arms. For one fleeting instant the years fell away, and I thought I saw them as they had once been, then the moment vanished, like an echo. Jarvis Lynch, Irene's brother, stepped up and took KC's hand in both of his own.

"You alright?" Lynch asked KC.

"They ran me over the hurdles a little bit," KC said. "But I'm okay. Who're those fellas?"

Irene led KC into their living room, where a thick-shouldered man and another one who kept his back to me dealt cards on the low table that fronted the couch. I placed the larger one's age in the mid-thirties, and when he stood, he was taller than I had expected, with a chest like a beer barrel and eyes that seemed to appraise and categorize all at once. A military M-65 jacket printed in camouflage was folded across the seat cushion beside him, and both Powell and I recognized the momentary once-over he gave us before he turned his attention to KC.

The second man was much shorter, lean and wiry, with a swarthy complexion and an unshaven, angular face that carried the haunted expression of an outcast, or the lone survivor of a catastrophe.

"This is Greg Reeves," Irene said to her husband, referring first to the tall one. "And Greg's friend, Chester Zachary. They're acquaintances of my brother's, out from Nevada."

"Sir," Reeves said.

Zachary said nothing, only nodded.

"Mr. Reeves and his friend drove out to help Jarvis and me move the whole herd up to the winter pasture," Irene continued.

"That was very kind of you," KC said. "Long way to come. I'm obliged."

"Happy to be of assistance, sir," Reeves said and looked as though he was waiting for an order to stand at parade rest.

"Well," KC said, "you all go on with your game or whatever it was you were doing."

"Let's get you out of that old coat," Irene said to KC. She lifted herself up on her toes and began to reach for his collar. "I made a fresh batch of cookies."

"In a minute," he replied, and gestured in Powell's general direction. "Grab those field glasses off that table behind you and come with me, youngblood."

Powell picked up a pair of binoculars by the leather neck strap and followed KC through the sliding glass door and onto a raised deck that offered a long view across a low, rolling field.

"You can come too, Sheriff," he said, and I noticed the look that passed between Reeves and Zachary.

The storm clouds that had begun to crowd the sky had taken on the color of dirty dish rags, and the chill wind seemed to slice through skin and bone. Sporadic drops of rain began to fall, landing on the topsoil with tiny puffs of dust, the air gravid with the odors of stagnant water.

"What is that smell?" Powell asked KC.

"Carp."

"Carp? The fish?"

"Train them glasses over that way," KC said. "Past the little buildings and the watchtower, off to the south."

"Is that Lake Rafferty?"

"Sure enough is."

"What the hell?" Jordan whispered. "Why does it look like that? Where is everybody?"

"They board up the buildings during the off-season," KC said. "The real question is, do you see any critters thereabouts?"

Powell lowered the glasses from his eyes and passed them to me. I had seen it before but took another look anyway.

"Birds don't migrate through the refuge anymore," I said. "Haven't done for years."

I returned the binoculars to KC and he slung the strap over his shoulder.

"Sheriff's right. FWS did a study that confirms it," KC said to my deputy. "My wife got her hands on a copy. Them birds quit migrating through here because the dumb sonsabitches introduced the carp into the lake."

"I don't follow," Powell said.

"The damned fish are native to Asia, not Oregon. Anyway, the fish ate all the water plants that the birds once used for food and nesting and what have you. Now the carp population's in the millions, the water's gone brown, and the birds don't bother stoppin' here no more."

"You've got to be shitting me," Powell said.

"Not even one little turd's worth. This world's full of irony, youngblood."

"Tell him the rest of it, KC," I said.

He narrowed his eyes and took one final look at what had once been a pristine mountain lake.

"The BLM and FWS have started to hire commercial fishermen to harvest the carp," he said finally. "Forget about a bird sanctuary; now it's the damn fish that brings in all the cash."

ON THE drive back to Meridian, the storm that we had seen gathering along the ridgeline erupted into a downpour. Fat raindrops collected on the windshield and slid off in the headwind like beads of quicksilver the thickness of my thumb.

"Did that guy seem off to you?" Powell asked, raising his voice above the sound of driving rain.

The runoff and yellow light from the instrument panel marbled Powell's face with strangely patterned shadows.

"Which guy?"

"Greg Reeves."

"I thought they both seemed fluky," I said. "And I'm not real copacetic having Jarvis Lynch hanging around, either. The man's become a political lightning rod. Irene and KC have never had it easy out there, and I wish folks would try not to make it any worse."

Powell nodded and seemed to be steeling himself for something.

"About that situation at the hotel—"

"You've already heard what I have to say on that topic," I interrupted.

"Thing is—"

"First thing in the morning," I continued unabated, "run both Reeves and Zachary through the system and see if either one of them has a sheet."

Powell nodded again and remained silent for the rest of the drive, but that left leg of his continued to bob up and down like a pumpjack.

It was nearly eight o'clock by the time the rainstorm passed through and we returned to the substation to retrieve my truck. I was tired and hungry and ready to get home. I had no doubt that my deputy felt the same way. I climbed out of Powell's Blazer, dug my own keys from my pocket as I crossed the unlighted parking lot toward my pickup.

I halted in my tracks as I approached the driver's side door.

"Everything okay, boss?" Powell shouted.

Some time during the two days we'd been gone, someone had slammed a chunk of concrete through the side window of my truck, climbed inside the cab, and used it as a public toilet.

CHAPTER EIGHT

JESSE AND I ate breakfast together at the kitchen table that morning, silent but for the melody of the wind chimes Jesse had strung up in the maple tree outside of our back door. When I looked up from my plate to reach for my orange juice, I found her staring at me.

"What's going on, Ty?"

"I don't know what you're referring to."

She leaned into the space between us, her shoulders cocked and forearms resting on the tabletop. She tipped her head to one side and seemed to be considering me anew.

"You haven't talked to me in days," she said.

"I've been in the city."

"Don't hooraw me, Tyler. You know what I mean."

The skin was tight along her cheekbones, and her eyes had begun to smolder.

"They dropped all the charges against KC," I said.

"I heard that on the TV and the radio. Tell me something that hasn't been all over the news."

"They kept him locked up in a jail cell for an extra day because they could, Jesse. No other reason. Just to rub his nose in it. The man's seventy-plus years old."

"Goddamn it, Ty," she said, her pupils constricting to pinpoints. "Can you just try to pretend that you can trust me with the truth? I found your clothes this morning wrapped up in a ball at the bottom of the sink in the mudroom. They reek like a barroom toilet. The dog wouldn't even sleep in there. Oh, yeah, and someone vandalized your truck."

"It isn't about trust, Jesse."

"Then what is it about?"

I am not one of those men who cannot articulate his feelings, but I am a product of my generation, and I hold fast to certain values that sometimes mystify my wife and daughter.

"There is a lot of ugliness out there, Jesse."

"You think you're protecting me?"

"It's always been my aim to protect you."

"Why do you do this, Ty? I'm a grown woman."

I re-folded my napkin with unnecessary care and placed it next to my plate.

"Because it doesn't help either one of us for me to lay my unfinished business at your feet," I said. "It's like digging for water under an outhouse."

There was something in my tone that even I didn't like hearing, something I wasn't proud of, and she slid her chair away from the table.

"That's lovely, Tyler."

She stood and picked up my plate of cold, uneaten eggs, carried it to the sink, and scraped it into the disposal.

"You're not doing me a favor by living behind a glass wall," she said, and walked out of the room.

I PUSHED through the door at the substation and strode past Jordan Powell without a word, still raw from my morning at home. He had the telephone receiver wedged between his shoulder and his chin and was scribbling something on a yellow legal pad.

"Wait a minute," Powell said as I hung up my coat and stepped into the back room for coffee. "He's right here."

"No, I'm not."

He covered the mouthpiece with one hand and said, "It's Laura Bursack from the coroner's office."

"Not now, Jordan."

"He'll call you right back," Powell said as he swiveled his chair away from me.

"Take a damn message, Deputy Powell."

"She already hung up."

"Goddamnit."

I carried my coffee to my desk, set it down hard enough to spill about a quarter of it across the blotter. I mopped it up with my handkerchief and took the file folder and pink phone message slip that Powell handed to me.

"I ran a background on the two guys we met yesterday at the Sheridans'," he said. "It's in the file."

"Thank you."

"The big one—Greg Reeves—he's a militia from Gabbs, Nevada."

"Does the Richfield station still do body work?" I asked.

"I think so," he said. "Did you hear what I just told you?"

"Something about Reeves."

"I said, 'he's militia.' So's the little squirrely guy. They were part of the dustup at Jarvis Lynch's ranch a couple years back."

That earned my attention. It also explained the man's odd behavior and bearing, and why there was something familiar about him. I recalled having seen him interviewed by the media both during and after the standoff.

"Did either of them do any time?" I asked.

"Catch and release."

"Shit."

"Yes, sir."

Outside, a sunbreak cast Meridian's main street into stark contrast with the pulsing thunderheads along the horizon. I could feel the drop in barometric pressure inside the depths of my skull.

"Run down and ask the Richfield guys to tow my truck in from the ranch," I said as I dialed the phone number for the morgue.

"What should I tell them to do with it?"

"They'll know."

LAURA BURSACK was as chipper on the telephone as she was in real life. Among her duties at County Hospital was to act as Meriwether County's appointed coroner. She possessed the kinetic energy of a passerine bird and the enthusiasm of a high school cheerleader, the precise reasons I had asked Jordan to take a message. As much as I appreciated her personality, I was not in the mood for it today, so I got straight to the point.

"Deputy Powell tells me you're ready to release the body?"

"I'm finished with him if you are, Sheriff," she said.

"What's your opinion on cause and manner?"

"Obviously, cause of death is a single bullet wound to the forehead," she said. "But I'm inclined to consult with you before I commit completely with regard to manner."

"You've ruled out suicide?"

She paused for a moment, and I could hear the casters of her desk chair rolling across the linoleum floor in her office and the snap of her door latch striking the selvage.

"There's virtually no stippling on the wound," she said, more softly now, and I wondered why she felt the need to lock her door. "That means the killshot came from at least thirty inches away."

"More than an arm's length," I said. "But I suppose it's possible he could have figured a way to do it himself."

"Are you serious?"

"I'm saying it's *possible*."

"You're messing with me, aren't you," she said.

"Devil's advocate."

"OK. Your crime scene report also mentioned a second bullet hole in the wall behind the victim."

"It's not unheard of," I said. "Sometimes a suicide needs to work up his courage."

"There was no residue or other evidence I saw that would corroborate that," she said. "You'd think there'd be powder on his ear, his face, something."

"Still . . ."

"Do you genuinely believe what you're saying to me, Sheriff Dawson?"

"No."

"I can't call it suicide. I'm labeling it as 'Undetermined/Pending' until somebody persuades me otherwise," she said. "Are you okay with that?"

"I'm keeping my investigation open, too."

"Any reason I shouldn't release the body?"

"No ma'am," I said. "I don't need it. I'll let PPB know they can come and pick up the victim."

* * *

I LOCKED the substation door and stepped into the morning, where the familiar smells from Rowan Boyle's diner carried on the breeze, but the shops and storefronts along Main had yet to open for business. I adjusted my gun belt and buttoned my duster, tugged the brim of my Stetson down low on my brow and walked westward, the orange glow of the sun at my back. A scrub jay called out from the top of a white oak beside the vacant lot that had once been a record store. The scorch marks from the conflagration that had razed the old building were still visible on the asphalt, as were the shriveled leaves of rabbitbrush and bilberry that grew wild along the periphery.

A few blocks further on, the spires of The Portman appeared as if from nowhere, amid a dense grove of tamarack. Built at the turn of the last century, the residents of Meridian still referred to it as the Gold Hotel, a reference to both the prices and the décor.

It is perched on a promontory overlooking the river, where the channel runs wide and deep and makes a gentle turn southward. What had once been a sixty-room Victorian beauty, the center of elegance and commerce for stockmen and their financiers, she stood more as a curiosity now; a remnant of an era bypassed by the interstate and whose only modern credential was its place on the historical register.

I stepped off the sidewalk, between the wrought iron entry gates, and onto the masonry footpath that bisected the gardens. The sound of the river drifted like a sigh as I passed beneath trellises draped with leafless wisteria, and the cordons and canes of dormant vines spiraled the stanchions.

A piked fence marked the stairway that led to the hotel's main entrance. Through the leather of my gloves, I could still feel the vestiges of hoarfrost as I gripped the brass pull, moved across the threshold and into an entirely different century altogether.

The foyer was warmed by a wood-burning fireplace positioned near the foot of a sweeping staircase that was wide enough to stand six men abreast. Overhead, a chandelier crafted by Tiffany bore the images of roses rendered in shades of claret and malachite and bathed the blockwood walls and velvet draperies with golden light. I paused a moment longer to admire a painting by Thomas Moran.

Though I had asked Deputy Chief Overton to order his detective home, I strongly suspected that he hadn't done so. He'd mentioned the hotel in his remarks to me, so I intended to find out for myself. I stepped up to the check-in desk and waited for the clerk to finish his phone call.

"Good morning, Sheriff," he said once he hung up.

"Do you have a guest by the name of Dan Halloran? Big guy, long sideburns, dresses like an LA pimp."

"I'm not supposed to say, sir," he answered, but angled his head in the direction of the bar.

"Much obliged," I said and moved across the lobby toward the lounge.

"Hollywood" Dan Halloran sat alone drinking a Bloody Mary at the mahogany rail, licking salt from the rim of hurricane glass and stealing glances at his own profile in the bar mirror.

As I approached, the bartender acknowledged me with a barely perceptible nod and Halloran turned in his seat.

"I thought I might find you here, Halloran," I said. "Of course, it wasn't all that difficult. It was either here or the Cottonwood Blossom, but the Blossom doesn't open 'til eleven."

"Charming. You country folks have an interesting sense of humor."

The name of the Cottonwood Blossom alluded to a slang term used by old-time cowboys, and referred to a recipient of frontier justice who'd been discovered dangling at the inclement end of a rope, most frequently a practitioner of cattle- or horse-theft.

"Our community takes pride in its history," I said. "We like to be sure that our visitors know where we stand."

"Take a load off your feet, Sheriff," he said. "You gotta try one of these cocktails. The bartender adds a float of Guinness and a slice of bacon to his recipe. It's pretty damn good. He put an extra slice in mine because I mentioned that I'm a friend of yours. Join me."

"I'm on the clock."

"Your loss. Breakfast of champions."

He shrugged and hoisted his glass to his lips, eyeballed me from behind the celery stalk and a skewer of stuffed olives as he drank.

"I can see that you're grieving," I said. "So I'll get directly to the point: the coroner's ready to release your partner's body."

Halloran's eyes moved to the window that looked out onto the hotel grounds. Though the flower garden had gone bare, the lawn appeared pristine despite the late season.

"It's always sad when a brother officer takes his own life," he said.

"That is a fact," I said. "It's good to start off your day with a nugget of truth. Actually, I've got another truth grenade for you, Halloran."

"What's that?" he asked and tilted his glass to his lips again.

"The official manner of death is being listed as 'Undetermined/Pending.'"

The stem of his hurricane met the bar with a force that rattled the silverware in the tray. Halloran glared at me as he wiped at his mouth with the back of his hand.

"I don't believe I heard you correctly," he said.

Outside the window, a single white swan paddled in slow circles across an emerald pond.

"The case remains open," I said. "But don't worry, detective. You have my word that I won't let go of this case until I find out exactly what happened to your partner. You know, in order to clear any misgivings folks might have about you or the PPB."

"Misgivings," he repeated.

"It's the least I can do for you, seeing as you're a brother officer and all."

WHEN I returned to the substation, I phoned Lieutenant Morgan at PPB Special Investigations.

"I just had a word with your Detective Halloran," I said. "He's still here in town, by the way. *My* town. I informed him that we're ready to release Clark Wehr's remains."

"You've locked the case down?"

"I'm afraid not."

"What's the problem, if you don't mind my asking," he asked, though he didn't sound particularly surprised.

"Among other things," I said, "the weapon from the scene had its serial number removed. Burned off. Nevertheless, I have reason to believe it traces back to the evidence room at PPB. It went missing from a case involving Wehr and Halloran. I suspect one of them carried it as a throwaway."

"How could you possibly know something like that?"

"I hold the state police forensics team in high regard," I said. "But I try not to involve myself too much in their methodology."

FIVE MINUTES after I had returned to my office, the phone rang. It was Deputy Chief Overton.

"What is this bullshit I just heard from Lieutenant Morgan?"

"I have no way of knowing which bullshit you are referring to," I said.

"How long does it take to close a suicide in Meriwether County?"

"As long as it takes."

"I thought I made myself clear to you last time we spoke."

His manner belied malevolence as much as irritation, and it sounded as though he were speaking through clenched teeth.

In large part, the settlers of this county—the whole damned state for that matter—were direct descendants of the pioneers, survivors of a frequently deadly two-thousand-mile trek along the Oregon Trail. Many of our antecedents drowned in river crossings, were killed in bloody, hostile raids, or died painfully and miserably from dehydration, starvation, or disease. But the ones who could endure the distance, from the Kansas Territory all the way through Nebraska and Wyoming, the people who forded the Platte River and the Snake, and crossed the Blue Mountain Range through passes with names like Flagstaff and Deadman in wagons made of wood and canvas? These men and women were not to be trifled with or condescended to, nor did one easily earn their trust or their clemency.

"You're not from Oregon are you, Deputy Chief?" I asked.

"You don't want to try my patience."

"That is not a tone you want to employ with me, sir," I said. "I strongly recommend you arrange for a vehicle to retrieve your fallen officer's body and order Halloran to get back home where he belongs. This conversation is concluded."

"That doesn't work for me, Sheriff."

"I don't work for you, either," I said, and killed the line.

CHAPTER NINE

THE NEXT MORNING, I was out the door well before sunup. The sky was cloudless and black, though the stars appeared to glimmer with uncommon urgency. The half-frozen soil made a noise like loose pebbles beneath my boots, my breath visible in the darkness. Even the horses in the remuda remained unusually silent, the only sounds the baying of coyotes in the distance and a pair of horned owls trading calls from somewhere deep inside the woods.

I slid into the barn as quietly as I could, switching on the overhead light only after I had shut the doors behind me. Drambuie nickered low in his chest when he heard me approach his stall. He rubbed his face against my pant leg when I unlatched the door to slip the halter on.

I spoke softly as I brushed and saddled him, both of us taking comfort in the familiar ritual. He followed me with his ears as I circled behind him, combed out his tail, and hooked his hoofs. I gently stroked his neck as I led him outdoors on his lead line, switched off the barn light, and waited in companionable silence as we both adjusted to the dark.

THERE IS a peculiar kind of quiet that defines autumn and winter. The wind suspires differently as it passes through the branches of the tall pines and the shallows of creek canyons, and the remote calls of wildlife can echo for miles within the gorge.

Drambuie and I picked our way along a rugged northwesterly course until we crossed the dry stream bed where I had blazed the tree bark all those years ago. The light on the horizon softened with the promise of sunrise, and I stopped for a short while for my horse to catch his breath. I lost myself to the hypnotic rhythm of the single light atop the radio tower at the far end of the valley as one by one the stars melted away.

Drambuie began to faunch and champ his bit as the first sunrays topped the ridgeline, wisps of vapor rising from the grass. Soft mist floated inside the cedar woods, and the uncertain glow that filtered down between the boughs seemed like the lace of Alençon.

I tied Drambuie's reins to a hitch post near the gate that led into the family plot. I drew a rag from the back pocket of my jeans and wiped away the dust and mud from headstones that marked the resting places for two generations of my family. I took a seat on the bench I'd constructed from the remnants of a fallen hemlock and lit a cigarette.

"Hello, Dad," I whispered.

PART THREE

NO SIMPLE HIGHWAY

CHAPTER TEN

WAIT. DON'T LIGHT that thing.

What?

I said don't torch that doobie, man. There's a cop coming over this way.

Shit. What should I do with it?

I don't know. Stuff it in your pocket. Hurry the hell up, he's, like, right on top of us, man.

Want to roll down your window, please?

He wants you to roll down the window.

I know. I heard him. I'm sitting right here.

You fellas okay in there?

We're fine, officer.

It isn't safe to park so close to the road like this.

Yeah, sorry. We were just getting a little sleep.

You don't have a place to stay?

No, dude. I mean, we're on kind of a road trip thing, and we just pulled off for a nap, you know. We're not vagrants or anything.

Didn't say you were. By the way, around here, some folks might consider the term 'dude' to be an insult.

No disrespect intended, officer.

I was just messing with you. But seriously, your friend looks like he's in pretty bad shape.

I'm okay.

Yeah, he's okay.

He looks a little peaked to me. You're sure you're all right? I used to have a bulldog when I was a kid. Had kind of a wheeze like you do. Snored like crazy. Sounded like a sawmill when he slept.

I'm okay.

If I was you, I'd have a doctor get eyeballs on you. We got one in Meridian, not far from here. Probably ain't in his office, yet, though. Still pretty early. The hospital's up the road a little ways further on, though. They're always open.

Thanks. I think we'll just get moving.

I see you got Montana tags.

Yes, sir.

What brings you out this way?

Like I said, just a little road trip. See America while we're young and all that jive. You know.

If you change your mind about seeing that doctor, there's a diner in town that isn't bad. Tell 'em Deputy Powell sent you. I'm just kidding, you don't have to tell 'em that. Anyway, you can get something to eat while you're waiting for the doc. Just a thought.

We appreciate it, officer. Thank you.
Don't park by the side of the road anymore, though, fellas. I'm serious.
We won't. Have a nice day.
Sure thing. You, too.

JESUS.
I know. Shit.
What the hell are you doing, don't light it now, asshole.
Now's when I need it. You saying you don't want a toke?
Just go back to sleep.
I can't sleep after that. My heart's pounding. Feels like it's coming out of my chest, man. I thought we were busted for sure.
Just shut up and let me drive.

WHAT'S WITH the racket, man?
I thought you were sleeping.
I was. Turn it down.
I thought you liked Zeppelin.
Not when I'm trying to sleep.
I was tired of the radio. The only station that comes in is some news channel, dude. It's like there's only one story over and over.
Well, turn it down, man—
Here, take this napkin and wipe your damn mouth. I think you're going to cough up a lung.
That isn't funny. I can barely breathe.
It's your own damn fault.
This again. Kiss my ass. And turn off the music. Seriously.
There. Happy now?
Better.
Here, listen to the radio: See what I mean? I swear I've heard this story fifty times.
What story?
This one on the damn radio. Old rancher guy keeps getting hassled by the FBI.
Why would the FBI want to screw around with an old rancher? He's not growing weed is he? That would be pretty cool if he was.
It ain't about weed, man.
Then what is it about?
I don't know, man. Go back to sleep. You're white as a sheet.

WHERE THE HELL is this, now?
Hospital.
Finally. Jesus.

Well?

Well what?

What are you waiting for? Get out of the car.

I can't walk all the way in there by myself. I can't make it that far, man.

I sure as hell can't carry you.

Why the hell not?

We don't need that kind of attention.

Are you kidding me? An hour ago, we were rapping with a pig in uniform by the side of the county road. With a joint in my shirt pocket. In the middle of fricking Hicksville. In the fricking dark.

I'm not gonna press our luck any more than we already have. That's all I'm saying. I'll take you as far as the door. They got people inside that can help you from there.

You going on without me, then?

I'm not gonna leave you, Shannon. But I can't stay here. Where's the gun?

I thought you were pissed off at me for having a gun.

I am. But you can't take it inside the hospital with you, can you? I just want to know where you stashed it.

Under my seat.

Okay.

Okay.

I'll check in later to see how you're doing. I'll come get you once they got you fixed up. Gimme your wallet.

What for?

So you won't have any ID on you. Give 'em a fake name when they ask.

I'll give 'em your name.

Don't even joke around about that.

Don't leave me here stranded. I'm not messing around.

I already told you I won't.

Swear to god?

Yes.

Say it.

I swear to god I won't leave you here stranded.

Where're you gonna be?

I don't know. I'll find something. Hole up somewhere I can find some food. Like back at that old cabin.

You can't go back to that place.

No shit, Sherlock. I'm just saying, someplace *like* it, someplace that might have some food and a real bed.

Like where?

You're starting to piss me off again, man. Don't worry about it, I'll figure it out. Now, put your arm around my shoulder and lean on me.

Slow down, it hurts when you walk that fast, man.

We go any slower, we'll be walking backwards. Prop yourself up for a second while I grab the door.

Can I help you?

This man is hurt. He needs a doctor.

Don't leave me stranded.

Say that one more time and I swear I'll kill you myself.

CHAPTER ELEVEN

DEAN STRICKLYN, the Portland attorney and owner of the fishing cabin in which Clark Wehr's body had been found had been stalling me for days. The case had bogged to a practical standstill, and I knew that if there was anything more for me to uncover, it would have to be done in the city.

I parked on Second Street, two blocks from the Willamette River, fed the meter, and walked to the law offices of Porter, Jax & Stricklyn. It was nearing noon, and I hoped Dean Stricklyn had not already slipped out for lunch.

The office receptionist was a petite brunette in possession of a bustline that was clearly aftermarket and eyebrows that had been shaped in such a way as to give the impression that she lived in a continuous state of astonishment. I introduced myself and was instructed to wait while she checked on Mr. Stricklyn's availability.

"I'd rather you not ruin the surprise," I said, and started down the hall.

The receptionist followed close on my heels as I brushed by her and made my way along a corridor paneled in burlwood, past the conference room and the closet-sized offices of the firm's paralegals, law clerks, and associates.

"You can't be back here, sir," she said to my back. "Mr. Stricklyn doesn't know you're coming."

"I suspect that on some level he does."

The doorway leading into the corner office stood wide open. An engraved plaque mounted on the wall informed me that I'd found the man I had been looking for.

Stricklyn unfolded himself from his button-tufted leather chair as I stepped inside his office. Over his shoulder, beyond the glass curtain wall, the sun glinted on the snowcapped slopes of Mount St. Helens. Fifteen floors below, a warning signal sounded as the center span of the Steel Bridge was lifted for a passing freighter.

I stepped inside and waited for a moment until the full weight of his attention landed on me.

"I'm Sheriff Ty Dawson, Meriwether County," I said, and made myself comfortable in his guest chair. "I've been trying to reach you, as you know."

Dean Stricklyn was a man of contradictions. I placed his age in the early forties, tall and stoop-shouldered, the vestige of a surgical scar on his mouth suggesting he'd had a harelip as a child. He gave the impression of self-consciousness about his height, but his unblinking glare belied an underlying ferocity that he seemed able to contain only through sheer force of will.

"I'm just leaving for a lunch appointment," he said.

"I'll join you."

I leaned into the caress of soft leather and took in the trappings of his legal practice as he gave in and resettled his seat. Elegantly framed landscapes in oil and acrylic flanked the sofa at the far end of the room while educational diplomas and a variety of honorary membership certificates lined the wall beside his desk. He eyed me with palpable hostility as I perused the photographs that choked the surface of Stricklyn's credenza, posing with local politicos and minor celebrities. I couldn't tell if this stage-set was intended to impress or intimidate others, or merely to remind him of whom he believed himself to be.

"It took me nearly three hours to drive here for a conversation we could have had over the phone," I said. "I've left you several messages. It makes me wonder why you would put me off that way."

"I didn't think there was anything I could add to your investigation."

"Not exactly your decision to make."

"What do you want, Sheriff?" he asked me, frowning at his wristwatch.

"What was your relationship with Detective Clark Wehr?"

"He was a casual acquaintance. I don't recall exactly how we met."

"And Detective Dan Halloran?"

"He was Clark Wehr's partner."

"You invited Detective Wehr to use your fishing cabin?"

"Yes."

"For what purpose?"

"So he could go fishing," he said, and tugged his French cuff across the face of his Patek Philippe.

"Did Wehr give you any reason to believe he was about to take his own life?"

"Of course not."

"Is that the mayor?"

"I beg your pardon?"

I made a gesture indicating his side table.

"In the photo," I said. "Looks like you and the mayor on the golf course. And that other one looks like you and Spiro Agnew. Your political allegiances seem unusually . . . elastic."

"And your political allegiances? What might they be?"

"I'm a political agnostic."

"I find that difficult to believe, Sheriff."

"I said what I meant. I always do."

He flashed a tight, dismissive smile at me.

"I think we're finished here," he said.

"Christ," I said, and gestured to the photo of Dan Stricklyn with the mayor on the fairway. "Golf is such a waste of everything that's measurable, don't you think? Land, water, money, time."

He made a move to get up from his chair, but I didn't budge.

"Why do you think Clark Wehr shot himself?" I asked.

"How would I know?"

"It seems clear that you were rewarding him for something," I said. "So why would a man who had earned your gratitude want to blow his brains out in your cabin?"

"Unfortunate coincidence."

"In my line of work," I said, "there are far fewer coincidences than there are secrets."

The twitch that touched the corner of Dean Stricklyn's mouth put me in mind of a nature film I'd once watched on television. The subject dealt with red pandas in the wild and how they frequently appeared to grin before they initiated an attack.

I CALLED the Meridian substation from a payphone near the waterfront. I listened as Griffin ran down a list of messages while I watched a colony of seabirds scavenge scraps of rubbish that had gathered along the littoral. The last of the messages Griffin read to me caught me by surprise.

I thanked him and rang off, then dropped another set of coins into the slot.

"Meet me at the oyster bar on Ankeny Street," Lieutenant Morgan said to me when he came on the line. "Dan & Louis. I'm sure you know the place."

"How'd you know I was in town?"

"Be there in thirty minutes."

"Slow down," I said, but I was speaking to a dial tone.

I fed the parking meter and made the short walk to the raw bar, took the stool nearest the door, and ordered a half dozen Yaquinas and an ice tea while I waited. Morgan showed up ten minutes later with a manila envelope tucked under his arm.

"You've got a lot of people riled up, Dawson," he said as he slid onto the seat beside me.

The lunch rush had already come and gone, and the lieutenant and I were alone in this corner of the room but for the middle-aged, bald-headed man behind the bar who busied himself shucking shells.

"You don't see me," Morgan said to the bald man who did not raise his eyes from his work.

"No sir," the man said. "I never do, Lieutenant. You ate yet?"

"Nope."

"Same as always?"

"Why not?"

I forked the last oyster off my plate, dredged it through some horseradish, and waited for the barman to disappear through the door that led into the kitchen before I spoke.

"How did you know I was in town?" I asked.

"I've got a detail set up on Stricklyn's office," Morgan said. "His residence, as well."

"So what am I, your stalking horse, now?"

"No, but you have become a useful distraction."

"Why do I feel as though I walked in halfway through the movie?"

"Because you did," he said. "Both of us did. It's just that I've got a seat a little closer to the screen."

He was about to say something else when the kitchen door swung open. We waited while the barman laid a linen napkin with silverware rolled inside beside a plate piled high with battered shrimp and fries in front of Morgan. He nodded to the lieutenant, then moved away without a word.

"Best fried shrimp in the city," Morgan said, and flattened the napkin across his lap.

"Due respect, Lieutenant Morgan, but I've got a hell of a drive ahead of me."

He wiped the crumbs of shrimp batter from his hands and peeled open the clasp that bound the envelope he'd brought. He slid a file folder from inside it and pushed it across the countertop to me. Inside was a small stack of eight-by-ten black-and-white photographs. Their quality was poor, grainy from deficient lighting and the magnification of a telephoto lens.

"I recognize Dean Stricklyn, but who are those two guys?" I asked.

"Fairly certain the one on the right is Clark Wehr. Probably doesn't look the same as when you saw him last."

"And the other? The one with his back to the camera?"

"We're not completely sure, but we've got a few guesses. He doesn't turn up all that often, but when he does, he's careful not to show his face."

"Where were these taken?"

Morgan shot a glance around the room before he spoke.

"Remember when I told you I'm watching Stricklyn's place?" he said. "I've also got eyes on the Countess. I told you about her—"

"I remember," I said. "These pictures were shot outside Ivy Novack's house?"

"No," he said, shook his head, and dropped a shrimp tail on his plate. "Those were taken in the parking lot behind the condominium she operates as a massage parlor."

"When?"

"Could have been pretty much any Thursday or Sunday night until about two weeks ago when it all stopped cold."

IT WAS approaching three in the afternoon by the time I walked back to my vehicle, stopped off at a deli on the corner, and bought a couple cans of RC Cola for the drive home. When I came outside again, a young man wearing a brown leather three-quarter, a turtleneck sweater, and woolen watch cap was pacing back and forth beneath the awning. His breath was coming out in plumes as he rubbed his bare palms together.

"I need to talk to you," he said.

His eyes cut sideways down the block, and he tucked his chin into the collar of his overcoat. The sky had darkened, and the atmosphere felt ripe with an approaching cloudburst.

"You must have me mistaken for someone else," I said.

"No, sir. No mistake. You just had a sit-down with the head of SID. I been following you since Ankeny Street."

"Listen, son. I'm tired, I'm frustrated, and I'm armed. I got a long drive ahead of me, so you're going to need to stand aside."

"Dan Halloran. Clark Wehr," he said as I began to turn away. There was an edge of desperation in his voice.

When I turned toward him, the skin beneath his eye began to twitch.

"Dean Stricklyn," he said. "Those names mean anything to you?"

My fingers grazed the Colt Trooper clipped to my belt.

He tilted his head in my direction, eyes locked on something at the far end of the street, and spoke to me out of the corner of his mouth.

"I know you're a cop," he said. "Only an asshole messes with a cop, and I'm no asshole."

"Spit it out. What do you want?"

"Chinatown's a couple blocks away. I can't be seen with you out here on the street. There's a little grocery store just inside the gate," he said, and hustled away.

I had driven all this way to try and shake out something that might breathe new life into the Wehr case. I found myself reminded that, more often than not, one's desires were not often manifested in the way they were expected.

Seven minutes later I passed into the city's Chinatown, spotted the tiny grocery market three doors down the block, but saw no sign of the man in the three-quarter coat and watch cap. The smell of cooking oil and seared meat drifted in the air, stirred an uninvited and ambiguous memory of my war, and just as suddenly fell away.

A tiny brass bell chimed as I opened the door and moved into the cloying heat and overwhelming aroma of sandalwood incense inside. An old woman behind the counter looked through me without expression, then gestured toward a door at the far end of a narrow aisle whose shelves had been stacked with kitchen wares, dried vegetables and spices, and canned goods bearing contents I could only guess at.

My right hand rested on my pistol grip as I twisted the doorknob with my left. The man in the three-quarter coat was leaning with one foot propped against the back wall of the stockroom, lighting a cigarette as I slipped inside and kicked the door shut behind me.

He had removed the watch cap he'd been wearing, his dark hair parted down the middle and long enough to brush the tops of his shoulders. His pale complexion spoke not so much of ancestry, but of a nocturnal lifestyle, with eyes that turned down at the corners, reflecting distrust like a man who once possessed something of great value but had lost it.

"What are we doing here?" I said.

"There's only two Asian cops in the entire PPB. Both of them work the other side of the river. If another white face besides you or me shows itself inside this room, we'll both know we have a problem."

"You've got two minutes, then I'm gone," I said. "You read me?"

He drew on his cigarette and studied me with aporetic eyes, as though there could be no turning back.

"My business partner and I are confidential informants for Wehr and Halloran. At least we were until a few days ago. Patrol cops found my partner in an abandoned clapboard by the river. Somebody hammered off his kneecaps before they carved out his tongue and put a bullet through his throat. Next thing I know, I hear Wehr killed himself and I haven't seen Detective Halloran in days."

"Not to be unsympathetic to your situation, but this sounds like Lieutenant Morgan's problem. Clock's running."

"Morgan hasn't been in that office two months yet; probably doesn't even know what's going on in his own house."

"What am I supposed to do with that?" I asked.

"I don't know if I can trust the man," he said, growing agitated. "If I guess wrong about him, I'm dead. You understand that, right?"

"My boots might smell like cow shit, son, but I understand the content of your statement perfectly well."

He began to pace the tiny room in a manner of an inmate.

"Look man, these SID guys have been pulling all the usual shit for years: falsifying search warrants, planting evidence, and running shakedowns. Everybody knew the game. But now? The cops got half the drug dealers in town teaming up with them against the other half. That's how they turned me and Buzzy."

"Buzzy is your partner."

"Was," he said, and took another drag off his cigarette. "They told us if we ratted out our competition, it'd be a good deal for me and Buzzy, right? We get a free ride on the collar and the other assholes go to jail. Narcs confiscate our competitor's stash, give it to us, and *we* put it right back on the street, like we're business partners."

"I'm still not seeing what this has to do with me."

"Shit," he said, shook his head, and crushed the butt beneath one of his eelskin zip-up boots. "Turns out, the goddamn cops are the most ruthless drug pushers in town."

"Like I said before: tell it to Morgan," I said. "He seems like good police. I don't know what else to say to you."

"You're still not hearing me, man," he said, and began pacing in a circle. "One of my handlers has killed himself, and the other one's gone missing."

"Wehr and Halloran."

"Yes."

I didn't know the source of his information about Wehr's alleged suicide, but while the kid might be short on details, he was correct about Wehr being off the board. I was vaguely troubled, though, to hear that he believed Dan Halloran to have somehow gone missing.

"You ain't from PPB," he continued. "You might be the only one I can trust.

It's like the whole narc unit's turned into a firing squad, except they're standing in a circle."

I slipped a pen and notebook from the pocket of my jacket.

"Write down your name and how I can reach you," I said.

He took a step away from me, his back against the wall.

"No chance, man. Next time you're in town, I'll find you."

THE SKY broke open when I was halfway home, a frog-choking downpour driven nearly horizontal by the wind. It was slow going as I made my way through the divide and was nearing midnight by the time I arrived home at the ranch, pulled my hat down low as I climbed out of the Bronco, and sprinted for the back door of the house.

Once inside, I peeled off my dripping Carhartt coat and hung it on a hook, poured myself three fingers of Jim Beam, and took a seat on the living room hearth and let the dying embers in the firebox warm the muscles of my back. Wyatt, our blue heeler, slipped through the gap where Jesse had left the bedroom door propped open, rubbed his muzzle on my leg, and curled up at my feet.

"I thought I heard you drive in," Jesse yawned as she moved down the hall.

She wrapped her arms around herself as though she'd felt a chill, stood halfway between the darkness and the firelight, and looked into my face.

"I'm sorry to wake you," I said.

"I wasn't really sleeping."

"I didn't expect to be so late."

"Are you alright?"

I nodded and patted a warm place on the stone beside me.

"Sit with me?" I invited.

"Okay," she answered, but chose to sit cross-legged on the floor beside my feet instead.

Rain ticked against the kitchen window as I watched the light and shadow play against her skin. I regretted and despised the distance I had put between the two of us because of my silence, the minefield I had inadvertently planted.

"I met a friend of yours today," she said.

"Is that so. Where?"

"He came into the thrift shop. It was my day to volunteer."

I felt the whisky warm my stomach, and I leaned down and scratched Wyatt behind his ears as I focused on my wife.

"Handsome man," she said. "Dan . . . something. Looks like somebody from the movies. He asked me to be sure to tell you he said hello."

CHAPTER TWELVE

THE NEXT DAY, I took the file folder Morgan had given me and returned to the Catonquin River Resort. The access road was cratered with potholes filled with rain runoff and brown mud and littered with boughs that had been blown down from the trees. I parked behind a hard-used Pontiac Tempest station wagon the color of cold oatmeal, a scuffed metal toolbox with its lid propped open resting on the drop-down tailgate.

I stood in silence, shielded my eyes against the ambient sun glare, and scanned the woods for any sign of Doug May, quiet but for the soft sound of the rushing river and the intermittent gusts passing through the trees. I tucked the file into my coat and moved off in the direction of the Stricklyn cabin.

It was there that I found the caretaker, balanced on an unsteady wooden stepladder with a hammer in his hand, making repairs to a section of gutter that had torn loose from the fascia and was swaying in the wind.

"You mind climbing down from there?" I asked.

"One second," he mumbled around the gutter spikes he had clenched between his teeth.

While I waited, I stepped beneath the overhang where the screen door slapped on creaking hinges, wedged it open with my toe, and peered inside. The crime scene tape had been pulled down out of the doorway, but the piceous remnant smudges of fingerprint dust still remained, like bone bruises, defacing the kitchen and living room.

I turned when I heard Doug May descend the ladder, and I slid the folder out from the lining of my coat. He glanced at me, then squatted to retrieve a bottle of TJ Swann out of a paper bag he'd left leaning against a rusted coffee can brimming with nails.

"'Mellow Days and Easy Nights,'" he quipped, and took a pull. "I was hoping you and I were finished, Sheriff. Don't forget that I'm the one who called you in the first place."

"I'm sorry, did I neglect to say, 'thank you'?"

My sarcasm wasn't lost on him.

"I'm just saying," he began. "Seems like I'm catching a lot of flak considering I'm one of the good guys."

"This isn't flak, Mr. May, it's follow-up. I need for you to take a look at this photo."

May tipped the bottle to his mouth again, then dried his lips with his shirt sleeve. He squinted at the photo for a moment before his face took on the color of a canned ham.

"Who is this man?" I asked. "The one who isn't Wehr or Stricklyn."

"I don't know," he said. "I can't see his face."

"You've seen him before."

May took a step backwards, as though if he created enough distance between the two of us, he could turn back time.

"Don't lie to me, Mr. May. The man's got ears like a taxi with its doors swung open. If you'd seen him before, you'd know. And I can see it in your eyes that you have."

"He may have been out here before."

"With Clark Wehr?"

May shook his head and cast his gaze deep inside the forest. When he touched the wine bottle to his lips this time, his hands were trembling.

"No," he said. "He was with Mr. Stricklyn."

"Were they out here more than once?"

He nodded.

"But I swear to god, I don't know his name."

"How about a woman from the city they call 'the Countess'? Have you seen her at Stricklyn's cabin, too?"

"I don't know anyone with a name like that."

He pulled his focus back from the middle distance.

"Mr. May, who told you not to talk to me?"

"Nobody."

I placed the photo back into the folder and handed him another of my business cards.

"I don't need your card, Sheriff. I've told you everything I can."

"That's an odd turn of a phrase: 'Everything you *can.*'"

"You know what I mean."

"I believe I do."

"I like this job. I used to like it, anyway."

"I bet you did. See you around, Mr. May."

AFTER LUNCH at Rowan Boyle's diner, I set off walking in the direction of the Gold Hotel to clear my head. I took the long way, meandering through quiet streets that had been named for spring flowers, past simple houses with wide porches, some decorated with jigsaw-cut bargeboards or disused lard cans planted with geraniums lining their windowsills. The sun broke through a rent in the overcast and I stopped for a moment to listen to the music that came from a leafless fruit tree whose branches had been strung with empty glass bottles colliding gently in the wind.

A short while later, I stepped into the hotel lobby and visited the uniformed desk clerk again.

"Is Dan Halloran still staying at the hotel?" I asked.

"Sheriff, I'm not supposed to—"

I placed my elbows on the counter and leaned into his space. He blinked at me and cut himself off in mid-sentence.

"This doesn't have to be difficult," I said. "Is Halloran a guest at the hotel or not?"

"No, sir. Not anymore. He checked out this morning."

"Thank you," I said, and began to turn away. "If he should happen to return, I want you to phone me right away."

"Okay, Sheriff Dawson."

"You call me right away. Day or night. Understood?"

The clerk nodded in response, but the expression on his face reminded me of a maltreated house pet.

Outside, I could feel the coming change in weather. The temperature felt as though it had dropped ten degrees, and the mountain peaks along the southern range had disappeared from view. I took the more direct route for my return to the substation, along the uneven sidewalk that skirted the old road and passed among the wildwood and ferns. I was coming to the bend in the pathway where the mountain laurel grows so thick you can't see daylight through the foliage when the first tentative raindrops began to fall. As I moved beyond the densest of the shrubbery, I saw the figure of a man I knew, standing fewer than ten feet away, knee-deep in the grass and pointing at my face, his forefinger and thumb cocked into the shape of a pistol.

"See how easy it would be," Dan Halloran said, grinning.

I lunged a single step toward him, took hold of his extended forefinger in my left hand while I drilled him with a crushing right jab to his nasal bridge. He folded to his knees and tried to focus on me as I forced his finger back upon itself, watching the pain swim in his eyes as I heard the snap of the joint giving way.

"If you ever come within a half mile of my home, my wife, or any member of my family again," I said, "I swear to Christ I will gut you."

I could hear the wet rattle at the back of his throat as he breathed, blood leakage from his ruined nose dripping off his chin.

"You're going to want to see someone about those injuries," I said. "There's a doctor a few blocks up that way, across from the park. Have a nice day."

CHAPTER THIRTEEN

THE FIRST SNOW began to fall the night before Thanksgiving, the eve of the Beaver Moon. A few of us had gathered together at the Cottonwood Blossom to celebrate Jordan Powell's twenty-fifth birthday. A swing band was setting up their equipment on the small stage near the back wall while Caleb and I waited at the bar for Lankard Downing to complete our table's order for another round.

I watched Jesse laughing at something Sam Griffin said to Powell, and I tried to recall the last time I had seen that expression on her face. In a far corner, a deaf couple shared a table, lost to one another in the formations of the other's lips and the graceful patterns they created with their fingers. I could not pull my eyes away from the rhythm and constitution of their singular language, somehow envious of their intimacy and communion.

Caleb tapped me on the arm and inclined his head in the direction of our group. A statuesque brunette wearing denim jeans that fitted her curves like she'd been dipped in blue liquid appeared from out of nowhere behind Jordan Powell. She covered his eyes with freshly manicured fingers and brushed a soft kiss on the back of his neck. I watched Jesse's expression go blank as her focus alternated between Powell and the new arrival.

I recognized the girl from the Benson Hotel, though I had only seen her from a distance at the time. In closer proximity, it was easy to see she belonged in this place like a Chateau Margaux belongs in a Dixie cup.

"So, who's this now?" Caleb asked me.

"The latest in a series of Powell's bad decisions," I said.

"Jordan Powell ain't kept two nickels from the same paycheck for as long as I've known him," Caleb said. He brushed a line of beer foam from his mustache with a knuckle and shook his head. "What's a girl like that want with him? Her nose is so high in the air, I believe she might drown if she got caught in a rainstorm."

Caleb and I collected the fresh pitchers that Lankard Downing pushed across the bar at us and delivered them to our table.

"You gonna introduce us to this little show pony, or what?" Caleb said to Powell.

The smile slid from my wife's face as Powell blinked in bewilderment and appeared to be at a rare and complete loss for words.

"Betsy Waters," the girl answered for herself, and waited while Powell fetched her a chair. The awkward and extended silence that followed was finally broken by an eruption of laughter from the other end of the room.

At some time long ago, Lankard Downing, the owner of the Cottonwood Blossom, had acquired a hand-sculpted sailing ship's bow-maiden, who occupied the wall between two billiard tables in full bare-breasted glory. Over the years, it had become a custom to outfit her with articles of lubricious attire when the first snowfall arrived. Someone had just decorated her with a pair of nearly transparent panties.

Betsy Waters excused herself and weaved between the crowded tables toward the washrooms while a pair of local girls moved in rhythmic unison at the center of the dance floor, eyes squeezed shut and swaying to the slow beat of the music.

"What the hell is the matter with you?" Jesse hissed at Powell once Betsy was out of earshot.

"I didn't know she was going to be here," Powell said. He looked around the table, from one man to the next, for support. "C'mon, guys. I barely know the girl."

"Sure thing, butterbean," Sam Griffin said as he tipped back his beer.

"Shasta's going to be here any second, Jordan," Jesse hissed. "If you've done anything to break that girl's heart, I swear . . ."

"I ain't gonna break nobody's heart, Miz Dawson," he said.

It was clear he was already half in the bag, that the boys had plied him with bunkhouse redeye before he'd even arrived here.

"Then you better get that expression off of your face right quick, boy," Caleb said.

"What expression?"

"The one that says you think that city girl pisses glitter."

Jesse shot Caleb a look that required no explanation.

"What?" Caleb said, shrugged, and turned his attention to the two girls dancing near the apron of the stage.

I spotted Betsy through a blue haze of cigarette smoke, pushing through a pair of batwing doors and back into the bar. She moved between the tables with the fluidity of a jungle cat, and I could see that Jesse had spotted her, too. We watched the girl make a beeline for the back of the barroom, take up a position beneath the bow-maiden, and proceed to act out a slow grind that culminated with her reaching up the sleeve of her blouse and coming back out holding a lacy brassiere. The place exploded with a burst of catcalls and applause as she twirled it overhead, roper-style, before fitting it over the maiden's bare chest.

Powell's face drained of color, and Jesse tossed her napkin on the tabletop and stood.

"I hope you're proud of yourself, Jordan Powell," Jesse said. "That's a real classy gal. I'm out."

I walked Jesse to her car and offered to come home with her.

"No," she said. "You stay. Sam and Caleb deserve to spend some time with you outside of work. It's not their fault that Powell's a jackass."

I watched her taillights disappear behind a curtain of slowly drifting snowfall and went back inside the Blossom.

Less than five minutes later, Shasta Blaylock arrived.

She was cradling a gift beneath her arm, a wicker basket wrapped in colored cellophane with an oversized crimson bow tied at the top. She searched the crowded room for familiar faces, pulled up short when she arrived at the table in time to witness Betsy Waters pressing herself into Jordan Powell's ribcage.

"Happy Birthday, Jordan," Shasta said, and placed the gift basket on the seat of Jesse's vacated chair. She could have ignited a small blaze with the rage inside her eyes.

Powell snapped to his feet and reached out to Shasta. He leaned in to kiss her, but she averted her lips, took a step backward, and looked him squarely in the face.

"Who's your friend?" Shasta asked.

"Nobody."

Shasta took the brunette's inventory and held her gaze.

"Who is this person to you, Jordan?"

"She's nobody," he said again.

"I'm walking out that door right now, Jordan," she said. "I'll give you one minute to meet me outside and explain yourself, or we're finished. I'm not fooling."

Shasta Blaylock's eyes glistened with humiliation as she inhaled, squared her shoulders, adjusted her purse strap, and took her time walking away. I stepped up beside Powell as he watched her pass through the doorway.

"That right there is shame you're feeling, son," I told him. "It won't do you any good right now, but what you need to remember is that you don't ever want to feel this way again if you can help it."

Powell remained stock-still as the door swung shut behind her. Caleb moved up on Powell's other side and placed a hand on his shoulder.

"You better get out there if you care for that girl," Caleb said. "She might kick your balls clear up into your throat, but I recommend that you take it like a cowboy if you intend to keep her."

Powell looked at Caleb, then at me.

"If you don't take Caleb's advice," I said, "tomorrow's going to be the first of a long stretch of worst-days of your life."

THE SNOW flurries had abated overnight, but the sub-freezing temperatures had formed a hard crust on the new fallen snow and a thick layer of sheet ice inside the water troughs. Earlier that morning, Taj Caldwell and one of the new wranglers had high-centered the flatbed on a hump in the service road, and daybreak found Caleb and me out in the elements helping them un-stick the rig.

The truck was weighed down with the hay bales and sack feed I'd ordered to restock the pole barn in the winter pasture, and without daily attention to the livestock during inclement weather like this, the losses owing to thirst, starvation, and disease would be unimaginable. And an unimaginably cruel way for them to die.

Caleb and I remounted our horses as the flatbed pulled away. I shook a cigarette out of the pack for my foreman, then lit one for myself. We sat together wordlessly in the frozen stillness, listening to a flock of geese making noises like a pack of feral dogs as they foraged in the short grass of the plashet.

Caleb and I took our time circling the periphery of the pasture, stopping off at every trough and flume to break away the rind of ice that would otherwise deprive the cattle of precious drinking water. Two hours later, I swung out of the saddle to check the level of the spring-fed pond and watched Drambuie paw the frosted collar of its rim before he dipped his head to drink from it.

Caleb emerged from the thicket a few minutes later, stepped out of his stirrups, and allowed his buckskin cutter to wander loose. He rambled to the lee of a windbreak formed of wild juniper and bog myrtle, squatted on his haunches, and burrowed pebbles from the soil. He broke off a stem of catgrass and chewed it while he lobbed the tiny stones into the reservoir.

"Sometimes," he said to me, "don't you wish your granddaddy had chosen to raise tropical fish instead of ranching cattle?"

A RIBBON of opalescence rose from the chimney as I treaded from the horse barn to the house. Inside, orange light flickered, the warm air sweet with the scent of willow wood.

I slid a cookie from a tray that still radiated heat from the oven and allowed it to cool in my palm. There was a hint of a smile on Jesse's face as I caught her reflection in the window over the sink. She looked away, brushed a lock of hair off of her forehead with her wrist, and returned her attention to skinning potatoes.

"The train's due at ten past twelve," Jesse said.

"It's always late."

"Don't you dare leave Cricket waiting all alone on Thanksgiving Day."

"What kind of father do you think I am?" I asked and moved off to the shower before she had the opportunity to answer.

CRICKET AND I were watching the Buffalo Bills beat the St. Louis Cardinals on the console in the living room when our dinner guests began to arrive. I muted the volume and opened the door as Caleb made his way up the porch stairs. His hands were gloved with oven mitts, balancing a bean casserole in a ceramic baking dish and a basket piled high with steaming corn muffins.

"Not a moment too soon," he said as he stepped across the threshold. "This tray's about to burn a hole through these damn gloves."

"Hello, Mr. Wheeler," Cricket said, and kissed him on the cheek as he made his way into the kitchen.

"Hello to you, sweetheart."

He placed his dishes on the counter and came back to collect a warm embrace from my daughter. Cricket's grandfather had passed away long before she'd been born, and Caleb was about as close as she would ever get to having one. Even so, he had been "Mr. Wheeler" to her ever since she'd been a little girl, and neither he nor I had ever disabused her of the privilege to display her proper manners.

"Gonna stick around a while this time?" he asked her.

"Only for a couple weeks. Just long enough for some home-cooked food and a load or two of laundry."

"Still can't get used to you being away at college," he said and looked off through the living room window. "You was just a button when I showed you how to rope that goat. You remember that?"

"I think I can still smell him on my hands," she said. "Come watch the game with us."

I poured Caleb a whisky and soda and brought it to the living room where he and Cricket had already settled on the couch.

"Not much of a game," Caleb said.

"Between Braxton and OJ, the Bills are the only offense on the field," Cricket said, and palmed a handful of popcorn from the bowl on the low table.

Fifteen minutes later, Sam Griffin let himself in through the back door. He was accompanied by Doc Brawley's silver-haired widow, Ruth, and a young man I had only met one time before, when he had first arrived in town to take over Doc's medical practice. Cheeks were bussed and hands were shaken and drinks were passed around. Outside, the color of the sky grew darker and a brontide rumbled through the pass.

Cricket surveyed the newly arrived guests, leaned toward Caleb, and whispered, "Where's Jordan?"

"I expect he's eating his turkey somewheres else this year," he said. "Seeing as he presently occupies the top spot on your mother's fecal roster."

"Why? What'd he do?"

"We can talk about it later on. Right now, I'm guessing she'd like you to pay some attention to the new medico."

The young doctor's name was Hunter Carlton, and judging by the conspiratorial glance Ruth Brawley shared with my wife, I concluded he had been invited to our home not solely because he was new in town or because Ruth worked as his nurse. My conclusion was confirmed when the ladies reacted with far more enthusiasm than seemed necessary when Cricket and the doctor discovered a shared interest in both contemporary films and horsemanship. It was equally clear that Caleb had picked up on it as well.

"Where are you from originally, son?" Caleb asked him.

"Grants Pass," he said. "But I did med school and my internship in California."

The doctor's tone was equal parts confidence and deference, with an element of humor laying in wait behind his eyes. He was of average height and average build, clean shaven with the youthful manner and demeanor of a high school athlete who never got much playing time.

"That explains it," Caleb said.

"I don't think I follow, sir," Carlson said. "Explains what?"

"Ordinarily," Caleb said, "when we get dressed up for company around here, we wear a shirt that's got a collar on it."

"I didn't have a clean one. That's why I wore the sports coat."

"A sports coat and a t-shirt. How old are you, anyway?"

"Caleb—" Ruth Brawley interrupted, but my foreman interrupted her right back.

"C'mon, doc," Caleb persisted. "How old?"

"I'll be thirty-one in September."

"Good god. I've got pairs of boots older'n you setting on the floor in my closet."

"I'm licensed to practice medicine, sir, if that's what's worrying you," he smiled. "In fact, I performed emergency treatment for a man who came into my office with a shattered nose and severely hyperextended index finger just a couple days ago."

Dr. Carlton slid a glance in my direction, but I couldn't quite decipher the message it contained.

"That man should consider himself lucky you were there," I said.

THE PHONE rang during our dessert of pumpkin pie and ice cream. I brought my plate with me as I excused myself and took the call in the kitchen.

The woman introduced herself to me as Cathie Fields, the charge nurse in the thoracic ward at County Hospital.

"Sorry to bother you on Thanksgiving Day, Sheriff," she said, "but I didn't know exactly what I was supposed to do under the circumstances."

"I'm sorry, but I don't know what we're discussing."

"A few days ago, a young man was dropped off at Admitting," she said. "He had no money, no ID, no nothing."

"Okay."

Her hand covered the mouthpiece on her end, the muffled hum of hospital chaos reverberating down the line.

"Apologies," she said. "Anyway, it was obvious that the patient had undergone significant trauma—a fistfight or a beating with a blunt object if I was to guess. Whatever it was had caused the fracture of several of his ribs, one of which left him with a pneumothorax—a punctured lung—a particularly nasty one."

"I appreciate your diligence, but I still don't understand why you and I are having this conversation right now, Ms. Fields."

"Earlier today, the patient was finally able to be moved from the ICU into the thoracic ward. We had to leave a chest tube in him that will need to remain in place for several days. These kinds of things often require a fairly lengthy recovery."

"You're aware that I have no authority with respect to indigent patients?"

"No, no," she said. "I understand. This isn't about money. The thing is . . . When we moved him from the ICU, naturally we moved his personal belongings as well."

"Naturally."

"When we did that, certain . . . *items* fell out of his pockets."

"What types of items are we talking about?"

"Several doses of what I am fairly confident is LSD, nearly three dozen amphetamine capsules, and a half-burned marijuana cigarette."

A ripple of animated conversation drifted from my dining room, and I took a sip of coffee that had gone cold.

"I understand," I said. "I don't believe I'll need to drive out there tonight, but I appreciate your notifying me. How much longer will the patient be remaining in your care?"

"I would guess a week, at least. More likely two. The lung puncture's pretty bad."

"Either I, or one of my deputies, will come up to interview the patient when he's physically able. Any guesses as to when he'll be up to it?"

"He can probably handle it tomorrow, if it's not overly rigorous."

"I promise not to use bright lights and rubber hoses," I said. "I'll just want to speak with him. In the meantime, I'd kindly ask you to seal the items you recovered in a plastic bag, record the contents and date of discovery on an adhesive label, and lock it in a secure place until we pick it up from you. Can you do that for me?"

"Of course."

"And one more thing: Please have your security staff keep a close eye on him. We don't want him to get up and walk away."

"There's little chance of that," she said.

"I appreciate the call, Ms. Fields."

"Happy Thanksgiving, Sheriff."

THAT NIGHT I dreamt of a forested hill in the frozen depths of Gimhwa Valley. I dreamt of the ceaseless concussion of Chinese artillery and the stench of charred wood and melted flesh. I dreamt of my MP unit and the night we had been ordered to escort three enemy combatants who had tortured and murdered defenseless US soldiers. These particular enemy combatants had ambushed a half dozen of our infantry, stripped them of their clothing and personal possessions, and over the course of several hours, systematically pierced their flesh to the bone using steel shafts that had been heated to the point of incandescence over a coal fire. Four of those GIs had suffered slow and agonizing deaths; the remaining two endured long months in the hospital wishing they'd died too.

I have witnessed the last light departing a man's eyes on more than a few occasions. I don't pretend to know the first thing about the human psyche and how some men are driven by compulsions of which they themselves have no understanding. But I have come to know that it is possible to be an occupant of hell without dying first.

I awakened, panicked, in the darkness, my eyes streaming and my cheeks slick with moisture, my heart tripping inside my chest. At first, I could not place the source of the anguished howl in my ears. A moment later, when I attempted to call out, no sound would come at all. I could no longer recognize a single one of the faces I had seen. Time had erased the essence of their features, even from my dreams.

CHAPTER FOURTEEN

THE CLOUDS THAT stretched across the mountaintops the next morning resembled sheets of fire. I stood on the gallery and watched my cowboys mount up and ride away, following the trail toward North Camp to shatter ice that had formed in the water troughs and scout the herd just as Caleb and I had done the day before. When I went back into the house, Cricket was standing at the mudroom door tying a wool scarf around her throat, preparing to drive me into town where I could finally swap the Diamond D ranch Bronco for my pickup.

She dropped me at the Richfield station, where my newly repaired truck was parked beside the service bay, then she drove on to meet up with me for breakfast at Boyle's diner. I paid the mechanic and took my truck to the lot behind the substation and left it there. Ice crystals glinted on the sidewalk as I strode along the empty street, and somewhere in the distance, the low rumble of the Southern Pacific echoed in the valley.

I was grateful for the warmth inside the diner, rubbing my palms together to revive my circulation as I scanned the room for Cricket. I found her seated at the counter, absently swiveling the floor-mounted stool in gentle arcs, exactly as she had done all those years ago when I would bring her here for ice cream sundaes as a child. Rowan Boyle had come out from his usual position flipping eggs and pancakes at the griddle and was sharing a laugh at something Cricket had just said as he poured coffee into her ceramic mug. He pushed his soda clerk's hat off his forehead and leaned a hip against the counter.

"Coffee, Ty?" he asked, and began to pour without waiting for my reply.

I hung my hat and coat on a wall hook, took a seat beside my daughter as Boyle returned to the kitchen. The jangle of silverware and the natter of a dozen idle conversations filled the empty spaces in a room already redolent with aromas of sweet syrup, toasted bread, and sausage gravy.

I blew the steam from my coffee cup and brought it to my lips. I turned my head to look at Cricket and found her staring at me.

"Is everything all right?" she asked.

"Why would you ask me that?"

She paused for a moment, gathering her thoughts, or perhaps her courage. "I heard you this morning," she said. "It was still dark out."

"Sometimes I have dreams."

She nodded but could not meet my eyes.

"Nightmares," she corrected. "Mom told me someone vandalized your truck. That's why it was at the Richfield."

"Comes with the job, Cricket."

She picked up her coffee mug and clutched it in both hands, warming her palms.

"You look tired, Dad."

"I'm a cowboy, a rancher, and a sheriff—"

"And a war vet."

"That too," I said. "Regardless, I don't close my eyes at night with an expectation of getting too much sleep."

She placed her cup down on the counter without having sipped from it.

"What happened to your hand?" she asked.

I shifted in my seat and looked out the window. A refrigerated Divco truck idled at the stop sign. The milkman in his billed cap and whites squinted out through his windshield, repositioned the sun visor, and pulled away inside a cloud of silver condensation.

"When you graduate next spring," I said, "do you plan on doing scout work with your mom?"

"If they're still making movies out here."

"They're always making movies out here."

"You're changing the subject."

"Trying to," I admitted. "Why are you looking at me that way?"

"The remark from Dr. Carlton last night—something about a man with a broken nose—what did he mean by that?"

"I already told you, I'm a cowboy and a cop. Sometimes things happen."

I climbed off my seat and walked into the restroom to wash my hands, mostly just to have something to do besides sparring with my daughter. There were no towels in the dispenser, so I dried them on my jeans. I caught my reflection in the mirror and turned away.

"Times are changing, Dad," she said when I returned to my seat.

"You kids have grown fond of saying that lately."

"Because it's true."

"Of course it's true. It's been true since time began. They didn't invent the concept down in San Francisco."

I noticed Rowan Boyle's profile through the window cutout in the kitchen door. He was about to come to take our order, but I shook my head and he returned to the cube steaks he'd left sizzling on the flattop.

"Things always *change*, Cricket," I said. "But they don't always get *better*."

"So that's your job now? It's up to you to make everything better?"

"Not everything. Just the things that I can."

"Bootprints in sand, Dad," she said, staring a hole in her placemat.

"I'm sorry you see it that way. Doesn't matter how old you get, you'll always be my little girl. You know that, right?"

"That's not fair," she said, and thought I saw the distant suggestion of a smile forming behind her eyes. "What does that have to do with it, anyway?"

"Everything," I said. "It has everything to do with it."

* * *

I COULD HEAR Powell and Griffin inside the office before I reached the door. I couldn't tell whether they'd been arguing, but the room fell into silence as soon as I stepped inside.

"You got your truck back from the body shop," Powell said, apropos of nothing, and bit into a cheese Danish.

"They had to replace the seat and dismantle the dashboard to get rid of the odor," I said, and turned my attention to Sam Griffin. "What are you doing back in the office already?"

I had sent him to County Hospital to retrieve the narcotics that the charge nurse had confiscated, and to interview our John Doe aspiring pharmacologist with the punctured lung.

"It wasn't much of an interview," Griffin said. "He was wired up like Jack Kerouac. Talking to him was like talking with a startled housecat."

"Did you get a name at least?"

"Eventually. His attention tends to wander."

"Coming down off something?"

"I don't think so," Sam said. "Wouldn't want to see what he's like when he's jacked up on black beauties, though."

Powell picked up the clear plastic Zip-Pak bag Griffin had brought with him from the hospital and dangled it in the air.

"I knew guys in 'Nam who'd gobble these things down like peanuts."

"Log that into evidence," I said.

"Already did."

"Then go lock it up."

"Roger that," Powell said. He placed his pastry on a square of paper on his desk and set off for the Sentry vault in the evidence cage.

Griffin had positioned a trash bin on the floor between his boots and swept wood shavings off his desktop from a pencil he'd been sharpening with a bone-handled jackknife. He folded the blade and slid it into an empty loop on his gun belt.

"You make the kid for a street dealer?" I asked.

Griffin shrugged.

"Maybe," he said. "But I gotta tell you, this guy is strictly low rent. More like a jackroller or petty thief dressed up like a hippie."

Powell returned from the back room carrying a cone-shaped paper cup filled with water he'd drawn from the cooler. He moved to the window, hitched his trousers, and half-sat on the ledge.

"Still, it seems like a lot of dope for a guy if he isn't bent on selling it," I said. "You said you got his name?"

"Sort of."

"Why do you like to make me work this hard for simple information?"

Griffin shifted his eyes in Powell's direction. It was clear my two deputies had already discussed this detail and found something amusing.

"Garcia," Griffin answered finally. "He told me his name is Jerry Garcia."

"That's a bullshit ID, Sheriff," Powell said. "Jerry Garcia's the guitar player—"

"I have a college-age daughter," I interrupted. "I'm aware of who Jerry Garcia is."

"Well, that's the only name he'd give me," Griffin said and leaned his bulk into the backrest of his chair. "Kept repeating it over and over."

Griffin shrugged again and stretched his arms over his head, weaved his fingers together, and cracked his knuckles.

"You think this guy is liable to rabbit-out on us?" I asked.

"Naw. He can't make it to the bathroom without somebody practically carrying him," he said. "I can book him into custody if you want me to, though; or cuff him to his bedrail 'til they discharge him. That way, at least we can roll his prints and try to find out who he really is."

I thought about that for a few seconds.

"Somebody dropped him at the hospital, right?"

"Yes, sir. Hustled him in, left him at the admitting desk, and took off."

"I'm assuming Mr. Garcia didn't share his chauffeur's name with you. Anybody from the hospital see the car? Get a decent description of the driver?"

"No, Sheriff. Nobody thought it was important at the time."

"In that case, let's leave the patient alone for the time being," I said.

"You sure you don't want to—"

"If we book him now, Sam, the accomplice will be in the wind. Let's stand pat and see whether his driver turns up on his own."

"Could be a while before he does."

"Could be never," Powell said.

"Maybe," I said. "But the patient's going to need to reach out for somebody to come get him when the hospital releases him."

Powell stood and tossed his paper cup into the trash.

"Get in touch with the charge nurse," I said, and pushed the telephone across the desk toward Sam Griffin. "Remind her to make sure hospital security keeps eyes on the guy while he's in recovery. The minute his accomplice shows his face, I want to hear from them."

THE FIRST call came three minutes later, at 8:47 a.m. It was a reporter from the big daily newspaper in Salem asking whether I had any comment regarding the conflict between US Fish and Wildlife and KC Sheridan. I told them I had none, mainly because I wondered what had taken them so long to pick up the story, and hung up without much further thought about the matter.

The second call came seven minutes after the first. This one was from the all-news radio station in Medford, and his question was very much the same as the newspaper reporter's.

"Somebody's yanking your chain," I said. "That matter's settled. Check the docket at the federal court."

"That's not my understanding."

I hung up without a further word and dialed KC's number.

"Why didn't somebody phone me, Irene?" I said when she picked up.

"What do you mean?"

My skull felt as though it was being constricted inside a garrote made of range wire.

"May I speak with KC, please?"

"You don't sound good, Ty."

"I'm okay, ma'am. Can you please put KC on the line?"

"I would, but he and a couple of the boys rode out to see after the cattle. Left about an hour and a half ago. Are you getting this nasty weather up where you are?"

"Goddamnit," I said, under my breath.

I hadn't meant to frighten her, but I knew that I had.

"Tell me what's the matter," she said.

"I don't exactly know yet," I said. "But I'm on my way out there, ma'am. Please don't talk to the press until things get sorted out."

"Until what things get sorted out?"

"I've got to go now, Miz Sheridan, but please do as I asked. No more press. Don't let Jarvis or anybody else utter another word."

Powell and Griffin were staring at me as I slammed down the receiver.

"Jordan," I said, "grab a couple Winchesters out of the locker and follow me to the Sheridans'. We'll take separate vehicles."

Griffin stood up and began to follow.

"I need you to stay here, Sam," I said. "Monitor the radio and stand by the phone. If you hear any unusual activity, give me a heads-up. Something's going on at the Sheridan place and I don't know what it is. Somebody's got the media fired up again, and I might need you to call the staties for backup. Or, hell, for all I know the state cops could be part of the problem. I don't know a goddamn thing."

What I strongly suspected was that Jarvis Lynch had been busy poking the beehive and was about to uncork something that couldn't be crammed back inside the bottle.

Powell came out from the back room with a lever-action rifle in each fist. I shrugged into my heavy coat and moved toward the door.

"If I can't raise you on the radio?" Griffin asked.

"Then use the phone and leave a message with Irene Sheridan. I'll get it eventually."

I PULLED off the county two-lane and onto the main access road that led to Sheridan's ranch, slowed to a near crawl as I looked for any sign of KC and Jarvis Lynch and whoever else might be riding with them. Gusts of wind pushed through the draw and bent the trees against a gunmetal sky, blowing clouds of dry powder off the branches.

Off to our right, the low-slung cinderblock structure that housed the wildlife refuge's visitor center sat vacant atop a short rise that abutted the shore of Lake Rafferty. Just beyond, the skeletal outline of the observation tower stood in relief against a snow-blanketed slope and put me in mind of a disused oil derrick. A length of steel chain had been slung across the entrance to the parking lot, and a message that read "Closed for the Season" had been painted in block letters onto a strip of reflective material and bolted to the face of the monument sign.

On the opposite side, the road curved generally northward past a drift of madrone and tanbark, and I spotted a pair of Hemmings County patrol cars forming a blockade across the cattle guard where KC's service trail had been carved into the brushland. Four men on horseback had formed up in a semicircle not far from the police vehicles and were clearly in the process of squaring off with three men in uniform. From this distance, the only participants I could distinguish with any certainty were KC and his horse.

Powell and I parked our trucks beside a culvert that ran along the rough shoulder and strode across a rock-strewn field toward the standoff. As we drew closer, I recognized Irene Sheridan's brother, Jarvis Lynch, straddling a nervous chestnut mare. I was expecting the other two to be Lynch's militia buddies from Nevada but was relieved to see it was two of KC's regular cowhands instead, though they were both armed with matching Henry repeaters. KC and Lynch carried 1911s tucked into holsters at their sides, but Lynch also had an M14 fixed on a web sling strapped across his back. KC had mentioned that he didn't believe the authorities were finished with him, and he had obviously ridden out here this morning prepared for that eventuality. Judging by the expressions each man wore, they had already moved beyond the discussion phase, and the situation teetered on the brink of turning western.

"What the hell are you doing here, Dawson?" Porter Brayfield said from the corner of his mouth. He had been glaring at me from beneath the stiff brim of his campaign hat from the moment I had climbed out of my truck.

Porter Brayfield had been the sheriff of Hemmings County since 1963. I had never been completely certain of his age, though I put him at least five years ahead of me, squinting into fifty candles on his next birthday.

"I should be asking *you* that question," I said. "The way it appears to me, you're standing in the middle of Mr. Sheridan's dirt road, openly brandishing firearms and preventing KC rightful access to *his* cattle. I have to admit I'm curious why that might be."

Brayfield was of average height, but constructed with a low center of gravity, with short legs and wide shoulders, and the pugilistic demeanor of a man who had devolved into an abuser after enduring a childhood of violence. His complexion was fair, chapped and reddened by weather, with lips that were so thin they more closely resembled an open wound.

He had wedged two of his green-and-white patrol vehicles at angles in the middle of the hardpan road and stood front and center before two of his deputies. I could tell that all three men were in full uniform beneath the foul weather gear they wore.

"KC Sheridan is trespassing," Brayfield said. "I'm here to turn him back around."

"Excuse me?" I said. "I don't believe I just heard you say that. KC's been using this road since you and I wore short pants to school, Porter. There's no need for all this armament. How about if everybody stows their weapons so we can talk to each other like civilized adults?"

"Tell them boys to go first," KC said.

Brayfield tilted his campaign hat forward on his brow and took two strides in my direction, close enough that I could smell the menthol from his chewing gum and see the rolls of fat that had developed on the back of his bald head. I could see over his shoulder that his men had made no attempt to move their M1 rifles from port arms.

I turned and scanned the faces of the four men on horseback fanned across the road behind me and didn't like what I saw there either. I cut my eyes sideways and noticed Jordan Powell's thumb positioned on the firing mechanism of the rifle that was squeezed tightly inside his gloved fists, and couldn't help but take cold comfort in the weight of the Peacemaker parked in my own holster.

"Everybody stand down for a minute, goddamnit," I said. "What the hell are you all doing out here in the snow with guns in your hands, anyway?"

"This section of road runs on my county, Dawson," Brayfield said. The whites of his eyes had turned pink and watery from the near-freezing wind. "On top of which it's encroaching onto federally protected land. Mr. Sheridan is no longer permitted to use it."

"You can't be serious," I said. "You came all the way out here carrying tactical firearms to make a claim like that out of the blue? Show me a court order."

I looked to my left and to my right, across a moonscape terrain of sharp rocks and scrub juniper, dotted with nothing more than temporary islands of snow-dusted ice. A barbed wire fence ran from horizon to horizon, broken only by the opening into which the Hemmings County squad cars had been wedged.

"How the hell am I supposed to feed and water my livestock?" KC asked.

"That's not my concern," Brayfield answered.

"Who's behind this, Porter?" I said. "USFW?"

He turned his face out of the wind, sucked out something that had been lodged between his teeth, and spat.

"My cattle're going to die in this weather," KC said.

"Did you not hear what I just said, Sheridan?" Brayfield said. "Your cows are not my problem." He rocked his weight onto the balls of his Sorel boots and thrust his free hand into the side pocket of his jacket. "Are you going senile or just deaf?"

Behind me I heard the unmistakable metallic clack of one of KC's cowboys levering a shell into the chamber of a .30-30 rifle. A half second later, every man who had been carrying a weapon had it shipped and cocked and locked, myself included.

"This shit's about to go pear-shaped, Brayfield," I said.

"Whatever happens next is not my doing, Dawson. This man has been informed that he's trespassing. I got no other way to say the words."

I heard a ringing in my ears, and I would have sworn the atmosphere took on the odor of burnt matches.

"If you and your men don't step aside," I said, "I do believe every last one of us could die right here on this goddamned road."

Brayfield said nothing.

"Are you a rancher, Porter?" I asked.

"You know that I'm not."

"Then you probably don't know that every single head of cattle in that pasture needs about fifteen gallons of water a day to survive; that means *every* damn one of them, *every* damn day."

KC exhaled, lowered his pistol, and rested it on his thigh.

"Let these men pass through this gate, Porter," I pressed. "If you don't, KC's entire herd is going to die a slow and agonizing death. That kind of thing won't win you any votes in your county. You know that is a fact."

For the first time since we'd begun talking, Brayfield appeared to be considering the consequences of what he had been ordered to do.

"Take a good look around you," KC said.

I craned my head to look at KC astride his horse and saw him as an old man for the first time in my life.

"You see any feed or water out here that ain't froze up solid?" KC continued.

"Shut your goddamned mouth, Sheridan," Brayfield said. "I'm tired of listening to you whine at me."

The ringing in my ears intensified and the edges of my vision flushed with hematic light. I leveled the Peacemaker, aimed squarely at Brayfield's orbital bone, and ratcheted the hammer.

"That's the last time you will express yourself to Mr. Sheridan in that tone of voice, Porter," I said.

"Get that gun out of my face."

"Nope," I said. "Somebody's set you up, Brayfield. But it's not too late to do something respectable instead."

He moved his eyes beyond the barrel of my revolver, across the rough topography, as I said, "You feel that? The wind's changed. Weather's breaking. I figure we got about twenty minutes before there's at least one news chopper circling above our heads. You don't want to be standing out here like this when they arrive."

I could see the wheels of his evaluation, how the situation had spun well beyond his ability to salvage it without some sort of compromise, his alternatives diminishing to a choice between political destruction or bloodshed.

"Here's what's going to happen now, Porter," I said. "You're going to let these men pass through because if you don't, it might be days or even weeks, but you can rest assured you'll see your life's plans come apart right before your eyes."

He ran his tongue across his dry lips and jutted his chin in KC Sheridan's direction.

"You know that I'm speaking the truth," I said.

"You'd better get this situation straightened out in one hell of a hurry, Dawson," Brayfield said finally. "That old man is snake-bit, and he don't even seem to know it."

CHAPTER FIFTEEN

"WHAT IN THE hell do you think you're doing?" I said.

I grabbed the receiver out of Greg Reeves's fist as he was still speaking and slammed it down onto the telephone cradle. Droplets of melted snow flew from my gloves and the folds of the coat I had not yet had time to shed, speckling the papers that were strewn across the countertop.

"I was talking to the *Las Vegas Courier*, asshole," he said.

Irene Sheridan rushed in from somewhere at the back of the house when she heard Reeves and me shouting at each other in her kitchen. She stood in the doorway and looked from Reeves to his friend Chester Zachary before noticing me.

"These two dumb sons of bitches aren't helping you as much as they think they are, Miz Sheridan," I said. "Pardon the expression."

"I don't understand what you mean by that statement, Ty," she said.

"If I had my guess, I'd say these two idiots have stirred up the news media and agitated the feds all over again. I believe Fish and Wildlife sent Porter Brayfield out to vent their frustrations on your husband and your herd."

"We've been down this road before, Dawson," Zachary said. "The feds haven't even begun to screw with KC yet. We know how they operate."

"That's *Sheriff* Dawson, and ten minutes ago, I had my Colt directed at another law enforcement officer's eye socket. Don't think for one second that I wouldn't use that same weapon on either one of you."

Reeves leaped out of his chair, stretched himself to his full height, and stared into my eyes.

"I've been mad-dogged by war criminals, son," I said. "Sit the hell down before you get so far across this creek you can't turn back. And tell your fool friend to stop using barracks language in front of this lady. I'm finished talking with both of you. You can leave."

They didn't, of course, but I ignored them as if they had, peeled my gloves off, and tucked them one by one into the pocket of my coat. Their testosterone levels had overwhelmed their common sense, and I knew that they'd leave the room of their own volition once the adrenaline burned off.

"Are KC and my brother all right, Ty?" Irene asked. "Did you see them on your way in?"

I hung my hat and coat on a hook beside Irene's back door, crossed my arms, and leaned against her kitchen counter. She appeared even more deeply fatigued than she had before, her expression that of a forest creature attempting to outrun a fire.

"Jarvis and a couple of your hands are looking after your livestock," I told her. "KC's still in the barn, I expect. Once he's finished putting up his horse, we're driving out to the county land office. We might have to go up to Portland after that."

"What happened out there?"

"Porter Brayfield and two of his deputies tried to blockade the trail that leads out to your winter pasture."

"Whatever for?"

"They accused you all of trespassing across federal property."

"That's crazy. There's no other way up there."

KC came in through the back door, wiped his boot soles on the floor mat just inside. He had mis-buttoned his shirt, and it hung crookedly under his jacket.

"We'd better get moving," was all he said.

SHERIFF BRAYFIELD had departed the scene at Sheridan's gate about the same time I had, but I left Jordan Powell behind to keep an eye on his two deputies while KC's brother-in-law and the cowhands checked on the Sheridan cattle. As KC and I passed by again, driving out toward the state road, I saw that the Hemmings County boys had stowed their weapons and gathered around the tailgate of Powell's pickup, and were sharing a Thermos among the three of them. The scene bore all the earmarks of an armistice, but I knew deep down it wasn't built to last.

We arrived at the Hemmings County land office a few minutes later. It was quiet, heavy with the chemical odor of cyanotype. We explained what we were looking for, and the female clerk behind the counter informed us that the civil engineer we needed to speak with was across the street having his hair cut.

Inside the shop, an old Graymark desktop radio was playing something by Conway Twitty and Loretta Lynn and the thermostat had been turned up so high it had fogged the plate glass window. A middle-aged man with long sideburns grown well beyond his earlobes looked at us in the reflection of the mirror as the barber shaved the back of his neck with an electric trimmer.

"Hello, KC," the man said from the chair. "What brings you to town?"

"I need to get a look at my parcel map."

"What's that? Can't hear you with these clippers buzzing in my ears."

The muscles in KC's jaw flexed as he pointed out the window.

"We'll wait for you across the street," KC said.

The man made a face and shrugged beneath the barbers' cape, gestured vaguely in the direction of his ears.

"Can't hear a thing. Why don't you wait for me over at the office? I'll be there in a couple ticks."

"Jesus Christ," KC muttered, pulling the door open. I half expected the handle to come off in his fist.

Five minutes after that, we watched the man with the Elvis sideburns trot across the street. A tiny brass bell chimed as he came inside.

"Apologies, KC," he said, and KC grunted.

The man's salt-and-pepper pompadour had been combed straight back off his forehead, and he smelled strongly of Vitalis and lime scented soap. In spite of the cold weather, he was dressed in khaki slacks and a short sleeved cubavera shirt with a collar that laid flat against his clavicle. He lifted a hinged leaf that was cut into the counter and stepped around the back, then smiled at the clerk and said, "I've got this, Marie."

"This here is—" KC began by way of introduction.

"I recognize Sheriff Dawson," the man said, and reached across to shake my hand. "Seen you in the papers once or twice. I'm Larry Lawrence, County Recorder."

"Pleasure," I said. "We've got a question regarding the Sheridan parcel. An issue concerning boundary lines."

Lawrence nodded and began thumbing through a large three-ring binder, found what he was looking for, and disappeared amid a warren of shelves stacked with rolled blueprints. KC paced the waiting area while Marie stole curious glances at us as she typed. Outside the window, fresh flurries of snow began to swirl.

Larry Lawrence returned to the counter and unfurled a roll of topographic maps and site plans stamped in blue with official-looking county markings, and weighted down the loose end with a tape dispenser. He slid a mechanical pencil from the plastic protector in his shirt pocket and directed it along the boundary of KC's property.

"This is your eastern edge right here, along the—" he began, but KC had run out of patience.

"I don't give a damn about that," he said. He planted an index finger on the access road and tapped it several times for emphasis. "All I want to know is whether this road runs across the goddamned bird sanctuary."

"The Rafferty Refuge?"

"Yes, goddamnit. You know what I meant."

The county clerk's cheeks reddened. He tucked a toothpick between his lips and lifted a magnifying glass and a ruler from the countertop. He leaned in and studied the blue lines more closely. He tugged at an earlobe, drew a pencil mark on the paper, and rolled the toothpick across his teeth. He placed the ruler near the mark he'd just made and studied something through the magnifying glass.

"See where this road curves along here?" Lawrence asked, but the question was rhetorical. "That's the point nearest to the refuge. Looks like it runs only fifty, sixty feet before it curves back into your deeded property."

"Does it cross over or not?"

Lawrence shook his head, but his expression did not match the gesture.

"Hard to tell," he said. "This map only shows where the road is *supposed* to be. I can only assume that's where it actually got built."

"What are you telling me?"

"Mr. Sheridan, even if it's off by a little bit, it can't be more than a foot or two because of this steep dropoff that runs beside the road. You wouldn't carve a trail that close to a culvert; the whole thing would wash out in the first good rain."

I could see KC's jaw muscles pumping again, and the way his eyelids began to squeeze together gave the impression he might throw something heavy through the front window.

"Is the damn road encroaching or not?"

The county recorder took a step back from the counter and removed the toothpick from his mouth.

"Only a survey team could answer that for sure," he said. "They're the ones who mark the official boundaries."

"You mean like the survey team that Fish and Wildlife sent over to my place a while back? The ones who tried to separate me from my reservoir? I imagine a team like that could *mis*mark a boundary, too, if they were of a mind to do it."

Larry Lawrence broke eye contact and made a face like he'd just stepped in something.

"All I'm saying is your road's *probably* not encroaching," he equivocated. "But even if it were, it doesn't amount to much. One foot over the line? For a distance of only fifty or sixty feet? Who cares?"

"Can we take that map with us?" I asked.

"It'll cost a dollar for a copy," he said, and I saw his Adam's apple rise and fall.

KC huffed and turned away toward the window, and I slid a dollar out of my billfold. Larry Lawrence came back a couple minutes later with the parcel map rolled up with a rubber band and handed it to me.

"I'm no attorney, Sheriff Dawson," the man said under his breath. "But in the event there is an encroachment, I'd say you had a decent case for adverse possession."

"I believe we're about to find out," I said.

KC'S ATTORNEY, Quentin Bahle, met us in Portland in the lobby of the federal courthouse. We found a relatively quiet corner where I could unroll the parcel map and bring him up to speed with more detail than I had been able to deliver to him on the phone.

"At a minimum," I concluded, "KC needs a court order that will allow him to keep using that access road until a proper new survey can be completed."

Bahle leaned in and studied something at the bottom of the page.

"This map's not even a year old," he said. "Look at the date stamp."

"Bullshit," KC said.

"Aren't those your initials in that box right there, KC?"

KC picked up the blueprint for a closer look, held it at arms length, and squinted for a few seconds before he thrust it back at the attorney.

"Those are my initials, but I didn't put 'em on that paper."

"Who did?"

"How in the hell should I know? Maybe the same lying sonsabitches that surveyed my private property without my permission."

I moved a short distance away, into a square of sunlight that streamed in through a window on the second floor and attempted to collect my thoughts. I felt a familiar ringing in my ears again.

"This isn't good," Bahle said to both KC and me when I returned to the conversation.

"So what am I supposed to do now?" KC asked.

The attorney drew a deep breath and gazed upward at the ceiling cornices, then drew back the sleeve of his suit jacket and glanced at his wristwatch.

"I suggest we do what you came here to do," Bahle said finally.

Fifteen minutes later, we were ushered into Judge Gerald Bonner's chambers, the same judge as had presided over KC's previous hearing. He was seated in his leather chair, inside a cloud of fragrant smoke that purled out of the calabash-and-meerschaum pipe he held.

"Hello again, Mr. Sheridan," the judge said, his outward manner deferential, but his tone reeking of mendacity.

"Your Honor—" KC began, but the judge cut him off.

"Counselor," he said, "I assume you're representing Mr. Sheridan, am I correct?"

"Yes, Your Honor."

The judge drew on the mouthpiece of his pipe, found that it had gone cold. He smiled and lifted his hand, eyed us from beneath unruly eyebrows as he bent his head, and fired the bowl using a Blaisdell lighter with the official seal of the academy at Quantico emblazoned on its side.

"Something wrong with my lighter, Sheriff Dawson?"

"You don't often see one from the FBI academy."

"You might if you sat on the federal bench," he said, and returned his attention to Bahle. "Mr. Bahle, is Sheriff Dawson also a party to this matter?"

"No, I'm not, Your Honor," I answered. "I'm here at Mr. Sheridan's request."

"I was not addressing you, Sheriff."

"Nevertheless, I—"

He shook his head and cast a glance outside his window. Three stories below, a bearded man stood on a brick pilaster, pontificating through a megaphone to a group of demonstrators that had begun to gather in the square, a barker at a modern-day sideshow.

"This is not a rodeo, a ribbon cutting, or a county fair," the judge said. "I observe the same decorum in my chambers as I do in my courtroom. You are excused, Sheriff."

"I beg your pardon?" I said.

He pursed his lips and cocked his head in a pantomime of puzzlement.

"You vex me, Sheriff," he said. "I'm beginning to believe you might have taken too many hard landings from your horse."

"Are you ordering me to leave?"

"Mr. Bahle," he said. "Please tell this man that if he doesn't vacate my chambers immediately, I will terminate any further discussion on this subject. With prejudice."

The judge's conduct and demeanor were not only odious, but an insult to the mantle that had been entrusted to him. It was clear that his desire to have me absent from the room had nothing to do with my legal standing in the matter, but rather because my livelihood was not dependent upon the bar. He was dismissing me because he knew I could not be manipulated, and because of that, would not be allowed to bear witness to the discussion among the parties, or as a consequence of it, to hold the judge accountable.

"I could find you in contempt, Sheriff."

"I could do the same with you, judge," I said as I opened the door to leave. "In fact, I already have."

The lobby was vacant as I strode through it, past the elevator that looked like an antique bank teller's cage, shielding my eyes from the harsh glare that reflected off the travertine floor. I put on my sunglasses and stepped out onto the portico at the top of the stairs to the courthouse. Tufted white clouds skimmed a sky bright with autumn sunshine, sidewalks and garden paths still damp from an earlier downpour. I lit a cigarette and leaned a boot heel against the stone façade and watched the temporary absence of precipitation bring the city streets back to life. The last red leaves of autumn were falling onto moss crusted pavers, and the air carried the riverine smells of iodine, wet sand, and grass.

It should have been an idyllic port city scene, but it was not.

The crowd that had gathered to listen to the man with the megaphone, the one I had earlier seen from the judge's window, had grown larger, their agitation palpable. A young man with sagging shoulders and the loose-limbed, elongated stride I associated with junkies and delinquents snaked through the assemblage, handing out flyers and bobbing his head to a rhythm audible to him alone. His hair flowed well beyond his shoulders, parted down the middle, and he wore a T-shirt printed with the likeness of a newly popular communist hero underneath a denim jacket. I looked off in the direction of the river, took a pull from my smoke, and when I turned back, the slouch-shouldered kid with the handbills was standing directly in front of me.

"You look like you got some free time to burn, Tex," he said. "Read this; it should be a real eye-opener for you."

"What did you just call me?"

"I called you 'Tex,'" he said. He grinned at some private thought as he appraised me. "Seriously man, the whole getup: the hat and the long coat and the boots."

"The only time I've been to Texas was for college. Earned a degree in philosophy before enlisting in the army," I said. "And based on that T-shirt you're wearing, I don't believe that I'd trust your judgment about anything. I think I'll pass on the reading assignment."

"Don't get hung up on the shirt, redneck. It's Che Guevara, man."

"I know who it is," I said and pressed the leaflet back onto his stack. "Don't you see any hypocrisy in handing out literature espousing pacifism and free speech while you've got the image of a mass murderer printed on your chest?"

"Like I said, it's just a shirt, dude."

"On the other hand, if it's the sheer numbers of innocent victims you're promoting, you might want to consider swapping your Guevara shirt for one with a photo of Mao or Josef Stalin."

"You need to mellow out, cowpoke."

"And *you* need to reconsider your own attitudes regarding prejudice, son. You stand here railing against bias based on heritage, upbringing, or outward appearance, but when you see me wearing a certain type of hat, you condescend to me? Check your own intolerance before you bang on someone else's door, kid. You're nothing but a pimple-faced hypocrite. Have yourself a groovy day."

I flashed him a peace sign and went back to my cigarette, which only irritated me more deeply because it had already burned itself down to the filter. I crushed it under my foot and dug inside my pocket for another one.

"Looks like the circus is back in town," a voice said from close behind me.

I slipped my lighter into my coat and turned to look into the face of the man I knew only as Wehr and Halloran's confidential informant. He was wearing the same leather three-quarter coat as before, when we'd met in Chinatown, but the watch cap was nowhere to be seen.

"How'd you know I was here?" I asked.

"Eyes and ears, baby. Eyes and ears."

At the far end of the sidewalk a young woman in tight jeans climbed off a ten-speed Schwinn bicycle and secured it to a light post with a chain and padlock. She tilted her face into the sunlight for a moment, and I watched her disappear into the crowd.

"What is it you want?" I asked him.

"Halloran's back in town," he said. "Somebody unleashed some damage on him, though. He looks like a raccoon, and he's wearing a cast on one of his hands."

I canted my head to one side for a better look at the informant and noticed he was grinning.

"Looks like your problem's been solved," I said. "Now that Halloran's reappeared, you can go back to being a snitch."

"Don't be like that, man. Halloran's only part of my problem. I still don't know who did my friend Buzzy, and Halloran's like a giraffe on an ice rink all of a sudden."

"I don't even know what that means."

"You're here on the right day, though," he said.

"Don't jerk me around."

"You familiar with the name Marcus Vessey?"

"No."

"I think you are, but you just don't know it yet."

I felt the hairs on the back of my neck stand on end.

"I can see by your face that you might know who I'm talking about," he said. "Say, you got another one of those smokes?"

I passed him the one I had just lit.

"You can finish this one."

"Oh, man," he complained, but he took it from me anyway and pulled a long drag. "Like I said before: you lucked out, came here on the right day. Want to see something fun? Check out the Stumptown Chophouse over on Ramser Street."

"I don't have time for this, pard. I'm hitting the highway once my colleague steps outside those doors."

"I ain't shitting you. Just hang out for a while. Watch what goes down in that bar around four o'clock this afternoon. I know you're gonna want to make time for this. Might make for a whole new definition of *happy hour*."

"Go talk to Lieutenant Morgan," I said. "I'm serious. I'm out."

"How many times I gotta tell you, man. I don't even know that dude. How'm I supposed to trust him?"

"You don't know me, either."

"Yeah, but you're a cowboy, baby. You gotta dig that."

CHAPTER SIXTEEN

QUENTIN BAHLE BORE an expression of outright exhaustion as he came down the steps a short while later, and KC's eyes were distant, glassy, like a man who had been hypnotized.

"Well?" I asked.

"The judge granted Mr. Sheridan seventy-two hours to get a new land survey."

"Which I have to pay for outta my own pocket," KC said. "Goddamn sonsabitches."

"It's a start," Bahle said. "I don't know what else to tell you."

I shook Bahle's hand and said goodbye, led KC down several city blocks to where I'd parked my truck. We waited for the pedestrian light, and KC looked across the street where they were changing out the letters on the Fifth Avenue Cinema marquis.

We climbed into my truck and pulled out from the curb. The cloud cover had returned, together with the promise of another downpour.

"I've got one more stop to make before we head home," I told him. "Shouldn't take more than an hour or so. Do you mind?"

"If it involves you buying me a drink, I don't mind at all."

A few minutes later, we had crossed the invisible line of demarcation between the city proper and the part nobody wanted to talk about. I turned south on Ramser and pulled into a poorly maintained parking lot notched with potholes and barbed with dead weed stalks. The spaces closest to the entrance had all been filled, so I pulled into a spot nearest the egress.

"Who the hell spends money on a heap like that?" KC asked.

He was referring to a late-1930s Ford coupe that had been chopped and channeled and painted a grotesque shade of purple metallic, parked a few spaces away. The customized Hemi engine was exposed to the elements and had chrome intakes and air filters, and polished exhaust pipes running the length of the chassis from the block to the rear wheel well.

"Looks like something my cat puked up before he died," he said.

A light rain began to fall as we approached the entrance of the Stumptown Chophouse. The place had been constructed of painted cinderblock, without discernible architectural design, and occupied the edge of what politicians would call a transitional area but regular folks would refer to as blighted. It was the only business in my sightline that hadn't either been boarded up or demolished outright but had somehow managed to exploit a shady notoriety that had refashioned it as skid row chic. A rectangle of faux river stone had been applied to the exterior beside the doorway, where a lighted neon sign with the place's name and an animated martini glass flickered and hummed in shades of violet, turquoise, and pink.

It took some time for our eyes to adjust to the low light as we stepped inside, navigated a hall festooned with framed photos of film stars, toward the clamor of cocktail conversation. Horseshoe-shaped booths upholstered in tufted Naugahyde flanked a tiny parquet dance floor and a stage set up for a small combo.

"Smells like an aquarium in here," KC said.

"If goldfish wore cheap aftershave."

A one-armed black girl wearing a fringed bikini gyrated on the top of a baby grand piano positioned beside the tiny stage. The piped-in music was some sort of listless jazz, and her eyes were focused somewhere very far away and bore the blank vacuity of an addict.

"You bring your wife to dives like this, Dawson?"

"Not on a bet."

We each ordered whisky neat from a waitress wearing a tuxedo jacket over a black leotard while I watched a buxom woman in a sequined dress and peroxided bouffant take a seat at the end of the bar beside a man I had only seen before in grainy photographs. I recognized him instantly, even in the low light of the room, the strange angles of his physiognomy and ears like catchers' mitts.

His wavy hair was parted on one side and oiled in a style once popularized by Dean Martin. He wore a two-toned bowling shirt and pleated slacks, his shirt pocket stuffed with Tiparillos. The bartender delivered their cocktails without taking their order and lingered, transfixed by the blonde's cleavage. The Blonde and Bowling Shirt touched the rims of their glasses together, but their expressions made clear that this was not a social ritual. I recognized the woman, too, but only by reputation and description.

KC drank in silence as I studied the man named Marcus Vessey and the woman they referred to as the Countess holding court, exchanging feral smiles and insincere handshakes with men who took turns sliding envelopes beneath the placemat at his elbow.

"Do these people have something to do with my problem?" KC asked.

I shook my head.

"I don't know for sure," I said. "I believe this might be about something else."

"Why do I keep thinking," KC said, squinting into the dim light at the bar, "that if I could drop every one of those bastards in the bowl and pull the chain, that the whole damn state would be better off?"

The tired saxophone music faded to silence, and the one-armed exotic dancer stumbled as she clambered down off the piano. KC tossed back the remnants of his bourbon, shook his head in disgust, and turned his eyes on me.

"You took on an ugly job, Ty Dawson."

"That is a fact," I said. "Let's get out of here."

* * *

JESSE WAITED to have dinner with me, and the two of us ate together in the dining room, Cricket having gone out with a group of her old friends from high school. I lit a pair of tapers and shook out the match as the candlelight dappled the walls and tablecloth.

"Your face looks hollow in this light," Jesse said.

"I'm alright."

"When was the last time you slept the night through?"

"I don't remember."

"It's been a long time since I saw any joy in you, Ty."

She was right, of course, but I didn't know if I was incapable or merely unwilling to address it. I had been raised on a notion of justice that required those of us who are able to come to the defense of those who aren't. No questions and no compromise. It was not a matter for debate or an evaluation of the cost. This was the code I had been brought up with.

Yellow candle flames the shapes of teardrops reflected inside Jesse's eyes as she looked at me, and I recognized the price of my isolation mirrored there. She deserved more, deserved better of me.

"I broke the nose of the man who introduced himself to you at the church thrift shop," I said finally.

She swallowed and set down her silverware on her plate but made no attempt to respond.

"He is a narcotics detective from Portland, and I suspect that he may have murdered his own partner in the service of political corruption. I believe him to be a dangerous man whose intentions are malicious and depraved, and introducing himself to you as a friend of mine was not only a lie but was intended as a threat. I also nearly snapped a finger off his hand."

Jesse lifted her wine glass by the stem and sipped. What little appetite I had brought home had disappeared together with the first words that had crossed my lips. I leaned back in my chair and refolded my linen napkin, stared into the wavering light.

"Was this the same person who damaged your truck?" she asked.

"Probably."

"So what's next, Ty? A car bomb?"

Though the words were laced with sarcasm, her fear and concern were genuine. I should have stopped myself right then and there, should have held my tongue and changed the subject. But I didn't.

"It also appears that an agency of our own federal government is attempting to take KC and Irene Sheridan's ranch away from them without their consent or compensation while people who claim to be their friends may be using them as political pawns."

"Ty—"

"I threatened to shoot the sheriff of Hemmings County in the eye after he disrespected KC."

Jesse placed her elbows on the table, knitted her fingers together, and rested her chin on them.

"You wouldn't have, would you, Ty? You wouldn't actually have shot him."

I wanted to draw my attention away from the quivering candle wick but could not.

"These people believe they can make the law up as they go along," I said.

"But you wouldn't have shot the man," Jesse said again. It was no longer a question, but a statement, a wish.

I drank off half the wine from my goblet in one pull, set it down softly, and smoothed the wrinkles from the napkin I'd laid beside my plate. I found myself questioning my own frame of reference: family homes with yellow windows, wooden stairways and porch rails and flowers planted in window boxes, and American flags that slanted out at angles from poles affixed to shingled buttresses. I had no desire to believe that those things had come in danger of losing their value.

"Seems like there's no honor in any of it, Jesse," I said. "I want to trust that what I'm doing is noble. Instead it's as though I need to bathe with lye and turpentine every night when I come home and scrub out the inside of my head with a wire brush before I can occupy the same bed as you."

THE DOORBELL rang as Jesse and I washed the dishes. When I went to answer it, I found Jordan Powell on the front door landing, shielding his eyes from the porch light I'd just switched on.

"Evening, Sheriff," he said, shuffling in the cold. "Is Miz Dawson at home?"

"Excuse me?"

"I'm sorry to bother y'all so late, but I really think I need to speak with your wife, sir."

He removed his hat and began to work the brim between his fingers. His breath was shallow, rapid, and the skin on his cheeks had colored in a way that suggested that he might have consumed a drink or two before coming over. I was about to call out for Jesse when I heard her step up behind me. I moved out of the way and Jesse took my place in the open doorway, cocked her head to one side as she appraised him.

"Hello, Jordan."

"Ma'am," he said, and glanced away.

A moth flew in out of the dark, beat its wings against the light fixture as she waited in silence for what seemed an uncomfortably long time.

"Is everything all right, Jordan?"

"Yes, ma'am," he answered, shifting his weight from one foot to the other. "I came to tell you I'm sorry for what happened the other night at my birthday."

"It isn't me you owe an apology to."

"You seemed pretty mad at me, Miz Dawson."

"Mostly I was disappointed."

"I understand."

I could see Jesse had no intention of inviting my half-drunk cowboy deputy into our house at that hour, so I brought a sweater from the rack and draped it across her shoulders.

"Shasta Blaylock deserves better, and you know it," she told him.

"I've already got things straightened out with Shasta."

Jesse raised an eyebrow and Powell's face colored more deeply.

"I really do, ma'am," he said. "And I also told Betsy where things stand with me and Shasta."

"Betsy . . . that's the chippie from the city?"

"She ain't a chip—Yes, Miz Dawson."

"Have you been drinking tonight, Jordan?"

"No, ma'am. Not much. Maybe a little bit."

"Is it true what you just told me? About Shasta and the other one? Cross your heart?"

"Yes, ma'am, it's the truth."

"You're a decent young man, Jordan Powell," she said. "I've always known you were."

He peeled his eyes off of the doormat and visibly relaxed when he finally lifted his head and saw the smile that softened Jesse's features.

"You ain't mad at me no more?"

"Maybe just a little bit," Jesse said, and bent into the light to kiss Powell on the cheek. "But tomorrow's a brand-new day. You'd best take one of the cots down in the bunkhouse now, or you'll have Ty to deal with in the morning, son, not me."

"Yes ma'am."

Jesse closed the door and looked at me. She kept one hand gripped on the latch, and I wished that I had some way to know what she was thinking in that moment.

I knew Jordan Powell to be a Vietnam combat veteran who still somehow managed to believe that people were basically good. He had survived his tour of duty and come home to a country who expressed their gratitude by heaping spittle and derision on him and his comrades-at-arms. Rather than sink into bitterness, Powell responded by quietly putting himself through two years of college before throwing in the towel on higher education and exchanging everything he had accomplished in his life until that moment for the unadorned life of a cowboy. I knew him to be youthful and energetic, generous almost to a fault, and a man who displayed not only his heart, but his entire being on his sleeve. He could also be headstrong and stubborn, willful, argumentative, and frustrating. But I'd never known him to duck a punch or shirk his duty, nor had I ever known anyone who threw himself into his own life the way Jordan Powell did.

When I looked at Jesse again, I saw that moisture had begun to well up in her eyes.

"What's happening to you boys out there is breaking my heart, Ty," she said. "I can see the signs in every one of you."

At first, I had mistaken the origin of her tears as grief, but her expression as she took her first steps away from the door told me she had exhausted the boundaries of her mercy. I went to bed that night hoping I was wrong about that as well.

PART FOUR

COLD RAIN AND SNOW

CHAPTER SEVENTEEN

JORDAN POWELL'S TRUCK was still parked outside the bunkhouse when I left for the substation the next morning. The predawn sky was deep blue and cloudless, maculated with starlight, and fading to gray within the halo that circled the moon.

The Chamber of Commerce had been busy decorating downtown Meridian while I'd been away in the city. I turned left and drove slowly down Main Street, deserted but for the presence of Rowan Boyle unlocking the front door to his diner. I flashed my headlights at him, and he tossed a wave to me as I passed by. Red and white holiday lights spiraled the trunks of leafless ash trees, and the conifers had been tied with red ribbon bows and tinsel garlands of every conceivable shade. Representations of candles and holiday wreaths had been fixed to the streetlight posts, and chaplets strung along the support cables of the town's lone traffic signal. Only one more day remained in the month of November, and Thanksgiving leftovers still occupied my kitchen refrigerator, but Christmas had arrived in full force in Meridian.

The inside of the office was so cold it stung my lungs, so I cranked up the heat and made coffee before removing my coat, muffler, and gloves. I checked in with the answering service, sorted through the mail, and scanned yesterday's newspaper while I waited for Captain Chris Rose from State Police CID to arrive at his office so I could call him. At a quarter to eight, I poured myself some fresh coffee, returned to my desk, and dialed his direct number.

We shared some small talk before I filled him in on what I had witnessed at the Stumptown Chophouse.

"I know Marcus Vessey," he said without having to look up the man's rap sheet. "Local legend in dipshit circles. Drives a purple rat rod with suicide doors and twice-pipes. He's a hard man to miss. They say he's the front for some of Dean Stricklyn's extracurricular enterprises."

"Is the Chophouse one of those enterprises?"

"Most likely."

Outside my window, the sky began to soften, and I watched the stars fade one by one.

"I must've seen ten different people come by to kiss his ring, and I was there for less than an hour."

"They also say he's Stricklyn's bag man."

"What's he into?"

"It's all rumors, Ty," he said. "But if I had to guess, I'd venture prostitution, pornography, and very probably narcotics."

"I have a surveillance shot of someone who looks a hell of a lot like him taken outside a condo the Countess uses as a cathouse."

"Who gave you something like that?"

Rose cut me off before I could answer.

"Never mind," he said. "I don't want to know."

He grunted, and I heard the protest of his chair as he stood and began to pace.

"Vessey's gone down twice already," Rose said. "For battery and sexual assault."

"If he gets popped again, they'll hang a 'habitual' tag on him, and he won't be out again until he's an old man."

"Third time's the charm," he said. "I heard he still likes to rape the occasional waitress in the parking lot after a shift."

"Come on, Chris," I said. "If *your* agency knows this, what the hell's PPB waiting for?"

He sighed as he stopped pacing and perched on the edge of his desk. I could picture his familiar scowl as he turned his back toward his office door.

"My advice?" he said quietly. "You need to watch yourself, Ty."

"What are you telling me?"

"That surveillance shot you mentioned? I'm guessing you got it from Lieutenant Morgan. He's so new to SID he still needs directions to the washroom, by the way. You have no idea—and neither does Morgan, for that matter—whether his man Halloran, or Stricklyn himself, isn't being tipped by Morgan's own surveillance team."

"And Marcus Vessey? What about him?"

"You and I don't call the play in the big city, Dawson."

I hung up and looked outside my office, trying not to feel as though I was being sucked down into a hole.

I LEARNED more about Vessey from the file Captain Rose sent to me over the Magnafax. I don't always appreciate modern technology, but at six minutes per page coming down the telephone line, the damn thing saved me a long drive to Rose's office in Salem.

Turns out Marcus Vessey had been born in Chicago. When little Marcus was still in diapers, his daddy got himself shanked to death by fellow inmates at Statesville, where his old man was doing a bit for aggravated sodomy on a ten-year-old neighbor girl. After his death, Mom became a triple-threat—exotic dancer turned hooker turned junkie—and expired two years later on the stained concrete inside a storage locker, the aftereffects of a speedball laced with cockroach poison.

Young Marcus took to the streets doing petty crime until he hooked up with a ring of auto thieves, acting as a spotter at the age of thirteen. After a stint in juvie, his psychotic and sociopathic inclinations ultimately earned him a position as an enforcer for a local bookmaker and loan shark. But Marcus administered his duties with a little more enthusiasm than the job required, and he had to disappear from the Midwest when the heat began to close in on him for his suspected complicity in the abduction of two men and a woman, and their subsequent demise at the wrong end of a set of power tools Marcus had stolen from the home of a part-time taxidermist.

I watched a redwing land on a leafless maple branch and wondered why a man like Dean Stricklyn would invite a vicious recidivist misanthrope like Marcus Vessey into his life or onto his payroll. In my experience, such men were loose cannons, or worse, and ended up working their own agendas without supervision or accountability, using a playbook that no one claiming membership in the human species would recognize.

So I picked up the receiver, dialed Dean Stricklyn at his office, and asked him.

"I'm familiar with the name," Stricklyn said. "I believe he manages a couple of nightclubs I frequent. I'd be happy to call and ask him to put your name on the VIP list at the door for you, Sheriff."

"I don't understand you, Mr. Stricklyn," I said. "Marcus Vessey's bloodline was contaminated or defiled somewhere along the evolutionary chain. Why would you want someone like him in your employ?"

He laughed.

"My employ? I have no idea what you're talking about, but I have to admit it is always entertaining to visit with you."

"Most killers that I've encountered are cowards," I said. "That's something you may not be aware of. Nice talking with you, Mr. Stricklyn."

JORDAN POWELL walked in through the back door of the office as I was hanging up the phone.

"Morning, Sheriff."

He wore the half-dazed expression of a man who had gone without much sleep.

"You don't have to tiptoe in," I said.

"Yes, sir," he said and slid into the back room. "I'll just hang up my coat and grab a cup of joe."

When he returned, he could not meet my eyes.

"You're looking a little penitent, son," I said.

His cheeks colored, and he blew steam off of his coffee.

"A little embarrassed is all."

"Just because you got liquored-up and came out to my house in the middle of the night?"

"I needed to apologize."

I swiveled in my chair to look him square in the face.

"I'm just razzing you," I said. "You did the right thing. Crow's a lot easier to eat while it's still warm."

"Roger that."

"Something else on your mind?"

111

Powell stood and walked over to my desk. He leaned a shoulder against the wall and looked out the window.

"You ever dream about it, sir?"

I didn't need to ask him what he meant.

"All the goddamn time," I said.

He inhaled deeply and looked as though he was in danger of drifting away.

"Sometimes I can't get it out of my head," he said.

"You never look at war the same way after you've fought in one," I said.

I gathered his empty coffee mug and stepped into the back room to get a fresh one for him while he collected himself. I knew from experience that sometimes memories came at you unbidden, without portent or forewarning. Any vet will tell you that you don't simply participate in combat; you don't just stand there and bear witness to a thing like war. No, it seeps in through your nostrils, through your ears and up your asshole and your pores; it makes a nest inside your guts and then it's in you and there's nothing you can ever do to get it out again. Go ahead, ask anybody who's been there.

"Sorry, Sheriff," he said when I passed his cup to him.

"Don't you ever say that word to me again, son. Not on that subject. You've got nothing to be sorry for."

He stepped back from the window and moved toward his desk and slumped down in his seat.

"You good to go, Jordan? Need a day for yourself?"

"No, thanks," he said, and showed the first sign of a smile. "I'm PFM."

Military-speak. Pure friggin' magic.

He sat in silence for several minutes as he finished his coffee and gradually returned to himself. I was all too familiar with the sensation. When he finally broke the silence, it was as if a new man had arrived inside the room.

"Last night," he said. "I shot a couple games of pool with a guy over at the Blossom."

I waited for more, but nothing came.

"Okay," I prompted.

"I was hanging out with one of the Hemmings County deputies."

I fought to keep the incredulity off my face.

"From the Sheridan standoff?" I asked.

"They don't think too highly of Sheriff Brayfield, either."

"There was a time when I thought he might be a decent man," I said.

"Then you ain't gonna like what his deputy told me."

"Spit it out."

"He told me that Brayfield aims to serve an arrest warrant on Mr. Sheridan."

"What? When?"

"From what I gather, Fish and Wildlife is planning to press charges."

"Charges for what?"

"Destruction of federal property. Same charges as before."

"They can't do that. They dismissed the case, let KC go. You and I both watched them do it."

Powell shrugged.

"I'm no lawyer," he said. "Just passing along what the deputy told me."

"When are they planning to do it?"

"He wasn't sure. Next couple days is what he figured. I guess a judge granted a seventy-two–hour stay. There's some procedures and whatnot to attend to beforehand."

I knew about the stay, had hoped the new land survey would put the whole thing to bed. If Powell's new friend was right, then KC was about to get tossed under the wheels regardless. The whole thing had been a show.

"Why would he tell you any of this?" I asked.

"I can't say for sure," Powell said. "But you get to know a guy when you're freezing your nuts off together in the middle of nowhere in a snowstorm."

"It wasn't a snowstorm."

"Sure felt like one to me."

I stood up from my chair and studied Powell again.

"You sure you're good to go, Jordan?"

"Yes, sir."

"Then grab your coat and gear and come with me," I said.

"Where to, if you don't mind my asking?"

"We need to tell KC what you just told me. But we've got one other stop to make along the way."

I PARKED my truck near the boat launch at the Catonquin River Resort. The sky had temporarily cleared of storm clouds, but the pine needles under my boots felt like a wet sponge and the branches of the tall trees sagged from rain.

I saw no sign of Doug May or his oatmeal-colored station wagon at the front office, so I reached into the cab and leaned on my horn. Powell stepped out of the passenger side and yawned, stretched his arms over his head, and called out for the manager. I was about to lean on the horn a second time when a heavyset man wearing yellow rain gear and carrying a garden rake shambled out of the overgrowth.

"What the hell?" he asked.

"Where's Doug May?" I asked. "I'm Sheriff Dawson, and I need to speak with him."

The man relaxed as he stepped out of the woods and moved closer to Powell and me. He pushed the hood of his slicker off his head and revealed a tangle of gray hair and a face that was the shape of a pie plate. His irises were the same shade as pond moss, his complexion ruddy from either brittle weather or strong drink, but my guess was both.

"He don't work here no more," the man said. "I'm Ned Bixby. My friends call me Bobo."

His handshake felt like uncooked bread dough, and the odor that emanated from his rain gear put me in mind of baitfish that had washed up in a levee.

"Have any idea where we can find Mr. May?"

He chuckled to himself and looked off toward the bend in the river. When he turned back, there was no mirth in his eyes.

"He was pretty bad beat up last time I seen him," he said.

"How bad?"

"If it was any worse, his face woulda been coming out the backside of his head. Hooked up his trailer and took off yesterday morning."

As we drove back to the highway, Powell removed his hat, rolled down the window, and allowed the fresh air to wash over him. His cheeks were flushed when he leaned back inside and cranked the window handle.

"About this morning—" he began.

"Everything we talked about stays between us," I interrupted.

"Thank you, sir."

"You don't need to say that again, either, Jordan. We've both seen the elephant."

He hesitated for a moment, picked something invisible off his pantleg.

"People always say they don't believe in god," he said. "But usually it's because of some horrible thing some other person did. That don't seem fair to me."

"No, I don't suppose it is. I guess it's the price of free will."

He pursed his lips and cocked his head sideways, like Cricket used to do when she was gearing up to ask me for something.

"You were river-baptized, right, Captain?"

Powell would call me that sometimes, in reference to my former military rank.

"Yes, I was," I said. "Not too far from here."

"Maybe you can tell me about it some time," he said without looking at me.

"That'd be fine," I said. "Anytime you want. You just let me know."

We turned onto the paved road and passed over a truss bridge that had been constructed as a project of the WPA. Down in the swale, a group of school kids stood on the shore skipping acorns and rocks across the creek.

"What's it like?" Powell asked. "The dunking, I mean."

"It'll change your life," I said. "But it won't change your past. You understand what I mean?"

He stared out the window and chewed at a hangnail on his thumb.

"Do they ever stop?" he asked.

"The nightmares?"

"Yes, sir. The nightmares."

"I don't know yet."

CHAPTER EIGHTEEN

THE BAROMETRIC PRESSURE dropped precipitously as we crossed the summit of Mt. Kanen and pushed into the pass, where a sprawling view opened far below. Off to the west, the wooded peaks marking the border of Hemmings County disappeared into the clouds, their slopes scarred by a patchwork of tree stumps and red soil laid bare by clearcutting before the boom had turned to bust. For decades, beginning in the Roaring Twenties, Hemmings County had been the wealthiest in the entire state. But by 1964, the logging industry and sawmill jobs had all but vanished, leaving a county boasting a geographical area the size of Delaware with a population of fewer than eight thousand human souls.

I stopped for gas at an Esso station when we reached the valley floor. I stretched my legs while the attendant checked the oil and cleaned the windshield, then climbed back into the cab and waited for Powell to return with a couple soda bottles from the machine. Across the road, a sheet had torn loose from a faded billboard advertising Sunshine Hydrox cookies and buffeted the frame in the rushing wind.

WE PULLED into KC Sheridan's place an hour later and parked next to a gray four-by-four pickup with Nevada tags. It had been modified for off-road performance, with a suspension lift and oversized tires, the grille and quarter panels caked with dried mud.

Three men occupied a plank table inside the workshop that abutted KC's horse barn, each of whom appeared to be field stripping a semi-automatic weapon. The smell of gun oil laced the air, and the table was littered with beverage cans and grease-blotted cardboard containers from a fried chicken franchise.

Two men had their backs turned to us, hunched over their work like combat surgeons. One was dressed in an M-65 jacket and camouflage pants he'd bloused into a pair of lace-up jungle boots. The other wore blue jeans and steel-toed Redwings and an OD fatigue shirt that still bore the shoulder patch of the 25th Infantry.

The man who faced us looked to be in his mid-thirties, had a shaved head the shape and texture of an ostrich egg, and eyes as featureless and empty as ball bearings. He stood up and glared as Powell and I stepped toward KC's back door. The other two remained fixed on their work and never bothered to acknowledge our arrival.

I rapped on KC's door with the ball of my fist, but no one answered, so Powell and I let ourselves inside, shipped the bolt behind us, and followed the drone of conversation that was coming from the kitchen. KC and Jarvis Lynch looked up at us from where they knelt beside a Dockash stove, warming their hands before the flames inside the box. The room smelled of fresh cheese biscuits, red gravy, and ham.

"Can't seem to keep easeful in this cold," KC said, and I heard his knees pop as he unfolded himself out of his crouch. "Never did get central heat in this place."

Jarvis Lynch remained where he was and said nothing, his eyes drifting from Powell to me before returning his attention to the fire.

"You don't appear surprised to see us," I said.

"I called your office a while ago," KC answered. "Deputy Griffin said you were on your way down here."

I worked my fingers out from my gloves, and Powell wedged himself into a warm spot closer to the woodstove. I craned my neck to look into the living room and saw no sign of the cadre of two from before.

"Where's Mutt and Jeff?" I asked.

"You referring to Reeves and Zachary?" KC replied. "Likely down to Lake Rafferty by now. They wanted to get a peep at the wildlife refuge."

"What in the hell for?"

"They don't have too many stagnant fishponds where they're from, I guess," Lynch smart-assed without bothering to turn in my direction.

"And what about those fellas out there in your shed, KC?" I asked.

"A few more friends from home," Lynch answered for him again.

"You really believe that's wise, bringing all these boys up here?" I asked. "You probably noticed things are a little tense as they already stand."

Lynch jumped up from his kneeling position.

"They didn't get here a moment too soon, if you ask me," he said.

"There are people who might interpret the arrival of out-of-state militia as a provocation of some kind, Mr. Lynch."

"Those people can kiss my ass, Sheriff," Lynch said. "The only provoking being done around here is coming from the same folks who claim to represent the law."

"I will assume you are not including either my deputy or me in that reference," I said.

The old man moved across the kitchen, rested his palms along the edge of the sink, and looked out the window. Light glinted on the patchy whiskers of his unshaven face.

"They set up a traffic stop last night," KC said softly. "Down where the access road comes off the highway."

"Wasn't anybody there when we drove in just now," Powell said.

"I suspect they'll only set up after dark," KC said. "Dollars to doughnuts he's got somebody watching from up there on the ridge during the day."

"He who?" I asked. "Who's watching from the ridge?"

"Sheriff Brayfield."

"What for?"

"Said he was performing sobriety checks. Set his roadblock just his side of the county line."

"The only people who use that road are either coming out to your place," Jordan said, "or going to the refuge."

"The refuge is closed for winter," Lynch said. "Remember?"

KC turned his attention back inside his kitchen.

"Them boys you just asked me about," KC said. "The ones you saw in my workshop? Brayfield stopped them as they drove in last night. Said he was fixin' on stayin' out there as long as it takes 'til this survey mess gets resolved. Obviously, that message was for me."

"Brayfield's lying," I said. "I believe the feds might be coming back for you, KC. I think the seventy-two-hour injunction was a ruse."

"That's what we figured," Lynch said.

I felt a ripple run down my spine that felt like ice water.

"You need to get your attorney on the phone right now, KC," I said. "We need to understand the situation before this gets any further out of hand."

"Ain't gonna matter," Lynch said. "That train left the station."

Jarvis Lynch folded his arms across his chest and leaned a shoulder on the wall.

"What is that supposed to mean?" I asked.

"You heard me, Sheriff," he said. "I got more men on their way here as we speak."

I LOCATED Irene Sheridan in the lower horse barn, at the end of a narrow gravel path a short distance from the main house. She was resting on the handle of a steel-headed rake, winded from mucking stalls, outlined by the dim light streaming from the cupola. Her silver hair had been pinned back in a bun, but several strands had come unfastened and fallen loose across her cheek.

"Sorry to interrupt you, Miz Sheridan," I said.

A horse in the far stall nickered low and deep as Irene turned toward the sound of my voice. She appeared to be resisting tears and had to clear her throat before she recovered the ability speak.

"Hello, Tyler," she whispered. "I must have been daydreaming."

The air was redolent with ammonia, horseflesh, and sweet feed, together with the loamy scents of alfalfa and damp clay. She took longer than necessary to deposit her rake on a spoke-wheeled utility cart that brimmed with soiled sawdust.

"It's trouble again, isn't it?" she asked.

"Yes, ma'am," I said. "I'm afraid it might be."

Her attention span took on the ephemeral quality of a firefly's light, her focus landing on everything inside the barn except my face.

"We should go up to the house and get Quentin Bahle on the telephone," I said.

"The attorney?"

Tiny particles floated inside a cone of disjected sunshine that quartered down from an air vent in the loft. As Irene Sheridan passed through it and moved with me toward the door, her parchment skin took on a translucence I had previously only associated with cerements.

"I'VE HAD a chance to look over the documents you signed when they released you from the jailhouse, Mr. Sheridan," Quentin Bahle said over the phone. "I really wish you would have shown them to me beforehand."

Jarvis Lynch, the Sheridans, and I were squeezed into a small bedroom that had been converted for use as the ranch office. Irene was seated on the only chair, and the rest of us were on our feet, arranged in a semicircle near the desk. The telephone seemed to be about the only modern component of the room, equipped with a precision microphone and speaker exactly like the one I had in the substation.

"Next time," KC said, "you're welcome to come and join me in the jail cell, too, so I don't make any more mistakes."

"I meant no criticism—" the attorney said.

"Hell you didn't."

"Okay," I said. "We're all a little barn sour. Mr. Bahle, can you tell us—in simple terms—where KC stands in all this?"

On the other end of the line, we could hear the sound of rustling papers and the closing of a door.

"Most of what was signed by Mr. Sheridan would be considered standard procedure," he said. "Acknowledgement that his personal effects were returned to him, a statement that he had been represented by legal counsel, and so on like that. But there were two small paragraphs appended to his acceptance of the suspended sentence."

I glanced at Irene Sheridan, watched her as she studied the tracery of veins and birdlike tendons of her hands, and saw that she was trembling. I gently placed my palm upon her shoulder. I could feel the rhythm of her breathing, and she felt so fragile that it seemed as though she might shatter into tiny pieces.

"The language in the first paragraph waived all of Mr. Sheridan's rights to an appeal," Bahle continued. "In the second paragraph, he relinquished all of what we call his '2255' rights. It is important to note that he did this unilaterally, meaning that Mr. Sheridan is bound to this waiver, but that the prosecution is *not* bound by it."

"Can you please clarify what that means?" I asked.

"In short, Section 2255 deals with collateral appeals; that is to say, that the defendant may appeal a verdict based upon any irregularity in the judgment. For instance, if a sentence was imposed in violation of the Constitution, or if the court acted without proper jurisdiction, or any of a hundred other reasons."

"I thought if I agreed to all the things I agreed to, so did they," KC said. "I thought it was, what do you call it, bilateral."

"I'm afraid not, Mr. Sheridan."

KC's face drained of color, and it looked like Irene was on the verge of fainting dead away. I leaned across and cracked the window open. The rush of frigid wind cut through the room.

"You're saying that the goddamn feds can change their minds, and KC can't do anything about it?" Lynch said. He looked like he wanted to crawl up through the phone wire all the way to Portland.

"We've heard they might attempt to come after KC again," I said. "Can they legally do that?"

"The prosecution has filed an appeal to enforce the sentence for destruction of government property that they claim should have been enforced originally. In other words, they're claiming that the judge had no right to suspend Mr. Sheridan's sentence in the first place, nor issue him a seventy-two–hour stay."

"And what do they claim the sentence is supposed to be?"

The silence that traveled down the line during those long seconds was the most devastating silence I had ever heard. Irene closed her eyes and massaged the knuckles of her hand.

"According to the statute," Bahle said, almost a dirge, "if the damage is in excess of one hundred dollars, the defendant is subject to a fine of up to a quarter of a million dollars and ten years imprisonment. Or both."

"Jesus," KC murmured, so quietly I couldn't tell if he'd intended it as exclamation or entreaty.

"That's double jeopardy," Lynch bellowed. "No way in hell even the feds can get away with that."

"You're not going to like this," Bahle said, "but it isn't double jeopardy because Mr. Sheridan isn't being tried twice."

"Then what the hell in god's green earth do you call what they *are* doing?"

"The court of appeals has sent the case back to trial court for 'resentencing.' The prosecution claims that the judge acted in error the first time, and he needs to correct the situation. In other words, they're sending it back and asking him to 'do it right' and fix what he did wrong before."

"I can't believe KC's left with no means for appeal," I said.

"Mr. Sheridan waived those rights in the document he signed."

"They goddamn tricked him!" Lynch shouted. "They knew that KC wouldn't know what he was signing."

KC seemed to shrink, his shame a living thing behind his eyes, his physical presence dissolving into a shadow of itself. It felt as if the air had been vacuumed from the room, as if all of us had been set adrift in zero gravity.

A cold white burn replaced the bitter metallic taste in my throat, a sensation I had come to recognize.

"We need to be level-headed here," I said. "What kind of timing are we looking at?"

"Jesus," KC whispered again.

"The ruling could come down within the next twenty-four to forty-eight hours, Sheriff Dawson," Bahle said. "Once it does, they'll issue an arrest warrant and come out to the ranch and take custody of Mr. Sheridan."

The tendons in Lynch's neck went taut, and he balled a fist and struck the office door so hard that a framed lithograph depicting longhorn cattle slid sideways off its nail and landed on the floor.

"I told you they'd pull some bullshit move like this," Lynch shouted. "No. This is not going to happen. Not on my watch."

"Excuse me?" the attorney said.

"Do you know what 'no quarter' means, counselor?" Lynch said.

The discussion that was mere seconds away from detonation was not intended for the attorney's ears. I thanked Quentin Bahle and cut off the call before any statements might be verbalized that could not be retracted.

I STOOD on the running board of my pickup and lingered for a final quiet moment before I climbed in. The low sun of late afternoon hovered in a narrow space between the outline of the mountains and the dense ceiling of storm clouds, mottling their undersides with peach-colored luminescence. Nearer to the house, in the work yard, a cluster of hard men threw horseshoes and drank beer in the remnants of the ebbing light, and the smells of burning cedar wood and charred beef fat drifted inside the smoke that carried on the wind.

"You sure you don't want me to stick around?" Powell asked from the other side of the cab. "I don't mind staying behind."

"Whatever Jarvis Lynch has planned is already in motion; probably been planning it for days," I said. "I don't want you getting caught up in the middle of it."

Powell looked away from me and squinted into the sky.

"What if KC don't let them take him in?" he asked. "Seems to me like they pulled a fast one on him."

Truth was, I'd been considering that question since we'd driven back from the city that first time. I didn't know exactly how or why, but something seemed inevitable about the whole damned situation. The conduct of the opposition was not only reprehensible, but the foundation of their legal strategy was both specious and perfidious. I passed my eyes across the landscape and heard the grit inside the brittle wind ticking against the windshield. Violence had been a part of human makeup since the first man drew a breath; I knew people who could kill you with a playing card.

"I'm inclined to back KC's play," I said. "But not at the cost of another Wounded Knee."

"The feds wouldn't take it that far," Jordan said, but I could see the doubts forming even as the words passed across his lips. "Would they?"

"The government?" I asked. "You and I both fought in wars they didn't even have the courage to declare. Ninety-five thousand US soldiers were killed, and neither you nor me came home victorious. Is that the kind of judgment that inspires confidence?"

He placed his palm on the passenger door handle and thumbed the latch button.

"This ain't the same thing," he said into the wind.

"Tell that to the feds," I said and climbed behind the wheel. "They don't respond well to being disagreed with."

As I threw the truck in gear, I peered into the workshop, where the same three newcomers now sat playing dominoes at the plank table that less than two hours ago had been strewn with the oiled mechanical components of semi-automatic firearms.

CHAPTER NINETEEN

GRAY TAILS of rainfall were draped across the Portland skyline as I came into the city. I parked on the street and buttoned my duster tight against my chin as I exited the truck, felt the raindrops palpate my hat brim and I glanced into the sky. Ripples of electricity pulsed inside the clouds, and I took cover inside a stairwell while I waited for the squall to pass. A jagged bolt struck a lightning rod fixed to the roof structure of a high rise across the street, but when thunder tore a seam in the sky directly overhead, I should have recognized the signs, a forewarning by semaphore.

QUENTIN BAHLE'S office was located on the fifth floor of a midrise with a peekaboo view of the Willamette River a few blocks from the courthouse. I peeled the foil wrapper from a stick of chewing gum as I awaited the attention of the young woman who occupied the receptionist's desk. She was engaged in an animated conversation with someone on the phone, gesticulating broadly as she complained into the microphone attached to her headset. She rolled her eyes as she noticed me, toggled a knob on the branch exchange switchboard, and angled her head to one side, like a bird.

"Help you?"

"I'm here for Quentin Bahle."

"Is he expecting you?"

"I doubt it."

Enormous teardrop-shaped earrings pitched like tire swings as she tilted her head sideways and examined me again. Her eyes locked onto mine as she fitted a cable jack into the board and whispered something unintelligible into her mic.

I moved to the seating area near the window to distance myself from her avian gaze, took a seat in a guest chair, and watched the rain pelt the glass and form runnels along the panes. Track lighting illuminated a reception space that had been painted in shades of ripening fruit and highlighted artwork that resembled what might have been swatches torn off a housepainter's drop cloth.

"Sheriff Dawson," Quentin Bahle said from somewhere behind me, "I wasn't aware you were coming."

"Neither was I until I found myself pacing my living room floor at three-thirty this morning."

He was wearing a polyester suit woven in a checkerboard pattern in hues of autumn foliage, with lapels so broad that the tips touched his shoulders. He forced a smile in my direction, tugged at his shirtsleeve and frowned at his watch.

"I have a ten o'clock," he said. "I don't have much time."

"I won't require much."

Bahle guided me into a conference room whose walls had been constructed from lime-colored glass, and he cast a glance down the length of the corridor before closing the door behind us. I waited as he stepped up to a sideboard and poured himself a cup of coffee from a chafer urn and brought it to his seat at the head of the table.

"Help yourself, Sheriff," he said, gestured me to a white Eames chair similar to those out in the waiting area, leaned back, and crossed his legs. My gaze wandered outward, beyond the room's translucent curtain wall, examined the maze of tiny offices and cubicles occupied by pink-cheeked attorneys freshly minted from law school.

"I'm the greybeard," Bahle said when he noticed me assessing his associates. "And to answer your next question, I'm barely forty."

I declined the coffee Bahle had offered me, hung my duster on a wall hook, placed my Stetson on the credenza, and took a seat directly across from him.

"The lawyers that are drawn to defense work are either youthful and idealistic," he said, "or reformed prosecutors looking for a payday before retirement."

"Which one are you?"

"I'm still too young for retirement," he said, uncrossed his legs, and shifted his weight in his chair. "You know that I can't talk to you about my clients."

"I don't need you to talk to me," I said. "I drove all the way up here because I need you to look at my face when I say what I have to say to you. I wanted you to see that I'm speaking the truth when I tell you that the situation at the Sheridan ranch is a tinderbox on the verge of going up in flames. That is neither colloquialism nor hyperbole."

"I've already explained the situation, Sheriff," he said. "What more do you expect me to do?"

The attorney looked as though he had already moved on from the conversation. I hadn't.

"I expect you to use all the influence, skill, and clout that you've acquired thus far in your profession," I said, "and to unleash every ounce of it for KC Sheridan's benefit. This 'resentencing' maneuver stinks to high heaven, and you and I both know it. If the feds keep pressing, and this situation starts to go sideways, it's going to be damn near impossible to stop the slide."

Bahle looked sidelong at me, picked a stray coffee ground off his tongue, but declined to respond.

It has been my experience that most human beings grow uncomfortable inside of protracted silences. I knew the maneuver, the stunt he was attempting to run on me, and I allowed it to hang there in between us.

The broad leaves of a potted ficus cast odd-shaped patterns of shadow on the conference room carpet, and I stood up to inspect it. The leaves felt rough and brittle in my hands, and I leaned down and dipped my index finger in the soil.

"This tree is dying," I said. "Needs water."

Bahle looked at me and checked his watch again.

I crossed to the sideboard and hitched a seat on it, shifted my focus to a piece of artwork that looked as though something had exploded inside the frame.

"The American judiciary takes pride in the maxim that it is preferable that a hundred guilty men walk free than to imprison one single innocent man," I said.

"I'm familiar with the statement."

"Inherent in that assertion," I said, "is the recognition that personal freedom comes at a price, and sometimes that price can be dangerous."

"I don't believe I follow your point, Sheriff."

"You have to admit that there would be an enhanced risk to the rest of us in having a hundred guilty—though un-incarcerated—criminals walking the streets in order to keep that single innocent man out of prison."

"It's just a saying," Bahle said and stirred the contents of his coffee cup with a plastic straw.

"If it's only a saying," I said, "you all should stop repeating it. Evidently, it is no longer true."

He made a move to stand up from his chair.

"Sit the hell down," I said. "It's not ten o'clock yet."

"I beg your pardon?"

"You espouse egalitarianism, but in practice, you won't lift a finger when an agency of the federal government drives a steamroller over the most basic rights of its individual citizens. You don't see something wrong with that, Mr. Bahle?"

"You're out of line, Sheriff."

"I assume you're familiar with the dubious history of the Rafferty Wildlife Refuge? If you aren't, you've got some catching up to do. And you'd better get to studying on it pretty goddamned quick."

"What is that supposed to mean?"

"Ten years in prison to a seventy-year-old man like KC Sheridan is a life sentence," I said. "Not to mention the monetary fine, which would ruin him. He and Irene would lose everything, including what's left of his life, for what? There are armed civilians out there right now who will not look favorably upon the US government rearresting KC Sheridan. Especially since the original charge was bullshit to begin with."

"The US government does not respond well to threats."

I plucked the chewing gum from my mouth, wrapped it in a paper napkin, and dropped it in a rubbish can.

"I said something very similar to my deputy yesterday evening," I said. "What I am passing on to you today, Mr. Bahle, is not a threat."

"No?"

"No. But don't mistake proper manners for weakness, or restraint for the absence of will. At the risk of repeating myself, Quentin, you need to pull in every favor, or whatever the hell else you folks use for barter around here, to get the prosecution to leave this thing where it was before they decided to take a second bite out of the Sheridans."

"I've already tried to explain to you that it isn't double jeopardy."

"Do you ever wonder why decent society has lost its trust in lawyers?" I asked. "Language doesn't matter as much as you think it does; referring to a vagrant as 'homeless' does nothing to improve his circumstances."

"You've made your point, Sheriff," Bahle said, glanced down at his cuffs.

"Have I?"

"I will do what I can," he said. "You have my word. But I would appreciate it if you'd inform Mr. Sheridan's supporters that acting aggressively toward USFW will have the agency seeing red. And that will not improve his bargaining position."

"Maybe USFW should be thinking more in terms of butternut and blue."

"That sounds like admiration in your voice."

"This is not a circumstance that I view in terms of 'sides,' Mr. Bahle. I'm only trying to express the gravity of the situation as I see it."

CHAPTER TWENTY

QUENTIN BAHLE departed for his appointment, and I used the telephone extension in the conference room to have the operator connect me to Lieutenant Morgan's office at Special Investigations. The detective who answered sounded like he'd been gargling rust remover.

"The lieutenant ain't in right now," a detective said. "Vice squad's busting fags down at Zorba the Greek's. Prob'ly got Morgan locked up in cuffs by now."

Someone in the background began to laugh.

"Oh, wait a minute," the detective continued. "Lieutenant's just walking in right now. They must have let him off with just a warning."

Morgan punched a button on his desk phone and came on the line. The background noise disappeared with a click as the other cop rang off.

"Don't mind these idiots," he said. "They still think that kind of shit is amusing. I'm glad you called, Dawson. It seems somebody in your charming little town put a beat-down on my prettiest detective."

"Must not have been reported in Meridian," I said. "I don't know anything about it."

"Like the Wild West down there, it seems."

"A man's got to hold on for the whole eight seconds, Lieutenant."

"Any movement on the Wehr case? I still have people crawling up my pants leg about that."

I thought I heard a hollow, electronic hum on my end of the call, then it was gone.

"Still working it," I said. "Listen, I need an address for the Countess."

Morgan didn't reply right away.

"Did I just hear you say that you want an address for the Countess?" Morgan asked. "What in the hell for? Never mind, it doesn't matter. No."

"Did you just tell me *no*?"

"I've still got a team watching her place," he said. "I can't have you waltzing in and blowing the whole thing up."

"It's a place of business."

"It's a brothel. You really want your picture taken popping in and out of a Portland whorehouse, Dawson?"

"You know some other way for me to speak to her?"

I could hear him grunt as he got up from his chair, heard the flat of his palm smack against his desktop.

"I cannot have you getting in the middle of my case."

"*You're* the one who handed *me* the photos."

"Not so you could screw up my surveillance."

"I can see I've caught you on a bad day, Lieutenant," I said. "I'll try not to look straight into the camera."

"If you get near her place without my say-so, I will park one in your ear."

"I'll assume that's just a colorful figure of speech." I said. "I'll be sure to say howdy to Halloran next time I see him."

"Well, you just might. I put him on medical leave until his hand heals up," he said, and hung up.

I looked out through the window, into the storm, as I passed through the reception area. I shrugged into my duster and nodded politely to Bahle's receptionist before I put on my hat.

She was slurping ramen noodles out of a Styrofoam cup, but the scowl she tried to pierce me with made it clear that she had been eavesdropping on the line.

"Y'all exercise a real special brand of law enforcement in this town," I said as I walked out of the office.

JORDAN POWELL was set to meet me at the Gold Hotel's bar when I returned to Meridian that afternoon. I hadn't eaten anything since before dawn that morning and my stomach had begun to growl, but I had one other matter to deal with before I sat down for lunch.

"Don't sneak off on me," I said as I stepped up to the hotel reception desk.

It was the same uniformed clerk I had spoken with twice before, and having seen me enter the lobby, he had begun to sidle toward the door to the manager's office.

"Good afternoon, Sheriff," he said, his pale features flushing pink as his eyes searched the windows and walls for something upon which to focus other than my face.

"Has Mr. Halloran been back here since you and I last spoke?"

"No, sir."

"Do you remember who I am referring to?"

"Yes, sir."

"City fella?" I persisted. "Dresses like a hustler, with a remodeled nose and a cast on his right hand?"

"I recall the person you're referring to, sir."

"And he hasn't been back to the hotel?"

"Not to my knowledge."

"Do we really have to do it this way every time?"

He opened the register and began to scan the pages.

I did not enjoy bullying service personnel, but the half hour I'd spent at Quentin Bahle's office had taxed my tolerance for passivity and indolence. I craned my neck and read the entries upside down as I watched the clerk leaf through the book.

"Mr. Halloran isn't here, Sheriff."

"I am grateful for your help," I said, and stepped away toward the lounge, beneath an archway that had been hand-hewn out of Brazilian mahogany.

I squinted through the dimness inside, found Jordan Powell seated at the bar alone, nursing a half-empty bottle of Dr. Pepper. Apart from the bartender, the parlor was otherwise unoccupied but for a middle-aged couple sharing a bottle of red wine beside the window at the far corner of the room. They were engaged in a muted dialogue, their voices lost behind the sigh of wind gusts and the scratch of hemlock branches on the glass.

"Been waiting long?"

"Only a few minutes," Powell said, absently toying with his coaster.

I fanned my damp coat across the back of the barstool next to me and climbed into my seat. When I looked up, Powell was studying me with something resembling concern in his eyes.

"I heard you throwing the steel at the desk clerk," he said. "You feeling okay, boss?"

"I recently found out that Dan Halloran's been placed on medical leave."

I watched Powell take in this information with a combination of cowboy stoicism and barbed muttering.

"Is that going to be a problem?" he asked.

"Not for me."

Powell told me he wasn't hungry, so I ordered a club sandwich and a cola from the bartender and turned my attention to the television that was positioned on a high shelf behind the bar. The sound had been muted and was tuned to some kind of celebrity game show.

"Any word from KC or Irene?" I asked.

"Not a thing. I spent the morning pulling a car out of a ditch, and Griffin's up in Lewiston working a break-in."

"Residential?"

"Hardware store."

"Injuries?"

Powell shook his head.

"Late night smash-and-grab."

I looked out the window at a sky that had grown turbulent and dark. The thunderstorm I'd encountered in the city had followed me southward, and though the rain had subsided, the low clouds skimming the snowline along the foothills had begun to quiver with flickering light.

"Hey, turn that thing up," Powell called to the bartender.

I followed the angle of Powell's sightline and landed on the windblown and unshaven face of a blond hippie-looking kid gawping at me from the TV screen. A news reporter whom I recognized from a network affiliate in Salem had her microphone pointed at the kid's face. Slightly out of focus in the background was the monument sign that marked the entrance to the Rafferty Wildlife Refuge.

"—charged in and took over the place," the kid said as the volume on the TV set came up.

The commentator followed up with something that I couldn't quite make out because Powell was hollering in my ear.

"I've seen that guy."

"Shut up for a second," I said.

"—armed takeover of the wildlife refuge at Lake Rafferty. So far, no injuries have been reported."

The broadcast returned to the anchor desk and an ongoing story about a rogue CIA operative named Philip Agee.

"Goddamnit," I said. "I was afraid they'd pull something dumbshit like this."

"I've seen that guy before."

"I heard you the first time. What about it?"

"He's not from around here," Powell said. "Him and another guy were driving one of them broke-dick Japanese pickups."

"What's your point?"

"What were they doing all the way out there in the boonies in the first place? The refuge is shuttered for the season, so they musta busted in. They told me they didn't have no place to stay."

"You keep saying 'they.'"

"That guy's buddy sounded sick as hell. Sweating like a pig. Couldn't barely breathe."

I felt the heat rush to my face.

"Hand me that phone you've got back there," I called out to the bartender.

I dialed the operator and asked her to connect me to County Hospital. I spoke to the hospital switchboard and was finally put through to Nurse Fields in thoracics, asked her to Magnafax me a photo of her patient with the punctured lung.

"Meet me at the office," I said to Powell. "Then I need you to spark your ass down to KC's place."

I dropped twenty dollars on the bar to cover the beverages and food I still hadn't eaten and watched Powell sprint toward the exit. By the time I arrived at the substation, Powell was already hovering over the machine, waiting for the image to transmit.

"What if it's him?" Powell asked as I came in. "What if it's the guy?"

The supply room smelled vaguely of chemicals, an odor reminiscent of ether and duck eggs that had been left out in the sun.

"If it's him, we'll put out a BOLO with the staties and every sheriff's office in south Oregon," I said. "If that jackass is running narcotics through our county, I want him."

Powell drummed his fingers on the counter as the machine hummed and buzzed with an electronic animation that I found somewhat unsettling. I paced the floor and worked through what came next.

"I'll meet you at the Sheridan place after I finish here," I said. "If that news reporter's still on scene, see if you can talk to her and find out if that idiot kid is still hanging around. He seemed to be enjoying his fifteen minutes."

"And if he's gone?"

"We'll check out the admin building at the refuge together, *after* we check in with KC. I want to see if KC's got any idea what's going on down there before we walk straight into a fresh pile of steaming shit."

Ten long minutes later, I tore the thin sheet of thermal paper off the roll and stretched it out flat on the counter. The image was little better than a high-contrast daguerreotype, but it was sufficient for Powell to make a positive identification.

"That's him. That's the guy."

CHAPTER TWENTY-ONE

"JARVIS TOOK HIS men down to the refuge after I got off the phone with Sheriff Brayfield," KC said. His expression was empty from fatigue.

We were standing in KC's workshop, a short walk from the house, where he'd brought me so that we could speak openly. What the old man really meant was that he did not want to talk within earshot of Irene, or where my deputy could overhear us. Jordan Powell waited outside the door, standing beneath the eave and stamping his feet to stay warm.

"I don't understand why you called Brayfield in the first place," I said. "Why didn't you talk to me first?"

"'Cause Brayfield's the one who started this shit show."

"And you thought you could talk him into intervening on your behalf with Fish and Game? You figured *he'd* be the one to talk them out of arresting you again?"

KC turned away from me, left furrows in a fine layer of sawdust as he trailed his fingers across the surface of his work bench, newly ashamed at having heard the callow nature of his intentions recited aloud.

"I think I heard Brayfield laughing at me," he admitted.

"Most people are better than we think they are," I said. "The rest are the exact opposite."

A fluorescent light that needed replacement sputtered overhead, the boards along the workshop's foundation discolored where decades of moisture had leeched into the grain.

"I thought I could talk reason to him, Ty."

I nodded. The daylight that showed between the wall slats had begun to soften.

"This has all started moving too fast."

"What about your brother-in-law?" I asked. "What's he intending to do?"

KC sat down at the same plank table where only a day ago I had watched Jarvis Lynch's friends field-stripping automatic weapons, and I took a seat across from him. The table's surface had been deeply scarred with markings carved with penknives and burned by cigarettes that had been left resting too long on the wood, and a bundle of Lucifer matches protruded from the mouth of a ceramic striker beside an ashtray bearing the logo of a chain of inexpensive motels.

"Jarvis told me that he's making a hard stand this time," KC said. "He says this is exactly what happened to him, only worse; expects supporters might show up here from all across the country once they hear what's happening to me and Irene."

"Is this the way you want it, KC?"

"I didn't ask for any of this. Jarvis promised me he won't tolerate violence or radical behavior."

I saw no advantage in stating the obvious—that his actions had already passed well beyond that line.

"How many men does he have with him, KC?"

He scratched at a patch of red skin on the back of his hand and cast his eyes to the floor.

"I don't know an exact count, but there can't be more than a dozen of 'em altogether."

"What kind of men are they, KC? Militia?"

He shook his head.

"Most of 'em are just regular men. Men with families who'd probably rather be home."

"I'm going to take Deputy Powell with me to have a word with Jarvis," I said. "But I also intend to speak with Porter Brayfield directly. I want you to know that."

"That's all right. I don't want nobody getting hurt because of me."

"Things are going to start moving with a life of their own now, KC. Brayfield's not likely to sit by while armed gunmen commandeer a government-owned facility."

"I don't want nobody hurt," he said again.

KC hadn't yet lifted his eyes from the hardpacked dirt floor. I reached across the table and touched him on the arm.

"I need you to look at me," I said. "I'm going to do everything I can in order to cram this situation back in the bottle. But you've got to make sure that Jarvis and his posse keep their heads cool."

His expression hardened, and the color seemed to drain from his skin.

"Why are they doing this to us, Ty?"

I thought about what I had said to KC's attorney about the blue and the gray, how ordinary people can be stirred by passions so deep and strong that they're willing to risk and lose everything for a cause.

The war between the Confederacy and the Union had been fought by ordinary people: farmers, tradesmen, shopkeepers, and their children, some as young as ten or twelve years of age. They fought hand-to-hand through thorn brambles and dense forests of hardwood strung with moss, across open fields with fixed bayonets, their lungs and eyes burning from black smoke. They were mowed down by the thousands by muskets and muzzle-load rifles and field cannon firing grape shot and lengths of iron chain; nearly three-quarters of a million souls were lost before it all came to an end, including at least fifty thousand noncombatant civilians, each and every casualty an American citizen.

How had this nation ever come to know a tragedy of such magnitude? Were the bureaucrats and demagogues who had brought it to bear ever made to answer for their hubris, or to suffer the burden of their shame?

"Tell me that you understand what I am saying to you, KC," I said. "Once somebody—anybody—squeezes the trigger, there won't be anything left to think about, no more decisions to be made."

* * *

THE ATMOSPHERE was unusually quiet as Powell and I crossed the vacant parking lot of the refuge, the silence broken only by the metallic rattle of the flagpole chain. A gust of wind blew through the panicles of brown oatgrass that had pushed between rift cracks that scarred the pavement. Even in the cold rain and snow, the air was dank, heavy with the odors of fish roe and algae.

Two armed men dressed in camouflage gazed down at us from the park ranger's lookout tower that rose up behind the administration building. Two more men roamed the open space between the stagnant lake and the main structure, low-slung and utilitarian, a dreary shade of pink that cannot be identified in nature.

I stepped up to a heavily bearded man whom I had not seen before at the Sheridan place, a man who now appeared to be acting as sentry for Jarvis Lynch. He was dressed in a green nylon parka, denim jeans, and snow boots whose soles had begun to come apart at the heel. The M1 carbine in the crook of his arm was of a vintage that had last seen service in my war. Jordan and I showed him our badges as we crossed over the threshold.

"I'm Sheriff Ty Dawson," I announced to anyone within earshot inside. "I want to speak with Jarvis Lynch."

Three men were hunkered down beside a woodstove, still bundled in heavy coats and gloves. The space had been intended for use as a visitor center but was now strewn with an assortment of camping gear and military-style sleeping cots. Casement windows along the rear wall had been swung out on their hinges, propped open with lengths of wood doweling in an effort to clear out the stench of mildew and human fecundity.

A mound of rubbish had been pushed into a corner, and the cushions from a threadbare sofa lay in a pile that suggested they had recently been used as a mattress. I recognized the man who advanced on Powell and me. He pushed back his hood to reveal the shaved head and flat expression I had seen the day before in KC's shop.

"You here about the kid we ran out of this place?" he asked and drove his gloved fists deep into the pockets of his coat. His voice sounded as though he'd swallowed steel shavings from a rattail file. "That's his crap piled over there in the corner. Feel free to take it with you when you go."

"We're not here for the kid," I said. "But since you've brought it up, care to tell me where he might have gone off to?"

"How would I know? Where do hopheads go when they tear ass for the hills?"

"He suggested on the TV news that you threatened him with weapons."

"Then he's a goddamned liar *and* a vandal," the man said. "Nobody got near that kid. It was all ass and elbows running for the woods the minute we showed up."

"You didn't speak with him?"

"Hell no. He took off like a scalded dog when he saw us drive in," he said, leaned a shoulder against the wall, and spat into a rusted paint can they'd been using as a cuspidor. "Look around, Sheriff. Take a whiff. This ain't our stink we're clearing out of here."

"Where's Jarvis Lynch?" I asked.

The bald man angled his head toward a small anteroom behind me.

"You come here to haul us off to jail, Sheriff?" Jarvis Lynch asked as he swept in through a screen door that opened onto an outdoor patio.

"You're in Porter Brayfield's jurisdiction, not mine," I said. "Meriwether County line is the other side of the paved road."

Outside beyond the glass, the wind cups on a weathervane began to rotate with such force that they became a blur. Beside the lake, spruce and fir heeled and thrashed from the gusts.

"How long do you intend to stay here, Mr. Lynch?" I asked.

"Long as it takes."

The man whose head resembled an eggshell lost interest, issued a grunt, spat into the can again, and sauntered back to the Schrader stove to rejoin his companions.

"These men aren't soldiers," I said. "They aren't trained for this. For starters, how are you going to feed them?"

"There's a pantry back there," Lynch said and gestured down the hall. "There's still some dry goods and whatnot that hadn't already been pilfered by the hippie kid, and the water still runs. KC and my sister's place is just up the way, if it comes to it."

"I will try to explain this to you as succinctly as I can," I said. "You've stepped into a whopping heap of crap right here, Jarvis. Here's your situation: KC's house and about two-thirds of his ranch is in *my* county; everything southwest of that road out is in Hemmings County. I do not represent the law in Hemmings County."

"That fat bastard Brayfield does."

I nodded.

"And the building that we're standing in belongs to the feds," I said. "Are you hearing what I'm saying to you?"

"Are we supposed to pretend that the government's not trying to steal KC's property?"

"Save it for the cameras, Mr. Lynch."

"You know as well as I do that this is all wrong, Dawson," he said. "I've stood down the feds before. I'm not going to sit quietly by and make believe they don't intend to throw KC into prison—again—and probably fine him so much money that he'll lose the ranch in the bargain."

"Can we take this conversation somewhere else?" I asked.

"There's nothing that can't be said in front of these men."

I scanned the room, took in the faces, some of whom I'd seen before, and did a rough accounting. Two in the watchtower, one at the door, three beside the heater; two more roved the perimeter fence between the building and the lake. I couldn't identify Greg Reeves or Chester Zachary, but they were around here somewhere, I had no doubt. That made a total of eleven men altogether, including Lynch.

"I spoke to Mr. Sheridan's lawyer earlier," I said. "He's taking one more crack at trying to persuade USFW to drop the charges against KC."

"Are you telling me that you believe that's going to work?"

"I'm not going to lie to you," I said. "It's a Hail Mary."

Jarvis Lynch looked at me as though I were speaking Esperanto.

"I've had it up to here with rules being made by people who ain't got to abide by them," he said.

"You may be right, Jarvis," I said. "But in my experience, when you go off half-cocked, things begin to circle the drain mighty fast."

"Folks need to hear about this, Sheriff. They need to hear about what's happened to KC. Same thing almost happened to me. It could happen to anybody."

"You're about to get your wish, then, I expect. Before long, you'll have TV and newspapers lined up three-deep outside those gates. They're going to have cameras pointed at you twenty-four hours a day. Don't make a mistake you can't take back, Jarvis."

He bit his bottom lip, worked his fingers underneath his hatband, and scratched his scalp.

"Does it seem right to you, Sheriff Dawson, that somebody sitting behind a desk in D.C. can just show up to work one day and write up a statute that carries the power of the law? No debate, no Congress involvement, and no vote? And then you know what happens next? If a citizen gets contrary to whatever the bastards wrote down, *they* go to jail, or a federal ranger shoots 'em."

"Tread carefully, Jarvis," I said. "I already told you. You and your people don't want to start something you can't walk back."

"That ain't my intention. I already gave the order: Nobody fires unless we're fired upon."

"Fired upon? Jesus Christ."

"Whatever comes next ain't up to me."

"And when they drive out to serve KC's arrest warrant?" I asked.

"Nobody's getting past us. We're setting up a blockade on the road."

"Are you sure this is still about KC?"

"It's about a hell of a lot more than that."

I tapped Powell on the arm and moved toward the door. Down a narrow hallway, the door that led into a tiny kitchen had been levered open with a felling axe. Inside, I saw Reeves and Zachary stacking tins of pickled meat and glass jars of vegetables on wire shelf racks.

"You want me to stay here, Sheriff?" Powell said under his breath.

I shook my head.

"Our authority begins about a hundred yards in that direction," I said. "But I want you to keep an eye on the Sheridans. Irene says she's got a room made up for you."

I heard the menacing croak of a raven, calling out from somewhere in the deep woods, wicked and low. I looked but could not find him in the shadows.

THE HEMMINGS County Sheriff's office was located on the ground floor of a three-story red brick structure that occupied a full city block, dead center of the town of Jericho, a monument to the long-departed halcyon days of the county seat. Constructed at the turn of the century, it represented a Victorian mélange of corbelled cornices and arched windows with granite sills, and still provided space to the County Department of Public Records, Public Works, District Court, the County Commissioner's office, and the Medical Examiner. Despite the outward elegance of the structure, the office of Sheriff Porter Brayfield looked like it had been decorated by an unemployed long-haul truck driver and the furniture procured from a rummage sale.

"I thought you'd be out looking for your BOLO," Brayfield said as I stepped inside his office.

"I was hoping you might be looking for the hippie kid, too."

"I've got bigger problems, as you damn well know, Dawson," he said. "But all things considered, I should have expected you to show up here."

"You and I need to talk before things get any further out of hand."

"I'm sorry, did I hear you right?" he said. "Did you just say '*Before* things get further out of hand'?"

He picked something out from between his teeth with his thumbnail and wiped it on his pants leg.

"Armed militia has taken over a federal facility in my county," he said.

"There are fewer than a dozen men out there," I said. "Don't make them out to be revolutionaries."

"I don't care what you call them, they got weapons and they're in a building where they damn well don't belong."

"They're idealists, Porter," I said. "They want their position heard, that's all. Let them air out their grievances, and this thing will work itself out without violence."

"Remind me again why I'm standing here talking with you. The last time we spoke, you had a revolver pointed at my eyeball."

"Because you don't always listen overly well."

"It's your turn to hear this, Dawson: I've got a passel of outlaw rednecks, outfitted with deadly armament, who have seized a government facility at gunpoint and are posing an imminent threat to the county seat. How would you expect me to respond?"

"Don't believe everything you think, Porter," I said. "Go on out there and have a look for yourself. I'll go with you."

"You have a puzzling manner of expressing yourself."

"I was just there," I said. "Unless those men are packing some sort of hidden missile system I failed to notice, they've got no weaponry that could possibly pose a threat to your town. The wildlife refuge is more than twenty miles from here."

"They are a dangerous and desperate militia. They would've murdered that young hippie kid if he hadn't got away."

"You sound like you've been breathing your own exhaust. The only thing those men want is news coverage."

"That's it. We're done," he said. "That's about all the give-a-shit I've got left in me."

Brayfield began to turn away, but I grabbed him by the shoulder and spun him around.

"What the hell's that supposed to mean?" I asked. "You're ginning up all this commotion because Fish and Wildlife wants to *re*arrest a seventy-year-old rancher over a matter the agency created out of whole cloth? Does that sound like justice to you? People are about to get hurt, Porter."

Brayfield unwrapped the cellophane from a peppermint he dredged out of the pocket of his trousers.

"It's out of my hands," he said and popped the candy into his mouth. "I put out a request for assistance through the PPB, the state police, and the Sheriff's Association. Deputy Chief Overton pointed out that since the takeover is on federal property, I should ask for assistance from the feds instead."

"Overton advised you to do *what*?"

"You heard me correctly, Dawson. The FBI is on its way as we speak."

"Do you have any idea what you've just done?"

CHAPTER TWENTY-TWO

I SLEPT THROUGH the night but awakened without rest. I dressed and took my coffee to the ranch office and looked over the paperwork that Caleb had left out for my review. By the time I finished reading, silver light had begun to appear outside the pebbled jalousies, and I carried my empty mug back to the house, lingered for a moment on the gallery.

The sunrise was little more than a narrow line, and rain descended from the clouds like campaign streamers affixed to a battle standard.

"I didn't hear you get out of bed," Jesse said.

She was seated at the breakfast table wearing a bathrobe that resembled a Navajo blanket, caressing a steaming teacup in both hands, and examining the newspaper she had spread across the tabletop. I gently moved her hair to one side and kissed the back of her neck. Her skin was warm and smelled of cinnamon and slumber.

"I didn't want to wake you," I said. "Is Cricket up?"

Jesse pulled her attention away from the paper and looked at me with an expression of concern.

"Cricket went back to school, Ty. She left two days ago."

I felt as though I were falling backwards from a great height.

"I wanted to see her off," I said, though I wasn't certain I had uttered the words aloud. "Who took her to the train?"

Jesse stood up from the table, and I heard her teacup rattle in the sink. When I turned to look at her, the planes and hollows of her cheekbones were illuminated with pale shades of morning sun.

"Looks like it might be a pretty day," she said.

"They often start out looking that way, don't they?"

Jesse ignored my remark and went outside to feed the chickens.

SAM GRIFFIN was replacing the ribbon on the typewriter as I stepped into the substation.

"Morning, Sheriff," Griffin said, and returned to his work.

I picked up my phone and dialed Captain Rose at state police CID. His secretary put me straight through.

"That's some kind of crap sandwich they've got brewing down south," he said without preamble.

"I might need some support on my side of the county line, Chris."

"Do you know something I don't?"

"Brayfield put out a request for assistance—"

"Must've bypassed us," he said.

"He said he was going to call you, but our friends at Portland Police advised him to process his request through the FBI."

I could hear Rose breathing, but that was all I heard for several seconds.

"Who the hell told Brayfield to do that?" he asked finally.

"Deputy Chief Overton."

"Christ on a bike."

"So, you appreciate the magnitude of my potential problem," I said.

Captain Rose began to pace behind his desk, and I heard the scrape of his footfalls on the chair mat. I waited for him while I watched Sam Griffin cross over to the shelf unit on our substation wall when the radio scanner crackled to life. Griffin thumbed the mic and answered the call as I pressed a finger to my ear to filter the background static.

Rose's voice came back on the line.

"I'm going to have to get back to you, Ty," he said. "Under the circumstances, this situation might have deteriorated beyond my pay grade."

"I'm heading down south in a few minutes," I told him. "I've got one of my deputies stationed at KC Sheridan's. You can reach me there or over in Jericho."

When I hung up, Griffin was standing at the corner of my desk.

"That was Powell on the radio," he said. "The feds have arrived."

"They've arrived where exactly?"

"Sheriff Brayfield's office," he said. Griffin's eyes dipped down the way they did when he didn't wish to be the bearer of bad news. "Powell thinks they're fixing to blockade the access road to the refuge. You want me to come along with you?"

"I need you to stay here, Sam," I said. "You remember what I said about how to reach me?"

"Yes, sir."

I repeated it anyway.

"If you can't raise me on the radio, leave a message with the Sheridans or with Jesse."

He nodded but made no move to step away.

"Something else, Sam?" I asked.

"Is this thing as FUBAR as it seems?"

"I don't want you out of earshot of the radio or the telephone," I said. "If this starts going down a sinkhole, it's gonna start going down fast."

"I got your six, Sheriff."

"I know you do."

THE STREETS surrounding the Hemmings County office building had already been cordoned off with sandbags and razor wire, the parking lot choked with unmarked cars and trucks bristling with communications antennae. Armed men outfitted in full tactical gear roamed behind barricades and jersey barriers, where spotlights fixed to mobile trailers had been positioned along the edges of the paved road, their lenses angled into the windscreens of oncoming traffic. It was the type of overt display of hegemony that thrives best at the intersection of avarice, ambition, and authority.

"Jesus," Powell said to me. "Looks like Firebase Henderson in Quảng Trị. All that's missing are the Hueys and anti-aircraft cannon."

"Don't let the feds hear you say that," I said. "They'll requisition them in."

Jordan Powell followed me through a temporary split in the wire and headed for the municipal building's main entrance. Inside, the lobby floor was a serpent's nest of electrical cables twice the thickness of my thumb that trailed through the sheriff's office doors and across the lot to one of three diesel-powered generators disgorging billows of black smoke into the wind.

At least a dozen federal agents crowded the Hemmings County Sheriff's office, half of them engaged in dissonant conversations using battery-operated field radios and telephones they'd commandeered from elsewhere in the building. I knocked twice on the door marked with Porter Brayfield's name and let myself in, though the man occupying Brayfield's desk was not Porter Brayfield.

"You're Tyler Dawson," the man said, but did not stand up. "Diamond D Ranch, Meriwether County. Would you like to know how I knew that, Mr. Dawson?"

He wore a government-issue haircut, his voice a clear baritone accustomed to command. Over his business suit he wore a blue nylon coverall with the letters FBI stenciled in yellow letters across the back. His freshly shaved cheeks were dusted with acne scars, and he stared at me with the wide-set eyes of a reptile.

"You're the FBI," I said. "I'd like to believe that knowing my name and my domicile is one of your lesser accomplishments."

He didn't smile but tipped his head and looked at me as though he were memorizing my face.

"Special Agent Nash," he said, introducing himself. He'd still made no effort to shake my hand or offer me a seat.

"I understand you've taken over this entire building," I said.

"You understand correctly, Mr. Dawson."

"*Sheriff* Dawson," I corrected. "I also understand you've issued orders to close the schools and public buildings in the town of Jericho, and that it is your intent to blockade the county road that runs through here."

It smelled heavily of aftershave and black licorice in the confines of the room.

"You are correct again," he said. "And, until further notice, there is also a curfew in effect from dusk until dawn. Is there a purpose to your visit?"

"Are you familiar with the KC Sheridan case?"

"Are you asking me whether I know why I've been sent to this tiny corner of our fine nation, *Sheriff* Dawson?"

"It seems to me that this situation doesn't rise to a level that requires military-style occupation," I said, and hooked a thumb toward the office window. "Is this the only move you've got in your playbook?"

"Can you please get to the point?"

"You folks make the laws and then proceed to ignore whichever ones don't suit your purposes. You don't see where that might offend people?"

"You asked whether I knew why I've been sent here," Nash said. "It was *not* to engage in a political discussion."

"How much popular support do you expect to enjoy after having placed this town under martial law?"

"This isn't martial law," he said, leaned back and crossed his ankles. "Maybe you should consider switching to Sanka."

"Is it true that all FBI agents are lawyers? You've still got the dirt from Pine Ridge on your shoes."

"I will repeat myself only once, Dawson. Listen carefully this time: This is not martial law, nor is this an occupation. We've been invited here to protect the citizens of Hemmings County, and more specifically, the town of Jericho."

"Take a close look outside," I said. "Does it appear any safer or more peaceful than before you dragged into town with your barricades and armored vehicles and sharpshooters?"

"Goodbye, Sheriff."

"If you restrict access through here, or take offensive action against the Sheridans or the men at the refuge, there will be pushback—"

"That's a warning of some kind?"

"That is a guarantee," I said. "I'm trying to tell you that I know these people. And once they get started, they will ride it all the way to the buzzer."

"I appreciate your input," he said.

He tore a page off a notepad on the desk and handed it to me. I folded it in half and slid it into my shirt pocket without reading it.

"One of my people took that message for you about half an hour ago," he said.

"Believe it or not, Agent Nash, we're on the same side."

"Is that so? I have it on good authority that you assaulted a Portland police detective and inflicted grievous injury on his person. I've been informed he is presently on a medical leave of absence."

"You have an incomplete understanding about the situation you've stepped into," I said. "There's a better way to deal with this."

"Close the door behind you on your way out."

I spotted Powell down the hall as I picked my way through the tangle of cords and conduit on the anteroom floor.

"I found the sheriff," Powell called out to me over the din. "He's in here."

My deputy was leaning on a door jamb, pointing into a room marked with a plastic sign that read "Storage." To his credit, I saw no visible sign of satisfaction on Powell's face.

Sheriff Porter Brayfield was seated on a folding chair tucked underneath a card table that had been set up with a telephone, a tape dispenser, and a stapler.

"What are you going to do about this, Porter?" I asked.

"You here to gloat, Dawson?"

"What the hell is the matter with you? There's nothing happening out there to gloat about. You've placed this entire end of the state in the crosshairs."

"I take it you met Agent Nash."

"*Special* Agent Nash," I said. "I have a hard time believing we're the same species."

"What am I supposed to do now?" Brayfield asked.

"Saddle up or shut up," I said. "Same as always. Those are the only two choices you ever had."

"Don't look so surprised, Sheriff Brayfield," Jordan said. "You asked for the damn bull, and the horns always come right along with him."

THE NOTE that Nash had handed to me was a message from Captain Rose at State Police CID, asking me to call him as soon as I could. I used the phone on Brayfield's card table, stepped into the storage room, and shut the door for privacy, though some part of me knew that privacy was a fantasy and that the feds out there were no doubt monitoring every call in the building, if not the entire town.

"Have you got an answer for me on that matter we spoke about earlier?" I asked, hoping that being cryptic might help.

"Not yet," he said. "I've got something for you on the BOLO, but you're not going to like it."

"That train left the station a long while back. I don't like much of anything lately."

"We found the kid you're looking for at a rest stop near mile marker sixty-three, northbound. One of my troopers is standing by at the scene."

"Roger that," I said. "We'll be right there to pick him up."

"I've got a crim team on the way. They'll meet you there."

It felt as though I'd been blind bucked.

"What the hell?"

"The kid's brains are spattered all over his seat covers, Ty."

"What the hell happened?"

"You tell me."

CHAPTER TWENTY-THREE

MILE MARKER SIXTY-THREE was a rural rest stop in the middle of nowhere, little more than a cinderblock outhouse with a drinking fountain. It was surrounded on three sides by ancient conifers and set into a hillside choked with squaw carpet and oxalis. A young state trooper paced a footpath across the unpaved hardpan and fallen needles, the crime scene technicians having not yet arrived. Someone living nearby had ignited a slash pile, and the white smoke hung inside the forest like fog, smelling of creosote and smoldering pine tar.

"Japanese pickup," Jordan Powell said as he crossed the open space from where he'd parked to where I stood beside the subject vehicle. "Montana tags. This is the same truck I saw before. The one I told you about."

"Is this the same driver?" I asked.

The victim's body had fallen sideways inside the cab, and Powell had to crane his neck inside, through the window opening, in order to get a good look at the man's face.

"That's the guy," he said.

Powell backed away a few steps, crossed his arms, and studied the compact pickup. I lit a cigarette and considered the scene from the opposite side of the truck.

"The driver's side window is rolled down," Jordan Powell called out to the state trooper. "Is this how you found him?"

"Everything is exactly as it was when I rolled up," the trooper answered. "Only thing I touched was the victim's neck, you know, to check him for a pulse."

"It was below freezing last night," Powell said to me. "Why would you roll down your window? To freeze your ass off while you think about killing yourself?"

"He didn't kill himself, he was talking to somebody," I said. "Maybe someone he knew."

"Or someone approached and asked him for help or some such," Powell said.

I placed my cigarette on top of a concrete parking block, weighted it with a loose stone to keep it from rolling away. I pulled the handkerchief out of my pocket, covered my fingertips as I worked the lever on the passenger door. I squatted on my haunches and studied the interior and the way the body had fallen sideways across the bench seat. Blood, bone, and organic matter spattered the passenger side window, at the center of which was a hole where the bullet had exited the victim's skull, passed through the glass, and ended up somewhere in the woods.

"The bullet exited through the back of his head," I said.

"The victim was looking in this direction, through the open window."

"Interacting with somebody."

"Someone who parked a single shot between his eyes. Are you going to say it, or am I?"

I dipped my fingers into the pocket of my coat and withdrew a penlight. I shined it underneath the dashboard and the seat. I found a large sandwich bag containing at least three ounces of marijuana secured to the underside of the glove compartment with strips of masking tape. I double-checked the seal on the bag and placed it on the floormat, turned the narrow beam to look beneath the seat.

"I've got a revolver over here," I said. "On the floor under the seat. Passenger side. Looks like a .32 belly gun. Two-inch barrel."

I heard a car pull off the paved road, figured it was Captain Rose's guys from CID. I didn't touch the weapon I'd just discovered, left it where it was for the forensics team to photograph and print.

"You suppose it slid across the floor while he was driving?" Powell asked. "Did he even try to reach for it, you think?"

"He couldn't have been reaching for it," I said. "The victim was looking straight into his killer's face."

I felt a catch inside my right knee as I stood up out of my crouch and went to retrieve my cigarette. Powell had moved from his side of the pickup and had begun slowly walking a circle around it.

I introduced myself to the two men who were gathering equipment from the storage compartment of an unmarked panel van, took the last draw off my smoke, crushed it on my boot heel, and field-stripped it. One of the techs looked familiar to me from the Clark Wehr crime scene, a man in possession of the interpersonal skills of a campsite raccoon. The other one I had never seen on the job before, tall, slight, and narrow across the shoulders, with the restive nature of a housecat. The thin one was reasonably personable, took off the cap he wore before shaking my hand, and I noticed a scar in the shape of a chicken's foot that started at his hairline and stretched down to his temple. I informed both of them about the revolver and the weed I'd discovered in the pickup.

"I want some close-ups of the victim's face," I said. "The dope and the gun, as well."

"This isn't our first crime scene."

"Let me approach this differently," I said. "Do you gentlemen have a Polaroid, or some other type of instant camera with you?"

"Yeah," the one with the scar answered me finally. "We got one in here somewhere."

"Good. Please use it to collect some shots of the victim's face, as well as the marijuana and the handgun. I intend to take the photos with me when I leave."

I looked beyond the tree line into a clearing dotted with ragwort and sword-fern, the atmosphere laced with silver-white haze. Something moved inside a shadow, and I spotted a six-point blacktail buck keeping watch over a pair of does grazing behind the boughs.

"Look here, Sheriff," Powell called out to me.

My deputy was standing at the rear of the victim's truck, gesturing toward the rear tires.

"Sonofabitch," I said. "I'll be damned."

"Two different treads."

I returned to the forensics van and tapped the more personable technician on the shoulder.

"I need some good close-up shots of the two rear tires while you're at it."

"With the Polaroid?"

"I would appreciate it. And a casting of the tire treads before you leave."

Jordan Powell was muttering something to himself when I stepped up beside him again.

"Problem?" I asked.

"I can't believe I didn't notice it the first time."

"You're referring to the tires?"

He shook his head and chewed a piece of loose skin off his thumb.

"Shit," he said.

I could have simply told Powell to let it go, but I knew it wouldn't do any good. He'd lose sleep over it for the next week if I didn't start talking him down.

"Did you approach the vehicle from the rear?" I asked.

His focus turned inward for a moment before he replied.

"It was early in the morning," he said. "I saw the truck parked there in a wide spot at the shoulder of the two-lane. I was coming from the other direction, so I just pulled over on my side and parked, walked across the road to talk to them. Welfare check, you know. I thought they mighta been broke down or something."

"So you came at them from the driver's side? From the front?"

"I guess I did. I noticed the Montana tags and started talking to the driver."

"Give yourself a break, Jordan," I said. "When the CID guys are finished taking pictures, meet me at the hospital."

He seemed surprised by what I'd just said.

"I figured I'd be heading back to the Sheridans," he said.

"You fixing to argue with me now, deputy?"

"No, sir."

"I need this man's accomplice to see you again. Up close and in person."

"Long way to drive just to rattle his cage, isn't it?"

"Do you know how to eat a Hereford bull all by yourself?" I asked. "One bite at a time."

"I don't think I understand what that's supposed to mean."

"It means we have more than one case to deal with."

I turned to have one final look at the deer in the clearing, but they had disappeared, withdrawn deeper into thicket.

CHAPTER TWENTY-FOUR

"REMEMBER ME?" Powell said as he pushed back the divider curtain. "'Cause I know who you are. You're the jackass who calls himself Jerry Garcia."

I watched the expression on the young man in the hospital bed move through the phases from surprise to panic to dread as he recognized Deputy Powell. The kid glanced at me briefly, but I was the lesser of his problems according to the criminal calculus in which he was presently engaged, and the kid's focus remained fixed on Powell as he tried to figure out how to play it.

His hair was tangled like wire, his manner tightly coiled and barely contained, a pressurized tank on the verge of rupture. His eyeballs shivered in their sockets, his hands clenching open and closed like the claws of a bird in death throes. It was clear that he was coming unraveled at having seen Powell again, so I stood to one side and allowed my deputy to take the lead.

"First thing we're going to do is drop the Garcia horseshit," Powell said. "Tell me your real name."

His Adam's apple bobbed as he swallowed, but he remained mute.

"I wonder what's in that bottle hanging there on the stand?" Powell asked me, and I knew he was setting something up. "Got a tube coming down out of it, poked into his arm with a needle . . . You s'pose that's pain killer of some kind? Does that suggest that this young fellow is suffering?"

"I suppose it does," I said.

Powell lowered the safety rail on the side of the bed and sat down at the foot of the mattress. He took hold of the kid's ankle through the thin bedcovers, squeezed it tightly as he gazed out the window.

"I had a buddy in 'Nam who was a tunnel rat, you know what that is?" Powell asked. "Never mind, it doesn't matter. Anyway, when I first arrived in Indian country this buddy of mine—this tunnel rat—he tells me, 'Rule number one: Make your first kill as quickly and quietly as possible. No shooting.'"

Powell pulled his eyes from the weather outside and turned his attention to the kid in the bed. Powell hadn't blinked since he had sat down, and the skin underneath his left eye had begun to contract.

"Man, I don't know how many people I ended up doing with my bare hands . . ." Powell said. "You know, I once crushed a man's trachea between my thumbs? Sliced a boatload of throats, too, severed some arteries . . . Real quiet though, you know, just like my buddy the tunnel rat told me to do. Turns out my friend was right because Charlie never *ever* heard me coming, never heard a damn thing, and look, here I am. I lived to tell about it, back home in the US of America. Sitting right here on your bed."

Powell stood and folded his arms as he looked down and studied the kid's face.

"Truth is," Powell continued, softer now, "the real casualty was *me*. The *civilized* version of me, anyway. That guy's gone for good, and that's no lie."

Powell didn't move, didn't pace, but continued to stare at the kid with his arms crossed on his chest, his expression a mask of malice and odium.

"What's your name, son?" I asked softly.

"Shannon," the kid said without pulling his attention from Powell.

His voice was a dry whisper, his fear like a living thing roaming loose inside of his skull.

"What's your last name, Shannon?"

"Drury. Shannon Drury."

Powell took a seat on Drury's bed again, patted the kid on the ankle.

"Do you know why my deputy and I came to see you today?" I asked.

Drury shook his head, but his attention remained locked on Powell.

"The hospital staff discovered narcotics in your possession when you checked in," I said. "But that's not the worst of it, Shannon."

I waited a moment for his anxiety to find purchase, to work its way all through his system.

"The worst of it is we found a loaded revolver and even *more* illegal contraband inside your partner's pickup truck."

Shannon Drury studied the two Polaroids I dropped onto his bedsheet, one each showing the handgun and the weed.

"You are about to enter a world of hurt," I said.

"But, I don't—"

"No, no, Shannon," Powell said. "You don't want to go down that road. You're about to say, 'I don't know about that stuff.' But, of course, you *do* know, Shannon. Just answer the man."

A sheen of perspiration reflected on the kid's forehead and face.

"You also burglarized a fishing cabin at the Catonquin River Resort," I said. "A man was shot to death at that location, and we have reason to believe you were there at the time."

"No, no, no, man."

"It might not seem like it right now," I said, "but you're in a position to help yourself, Shannon."

"No, man," he said. The neckline of his hospital gown had begun to soak through with sweat. "This ain't right."

"There's no point in trying to lie to us," Powell said. "It won't help you or your buddy. Show him, Sheriff."

I had intended to withhold the Polaroid photos as my hole card in case the kid asked for a lawyer, but it looked to me as though Powell was on the verge of breaking what little resistance remained. I tossed two of the less gruesome pictures of the dead man onto Drury's bedspread. He glanced at them long enough for recognition to set in and began to dry-heave. Powell pushed a bedpan toward the kid's face, then stepped to the window and looked out at the gray sky again.

"Do you know how many steps it takes to walk a jail cell from end to end?" Powell asked without turning his attention from the weather. "You're about to find out, Shannon."

"Save all of us some time and trouble," I said. "Give us your friend's name. You can't help him anymore."

"Jack," Drury answered. It was clear that the fight had gone out of him. "His name is Jack Strong."

"Tell us what happened at the Catonquin River. What happened that night at the cabin?"

"DO YOU believe him, Sheriff?"

"Some of it."

I was standing outside with Jordan in the lee of a rock wall at the hospital's entrance, the susurrus of the river echoing against the stones. I blinked hard as the sun revealed itself through a small break in the cloud cover. Over Powell's shoulder, I could see the diaphanous layer of snow on the road had melted during the course of the day, leaving water to gather in pools along the roadside and in the pavement depressions that would turn into black ice overnight.

"You think they actually heard the two gunshots?" Powell asked.

"That part I believe."

"And the car?"

"I'm inclined to believe that part, too."

If Jordan Powell was a horse, I would have said he'd gone barn shy. From the moment we'd departed Shannon Drury's room, he had not been himself, some part of him having drifted away.

"Where does that leave us?" he asked.

"We now know that a third party was present when Clark Wehr was shot," I said. "And this Drury kid can testify to it."

I accompanied Powell to his truck, watched our shadows angle out in front of us, then dissolve into nothing as the sun vanished again. He unlocked his door and gazed off toward the bend in the river where a curlew perched on the twisted fingers of a fallen tree limb and white water sluiced across shattered blocks of basalt.

"Where to now?"

Powell's question was barely audible, as though he had been speaking to himself.

"I want you to head on back to KC's," I said. "Check in with me when you get there."

Powell took off his hat, wiped a forearm across his eyes, climbed into his truck and rolled down the window.

"I got that kid killed, didn't I?" Powell said. "Jack Strong."

"Why the hell would you have something like that in your head?" I asked.

"Detective Halloran knew about those tire treads. I told you about it when he was standing right there next to you at the scene. When you put out the BOLO . . ."

"Don't borrow other people's grief, son," I said. "Those two boys called their own play."

Powell looked down from his seat, in my general direction, but not at my face.

"You did a fine job up in that hospital room, Jordan," I said. "You might've finally broke this thing open. It was a solid interview."

He nodded, passed the back of his hand across the hollows of his eyes again, and put on the pair of sunglasses that had been resting on his dashboard.

"I never knew you were a tunnel rat," I said, trying to draw him back from the chasm.

"I wasn't," he said. "But I knew a couple of guys who were."

"It was a spooky damned story."

He turned the key in his ignition and tugged his door closed.

"It was a spooky damned war," he said, and drove away.

MY GRANDMOTHER had been raised Catholic, and my grandfather Methodist. When the two had sought to wed, neither of the families would condone the union on religious grounds, so the young lovers eloped to Oregon where both were baptized in the Applegate River before taking their vows.

I grew up Presbyterian and still attend the same church I attended as a child, directly across the street from St. Stephen's, the only Catholic basilica at this end of the county. I have retained precious few memories of my grandmother, but among my favorites are those rare occasions when she would sneak me off to St. Stephen's with her, and it all had seemed so very clandestine—a covert pilgrimage to a place of sanctuary recalled from her own distant youth.

Afterward, she would treat me to ice cream at the drugstore counter in downtown Meridian, where she would swear me to an oath of secrecy, and I would wonder aloud as to why the priests got to wear such spectacular garments, while the minister at my church showed up every Sunday in the same shiny sports coat and striped necktie. Though I had no awareness of it back then, Catholics were looked upon with a certain amount of suspicion by outsiders, their rituals considered both mystical and exotic. As I grew older, I began to strongly suspect that Catholic children were admonished to steer clear of Protestants for many of the same reasons.

The rose window in St. Stephen's tower shone like an opal on a backdrop of night sky as I drove home, the valley floor beyond my headlights lost in moonless dark. I pulled into the driveway and parked beside the rectory, left my Stetson on the seat, and went inside.

The narthex smelled of incense and candle wax, the atmosphere was still and warm, suffused with the dim flicker of votives. I took a seat in the very last row of the nave, where I could hear the faintest traces of the choir rehearsing in a distant chamber. The sacristy door squeaked on rusted hinges, and I looked up to see Monsignor Turner lock the door behind him before he crossed between the pews and came to greet me, dressed casually in his black slacks and clerical collar.

"Good evening, Sheriff Dawson," he said. "What brings you to my oratory?"

His tone was like a steel handshake inside a velvet glove, with eyes that smiled when he spoke, but brooked no prevarication.

"I saw the light in the Catherine glass and decided to stop in."

"God doesn't mind which of His houses you visit, you know."

"No," I said. "But Pastor Dunn might."

The sound of the monsignor's laugh reverberated on the masonry.

"You know that Pastor Dunn and I play canasta together every Tuesday night," he said.

The air inside the nave was like a silver haze cleaved by blades of yellow incandescence, where antique hand-carved renderings depicting the stations of the cross glowed in the light that bathed the walls. I glanced away from the Monsignor to the carving that hung beside me and noticed it was station number three.

"Is something troubling you, Sheriff?" he asked.

I took so long to answer that he must have thought I had ignored his question. He followed my eyes, saw where my attention had drifted.

"It's called the Via Dolorosa for a reason," he said.

"I just needed a quiet place to do a bit of reckoning."

It was his turn to go silent. He pursed his lips and glanced in the direction of the altar.

"Interesting choice of words," he said.

"I have an interesting set of problems to sort out."

"I've grown fairly good at maintaining confidences."

I smiled and looked into his face, and thought I saw a trace of sorrow there.

"I'm counting on that, Monsignor."

He studied me for one more long moment and made the sign of the cross in the air between the two of us.

"*Kyrie eleison*, my son," he whispered.

CHAPTER TWENTY-FIVE

THE NEXT MORNING, they showed up on horseback by the dozens, nearly seventy-five at final count, following in a line behind a single rider flying Old Glory from a pole tucked into a leather pouch strapped to her stirrup. Some of them led strings of mules strapped with pack rigs loaded down with crates filled with food, blankets, and supplies collected from schools, businesses, families, and churches. The local fire department even sent a Jeep pickup, its cargo bed stacked high with pallets of bottled water that had been tied down with rope.

The caravan followed the course of a dry creek bed that passed beneath a long-abandoned shoofly bridge before it cut across a corner of the wildlife refuge a mile north of the federal roadblock and a half mile deep into Meriwether County. My county.

Television news crews, wire service photographers, and stringers lined the shoulder of the gulch where the creek bank rose up and looked out across a stretch of valley that rolled all the way to the foothills. Some of the riders were smiling as they rode past the cameras, others wore the taut expressions of awareness as to what was likely to follow as a consequence of their arrival. Federal agents may have failed to prevent access to the activists this first time, but it wasn't likely to happen again.

I ate a cold egg sandwich for breakfast as I throttled southward toward Jericho and KC Sheridan's ranch. Jesse had left the sandwich in a brown paper sack in the icebox for me with a handwritten note stapled to it that read, "Please be careful, Ty," together with a scripture from the Psalms. The snow flurries and wind grew stronger, my wipers scarcely able to keep pace with the ice crystals forming at the edges of the windshield, and the coffee I'd brought with me in a Thermos was eating a new hole in the lining of my stomach.

The news accounts on my truck's AM radio echoed the newspaper headlines I'd seen at home: the aural equivalent of "Armed Protestors Occupy Federal Land," and "Militia Members Take Over Government Buildings in Oregon," magnified by verbal exclamation marks and augmented by telephone interviews intended to stoke apocalyptic paramilitary fantasies from coast to coast. The situation seemed to have already metastasized far more rapidly than anyone could have imagined, and I knew that any reaction from the feds was likely to be an *over*reaction. Any guess as to where it all might spiral from there was simply too ugly to contemplate.

The Sheridan house was neat as a pin when I arrived, Irene's grooming and attire impeccable, as though any order she imposed upon herself could somehow counteract the chaos that had recently come to define her life. I followed her into the kitchen, where she offered me a cup of hot tea from a samovar she'd set out beside a tray of freshly baked cookies.

"Your deputy is a wonderful young man," Irene said and led me to a seat on a davenport near the living room window. "A real gentleman. I just thought you should know that."

"I appreciate your saying so, ma'am," I said.

It was painful to watch her exerting so much effort to avoid the very subject that had brought us together in the first place. Outside, I could see that the snowfall had subsided, but the atmosphere seemed frangible and on the verge of fracture. Irene told me that Jordan Powell had awakened before daybreak and had driven down to the wildlife refuge before either she or KC had arisen from their bed.

When KC entered the room a few minutes later, his shoulders sagged and a furrow carved across his brow as if he'd spent a lifetime in worry. He wore faded blue Levis with no belt, a long-sleeved western shirt with snap buttons, and no boots on his stockinged feet. Irene stood and pasted down an errant lock of his hair with fingers that she dampened with her tongue.

"How are you holding up, KC?" I asked. "All this ruckus has got to be scraping your last nerve."

"Don't worry about me," he said. "I got thick bark."

But his expression remained empty, devoid of comprehension, devoid of anything at all, like a person who had undergone electroshock therapy.

"You heard anything from that goddamn attorney of mine?" he asked.

"I expect he'd be reaching out to you, sir, not to me."

"S'pose you're right," he said, and his attention drifted. "It ain't all the hullabaloo driving me crazy, though; it's the damned waiting. That reminds me, we got a phone message for you. Came just before you drove in."

"I'll go get it for you," Irene said.

"Don't trouble yourself, ma'am. Just tell me where to find it."

"I wrote down the name and phone number on a note pad in the office," Irene said. "You go right ahead and use the extension on the desk in there, Tyler."

I saw KC's face reflected in the windowpane as he gazed down the slope in the direction of Lake Rafferty. The harsh light from the table lamp touched his face unkindly, and the hollows of his eyes were lost in shadow. It seemed as though I could see straight through him in that moment, and I had to look away.

"THOUGHT YOU'D want to know," Captain Rose said to me, "that the tires on the dead kid's pickup match the plaster casts from the Wehr murder scene."

"Way ahead of you, Chris," I said.

"I also got an ID—"

"Jack Strong."

"*Jonathan August* Strong, wiseass. Age twenty-four. Occupation: Shitbird. Strong arm robbery, and possession-with-intent to distribute."

I adjusted KC's office chair so I could look out through the sliding glass door. A gust of wind blew fresh powder from the quoins and weatherboards and dusted the branches of a leafless shrub protruding from a weed-choked planter box.

"I've got Mr. Strong's accomplice under house arrest at County Hospital," I said. "He's recovering from a punctured lung. His name's Shannon Drury."

"Couldn't happen to a nicer guy," he said. "I hope it hurts like hell."

I could hear Irene and KC's voices through the heater vent, though I could not make out their words.

"I've got the county coming apart at the seams down here, Chris," I said. "Are you going to send some manpower to back me up or not?"

"Still waiting for an answer from the bosses."

"Tell them to be sure to take their sweet damn time," I said. "Do they read the papers?"

"This is politically sensitive shit, Dawson."

"You'd better not be slow-walking me."

I carried the phone to the far corner of the office, tugged the cord out from where it caught beneath the desk chair. I pulled open the sliding glass door a few inches and felt the bracing rush against my face.

"You want to hear what I've got for you or not?" Rose said, but went ahead without waiting for me to reply, his tone restless and edgy.

"I've only got the jacket on Jack Strong, the dead kid," he continued. "But I think it's a safe bet that he and your guy Drury have been working together for a while. Strong's got warrants out in two states, the most recent being robbery and assault on three liquor store employees in Missoula. They broke in, one of them beat the manager senseless with a tire jack, bound and gagged a female employee and dumped her in the freezer, then proceeded to kick the living shit out of the security guard. Crushed the poor guy's orbital bone and left him blinded in one eye, but apparently not before the guard landed a few good licks against the kid you've got in your hospital. That's the security guard's duty weapon you found in the pickup truck."

Captain Rose went on to tell me that the two young men had been operating primarily in Utah and Montana as crossroaders. They'd travel the back roads and stake out small-town liquor and grocery stores by sitting in their vehicles and watching the store's owner through binoculars. Most of the businesses had safes they kept behind the counter, near the register at the front of the store. Strong and Drury would eventually get the safe's combination either when the owner made the night count-out or when he opened it to seed the register before he opened the doors in the morning. Then the two would break in after hours and empty out the contents. Until recently, their crimes had not been violent in nature.

But they got unlucky on their last job. Everyone did. The night manager, a second female employee, and an armed security guard were drinking beer inside the walk-in cooler at the back of the store when Strong and Drury broke in.

"You want me to send a man over to the hospital to keep an eye on your suspect?"

"I would appreciate that," I said. "And please get me some help down here."

Rose had started to say something, but I wasn't listening. Through the window I could see Jordan Powell's truck speeding up the paved road, throwing a rooster tail of snowmelt and rainwater high into the air behind him.

"I've got to jump off, Chris," I said. "I think the shit may be hitting the fan."

I hung up the phone and watched Powell's vehicle slide sideways at the final corner, then fishtail and straighten out just in time to pass between the gateposts unscathed.

"I WAS hoping you'd be here," Powell said as we rumbled across the cattle guard less than five minutes later. "I believe they're fixing to set up a parley. They agreed to allow you to act as go-between."

"Who agreed?"

"The FBI and Jarvis Lynch."

We topped a shallow rise in the road, and I got my first look at what the landscape had become. The feds had parked their vehicles at angles across the centerline about a hundred yards beyond the entrance to the wildlife refuge headquarters. Jersey barriers and ropelines defining the shoulders on both sides of the pavement, the road itself blocked off from edge to edge by uniformed personnel manning positions behind rows of sawhorses stenciled with lettering that warned against approaching their defensive perimeter.

"It's like the DMZ out here, Sheriff."

"Looks like you got those helicopters you were mentioning earlier, too," I said.

"Choppers showed up around sunrise this morning," he said. "First one I spotted belonged to Channel 7. That other one, the white one a little further out, might also be a TV station, but I'm not sure. Never got a good look at the markings."

"The one circling the crowd appears to be military."

"It's a Huey, sir," he said. "I'd know that sound anywhere."

The pavement was slick with runoff, the knuckles on both of Powell's hands blanched white as he squeezed the wheel, the skin at the corners of his eyes drawn tight. It appeared he may have shaken off the darkness that had crept up on him the night before, though it was difficult to tell.

"Lynch told me that the feds cut all the power to the refuge building after the horse caravan arrived," Powell said. "Waited 'til the civilians unloaded and left before they pulled the plug."

"Doesn't look to me like all of them went home," I said.

At least two hundred people were lined up behind the barricades, a good many of them from the media, but at least a couple dozen of the horsemen had remained behind, still mounted and easy to distinguish in the crowd. One of the horses spooked when a news chopper swept in for a low-angle camera shot, sending gouts of runny mud into the air as the frightened animal arched its back and windmilled into a cluster of wide-eyed onlookers.

"If that animal gets its bill in the ground again, he'll come undone for sure," I said. "He doesn't appear overly fond of aircraft."

"Them helicopters're here for the long haul," Powell said. "They ain't going nowhere until the bitter end."

"Is Jarvis Lynch aware of that?"

"Hard to tell what that man's aware of," Powell said and risked a sideways glance at me. "His bunch got a real big boost out of seeing all them townfolk riding in with water and food and whatnot and carrying the colors."

"FBI's got cameras and sharpshooters aboard their birds," I said. "Make no mistake about it. I'd bet my last five dollars they've got snipers set up in the trees out there, as well."

Powell turned off the road and into the refuge parking area. The Stars-and-Stripes the riders had carried with them had been hoisted to the top of the flag-staff and fastened to the halyard upside down, the signal of extreme distress and imminent danger to life and property. The atmosphere felt friable and thin as I stepped out of the truck, breathed deeply of the near freezing air, and felt it burn deep in my lungs. I exhaled a cloud, and the momentary silence was shattered by the hammer of a woodpecker, sounding like machine-gun fire from inside the thicket, amidst the murmur and the thrum of curious onlookers being detained behind the federal blockade.

Lynch's compatriots, Greg Reeves and Chester Zachary, intercepted Powell and me as we approached the front door of the building. Each of them was dressed in army surplus winter gear, their weapons slung over their shoulders from straps of webbed material. They had been smoking cigarettes beside a small woodfire they'd built inside a ring of painted stones. Zachary acknowledged Powell and me with a brief nod, tossed his half-smoked butt into the flames, shouldered past us, and went inside. Reeves remained behind, occupying the open space between us and the door.

"They think we're a bunch of rodeo clowns," Reeves said, and angled his head in the direction of the roadblock. "Like all they have to do is turn loose the bronc and we'll run up the boards."

His complexion was raw from the cold, unwashed and unshaven, and the tone of his voice was both bitter and defiant. His pant legs were sodden, crusted with mud from his knees to his bootlaces.

"I would advise you not to get too self-congratulatory over a show of community support," I said. "The citizens of Jericho are good people, without a doubt. But that's the Federal Bureau of Investigation manning the wire."

"I know damn well who's on the wire," he said. "They have no reason to be here. If they think they can kill us over this, they're gonna have to die, too."

"Slow down there, Seabiscuit," I said. "Nobody's dying. Not today."

"You got a perfectly good smolder going inside that fire ring," Powell said. "How about we all wander over and defrost ourselves."

Jarvis Lynch pulled a wool beanie down around his ears as he stepped out of the doorway and came to where Reeves and Powell and I now faced one another across the campfire. Lynch leaned down and grabbed a chunk of wood from a stack of quartered tree limbs and tossed it on the faltering flames. He repositioned it with the toe of his boot and waited for it to catch, watched a spout of glowing embers rise in the convection.

"Sheriff Dawson's right," Lynch said. "Nobody fires unless fired upon."

"That's not exactly what I said, Jarvis."

One look at Lynch and Reeves was all it took to see that the elements and stress had already begun to take a toll on all of them—ordinary men who viewed themselves as having been pushed to the brink through no fault of their own.

"Did your deputy inform you that we'd like for you to act as intermediary for a parley?" Lynch asked me.

"He did."

"Should I assume you're willing?"

"It's what I've been trying to convince you to do from the get-go, Jarvis," I said. "But before I talk to the feds, I'd like to go inside and have a word with your people."

"There's no need for that," he said. "I speak for them."

"You don't listen for them, too, do you?" I asked and moved toward the front door.

The windows that had been propped open with broomsticks last time I had visited had done nothing to disperse the odor and fecundity inside. In fact, if anything, the situation had been made worse due to the absence of electrical power that the authorities had cut off, power they desperately needed to operate the heating and lighting equipment, but also the pumps that ran the water well and sewage system.

I pressed my way through to the center of the main room where most of the men had gathered, warming themselves inside the circumference of heat that arced out from the woodstove. Lynch stepped up beside me and called out for the men's attention. I recognized many of them from KC Sheridan's.

"Those are trained federal agents out on that road," I said. "They've been invited here by Porter Brayfield, the Sheriff of Hemmings County, and he did so because this is federal property you're standing in."

I paused for a moment and scanned their faces. These men were not mercenaries, revolutionaries, or warriors; these men were dry soil farmers and cattle ranchers, sport hunters and fly fishermen who waded creeks and river shallows for redsides and cutthroat, and drank domestic beer from tin cans that they pulled from coolers filled with ice they cracked by hand.

"The US government does not employ part-timers to protect its possessions," I said. "It defends them with heavily armed professionals."

Jarvis Lynch took the opportunity to step into the gap and break the freighted silence.

"I'll remind you it was a US federal agency that tried to steal *my* cattle, too," Lynch said. "That very same agency built a fence—an *illegal* fence—for the purpose of denying KC Sheridan the use of his own range water. Now they've gone back on a deal they made with him so they can steal his entire goddamn ranch."

The men stirred in the semi-darkness, many of them nodding in agreement.

"Where is it supposed to end, Sheriff?" one of them called out.

"Have any of you noticed the little red lighted dots?" I asked. "The ones that dance around on your chest? Or maybe you've seen one of them glowing on your buddy's forehead?"

A voice came from the back of the room. It was one of the men I'd seen before at KC's place, attending to his weapon and playing dominoes in the old man's work shed.

"I've seen 'em," the man said. "Most of us has."

"That's called an Aimpoint Sight," I said. "It's one of the newest pieces of gear they've got. When you see that little red glow, it means a trained sniper's got you scoped, and that tiny light is where the bullet's gonna blow a hole through you when he's told to squeeze the trigger."

The silence was complete but for a spring retractor on a screen door that had worked its way undone, rattling in the doorframe as I looked the men over, one by one.

"I don't want there to be any misunderstandings," I said. "So, I will repeat myself: Those men outside are highly trained and heavily armed. They will shoot you if they're told to."

Chester Zachary stepped forward out of the dark from his place beside the woodstove.

"I didn't drive all this way to get myself killed," he said. "But sure as hell, Sheriff, it ain't right what's going on here with the Sheridans. I came here for my kids. That's the truth of it."

The throb of approaching chopper blades grew louder, rattling the glass inside the window mullions. One of the men nearest the glass worked the action on his assault rifle and dropped into a crouch. Two others took up positions next to him. The thin layer of snow that had fallen overnight roiled in dusty waves of rotor wash as the aircraft made a final pass over the roof and dopplered away.

"I don't want to die out here in the goddamn snow in goddamn Oregon," another one volunteered, and the room returned to anxious silence. "But I ain't going home without a hard stand. I don't claim to speak for nobody else, but that's the way I feel about it. If we let these people get away with it this time, they'll by-god do it again. And worse."

"Y'all don't need to quote Jefferson and Publius to me," I said. "I'm not your enemy. I wanted you to understand what's happening out there, and I don't care to witness any bloodshed. That's all I wanted to say to you."

Jarvis Lynch followed me outside. The hollow electronic bleating of a voice projected by a megaphone pealed through the cold, but I couldn't decipher the words.

"What the hell are you doing, Dawson?" Lynch said once we were out of earshot. "Are you trying to put the scare in my men?"

"If they're not scared already, then they're stupid," I said. "I just needed to see for myself where they stand."

The rim of the high bluffs glowed momentarily beneath a sunbreak. I reached into my pocket and offered Jarvis Lynch a cigarette, but he declined.

"I've seen war, Mr. Lynch," I said. "I've participated in armed combat, and I've seen men killed, and killed badly. But I don't believe I ever fought beside a man who wasn't exactly as afraid as I was."

I turned my back to the wind and lit a smoke for myself. I drew deeply and looked into Lynch's face, gestured toward the dismal cinderblock structure, heard the snap of flag canvas in the chill breeze and the ring of the grommet scraping the spar.

"I can see for myself that the men inside that building aren't stupid," I said. "Back in Korea, I would've laid down my weapon on the spot if I ever once believed I was following a leader who had any interest whatsoever in dying as a martyr. Tell me that's not who you are, Jarvis. I want to see your eyes when you swear to that, then I'll go and set a parley for you."

CHAPTER TWENTY-SIX

THE CROWD FELL silent when they spotted me walking, alone, down the centerline of the road. Half-melted snow sluiced beneath my boot soles, the dull pulse of helicopter rotors tracing wide circles overhead. There was an emptiness where the wind should have been, in its absence only silence and cold. Even the clouds appeared immobile, reefed and stalled in midair like frozen sheets of silver glass.

I had made it roughly halfway to the barrier when Porter Brayfield ducked beneath the ropeline and moved toward me with a stride and posture that was intended solely for the benefit of the news cameras. I stopped and waited for him to reach me at a distance I judged to remain out of earshot of the press.

"Jesus Christ, Ty," he said under his breath, his voice hoarse and strained. "The feds are outfitted for warfare. My courthouse building looks like an FOB in Da Nang."

"You invited them here."

"You've got to help me out," Brayfield said. "How could I have known it would be like this?"

"How could you *not* know, Porter?" I said and resumed my course toward the federal blockade.

"No matter what happens next," he said, "all the blame's going to land on me anyway, isn't it?"

The mechanized whirr of camera shutters grew louder as I moved closer to the sawhorse deadline. Brayfield kept walking in lockstep beside me, grousing to me out of the side of his mouth.

"I believe God leaves His fingerprints on every soul, Porter," I said. "Some ignore it for their entire lives. Others turn their backs on it knowingly. I wonder which one you are?"

Reporters began shouting questions at me from out of the crowd, but I said nothing until I halted about ten feet away from Special Agent Nash. Two Chevrolet Suburbans had been parked at angles in the middle of the roadway, their bumpers nearly touching, forming a shape resembling an arrowhead. Nash passed through a gap between the sawhorses and took a position at the tip of the spear.

"You should step aside, Brayfield, and let Sheriff Dawson and me speak," Nash said.

"This is Hemmings County," Porter objected, but Nash stopped him mid-sentence with an upraised palm. Somehow the gesture seemed even more condescending and insulting than the interruption itself, the news cameras capturing every moment of Brayfield's humiliation. But it wasn't quite finished.

"Please stand aside," Nash told him again, louder and more clearly this time. "You've abdicated your authority in this matter. You have—how would they describe this in diplomatic circles?—surrendered your portfolio."

Brayfield tried to grab hold of me as one of the sentries lifted the rope, but he stubbornly remained on my side of the line, seething and impotent.

Nash and I ignored them all, eying one another from a distance of five feet in the middle of a frozen rural road.

"I will remind you that where we are standing you have no jurisdiction whatsoever, Sheriff Dawson," Nash said to me.

Nash had traded his business suit and coveralls for a tactical uniform of green and tan camouflage, and a utility belt with a .45 caliber pistol and a flashlight the length of my forearm was strapped across his hips. The dusting of acne scars across his cheeks appeared more pronounced than before, aggravated by the weather, or perhaps he was flushed with aggression.

"Walk with me about three hundred feet in that direction," I responded. "And we'll have a different conversation altogether."

Both sides were well aware of my role here, so the only reason for Nash's display of belligerence was for the cameras, though I didn't understand how it would win him much support at this end of the state. I was uncertain as to whether it was a negotiating posture or a defect in his personality.

"As you know, Jarvis Lynch would like to have a word with you," I said. "Face-to-face, in front of the media, and without risk of personal harm, arrest, or reprisal. He has asked that I remain here to stand witness."

"Mr. Lynch and his militia are guilty of—"

"That was a yes or no proposal, Special Agent Nash," I said. "What's it going to be?"

JORDAN POWELL escorted Jarvis Lynch as far as the intersection of the main road and the refuge's parking lot, as I had instructed him. I watched Powell scan the tree line for any sign of deceit or abrogation on the FBI's part as Lynch moved slowly up the road toward Nash and me. Lynch walked slowly and deliberately, with arms extended outward, at waist level, as a demonstration of his peaceful intent.

"Stop there," Nash said as Lynch reached a point about ten yards away from us. "Open your coat and turn slowly in a circle."

"I decline to do that," Jarvis said, and kept walking.

"I ordered you to stop," Nash said. "Open your coat and turn slowly—"

"Open *your* coat and turn in a damn circle," Lynch said, and continued moving forward, closing the gap. "I know you've got a half-dozen snipers with my skull in their crosshairs right now. Speak to me like a human being or this conversation ends now."

"You don't dictate the terms."

"Take a look around you," Lynch said. "There're cameras and reporters everywhere. This is still America, friend. If you're going to murder me, you're going to have to do it out in the open for a change, in front of the entire world."

"It was you who said he wanted to talk."

"We have only two demands: First, drop the ridiculous charges against KC Sheridan and leave him and his ranch alone. The second demand is for you all to go on back home. Let the town folks reopen the schools and businesses and get on with their lives. Go back to Quantico or wherever you mobilized from, and we'll do the same. That's it. That's all we're asking."

"The United States government does not negotiate with terrorists."

"Did you just call me a terrorist?" Lynch asked and turned toward the cameras. He wore the facial expression of a man who had just experienced a personal violation. "Did you people hear what that man said to me? Peaceful protest has become an act of *terrorism*?"

The sky seemed to groan beneath its own weight as Lynch paced the width of the road, shaking his head as though trying to assimilate the contents of his own statement, the news cameras recording his every move.

"Peaceful protests do not ordinarily include the brandishing of firearms, sir," Nash said.

"I'm not armed."

"The men occupying the headquarters building most certainly are."

Jarvis Lynch laughed aloud.

"You've got two men standing beside you dressed in full kit and camo," he said. "Both of them have their palms on the butts of their pistols as I stand here. *My* men at the refuge—all the way back there—carry weapons for their own protection. I had to walk out with my hands raised like a criminal in order to have a dialogue with you, for Chrissake."

"You and your men need to lay down your arms," Nash said.

"You first."

"This is not personal, Mr. Lynch. There are laws, and we're here to enforce them. No one has to get hurt."

"And yet you rolled into this place like an occupying army."

"We are responding to the hostile takeover of federal property."

"The damn doors weren't even locked," Lynch said. "We're twenty miles from town. All of this is a bad joke."

"We're only repeating ourselves now, Mr. Lynch," Nash said, turning in quarter profile for the cameras. "Relinquish the property and we will be as lenient as possible regarding the charges against you and your militia."

Jarvis Lynch looked first to me, then centered his focus on Special Agent Nash.

"You have no intention of considering anything I've just said, do you?" Lynch said softly, his tone burdened not with defeat but sorrow. "You have just demonstrated exactly why we need to do what we are doing. You've left us no other choice. No choice at all."

Lynch stepped toward the knot of journalists and press cameras and came to a halt just short of the crowd-control rope. For one prolonged, unsettled moment, the atmosphere was unstable and tense, but the silence was broken by the sudden outcry of dozens of voices shouting questions inside a crescendo of reverberation from approaching rotary aircraft.

"All we are asking," Lynch said as he raised his arms in a gesture that restored a ragtag sense of order inside the crowd, "is for the federal government to admit they made a mistake when they reneged on their release of KC Sheridan. And to drop the charges against him."

"Stand down, Mr. Lynch," Nash said.

"Not going to happen. The only thing Mr. Sheridan is guilty of is removing a chain link fence that *you* illegally erected on *his* property in an attempt to deny drinking water to his cattle. That's what this whole thing is about. Simple as that."

An ephemeral calm descended as Jarvis Lynch scanned the faces in the crowd one at a time.

"It gets to the point that even when you try to do the right thing," Lynch continued, "you know that you're being played. When you try to set things straight, it seems like they just keep on ignoring you, or they hand out a bunch of condescending claptrap, then turn deaf again. After a while you decide you can't go on forever playing defense—nothing happens, nothing ever improves."

Jarvis Lynch moved his eyes skyward, in the direction of the advancing choppers.

"That's all I've got to say," he said, raising his voice above the beat of the blades. "Residents of Jericho, I'm very sorry about what they've done to your town. It didn't have to happen this way."

He departed without a further word while questions were shouted at Lynch's back long after he was out of earshot.

THAT NIGHT Jesse brought a half gallon of ice cream and two spoons into the living room and sat quietly beside me on the couch. I muted the volume on the television console and the room seemed to draw in upon itself, the only light provided by the flames inside the fireplace and the blue glow of the picture tube, noiseless and still but for the rain ticking against the window. The television screen continued flickering with dismal images of pandemonium being visited upon our quiet county and the escalating number of ordinary people that had been labeled as provocateurs, gathering in the dark and the cold in the middle of nowhere, subjected to containment behind paramilitary barricades and sawhorses, concrete barriers and rope lines manned by uniformed men with flat affects who probed the snow-crusted no-man's-land with the stark beams of searchlights, armed with weapons of war.

"I had no idea it had gotten so out of hand," Jesse said, the screen's luminescence reflecting on her smooth skin. "Where did all those people come from?"

"Hemmings County mostly," I said. "There're rumors of caravans coming all the way from Kansas, Missouri, and Texas. Why are you looking at me that way?"

"I wish you'd talk to me about it, Ty."

"If I was inclined to talk about it with anybody, it'd be you."

"I'm sitting right here."

"I know it."

Wyatt was curled up on the floor at my feet, lost in a dream, his paws and musculature twitching as he made muffled barking noises down deep in his chest.

"I saw you on TV earlier today," Jesse said. "You looked so calm."

Jesse offered me a spoonful from the ice cream container.

"Both sides are talking past each other," I told her. "It's difficult to tell whether I am a source of stability or agitation, so I got out of the way and came home."

A stream of pine sap leaked out from a log inside the firebox, hissed and ignited as it dripped onto the coals. I felt Wyatt startle awake at the sound. He looked into my face for reassurance before settling down, resting his muzzle on my boot.

"Irene and KC are like two people standing at a siding watching trains collide in slow motion," I said, "just hoping the trains don't slide clear off the tracks and roll right over the top of them."

Jesse was staring into the fire. She touched the back of her wrist to her face and brushed at the moisture that had pooled in her eyes. I stood and switched off the television, returned the ice cream to the freezer, and sat down on the hearth.

"What happens now, Ty?"

"I wish I knew."

She bit her bottom lip and nodded but did not turn her focus from the flames.

"I may have misjudged Jarvis Lynch," I said.

CHAPTER TWENTY-SEVEN

I AWAKENED the next morning to learn that two events had occurred during the night that appeared to have no relationship to one another. The first occurrence I heard from local news coverage: Two males had sustained significant injuries at the hands of FBI personnel shortly after one a.m., out on the bleak and empty stretch of county road that had become the site of the FBI blockade.

A man in his late thirties, identified only as the owner of a small business and a resident of Jericho, had been arrested after shattering the windshield of a government-owned Suburban with a rock the size of a softball while an agent had been sleeping on the backseat. It was further reported that the perpetrator resisted violently in the course of his arrest and was injured in the FBI's attempt to subdue him. During the altercation, a member of the press who had been taking photos of the event found himself caught up in the melee and was later dragged away and vigorously discouraged from photographing the feds in the dispensation of their duties. The photographer was charged with interfering with an officer, but was subsequently released after a relatively brief detainment, though his camera and film had somehow been irreparably damaged during the incident.

"I was angry, I was upset," the stone-thrower said as he was climbing into his car following his release from a holding cell. He wore a welt the size of a golf ball over his left eyebrow and another on his left cheek. His lower lip also appeared to have required several stitches.

"I live here in Jericho," he continued. "I have a family and a business here. I heard that some out-of-state militia group took over the wildlife refuge, so I went out and had a look for myself. It's not a takeover at all. It's, like, ten guys freezing their butts off out there. It's no armed occupation either. Hell, it barely qualifies as a sit-in."

I would have found humor in the man's assessment except that I knew from personal experience there is no group of humans more treacherous than bureaucrats with access to military armament, especially bureaucrats who find themselves to be the subjects of derision. I had also come to the cynical belief that in almost any protest demonstration or similar display of public outrage, there are roughly a half-dozen people in the entire crowd who know what's actually going on. Everybody else is just there for the party.

At the confluence of these two forces lay the killing fields, with neither faction in possession of the self-restraint or prudence for the exercise of either forbearance or abnegation. Capitulation was not a part of the vocabulary of control, and I had no doubt that Special Agent Nash was experiencing the incipient sensation of the lash at his back.

I turned up the sound on the TV when I recognized Larry Lawrence, the

Hemmings County Recorder with the Elvis hair, being interviewed onscreen by a pool reporter from one of the networks. He had traded his cubavera for a paisley shirt with a zipper down the placket, but his salt-and-pepper pompadour remained immobile in the stiffening breeze.

"What's happening to the Sheridans throws a shadow across everybody in this country who owns property," Lawrence said. "And I'm telling you, that is one heck of a lot of people."

It was becoming clear to me that the tide of press coverage had undergone a subtle transformation overnight, likely due to the FBI's maltreatment of the photographer. But there had been something vulgar and vaguely spurious in the media reporting from the outset, and I feared that KC and Irene Sheridan would find themselves to be the final victims after the entertainment value of their story had been exhausted, subsumed by the media's systematic marketing of fear and distrust they tried to disguise as information.

I tossed the cold dregs of my coffee into the kitchen sink and went out on the gallery to check on the weather. I judged it would be another hour until daylight, so I whistled for Wyatt and called for him to come with me to investigate the thin line of yellow incandescent light I noticed spilling out from between the barn doors.

The air smelled of ozone and pine tar, and the hollow call of a spotted owl echoed out of the darkness as we picked our way along the narrow gravel path. Wyatt weaved between the shrubs, nose pressed nearly to the soil, as I pushed one of the heavy barn doors across its sliding track and stepped inside.

Taj Caldwell, one of my longtime cowhands, was seated on a three-legged stool making repairs to a woven latigo he'd snubbed onto his saddle horn for leverage.

"Little early for you, isn't it?" I asked.

Taj had a square jaw and eyes like buckshot, his posture straight as a pry rod, his features angular and hard like the cutting edge of a surgical instrument.

"A man's saddle is his workbench and his throne," he said and grinned at me. "Ain't that a fact, boss?"

Wyatt had followed me inside and had begun to hunt the open space between the groom stalls, tracking the scent of one of the barn cats.

"That is a fact," I said, whistled for the dog, and turned to walk back to the house. "I saw the light was on and came down here to make sure everything was copacetic. I'll leave you to go on about your work."

"You don't need to amble off just yet," he said. "It's been a minute since I seen you around the ranch, boss. You been plenty busy, I know that for sure. I guess it's a hell of a dustup they got going down in Jericho."

"That it is, Taj."

He returned his attention the length of fresh rope he'd been handling, coaxed a flame out of a butane lighter and worked it along the edges, singeing the stray hairs away.

"Old man Sheridan's got some grit, though, don't he?" Taj smiled as I moved toward the big doors to leave. "It's like he's teaching them city boys that *tellin'* a man to go to hell and *makin'* him do it are two entirely different propositions."

I LEARNED about the second event that had taken place during the night a couple hours later. The news arrived in the form of a phone call that came in while I was scanning the headlines of the Salem morning daily at my desk at the Meridian substation. I picked up the receiver and looked out the window across an empty street blushing with crisp morning light that was the color of fresh heather. "You'll never guess what we found in Darktown," the caller said.

"I don't recognize your voice," I prevaricated, "so I will assume we don't know each other and will therefore forgive you for not being aware that I don't tolerate people speaking in that manner."

I could hear the caller smiling inside the small measure of silence that hung between us before he responded.

"Shall I assume that you will also forgive me for not giving a shit as to your tolerations?"

"Goodbye," I said, and hung up.

My phone rang again a few seconds later.

"State your name and your business, or get off the line," I said when I picked up again.

"You seem in need of a vacation, Sheriff. I was phoning you because I have some information that is pertinent to a case you're working on."

"You must not have heard what I just said. I won't repeat myself."

"This is Deputy Chief Overton," he replied. "Portland Police Bureau."

"A little early for you to be in the office, isn't it?"

"I thought you'd want to know that Detective Dan Halloran was found dead shortly after two a.m. this morning. He had been murdered. Murdered bad."

"I'm sorry, it sounded like you just said that Detective Halloran is dead."

"We found him in a parking lot in Dark—across the river. Homicide tells me it took some time for the detective to give up the ghost."

A wind funnel rose up in the center of the street, swirled along the dividing line for a full block before it died away.

"I can tell you're deeply troubled by his passing," I said.

"Detective Halloran was alive when someone fed him feet-first into a gas-powered log-shredder. They dropped him in up to his waist, just far enough to mutilate him from his feet all the way to his genitalia, Sheriff Dawson. He bled to death with his torso still wedged in the blades of the machine. I am calling you as a professional courtesy so that you can stop spinning your wheels and move on with your life."

I thought back to the last time I had encountered Dan Halloran.

"Are you still there, Sheriff?"

"I'm here."

"You've got nothing to say to me?"

"I understand that it was you who advised Porter Brayfield to requisition the FBI into his county. Whatever happens down there as a result of that decision is on you, Overton."

"You're way out of your depth, Sheriff."

"If harm comes to the Sheridans or anybody else down here, I will take your scalp," I said.

"I don't abide the issuance of threats."

"I don't bother making them," I said. "Actions have consequences, Deputy Chief, that's what I am telling you."

"I called you this morning because I thought you'd want to know about Detective Halloran. You can cross him off whatever list you've conjured up regarding Clark Wehr's suicide and call it a day. It's over. Take the week off at the fishin' hole or whatever it is you do in Hicksville."

"The manner of Wehr's death has not been determined."

"I heard rumors that the army used American veterans of the Korean War for psychological experiments. I never knew they allowed any of the test subjects to return to society."

"I believe your personal hard-on for me has begun to cloud your cognitive abilities," I said. "Thank you for the call, Deputy Chief."

"Close the case."

"My condolences to the PPB on the loss of another one of your detectives."

"Close the goddamn case, Dawson."

"CID. Rose speaking."

It was unusual for Captain Rose to answer his own phone, even at this early hour, and I could tell by his tone that he was already shot through with fatigue.

"I need for you to double up security on Shannon Drury at the hospital," I said.

"The kid's handcuffed to a hospital bed, for Chrissakes, Ty. He's not going anywhere."

I repeated what I had just learned from Deputy Chief Overton.

"Jesus," Rose said. "A log-shredder?"

"You won't find me weeping over it."

"The man was a cop, Ty."

"Dan Halloran was a shitweasel. And the shitweasels have apparently begun to feast on their own kind. I don't want anything to happen to my prisoner."

I heard Rose kick his office door shut, muffling the distraction of ringing telephones on his end.

"Yeah, well," he said, "in other news: I got a call from Montana, and they want to extradite Drury to face charges against him back at home."

"Fine with me," I said. "Let Montana feed and house him. One condition, though."

"What's that?"

"They have to agree to send Drury back here posthaste if I need him as a witness. Why does it sound as if you're about to drop another shoe?"

"Word came down from Mount Olympus regarding the backup you requested."

"Good."

"Not good."

The hollow void on the phone line was superseded by a high-pitched ringing in my ears and the sensation of a knife blade made of ice scoring the flesh down the length of my spine.

"There must be something wrong with my telephone," I said.

"You heard me correctly."

"There's a convoy of KC Sheridan supporters driving in from Kansas, Missouri, and—"

"I am aware of that."

"There's already been trouble down there," I said. "There's going to be more."

"It's out of my hands, Ty. I'm sorry."

Off to the east, beyond the peaks, a pale ring of light encircled the rising sun.

"Explain that to me, Chris."

"Believe it or not, there's shit that goes on around here that is beyond my pay grade."

"Speak slowly, so I can understand."

He paused a beat and I waited, pressed my palm against the freezing windowpane.

"It came all the way down from the State AG's office," he said.

"Why would the attorney general get involved in sending state police backup to me?"

I heard the captain sigh as he hefted himself out of his desk chair to pace the floor.

"Someone placed a call to the Portland mayor's office," he said. "The mayor called the AG, the AG called the governor, and the governor called my boss."

"Who set it in motion?"

"I should also mention that the word 'toxic' came up repeatedly in those conversations," Rose said. "I took it as a reference to the general circumstances, not you personally, Ty. But I've got to be honest here, I'm not a hundred percent certain about that."

"Who called the mayor, Chris? Who tipped over the first domino? It was someone at PPB, wasn't it?"

"I've been telling you," Rose said, "command has been keeping an eye on this thing from the start. The feds don't want another Kent State or Pine Ridge. Neither does our governor."

"The feds didn't want *those* events to happen, either, but they ended up with both," I said. "Why would anybody trust the quality of their judgment this time around?"

There was a heavy thud and the resonance of rattling glass as Rose's fist made contact with his desktop.

"The goddamned governor has a combat unit from the Oregon Guard on standby as we speak, Ty," he shouted. "Do you get that? They feel that the risk of violence will intensify if additional police jurisdictions become involved."

"Did you just use the term 'intensify'?"

Seconds stretched, and I felt the heat drain from my skin and the racing of my heart begin to regulate inside my ribcage.

"Is that the way we operate now?" I asked. "Lawyers dictate our actions, so we end up playing defense with our lives?"

"Spare me the sanctimony."

"You know as well as I do that all of those assholes are hypocrites," I said. "The suits in Salem claim to be 'stunned' by the federal escalation, but they know those guys showed up kitted-out for war."

Rose offered no reply. There was nothing left to talk about. There would be no peaceful end to this, not now. Somebody leaves or somebody dies, it was going to be that simple.

"You've gotten good at this, Captain," I said finally.

"Was that an insult?"

"None was intended," I said. "But it might well prove to be a curse."

CHAPTER TWENTY-EIGHT

THE STORM CLOUDS that had gathered along the inland range all morning had begun to move slowly westward, inundating the landscape with sleet and freezing rain as the first of the Kansas convoy approached the Oregon state line.

I stood beneath the eave on the Sheridans' terrace and looked down the slope in the direction of the Rafferty Wildlife Refuge. I picked up a pair of field glasses but couldn't see through the precipitation. From inside the house I could hear the murmur of noise from the TV in the living room but could not decipher the content. I returned the binoculars to their place on a nail as Jordan Powell pulled open the sliding door and poked his head out through the opening.

"KC's back," Powell said.

The living room seemed stiflingly close as I stepped inside, and the air smelled of scorched coffee grounds, bacon grease, and the smoke from the maplewood logs in the fireplace. When I arrived half an hour earlier, Irene Sheridan had pressed an enameled steel campfire mug into my fist and informed me that KC and one of his cowhands had gone out to check on the herd some time before daybreak. I sniffed at the mug's contents, an aroma that reminded me of kindled chicory, and left it to cool on a lamp table beside the couch where Jordan Powell sat watching the morning news. Irene had been distracting herself with household chores and carrying on an unintelligible monologue under her breath ever since.

"How long has she been like this?" I whispered to Powell.

"Since yesterday. The old man ain't doing much better'n she is."

We watched as KC and his stockman stomped their feet on the mat outside the back door, shook the moisture out of their dusters, and hung them from pegs on the wall. The ranch hand removed his hat and placed it on the coat rack. KC kept his on, shot a glance past my shoulder at the television screen, and I saw the muscle in his jawbone begin to flex.

"How're your cows holdin' up, Mr. Sheridan?" Jordan asked in a bid to refocus KC's attention.

Sheridan shifted the grim set of his eyes from the picture tube and pinned my deputy with them.

"They're fine," KC said. "No thanks to Porter Brayfield and all the rest of them idiots. My whole goddamn herd would be froze up solid, layin' on their backs with their feet in the air if your boss hadn't stuck a gun barrel in that fat bastard's face."

There was a time when I had believed that the architecture of the world's future was being constructed by the innovative, the wise and resourceful, moving forward with great deliberation; that options were being considered, opinions expressed, and that only the fittest of plans would be set into motion, expedited with boldness and integrity. But to the extent that had ever been true, the valiance of ideals had since degenerated into self-aggrandizing deceptions, atrophied to the degree that the courageous or outspoken were routinely and casually sidelined by ideologues with meretricious designs, the foundations of their hustles and hoaxes laid without form or foresight, and constructed by functionaries vested with authority that exceeded ability, taking action by fiat, motivated by crisis, and later legitimatized by the protean concurrence of sycophants.

Chairman Mao said that political power grows out of the barrel of a gun.

Until recently, I had considered his remark as either parable or hyperbole.

I glanced out the window, beyond the cold rain and snow. Somewhere out there, a mile-long cortege of station wagons and pickup trucks, sedans, panel vans, flatbeds, and vehicles of every description navigated the high mountain passes, and at this very moment bore down on a two-lane stretch of unremarkable county highway, where our own federal government had seen fit to cordon it off with barricades of concrete, razor wire, cyclone fencing, and armored weapon emplacements.

"The backup I requested from the state police is not coming, KC," I said.

"I thought you had a friend over there," he said.

"Strings were pulled. Somebody in Salem didn't want to risk state troopers getting caught in the crossfire."

Irene watched us silently from where she stood beneath the kitchen archway and tugged at a white handkerchief she had pushed into the sleeve of her cardigan sweater. KC looked at his wife for a moment before nodding his head in the direction of the television console.

"You're telling me they're aware that all those folks are coming here from Kansas and wherever else?" he asked.

"Yes, sir," I said. "They're aware."

His expression registered incredulity. He removed his hat and began to straighten the brim. It was clear he hadn't slept in some time.

"I should make some kind of statement on radio and the *teevee*," KC said softly, licked his cracked lips, and gazed past the window frame. I could tell he was thinking the same thoughts as I had been. "I should tell them all to turn back and go home."

"You can't show your face in that crowd down there right now," I said. "Too many things can go wrong, KC."

"Ain't gonna get no better when the Kansas folks start rolling in."

"There might be a safer way," I said.

The pendulum clock in the hallway marked the seconds as KC stared out the window and considered what I had said. In my peripheral vision, I saw KC's cowhand's eyes move from me to KC and the belated realization dawn inside them.

"You can't turn yourself in, Mr. Sheridan," his cowboy said, the first time he had spoken since he'd come inside the house.

KC turned and looked the man straight in his eyes. KC appeared as though he was about to say something, but thought better of it. He placed a hand on the man's shoulder and squeezed.

"I appreciate your help with the herd this morning," KC said. "You go ahead back to the bunkhouse now."

"How 'bout if—"

"You go on, now."

The rowels of his spurs rang like temple bells as we all watched him cross the room to collect his coat off the peg on the wall, press his rain-dampened hat into place on his head, and step out the door without a backward glance. Once he was gone, KC pursed his lips and took a lingering look at his wife. Irene didn't blink as she held on to his gaze, didn't tremble, didn't move, did not shed a tear. This time, I could not guess what KC might be thinking, did not even try.

"Piss on the fire and call in the dogs," KC said finally. "This hunt's over with."

"Are you a hundred percent certain?" I asked him. "There's not going to be any do-overs."

"I can't let no more people get hurt 'cause'a me."

"MAIN THING is to keep this whole deal on the quiet until KC's safe and sound in Meridian," I said. "This place'll light up like Manassas if anybody spots him being driven away by the feds."

"Or by anybody else with a patch on their sleeve," Jordan said.

We had left the Sheridans so they could have some time to themselves while Powell and I worked out the details of getting KC from his ranch to my substation without either side hearing about it and jumping the gun. I would have taken Sheridan with me right then and there, but I wasn't about to make a fugitive out of him without KC's attorney hammering out some kind of back-channel agreement with the authorities beforehand. No handcuffs and no perp walk; just a televised statement from KC to the press and the public that might bring this standoff to a peaceful conclusion. The old man had been crystal clear about what he wanted.

"You tell that sonofabitch lawyer to do it exactly the way that I told you," he'd said to me as I walked out the door. "If he doesn't, by god, all bets are off. They can lock me in the penitentiary, but Irene and Jarvis and everybody else out there gets to go home. No charges, no fines. No tricks this damn time."

"I'll tell him."

"You do that, goddamn it, Ty."

There was a momentary break in the weather, and Powell and I followed a winding dirt path that led from the main house to the maintenance shed where KC kept his tractors and implements. I forced open a door that had swollen from moisture, dusted cobwebs from the frame as I led the way inside and tugged on a pull-chain that illuminated a bare bulb overhead.

"I'll have to go back to Meridian, coordinate with Nash to let KC through the blockade without making a scene," I said.

A gust of wind rattled a small square of window glass at the far end of the shed and the rainclouds burst open again.

"There's only one way back to the main road," Powell said. "And they got security details at both ends of it."

"But the crowd's only gathered at the south side of town . . ."

"The direction the caravan's coming in from."

I began to pace and lit a fresh cigarette.

"We could use the fire road that runs through KC's winter pasture," Powell suggested. "Pick up the logging trail along his back fenceline and then the two-lane just shy of where Nash has the blockade detail set up."

"Assuming KC's lawyer and Nash reach an agreement," I said, "we can roll out at first light. KC can be in Meridian before anybody even knows he's gone."

The atmosphere took on an abnormal stillness as long seconds ticked past and the wind shook the loose glass in the mullion again.

"Do you trust him?" Powell asked.

"Nash? I think he's a coward and a political tool."

I took a draw from my cigarette and slowly exhaled, watched the thin blades of light cleave the smoke as it bled out through the cracks in the boards. I was of no mind to defend FBI Special Agent Nash, but like it or not, he was the card we had drawn.

"You know, I've enjoyed staying here with the Sheridans," Powell said, and tipped his head in such a way as I could not see his eyes. "I'd hate to see anything happen to the old man."

"You want to drive him out of here?"

The light caught the side of Powell's face when he angled his face to look at me.

"I'd like that very much," he said without turning away. "You know, sir, some folks are going to say KC was a fool for surrendering just when the cavalry was set to arrive."

"And what do *you* say?"

"I'd say those folks are dead wrong," he said. "They didn't see what we've seen here. I'd say Mr. Sheridan's one of the finest men I've ever met."

"KC's going be counting on you, Jordan," I said. "So am I."

"I know it, sir."

I thought I saw his lips twitch into a smile, or maybe I only imagined it.

CHAPTER TWENTY-NINE

IT WAS a little past three in the morning when I gave up hope on any chance of sleep. I gathered my things and drove the winding highway to the substation, the starless, leaden, and confining quality of the atmosphere like a living being constricting my skin, the low moan of the pavement a prolonged soul whisper in the dark.

At the office, I made coffee and reread the case files on the Clark Wehr shooting, Shannon Drury's rap sheet, and the crime scene assessment of the murder of Jack Strong. Standing at the rear window, I peered down the alley and watched a small passel of opossums working to pry loose the lid from a rubbish can. My mind wandered back to the senselessness of the violence the two crossroaders had visited on a young couple and a moonlighting cop in a Montana convenience store, and the utter absence of luck that had accompanied them in their getaway, landing the pair in an abandoned fishing cabin where they became the unwitting witnesses to a murder.

There was no doubt in my mind that Jack Strong had been killed because he and Drury had simply been out there that night in the woods at the Catonquin Resort, but with Dan Halloran dead, the only thread that remained was the cabin's owner, the politically connected attorney Dean Stricklyn, and he sure as hell wasn't talking to anyone.

Around 5:15, I heard the back door to the office swing open and saw Sam Griffin carrying a cardboard container piled with doughnuts so fresh I could see the steam rising off them as he stepped in from the cold.

"Didn't figure you'd get much sack time last night," Griffin said.

"You know how it is," I said. "Standing by for standing by."

He handed me the pastry box and turned back for the door.

"Help yourself," he said. "I got something else out in the truck."

A couple minutes later, he carried in a small desktop TV with rabbit ear antennae and a plastic handle built into the casing. He placed it on the side table beneath the cork board where we pinned the bulletins and most-wanted posters, plugged it in, and angled it so we both could see the screen from our desk chairs.

"Going to be a long morning," I said.

"Have a doughnut, boss," he said. "Helps reduce the pucker factor."

Griffin had been briefed on all the moving parts of the plan and the clandestine extradition of KC Sheridan before the expected arrival of the Kansas convoy. It felt good to have someone else in the room with me who understood the stakes. I folded a paper napkin around an old-fashioned doughnut and took it to my desk, glanced out the window, and calculated that we still had a good two hours remaining between now and daybreak.

I felt Griffin's eyes on me, reading my thoughts.

"What time are we expecting Powell and Mr. Sheridan?" Griffin asked.

"Depends," I said. "I still haven't heard whether they've reached an agreement between KC's attorney and the feds. Nobody's going anywhere before that happens."

"Tick tock."

I nodded.

"The whole thing turns into a goat rodeo if the convoy arrives before Powell gets KC out of there."

Griffin tried to tune in the morning news broadcast out of Salem, but their images were little more than outlines in a static haze, so we were forced to settle on a network feed coming up to us from California. We sat through an interview with cast members from *The Rocky Horror Picture Show*, followed by a piece about corporate toy giant Mattel cooking its books in an effort to mislead its shareholders.

Going unreported was anything having to do with KC Sheridan or the turbulence in Jericho, Oregon. Also unreported: Following years of outright denials, the People's Republic of China released the cremated remains of two US Navy airmen they'd shot out of the sky nearly a decade before. Their ashes had been handed over to representatives of the International Red Cross at the border between Hong Kong and the Chinese mainland.

"Ten years of lying . . . for what?" Griffin said. "Who the hell's running this world?"

"If voting changed anything, they'd make it illegal," I said, stood, and turned down the sound.

The phone rang while I was in the restroom. By the time I'd washed my hands and returned to my desk, Griffin had finished the call.

"That was Quentin Bahle," he said. "They have an agreement. Bahle's bringing the paperwork down here for Mr. Sheridan to sign before he takes him from here up to Portland."

I should have felt some measure of relief. The wall clock read 6:52 a.m., a little over forty minutes before sunrise, and the day had only begun to flush with predawn. I immediately picked up the phone and dialed KC Sheridan at home to tell him it was a go, and I counted eleven rings before Irene picked up. I could hear the thickness of her voice, the stiff and fragile management of what remained of her composure.

"You just missed them, Tyler," she whispered. "I can see their taillights on the service road."

"Who the hell gave them the green-light?"

SOMEBODY LEAKED, and what should have been KC's clandestine and orderly extraction was going to hell in a handcart, right in front of my eyes.

By 7:48 a.m., the broadcast on the portable television broke away to a live aerial that could only have been shot from a moving helicopter. It showed a

ribbon of surface road snaking between clusters of dense growth that had matu-
rated amid plantation stands destined for the lumber mill. From above, a wide
shot showed the forest floor patched with fresh white powder, the narrow road
hemmed in along its shoulders by hillocks of accumulated ice and snow. A single
vehicle was moving with great caution along the centerline, a lone Ford pickup
truck, its headlights probing the colorless landscape.

"WHAT ARE you doing here?" Quentin Bahle said to me as he stepped across
the threshold into my office, the handle of a scarred leather portfolio clutched
tightly in his fist.

"You haven't been listening to the radio on the way down here?" I asked.

His eyes appeared to palpitate inside their sockets, and he looked through
Sam Griffin as though he was invisible as they locked onto me.

"Reception was for shit passing over the divide," Bahle said. His attention
roved to the TV screen. "What the hell is going on?"

"My deputy and your client have lost the element of surprise," I said.
"Somebody leaked the plan, goddamnit."

Bahle sighed and dropped into an office chair without taking the time to
remove his overcoat.

"I thought you were supposed to be driving him," he said.

"You misunderstood," I said. "There's a lot of moving parts to this, Mr. Bahle."

The attorney squinted and leaned forward for a better angle on the screen.

"Can you tell where they are?" Bahle asked.

"What did you say?" Griffin said and turned down the volume.

"Where are they?" Bahle repeated. "Can you tell?"

Griffin looked at me and shrugged. He made a move for the volume knob, but
I stopped him.

"Leave it down low," I said.

I'd been watching since the broadcast began and was intimately familiar with
the route that Powell and KC were taking.

"They're about three miles from the intersection with the county road," I
said. "After they get waved through the FBI checkpoint, it's a straight shot to
Meridian."

IT STARTS off like a high-pitched hum that emanates from a great distance.
Minutes crawl by and the only thing I can hear is the ringing inside my own ears.

A second vehicle had moved into the frame seemingly out of nowhere, maintaining an even distance, perhaps a hundred yards behind Jordan's pickup as they
approached the intersection. When the aerial news camera panned out wide, I
could see that the checkpoint had been repositioned from its previous location
out on the county highway to the service road on which Jordan was now traveling.
Two government-issue Suburbans had been parked at spearhead angles about a
half mile ahead of Powell's location, and I knew he had not spotted them yet.

"Is this a part of the plan you worked out?" I asked Quentin Bahle.

I felt an unwelcome heat developing inside my skull and could no longer recognize the sound of my own voice.

"No," Bahle answered. "I have no idea what this is."

"I know what it is," Griffin said.

So did I. I studied Bahle's expression and recognized what I saw there.

That son of a bitch.

"Inform Mr. Bahle what he is witnessing," I said to Griffin.

"It's a tactical maneuver," Sam said.

"Tactical maneuver?" Bahle asked. "To what end?"

"Shut up," I said, my eyes fixed on the picture tube.

Powell turned a corner, slowly brought his pickup to a stop at least a quarter mile short of the two Suburbans he now saw; the vehicle that had been tailing them pulled to a halt as well, maintaining its hundred-yard buffer.

Griffin stepped up beside me and we both watched, transfixed.

The cadence of my pulse began to pound inside my throat, and pinprick beads of cold sweat crested the pores of my skin. I could no longer accurately assess the passage of time, but I estimated at least two minutes passed without a single move from anyone appearing onscreen. I heard my heartbeat in my eardrums.

Suddenly, a puff of silver bloomed from Powell's exhaust pipe, and we watched his truck begin to inch forward. A pair of riflemen, outfitted in camouflage and combat boots bloused at the ankle, exited one of the government Suburbans and leveled their weapons in the direction of Powell's windshield. Powell did not pause but pressed forward slowly until he was half the distance of a football field from the armed agents and their roadblock.

Any military veteran could see that the two riflemen had moved to full alert, and I was sure Griffin was holding his breath for the same reasons I was. It was clear the men had no intention of allowing Jordan and KC to pass, but instead were preparing to detain them. It was clear that Jordan recognized what was happening, too.

The rear end of Powell's truck slid sideways as he hammered the accelerator, lurching for the narrow gap between the road shoulder and the federal vehicles. Powell fishtailed, recovered momentarily before plunging headlong into a drift of castoff from the snowplows, his tires driving deep into the bank and launching great arcs of pulverized ice crystals and gravel behind him.

"What the—"

"Shut the hell up, Bahle," I said, unwilling to avert my eyes from the screen.

The silhouette of a military chopper passed between the aerial news camera and the scene that was unfolding below, its altitude so low that the picture was obscured by its rotor-wash. When the air finally cleared, we could see that Powell's truck had stalled and bogged down in the drift. The FBI riflemen kept advancing on foot, widening their angle of approach, moving with studied deliberation.

"What happened to the deal, Bahle?" I asked, though I received no reply.

The armed agents halted as the driver's side door of Powell's pickup wedged open, the splayed fingers of both of Powell's hands extended out through the opening. The passenger side door cracked open a moment later but appeared as if KC was holding it from inside the door frame, maintaining his position in his seat.

Powell slid out from the driver's side and crabbed sideways into the freezing air, arms extended outward in the manner of a cruciform. We could see his lips move as Powell called out something to the agents and moved his left hand with exaggerated deliberation in the direction of his coat buttons, but something made him pull up short. Powell froze and raised his arms above his head again, then turned his head sharply in the direction of the deep woods.

"What's he looking at?" I said. "He sees something."

The military helicopter circled in front of the camera again, this time making a slow, shallow pass before it crossed the frame for a second time. As the screen image cleared of airborne interference, it appeared that Powell had dropped down to his knees. He remained that way for long seconds, buried to his thighs in snow. Then he pitched forward suddenly, inside a small cloud of dark mist, and toppled face first into the drift.

The news chopper banked sideways at a sickening angle, and the entire image slid out of the frame.

"Did you see that?" Griffin shouted.

"Sweet Christ," I heard myself whisper. "What the hell have you done, Bahle?"

The picture went black, then began to flash between visual static and poorly focused images of Powell's stranded pickup and his supine body lying motionless beside it. I glanced at Sam Griffin, could see his lips move, but I could no longer hear him for the deafening roar in my head. His eyes were still locked onto the screen.

I turned back to the TV in time to witness the glass of Powell's truck windshield pucker once, then twice more in split-second succession before the video feed was replaced by a test pattern.

IT STARTS off like a high-pitched hum that emanates from a great distance, closing in on me, escalating to a nearly unbearable bellow deep in my auditory canal. My field of vision contracts to a single point of cynosure, crimson and blurred at the edges, and I begin to feel some nameless part of my humanity slide away.

PART FIVE

SLIPKNOT

CHAPTER THIRTY

KEMUEL CLEMENT SHERIDAN was pronounced dead at the scene at 10:54 that morning by the Hemmings County coroner. Meriwether County Deputy Jordan Powell was transported by med-evac helicopter to the hospital in Meridian, comatose, the surgeons unwilling to opine on his prognosis.

By 1:00 p.m. that same day, the first wave of the FBI's extraction out of Jericho had been initiated. By 3:00 p.m., their evacuation was complete.

The feds had left the ground floor of the courthouse building looking as though it had exploded from within, having abused it nearly to the point of demolition. Special Agent Nash and the six men he had assigned to the road-block details were the only agents left behind to provide testimony. They had been transported to a federal office building in downtown Salem, where they had been directed to make themselves available to Oregon State Police investigators, to whom Powell and KC's cases had been assigned.

BUT NONE of that had yet occurred as I switched off the television set in my office and dialed the phone. My first call was to Agent Nash, but I was informed that he could not be reached. My next was to Captain Rose at CID, but I was told the same thing by the switchboard operator in his office. I slammed the receiver into the cradle with such force it fractured the handset, a single remnant note from the bell mechanism inside it lingering in the silence, as though the entire world had drawn a breath and was waiting for some signal to exhale.

Quentin Bahle attempted to break the silence, but I cut him off before he could.

"Get your ass out of my sight," I said.

Bahle seemed shell-shocked as he rushed out the office door. I didn't have to ask him a second time.

I took Sam Griffin with me and drove southward to see about Powell's condition, arrange for the retrieval of KC's remains, and inspect the scene of the shooting before it was overrun, trampled, and destroyed by the state's investigators.

By the time Sam and I pulled to a stop on the shoulder of that remote service road on the outskirts of Hemmings County, KC's body had already been removed by the coroner. But both KC's and Powell's blood was still abundantly in evidence, mixed with the mud of a roadside snowbank and indelibly stained into the fabric on the seat of Powell's bullet-ridden pickup.

A uniformed state trooper attempted to stop Griffin and me as we ducked under one of the strands of yellow tape that had been strung up everywhere, but I badged him and recited both of our names for his crime scene log. The trooper had odd-colored patches of skin on the flat planes of his face, and he eyeballed Griffin and me with a combination of pity and condescension.

"This is an active scene," he said. "You can't go in there."

"My deputy was driving that truck," I said. "This man and I will go where we goddamn please."

"We're still processing—" he began.

Sam and I were a hundred feet away by the time the trooper gave up trying to corral us.

On the inside of the barricade, the service road that Powell had been driving on began to make a gentle curve to the northwest. Beyond that point, it became a mile-long straightaway that terminated where it intersected with the county two-lane.

"They could have spiked the pavement anywhere along that straight stretch if they'd wanted to," Griffin said. "Plenty of visibility, plenty of shoulder. Nobody would'a got hurt."

I felt that familiar sensation burning underneath my skin again, and gazed along that unrestricted expanse of asphalt, true as a rifle barrel clear to the highway.

"They should never have been stopped out here in the first place," I said. "They told me we had an agreement. They were supposed to have had free passage."

Griffin followed me as I backtracked to where we'd started from. We split up and moved along the brow of an escarpment toward the point where Powell's truck still remained highbanked in the drift, each of us describing a wide arc between stands of scrub and cedar. I halted behind a cluster of blue spruce and sweetgale, at a distance of about thirty yards from the truck. I studied the angles and terrain, the sightlines and the pitch of the sun, then ran my fingers across the bark of the low branches. Griffin knew what I was doing. I could see that he was doing the same thing I was. I waited for him to look up from his work and waved him over.

I took a step back and squinted into the glare. Everywhere I looked were cops, cameras, and notepads; yellow tape, crime scene technicians, and troopers, but not a solitary member of the press. Every few seconds, one or another of the state's investigative team would cast a glance in our direction, their expressions unreadable. When Griffin stepped up beside me, I turned and spoke softly so we wouldn't be overheard by CID personnel.

"This is a kill zone," I said. "An ambush position."

Griffin's eyelids went tight, but I detected no surprise in them.

"Have a look at the limbs on this spruce tree," I said. "The branches have been notched."

Griffin removed his gloves and ran his bare fingers over the rough bark. His expression registered nothing, no shock or bewilderment, only the grief of recognition. The blockade detail had been moved to this location for reasons yet unknown. But it was clear that a sniper cell had been positioned out here for a kill, and that was exactly what they had accomplished.

I stood in the shadows and watched Sam Griffin work his jaw, trying to clear his ears and process the implications of what we had just seen. My imagination wandered seven thousand miles away, envisioned those lonely and desolate places where tens of thousands of young American GIs had been killed in villages with names that people back at home could not pronounce or even identify on a map. The relevance and gravity of words and images fell away at that moment, meant less than nothing to me, and devolved in entropy, a collage, an abstract composition constructed from shattered fragments of noise and broken light. Could anyone tell me how in hell the world was now a better place after the assassination of a man like KC Sheridan, and perhaps Jordan Powell as well?

TWO HORSES roamed inside a patch of sunlight that shone on the Sheridans' paddock. One side of the barn was cloaked in shadow, and melting frost dripped from the eaves as Sam and I crossed toward the back door to the house. Jarvis Lynch's truck was parked crossways to the garage, a dog-eared corner of a bumper sticker flitting in the breeze.

I removed my hat when Irene Sheridan came to the door, her face void of color or emotion. We stepped inside, and Irene moved close to me, looked into my face, and began to shriek. I had never heard a sound so freighted with grief, a sound so desolate and so broken. This was not an outward cry, of railing against god or man—it was the feral howl of a human soul that had been clawed out from inside, rent into tattered pieces, shredded and abandoned.

Irene began to pummel my chest with her birdlike fists, and Sam made a move to control her. I stopped him with a glance, and he stood aside while she continued to lash out at me, hammering until her shoulders sagged and she collapsed into my arms.

I carried her into the bedroom she had shared with KC for more than five decades, placed her on the mattress, and drew a blanket over her. There were no tears in her eyes when she blinked up at me, only emptiness, and a kind of revulsion I never wish to see again in the expression of another human being for as long as I live.

JARVIS LYNCH was watching the news on TV in the living room with Greg Reeves and Chester Zachary when I came out from the bedroom.

"What're you looking at me that way for?" he asked.

"Turn that off," I said. "We need to talk."

Lynch didn't respond, and Greg Reeves eyed me with contempt.

"How long before they come to take the ranch away from her?" Reeves asked me.

With the feds packing up and mustering out, these men were left with nowhere else to direct their outrage and frustration. It wouldn't be long before the press evaporated from the scene as well. I understood the animus, but it didn't mean I had to put up with it.

"You men brought this on," I said. "Now you need to fix it."

"Care to explain what the hell that's supposed to mean?" Lynch said.

"The feds are bugging out as we stand here, and the Kansas convoys are going to start to show up any minute," I said.

"Let 'em come."

"Wrong attitude," I said. "You need to read KC's statement, Jarvis."

"What statement?"

"The one KC was going to read on TV after he turned himself in this morning. The whole point of his surrender in the first place was to avert a full-scale shootout. We're still going to get one if you don't set yourself in front of that convoy right quick, before they go to hell. Those people need to hear KC's words, and they need to hear them now."

Lynch chewed his lip and looked away.

"I ain't gonna speak to nobody," he said.

"Why don't you do it?" Reeves asked. "You're the sheriff."

"It's gotta be either Lynch or Irene, nobody else's words will carry any weight," I said, and turned to Jarvis. "It's obvious Irene isn't up to it. You gonna cowboy up, or what?"

Lynch peeled his eyes off the carpet and seemed to draw courage from the company of his two friends.

"We still got men out at the refuge," Lynch admitted. "They've been with us the whole way along. I don't suppose we should show the white feather now."

"Don't you dare speak to me about loyalty," I said. "You carpetbagging sons of bitches coming out here fanned the flames that started this whole mess. None of it would have happened if y'all had just stayed home. You don't get to lecture me on that subject, Lynch, you understand me?"

Greg Reeves leapt to his feet and took a step toward me.

"You move any closer to me, boy, I will drop you," I said. "I am not joking. Sit your ass down."

I saw Reeves lower a shoulder and knew exactly what was coming. I stopped him with a right jab to the bridge of his nose and doubled him over with a left that drilled deep into his solar plexus. He cupped his nose and stared at me as his knees gave out on him. A gout of blood rushed between his fingers, down his chin, and onto the floor.

"*You* lit this fuse, Lynch," I said. "You'd better snuff it out. KC's already paid for your poor judgment. So did my deputy. And so has your sister."

Griffin dragged Reeves across the floor by his collar and into the kitchen, where he left him to bleed on the linoleum.

"Time's running out, Jarvis," I said. "More blood will be shed, and they'll do it in your sister's name. Count on it."

CHAPTER THIRTY-ONE

TWO DAYS LATER, I received a phone call at the office, a female voice announcing to me that Captain Rose, Criminal Investigations Division, Oregon State Police, would be on the line for me in a few moments.

The nature of our personal relationship had deteriorated over the course of the past three days. Because Powell had been a deputy under my jurisdiction and the FBI was directly involved in what was now being termed an "incident," the case had been turned over to the state police. As head of CID, Captain Rose had been placed in charge of it. I had shared my findings with him regarding the sniper's notches Griffin and I had identified in the trees, but I had been left largely out in the cold in terms of the investigation.

"We're still not releasing the autopsy results to the public," Rose said to me without salutation or preamble. "But I wanted you to know that the official statement is that KC Sheridan died of exsanguination."

"He bled to death," I said. "You're going to announce that he bled to death? You know that the rest of the known world watched the whole thing on TV, don't you?"

The truth was, the origin of my hostility had almost nothing to do with Rose's status as the leader of the investigative team and almost everything to do with the fact that he had failed to back me up when I had initially requested extra personnel. For Rose's part, I knew he was aware that I believed that if his troopers been there when I'd asked for them, this entire situation would have played out differently; KC would still be alive, and Powell would be home mending fences with his fiancée. But the fact that Captain Rose had never allowed for any professional accountability on his part well and truly pissed me off.

"And please remember, I've still got a deputy with a sniper's bullet lodged in his skull."

"There's no hard evidence of snipers, Ty," he said. "No video, no corroborating witnesses—"

"The video tape was confiscated, and the only witnesses are the defendants."

"Do you want to hear what I have to say, or not?"

"Depends. Are you going to tell me something useful?" I asked.

"It wasn't personal, goddamnit, Ty."

"The hell it wasn't."

"I meant—"

"I know what you meant," I said. "Just tell me about KC."

I heard Rose breathe into the phone.

"Three rounds through the windshield," he said. "One missed completely and passed through the seat cushion, one passed through Mr. Sheridan's windpipe, and the third caught him beneath his left eye and exited through the back of his head. Coroner says he died instantly from the effects of the third projectile."

"What do Agent Nash and the assassins have to say about it?"

"That's not a word we're applying to this," he said.

"Answer my question."

"You've read the interviews."

"They were redacted. Heavily."

"That's the way it works with these people, Ty."

"I don't want to hear any more about jurisdictions and chains of command," I said. "I especially don't want to hear that they shot Powell because he was going for his gun. We've all seen the footage on TV. The sonofabitch who tapped the trigger on Sheridan and Powell is a straight-up murderer. In two days' time, that bastard and all the rest of Nash's team will be back at home in D.C. dining on lobster tails and rice pilaf."

What I elected not to bring up with Rose again was that the feds had not only confiscated the film footage from the news helicopter but had quarantined it so that no one could even view it. I could not blame Rose for that, nor was it my desire to place blame on him for anything beyond that of which he was already well aware.

"I want a word with Nash and his men before they leave the state," I said.

"Not a chance in hell, hoss."

"They can't make blanket assertions about Powell and KC being an armed threat to them and simply disappear back to Washington."

"Powell's a cop, of course he was armed," Rose said. "And KC was found with a .45 revolver in his lap."

"It was in his lap, Chris. It wasn't in his goddamn fist."

"I'm not litigating this with you," he said. "I'm telling you the feds have been cooperative so far. We're allowing them to return to Quantico to face an internal FBI inquiry that will run parallel to our investigation."

"A rigorous and unforgiving reckoning, no doubt."

"You've got to let the system sort this out, Ty."

It was the lying I had come to hate. As an officer of the law, I am allowed to lie outright to a suspect in the course of an interview; to utter whatever comes to mind if it might result in a confession, or perhaps rattle loose some small bit of information that I might be able to squirrel away for later. It was often an effective tactic, but what did it say about a system that encouraged the enforcers of the law to break the basic tenets of civilized society in service of taking rule breakers off the board? Where did the truth reside if everybody in the room was a cop?

"The system's rigged, and you know it, Chris."

"You've got to stop saying shit like that," he said. "You're starting to sound like a crazy person. I'm telling you that as a friend, Ty."

* * *

I LIT a wooden kitchen match with my thumbnail, touched it to the wick of an oil-fired lantern on the table beside the willow rocker on the porch. The sun had long since sunk behind the mountains, and the yellow flame inside the tapered torch glass shivered out a ribbon of oleaginous black smoke into the cold. I heard his footfalls on the gravel long before I saw him step out of the dark and climb the stairs up to my gallery.

"Third night in a row I seen you up here drinking by yourself," Caleb said.

"These kinds of days lend themselves to it," I said.

He hooked a finger through the top rail of a Wakefield chair, dragged it across the floorboards, and joined me inside the circle of lamplight.

"Maybe they do," he said. "But I don't care to see a man drinking alone."

I poured four fingers of Jim Beam into a jelly glass and passed it to him. I could smell the citrus of his hair tonic and the scent of soap in the creases of his snap button shirt. The diffused light reflected on his freshly shaven jaw as he angled his head in the direction of the barn.

"I seen you take Drambuie up the trail this afternoon," he said. "Did you get out there to check on the stock?"

"I trust you to see that the cows are taken care of," I said. "Drambuie and I rode up to the Stone Garden so I could have a few words with my people."

"How're they doing?"

Caleb brought his glass to his lips, tossed off half the contents, and dried his mustache with the back of his hand without breaking eye contact with me.

"The folks in the Stone Garden aren't prone to changing too much anymore," I said.

"That is a fact. But your grandpap and your old daddy always did dispense some sage advice as I recall. Your momma and grandmomma, too, for that matter."

"I haven't known you to keep a notion to yourself too often, either, Caleb," I said. "You got something on your mind?"

He threw back the remainder of his whisky and set the empty glass beside the bottle on the table.

"How about pouring me another one first," he said. "There's a big hole in the top of that jelly jar."

He sipped a little slower this time, and I saw his eyes drift off among the cottonwoods that grew in rows along the banks of the dry creek.

"Did you get your problems sorted out while you were up there at the Garden, Ty?"

"A few of them."

The nightsong of a mockingbird echoed from somewhere in the pine woods. Caleb cocked his head and listened.

"I'm worried about Powell too, you know," he said. "You ain't alone in that."

"Doesn't seem right, the world going on like nothing ever happened, like KC and our cowboy were never here."

The mockingbird stopped singing, and the only sound remaining was the whispering of wind inside the trees.

"The Lord has some tough ways sometimes," Caleb said, and leaned back in his chair. "Sometimes it feels like it's us needs to forgive Him, don't it?"

CHAPTER THIRTY-TWO

A HIGH PRESSURE system had temporarily forced our winter northward. The morning was as blue as cobalt, cloudless, and bright as I rolled up on a midrise condominium building located at the edge of a genteel northern skirt of downtown Portland. This was where the Countess operated her business from a fourth-story penthouse unit with a view that looked out on the Willamette.

I climbed out of my truck, could smell the fishkill and algae from the riverbank, charging a breeze that felt more like May than December. The bare branches of ash trees along the wide boulevard seemed alive with the noises of grackles and starlings.

The building was shaped like an oxbow, its entry access protected by a fortified wrought iron gate and electronic intercom lock system. I pressed the button beside the tiny plaque engraved with the number 403 and waited. I easily spotted both of Lieutenant Morgan's surveillance teams, set up as they were in nearly identical unmarked police vehicles and parked on adjacent corners across the quiet street.

A buzzer sounded and unlocked the gate. I crossed a tastefully landscaped courtyard and took the stairs to the fourth floor. A slender young woman wearing a sleeveless smock dress the color of ripened watermelon waited for me at the door. She waved to me and displayed the smile of a former prom queen.

"Hello, doll," she said.

Her complexion was like buttermilk, untouched by the sun, and someone had taught her how to move as though she did not touch the floor. I waited until we were inside, with the door shut tight behind us, before I showed her my badge and identified myself.

"Aw, that's sweet," she smiled, folded her arms behind her back, and leaned a shoulder on the doorframe. Her voice was smooth and easy, a sultry southern breeze in the magnolias. "Where y'all from?"

If she was the least bit uncomfortable having a law enforcement officer on the premises, she did nothing whatsoever to show it. I asked to speak to the Countess, and the girl actually began to laugh.

"Nobody in here calls her by that name, sugar."

The anteroom smelled of gardenia and cut grass. The walls were decorated with tropical-themed wallpaper depicting palm fronds and pandanus leaves, and a set of bamboo furniture had been neatly arranged in the corner. Framed lithographs displayed tranquil scenes from a pre-Castro Cuba that had probably never existed.

"Can we move this along, please?"

"I'll be right back," she said, and disappeared through a doorway strung with beads made from the husks of polished nuts.

I was inspecting a print by Roberto Juan Diago Querol when the woman known outside these walls as the Countess passed through the beadwork.

"I don't receive visits from cowboys in full regalia very often," she said and offered her hand. "Ivy Novack."

She was a statuesque woman in her early forties, taller than average, with posture that suggested familiarity with the runway or the pageant circuit, and shoulder-length hair that was the color of fireweed honey. She was dressed in a pearl-colored jumpsuit, pulled in at the waist with a belt woven from strands of rough jute and tied at the front in the manner of a martial artist.

"I was wondering how long it would take until you came to see me," she said.

"You know who I am?"

"Yes, I do."

"Then you can probably imagine what I came to speak with you about," I said.

"Oh, we're not having this conversation here, sweetheart," she said. "Let's talk at my house. You drive."

WE DROVE into the wooded foothills overlooking downtown, parked in the driveway of a sprawling, low-slung, prairie-style house that could have been designed by Frank Lloyd Wright. I followed behind her along a stone footpath, passed under a trellis threaded with dormant trumpet vines, and entered the house through a side door inset with translucent circles that resembled the bottoms of wine bottles.

Inside, a gas-fueled fireplace, open on all four sides, dominated the center of an expansive living room, where she showed me to a leather sofa that was the exact same shade as a ghost flower. She looked at me from over her shoulder, offered me a Boodles and tonic as she mixed one for herself from a bar trolley. I declined the cocktail, but my attention landed on a framed photograph she had placed in a position of prominence on the mantel while I waited for her to finish making hers.

"It's the only photo I have of just the two of us," she said. "Clark didn't like having his picture taken."

Ivy Novack sat down beside me, closer than seemed appropriate at first, and told me about how she and Clark Wehr had met, how she had been walking her dog along Preston Avenue and Wehr had pulled over his convertible Porsche and introduced himself. She said that he had seemed to be completely unaware of her occupation at the time.

"My dog died about a year later," she said. "I still miss that sweet little guy."

At the outset, she had lied to Detective Wehr, terrified he would cut off their relationship, like they all did, when he found out how Ivy made her living. But she was beautiful, intelligent, and kind, and Clark Wehr was a pragmatic man, and the two ended up falling in love.

"Who else knew about your relationship?" I asked.

An alluring, paper-thin gap showed between her front teeth, and her meticulously penciled eyebrows arched when she smiled.

"Oh, everyone knew, darling."

"Including Dan Halloran?"

"Clark and Danny were partners," she said. She used her thumb to wipe a pink crescent of lipstick from the rim of her highball glass before placing it on a coaster. "The boys would feed me information—about vice raids, stings, and that sort of thing—and eventually began to introduce me to the right people in town."

She bent forward, plucked an unfiltered cigarette from an ornately decorated hinged box on the table.

"People like who?"

"Would you care for one?" Ivy asked.

"No, thank you."

"Let's step outside," she said. "I don't like to smoke in the house."

The breeze was light, washed with sunlight. I lit her cigarette for her and leaned my forearms on the handrail, admiring her view of the city.

"Who did Wehr and Halloran introduce you to?" I asked again.

She exhaled a funnel of tobacco smoke and examined the skyline.

"Slow down, cowboy. I need to know."

"Need to know what?"

"Who you are."

"We've already been through that."

"We've established your name and what you're interested in," Ivy said. She turned and looked at me with uncommon directness, rested both of her elbows on the rail and pressed the small of her back into it. "But not who you *are*. What, exactly, are we doing here, Sheriff Ty Dawson?"

The sun glinted on the ribbon of river that bisected the city, and I followed the course of a merchant vessel as it passed beneath the spandrels of St. Johns Bridge.

"Do you feel safe?" I asked.

Ivy Novack laughed without humor and tucked a loose curl into place behind her ear.

"I've got PPB eyeballing me practically twenty-four hours a day," she said. "I assume you spotted them outside."

"Is that a 'yes,' or a 'no,' Miz Novack?"

"I can see by your ring that you're married."

"My wife's name is Jesse."

"How would you feel if someone you trusted—that *both* you and Jesse trusted—walked into your kitchen, smiled, and blew a hole through the center of Jesse's forehead?"

Her eyes moved off mine, beyond the sliding door, and found their target on the mantelpiece inside the house.

"I saw you at the Stumptown Chophouse in the company of Marcus Vessey," I said.

"I don't imagine that you have respect for everyone with whom you associate in your work, Sheriff."

Her aspect and body language stiffened, and she pulled her attention away from the old photo and focused it on me again.

"I file my taxes every year just like you do," she said. "I need a visible means of support in order for my situation to function properly."

"Vessey launders your money."

"I'm an investor in Dean Stricklyn's restaurant business," she said, and crushed her cigarette into a cut crystal ashtray on the patio table.

I reached into my pocket, unfolded the black and white surveillance photo that Lieutenant Morgan had given to me and showed it to her.

"Is this Vessey?"

Ivy's eyes grazed the image and the muscle at the corner of her jawbone began to flex.

"Marcus Vessey might be the worst man I've ever known," she said. "He ruins people."

"Do you think Vessey killed Clark Wehr?"

"Do I look like a woman who would break bread with a monster who could murder my man in cold blood? I need another cigarette."

I unsnapped my shirt pocket and shook one of mine out of the pack and lit it for her.

"Vessey is a disease," she said. "A rapist who destroys people from the inside. He wouldn't have what it takes to kill a real man like my Clark."

She drew deeply from her cigarette. I elected not to share with her my conviction that most murderers were both cowardly and craven at their cores, and that ending a man's life took no special skill or strength of purpose.

"After I'd first started working with them—"

"Working with whom?" I interrupted.

"Stricklyn and Vessey."

A rose-colored patch appeared in the hollow of her throat, as though the mention of their names had caused her blood pressure to spike.

"One of my newer girls showed up in town with her younger brother," Ivy continued. "Her brother was nineteen, maybe twenty years old, and needed work. They both needed money to get themselves settled, so I introduced the kid and one of his little friends to Marcus Vessey. Stupidly, I figured he'd put them to work in the restaurant bussing tables."

Her eyebrows knitted together as she paused and gazed out at the river.

"Next thing I heard," Ivy said, "both of those boys were moving dope for Marcus. Then one of them got pinched, and that was it."

"That was it *how*?"

"Vice cops turned the poor kid into a snitch. Not long ago, someone took a sledgehammer to his kneecaps, shot him in the throat, and he ended up choking to death on his own blood."

I'd heard that story once before. From Halloran's CI.

I knew from experience that some men lose themselves in moments of crisis, and the world seems to fold in on them, to disintegrate and fade to black. Others flourish inside the cloud of chaos, where both mind and body operate synchronously, and time elapses at a pace of its own determination. I have found that I am of the latter breed.

I don't know how long my mind had been racing, but when I looked at Ivy Novack again, she was gazing strangely at me.

"I asked you a question earlier," she said. "Who are you really, Sheriff Dawson?"

"I believe that Dan Halloran murdered Clark Wehr," I said. "But I can't prove it yet."

She averted her eyes for the first time since we'd met, and I studied her for a reaction.

"You think Danny killed my Clark?" she asked. "His own partner?"

"Yes, ma'am, I do."

She stood and moved to the corner of the balcony. She arched her half-smoked cigarette beyond the railing, watched the tail of sparks fall to the lawn down below, and slid her hands into the pockets of her jumpsuit, her back to me.

"That isn't everything, though, is it?" she asked.

"No, ma'am. Turns out, it's not even close."

"I can't stay here in the city if I tell you what I know," she said.

"I'm aware of that."

She turned and looked into my face without shame, without mercy.

"Do I have your word you will help me get out of here if I help you?"

"Are you going to be square with me?" I asked.

"Let's talk inside."

"YOU'VE GOT the balls to show yourself in here after what you did?" Morgan said as I walked into his office an hour later. "You blew up my surveillance."

"The Countess knew all about it, Morgan," I said. "They weren't real subtle."

"Bullshit."

"Who's the guy you've got tailing me? The one who refers to himself as a Confidential Informant?"

"Are you high on something?"

"That's Marcus Vessey in the photo you gave me, by the way. The guy with the ears."

Morgan leaned back in his chair and studied the framed pictures on his wall.

"But you already knew that, didn't you?" I said. "You knew that when you first handed it to me."

"What do you want?" Morgan said, planting his focus on me.

"I used to know a decorated Vietnam combat vet who had to sleep with a nightlight," I said. "He was afraid of the dark ever since he'd manned a forward listening post in Indian country."

"You're a hard man to understand," he said.

"Why are you running me?"

"As usual," he said, "I don't know what you're talking about."

"The jury's still out on you, Lieutenant," I said. "But for the time being, I'm going to choose to keep believing you're one of the good guys."

"Next time," he said to my back as I stepped out the door, "call me and ask permission before you rathole one of my stakeouts."

I turned and addressed him from the center of his doorway.

"The next time I call you," I said, "I will expect your complete cooperation."

"Cooperation with what?" he said, grinning. "Like you say 'jump,' and I say 'how high'?"

"More like, I say 'jump,' and you just do it."

AFTER LEAVING Morgan's office, I stopped in at a Mexican grocery store across from the courthouse. I ordered a plate of tacos and an RC Cola from a man wearing a white apron and a paper hat working the counter and took a seat at one of the small tables near the window. About half a block down, I saw a beat cop frog-marching a handcuffed suspect into the rear entrance of the courthouse.

"You don't want to be here, Sheriff," Judge Bonner said from somewhere behind me.

I had not seen him walk in. In fact, I had not seen him since he'd invited me out of his office during his meeting with KC and Quentin Bahle. I did not have to think too hard in order to imagine how he knew I was in town.

"I believe the fact I'm sitting here in front of you argues otherwise," I said.

"Go home, Dawson. It's over."

I cut my eyes outside the window again, but the beat cop and his arrestee had already disappeared inside the building.

"I've just had a premonition as to what your future's going to look like, Judge," I said.

"Let me give you some advice: If you're planning to orchestrate some sort of personal Armageddon for me, it's not wise to tell me about it first."

"During the Civil War," I said, "a general would sometimes notify his enemy counterpart of an impending attack. It was intended as a gesture of gentlemanly honor, for the purpose of allowing his opponent the opportunity to surrender before blood was spilled."

"And you think that's analogous to our situation here?"

"Next time I see you," I said, "I'll be whistling the song they call *Deguello*."

He studied me, looking for some sign of insincerity or deficiency of purpose, and found none.

"You should probably leave now, Judge," I said. "My food is getting cold."

* * *

I PARKED near the back door to St. Stephen's basilica on my way home. The late afternoon sky had taken on the color of antique ivory, and the wind out of the west felt arctic and dry, restless with electrical currents.

I dipped the fingers of one hand into the wall font near the door to the sacristy. I took a seat in a pew in the last row of a nave that was otherwise vacant of parishioners and closed my eyes. I had never been educated in the liturgies, possessed no intimacy with the petitions, devotions, or novenas which might have pacified the malignity and rancor inside my head. Instead, I breathed deeply of the warm scents of incense and melted beeswax and opened my eyes when I heard footsteps in the aisle beside me.

"I was very sorry to hear of your loss," Monsignor Turner said. "I know you men were close."

"I appreciate the sentiment."

He clutched a leatherbound Bible with both hands and was dressed as before in black slacks and clerical collar, though, this time, he wore a stole of purple silk draped across his shoulders. His eyes shone like pewter, reflecting the segmented light of the stained glass in the window openings.

"You're welcome here any time," he said. "As I said before, it's the same god who lives here as across the street."

"Seems like He dresses better here."

A smile touched the corner of the monsignor's lips, but his attention roved toward the chancel and lingered there.

"It's not a visit to Lourdes," he said.

"That's not what I came here for."

"Something you'd like to discuss in confession?"

"Not yet."

His focus returned to me then, and he nodded in a manner that suggested he understood my meaning.

"I'll leave you to your thoughts," he said, and began to walk away.

He had made it nearly all the way up the aisle when he stopped himself and addressed me from the narthex.

"Peace be with you, Sheriff Dawson," he said.

Something in his tone registered as admonition.

"Peace be with *you*, Monsignor."

CHAPTER THIRTY-THREE

JESSE WAS HUNCHED inside the chicken coop when I got home that afternoon. She was holding a galvanized bucket overflowing with soap suds in one hand, scrubbing the nest boxes with a wire brush. The hens were roaming free, scratching at the soil in a planter where a paper bush was glowing in the last blush of sunlight from behind the ridge.

"Something's killing the pullets," Jesse said and blew a stray lock of hair from her face.

Wyatt heard my footfalls on the gravel, lost his footing as he raced around the corner of the house, scattering the chickens, and sliding to a halt against my boots. I bent down to scratch him, and he rolled onto his back, making a mewling noise deep in his throat.

I stepped into the chicken coop to give Jesse a kiss, but she gently elbowed me away.

"Wait until I've had a chance to shower," she said.

I followed Wyatt to the back door and heard Jesse call out behind me.

"Oh," she said. "Shasta Blaylock's down in the office with Caleb."

"Is everything alright?"

"What do you think?"

CALEB WAS kneeling on his haunches, feeding kindling into the Belleville furnace while Shasta Blaylock watched him from my swivel chair as I walked in. She was bundled inside a hand-knitted woolen sweater, the pigment of her nose and cheeks reddened by emotion.

"Hello, Mr. Dawson," she said. Her voice was raw, haunted by thoughts she could not fully articulate.

Caleb blew the flames to life inside the woodstove and shut and latched the iron door. He stood and tucked his hands into the pockets of his jeans.

"Shasta's just come back from the hospital," he said, measuring his tone with care, and cast his gaze out through the jalousies.

"Jordan's still in a coma," she said. "Doctor won't say if they think he'll live or—"

"It's early going yet," I interrupted. I didn't want to hear that next word cross beyond her lips.

"Folks at the hospital won't let me have a say in how they care for him," she said. "They barely speak to me; told me it's because I'm not family."

"You're his fiancée," I said.

"That ain't kin enough, evidently," Caleb said.

"It's why I came to talk with Mr. Wheeler. I've never met any of Jordan's people."

"It's 'cause he ain't got any people," Caleb said. "Never gave me no names or next of kin or nothin' when I hired him on to work here, Ty."

Shasta's resolve seemed on the verge of breaking down again. I sat down on the desktop beside her and offered her my handkerchief.

"We hadn't even picked a place for the wedding reception yet," she said to nobody. "Jordan would just laugh and tell me we had all kinds of time. Big lie that turned out to be."

She wadded my hankie into a ball and pressed it to her lips but would not permit herself to cry again.

"I'll make a couple calls," I said. "We'll get things straightened out."

I was certain that she had not heard what I'd just said, but after a few seconds she nodded.

"I was really mad at Jordan the last time I talked with him," she said. "I wasn't nice to him at all."

I reached my hand toward her, and she laid her fingers in my palm. I squeezed them gently and looked down at the simple diamond solitaire she wore.

"That's how love goes, darlin'," I said. "That's how she rolls sometimes. Jordan knows that. Those aren't the last words you'll ever say to him. Not by a long shot."

She swallowed hard and gripped my hand inside of hers as though it might require all her will to make it through the afternoon.

LACY SMOKE drifted from the stone chimney as the fire died inside the living room. I could see the orange pulse of embers reflected in the window as Jesse and I sat on the gallery and looked into the clear night sky at stars we hadn't seen for weeks. I could barely make out her features in the dark, sitting in the willow chair beside me, her face illuminated only by the quiver of the fading flames and the single lamp we'd left on inside the house.

I told Jesse about Shasta Blaylock. I also spoke about my conversations with Lieutenant Morgan and Judge Bonner, but made no mention of having met with Ivy Novack or what the two of us discussed.

"Morgan has been withholding things from me about the nature of his surveillance team."

"You think he could be involved in blackmail?" Jesse asked.

"I don't know. Maybe more than that, maybe nothing. I'm not entirely sure."

"You used to spend your time with a better class of people, Ty," she said. "Before they made you sheriff."

"I thought you wanted me to talk to you."

I leaned in for a refill of Jim Beam but thought better of it. Instead, I sat my empty glass on the low table between Jesse and me.

"Even you can't fix everybody," she said, tucked her legs up sideways in her chair, and studied me.

"I'm not trying to fix anybody," I said.

"Then what are you doing?"

She seemed unusually vulnerable and defenseless when she looked into the dark, into the forest, as she waited for my answer.

"In the war," I said, "I saw a man die from an infection. It was a slow, ugly, and agonizing death. It was also entirely preventable. Someone could have stopped it."

Her eyes probed mine as if to seek the true meaning of my words.

"Are you ever planning to come back?" she asked.

"Back where?"

"Back here. Back to the ranch. Back to me."

She picked up a clear glass vase she'd filled with tiny seashells we had collected together from the shore at Cannon Beach and turned it in her hands.

"Why are you so angry with me?" I asked.

"I'm not angry with you," she said. "I'm angry *about* you."

"You're the second woman in one day who's given me a headache splitting words apart."

"What is that supposed to mean?"

"I have no idea," I said. "I'm just tired."

"You can't let evil men have power over you, Ty."

"What exactly is it that you think I do when I leave here every day, Jesse?"

She turned her eyes and looked through the window glass into the empty house, and let my question float away.

CHAPTER THIRTY-FOUR

WE SPENT THE next day burying our friend.

Jesse, Caleb, me, and most of the ranch crew drove in a procession down to Jericho and prayed KC Sheridan into the ground. The temperate weather had continued to hold, the sky a cloudless blue as we stood and watched a good man being lowered into a hole, but the sun never seemed to climb up high enough to issue any warmth. There was little cause for optimism despite the pastor's words, not here, not yet.

Jarvis Lynch stood alone beside his grieving sister, his companions having departed back home the day before, there being no further reason for them to remain. Lynch and Irene had delivered what had turned out to be KC's final words to the arriving caravan from Kansas, delivered them the very day that KC died. At first, it seemed the crowd might turn on them, but it was Irene who finally put an end to the whole thing.

The Kansas convoy had pulled into town as the final wave of FBI were heading out, the only contact between the factions occurring as the new arrivals pelted the government vehicles with rocks and glass bottles. There were no injuries, nor arrests. Almost all of them left Jericho a short time afterward, before the moon had even showed itself that night.

On our way from the cemetery to Irene Sheridan's house, we drove past the county building. A panel van and dump truck with a contractor's logo painted on the door were parked outside the entrance, removing broken sheetrock, shredded electrical cable, scrap metal and damaged carpeting in preparation for interior repairs. Bent and twisted rolls of concertina wire and lengths of painted two-by-fours that had once been used for barricades were heaped in piles in the dirt beside the dumpsters on the vacant lot next door. Everybody in our car surveyed the remnants of the damage as our cortege rolled slowly by, but no one dared to break the silence with a word.

SOME TIME shortly after noon the next day, Chris Rose showed up at our front door. He handed Jesse a bouquet of white irises when she answered the bell, paid his respects, and stepped outside to find me on the gallery.

"I know this is a bad time," he said to me. "You know I'm sorry as hell about KC and your deputy."

All my emotions had been spent, rendered to the bone after the past few days, and I simply no longer felt justified in directing any further enmity at Chris Rose. I shook his hand and offered him a drink, which he declined. He looked strangely at me and angled his head in the direction of my office down below.

"A word?"

We walked along the path without speaking, the sunshine thin and fissile. I sat down in the rolling chair behind my desk and Rose took the one behind Caleb's. His focus landed on a rodeo poster from the county fair last summer, one with a photo of Paul Tucker, one of my ranch hands, astride a bull named Desolation. Rose seemed to be building himself up to tell me something, and at a loss for words.

"In my experience," I said, "bad news don't get any better by waiting to tell it. What's on your mind, Chris?"

He looked into my face, and without a further word, withdrew a cassette tape box from the breast pocket of his jacket. I popped a Willie Nelson tape from the player on the shelf and replaced it with the one that Rose was handing me.

"What you're about to hear stays between the two of us for now," he said.

"Whatever you want."

"I'm dead serious, Ty."

"Understood."

He studied me, tipped his head slightly, and I pressed *play*.

"Is that Agent Nash's voice?" I asked.

"Yeah, it is," Rose said. "Listen to this part. Listen what he says to me right here."

Three minutes later, I felt as though I'd been field-dressed, hung, and bled out from a limb.

"Jesus," I said. "He found out about an offer to buy KC's property?"

"Multiple offers. From the same buyer," he said. "You'd think he would've mentioned it to you, Ty."

"Not really. KC got offers all the time. Turned every one of them down flat. Legacy can be a heavy burden."

"Looks like this one might've run out of patience with him."

KC was nothing if not independent, a loner to the end.

"How did Nash tie Stricklyn and his bunch to it?" I asked.

"You mean the judge and all the other assholes?" Rose said. "He wouldn't say yet. We're still in 'Let's-Make-a-Deal' mode."

"Do you believe him?"

"Do you?"

I squinted at the window glare and felt the blood vessel in my temple begin to twitch.

"Will he testify?" I asked.

When I looked at Rose, his head was slowly moving up and down.

"When are you picking them up?"

"Tomorrow," he said. "I came here to ask you if you wanted to come along. Looks like your instincts might've been right after all."

I SPENT the remainder of that afternoon with Caleb Wheeler, Sam Griffin, Taj Caldwell, and Paul Tucker on my porch, drinking and watching the sun slide off the trees. I had an early appointment the next morning, but we passed that bottle of Kentucky whisky from hand to hand, remembering KC Sheridan, and telling stories about Jordan Powell. I could feel the better angels of my good judgment abandon me with every swallow. But I didn't let them stop me. Didn't even let them slow me down.

CHAPTER THIRTY-FIVE

I WALKED IN to Quentin Bahle's office unannounced, closed the office door behind me. Silver light was glinting off the river outside his window.

"You look almost as surprised to see me right now as you did the other morning at my office," I said. "Why is that?"

"I never got the chance to tell you how sorry I am about Mr. Sheridan and your deputy," he said. "How was the funeral?"

"Never should have happened."

"A tragedy, without a doubt. How is Mrs. Sheridan holding up?"

His tone was circumspect, unsettled, but somehow patronizing, and I recognized him in that moment for exactly what he had proved himself to be: A man who believed that the mere possession of a bar card cloaked him with superiority, acted as camouflage for moral incertitude, and compensated for an ordinary mind.

"You misunderstand my meaning," I said. "It never should have happened because you told me you made a deal with the feds for KC's safe passage."

"You're under a great deal of stress, Sheriff."

"A good man is dead because of you. Another one is in God's waiting room."

He shot out of his chair and leaned across his desk at me. A spherical paperweight made from Venetian glass rolled off the edge of his desk and landed on the carpet.

"Mr. Sheridan is dead," he said, "because mobs don't make laws in this country." The pitch of his voice seemed to have elevated by two octaves as he stabbed his index finger at me. "And men like Jarvis Lynch and his kind act as though they're making some noble stand for the cause of freedom by not paying their property tax bills. Grow up, Sheriff."

I hooked my thumbs on my gunbelt and stood to my full height.

"You're better than that, though, aren't you, Mr. Bahle," I said. "Because your involvement in any cause emanates from safely behind your little desk, dictating letters to the editor of your local paper. Or airing out your petty grievances among your peers around the clubhouse bar after an afternoon spent on the links."

"Mr. Sheridan should have sent his brother-in-law packing the day he showed up at his house."

"You're saying KC deserved what he got? And what about Jordan Powell? Powell is in a coma leaking blood out of his brainpan because he was sitting in the driver's seat of that truck. You thought I'd be sitting there. You thought I was supposed to drive KC that day. The bullet that put Powell in the hospital was meant for me."

"You need to leave, Sheriff."

Bahle picked up his telephone handset and began to dial. His eyelids began to quiver like a junkie on amphetamines, jacked to the gills.

"Put that phone down and speak to me like a man," I said.

He replaced the receiver with exaggerated care, struggling to maintain eye contact with me.

"The KC Sheridan I knew was a realist," I said. "He found idealism to be a pain in the ass."

"I represented the man. I think I know who he was."

"Do you attend services, Mr. Bahle?"

"Why would you ask me something like that?"

"Because you behave like someone in search of atonement."

"Atonement for what?"

"That's the question, isn't it?"

He slumped back into his chair, an expression of bemusement on his face.

"Have you always been a bully, Sheriff Dawson?"

I heard myself laugh out loud.

"Is that how you still see the world?" I asked. "Through the eyes of a help-less ten-year-old?"

"You're making my point for me," he said.

"Maybe it's not always about the other guy, Mr. Bahle. Maybe it's you. Maybe you bring this kind of damnation onto yourself. Maybe you're weak, and you give off an odor like raw meat to predatory animals."

"I suggest you take more care with your choice of words," he said. He had meant it as a threat, but we both recognized his statement as vain hyperbole.

"It's easy to think you hit a home run when you were born on third base," I said. "Painting yourself as a hero is growing tiresome. You need a new song, Bahle. In fact, you need a whole new band."

I picked up the glass orb that had fallen to the floor, placed it at the center of his desk blotter. I stepped across the room and opened Bahle's office door, held it that way so that Captain Rose and his two uniformed state troopers could move inside and slap the cuffs on Quentin Bahle.

I WAS leaning on the fender of a state police squad car, smoking a cigarette in the sunshine outside on the street, watching Chris Rose perp-walk Federal Court Judge Gerald Bonner out the front doors of the courthouse. When Bonner stepped within earshot, I began to whistle a tune familiar to anyone who knows the history of the Alamo.

"I offered you a chance for surrender with at least a shred of dignity attached," I said. "After this, your whole family is going to treat your name as a cautionary tale."

His eyes bored into mine, but there was nothing left behind them anymore. I would have found it pathetic, but this man was a grifter and a murderer. In my grandfather's day, they would have bounced him off the rafters of a barn and passed a whisky bottle while the body was still twitching.

An hour later, Rose found me at the same oyster bar where I had first met up with Lieutenant Benjamin Morgan. Rose took a stool beside me and ordered a dozen Netarts on the half-shell and stared blankly at the mirror on the wall behind the bar.

"That's a new one for me," Rose said. "A federal goddamn judge."

I made eye contact with him in the mirror. There was a network of crisscrossed lines across his forehead I had not noticed before.

"That judge conspired with KC Sheridan's attorney, colluded with Stricklyn, and lied outright to a federal agent," I said. "Judge Bonner might as well have pulled the trigger himself."

"They're putting him on suicide watch."

"Why bother? The man's a tumor."

"He's a federal judge, for chrissakes, Ty. At least, he used to be one."

"The asshole practically ordered the hit," I said. "Nash looked you in the face and told you that the judge had said KC wasn't turning himself in at all, that Sheridan was making a run for it. That was an outright lie that would result in only one outcome, and Bonner knew it."

The barman slid an iced plate of shelled oysters in front of Rose, took one look at the expression on his face, and walked away. Rose glanced down at the plate and pushed it to one side.

"Still," Rose said. "Suicide watch? That's some messed-up shit."

"Like I said: Why bother?"

"Nobody wants a judge offing himself on their watch. Not here. Not now."

And there it was.

The black cloud that hung over this city had nothing to do with weather. It was the headwind I'd been facing all along. Last year, six uniformed officers of the Portland Police Bureau had been killed in separate incidents, every one of them by gunfire. The last time even a single officer had been killed in that manner was nearly thirty-five years before, back in 1941. What did that tell you?

Add that to the legacy of corruption made so widely public by the Senate investigation, the current sociopolitical landscape felt like a flash fire poised and ready for ignition. The problem was that those who were the most corrupt of all were not only surviving, they were thriving, using the restive and anxious atmosphere to their advantage.

"Was that *Deguello* you were whistling when I came out with the judge?" Rose asked. "What the hell was that about?"

"Maybe it's time somebody actually hosed out the bowl," I said.

His eyes took on a faraway expression, the way they would when he pretended not to have heard something I said.

I DROVE by the Countess's condominium before I headed home. The street was so quiet I could hear the sound of ships' bells from the river, and I couldn't help but notice the absence of Morgan's surveillance team.

I followed Ivy Novack into the small room she used as an office. I took a seat and watched her open the draperies. She tossed her hair and angled her face to catch the light as she perched a hip on the low sill.

"Troopers arrested Judge Bonner and Quentin Bahle earlier today," I said. "I wanted you to know."

"And so it begins," she said.

"As you knew it would."

She turned to face me, but in the sun's glare, I could not make out her features, only her silhouette lined out against the glass.

"I didn't see my little surveillance shadows parked outside this morning," she said. "I should have known something was going down. Have they all gone home?"

I wrote down my phone numbers for her, both at the substation and the ranch.

"How much longer do I have?" she asked.

"Probably not long. You can come with me now, you know."

She held a long silence then turned her face to the view outside her window.

"No, but thank you, Sheriff. I don't believe I'm quite ready to leave yet."

CHAPTER THIRTY-SIX

THE ALARM CLOCK beside the bed said it was a little past four when I slipped out and crept into the kitchen to make coffee. I could tell that the barometer had dropped during the night, felt the damp chill that presaged the return of winter weather.

About the time I was spooning coffee grounds into the percolator, Caleb Wheeler was nearly two miles away, riding horseback across the cattle guard that marked the entrance to Amantes Camp. He was getting an early start, checking for breaks in the fence wire in preparation for rotating the herd down from the north pasture. He had been about to climb down from his mount to unchain the gate when he caught a movement in a clump of tall grass beside the cow path. He swung his gelding around and built a loop in his reata as he moved in the direction of the rustling he'd heard inside the undergrowth.

"If you're all the way out here this time of the morning," he called into the dark. "You're either lost or looking for trouble. If you ain't lost, then you found what you're looking for."

A male figure wearing a Navy peacoat, woolen watch cap, and ski gloves stepped out onto the dirt road with his hands raised over his head. The paleness of the exposed skin of his face appeared to glow beneath a moon whose light had begun to fade behind a skein of drifting cloud.

"I was looking for Sheriff Dawson," he said.

"Well, then you got two problems: You missed him by a long-damned ways, and I don't believe you anyhow."

"He knows me."

"That there is some grade-A bullshit, too, son. 'Cause if you knew him, you wouldn't be stumbling around all the way out here. Not to mention, as long as I've known the man, I don't recall him to have ever received a single visitor at this hour of the morning."

"I guess I kinda got turned around in the dark."

Caleb swung his loop and dropped it over the trespasser's head and shoulders. Wheeler's horse did what it'd been trained to do and backed up, took the slack out of the rope, and Caleb grinned while he watched the man fall to his knees in the loose dirt.

"You'd best try to keep up with me, boy," Wheeler said, and dallied the rope to his saddle horn. "This animal don't like to walk slow."

JESSE WAS still asleep when I got dressed and brought the cold dregs of my coffee to the kitchen and poured them down the sink drain. My wife had strung up wind chimes in the maple branches, and I poured myself a fresh mug and listened to their music decorate the breeze. I got lost in the sound momentarily, snapped out of it when I heard Caleb's pitched whistle coming from somewhere down near the snubbing pen.

I threw on my coat and jogged in the direction of the corral. I spotted Caleb astride his gelding in the gray light, and immediately recognized the narrow-shouldered city kid he'd snagged inside his catch rope.

"Tell me why I shouldn't shoot you in the legs and leave you for the coyotes," I said to the kid. I knew him only as Dan Halloran's confidential informant and found myself furious that he'd had the balls to show up at my door.

"That'd be murder," the kid answered.

"What it would be is sensible home security. I'm wondering why a drug dealer and a snitch is trespassing on my ranch. This is where I live, goddamnit. This is where my *family* lives. I'm wondering what possible good could come from you being all the way out here. Makes me wonder if you're by yourself. Makes me wonder who sent you. Makes me wonder how you got here. You got any answers for me? Let's start with your name. In all the time I've known you, I never once heard you say it."

"Want I should turn him loose, Ty?" Caleb asked me and spat a stream of tobacco juice into the dark.

"Not until he tells me his goddamn name."

"My name's Rick Bosworth, but people call me 'Bosco.'"

"I won't be doing that," I said.

I could see that he was filthy, his jeans and peacoat dotted with burrs and seedheads that had worked their way into his clothes. There was desperation in his eyes and the set of his jawline, something he had not shown in our previous encounters.

"Join me in the workshop once you've got your horse cooled out, Caleb," I said. "I don't want this piss-trumpet in our office, and I sure as hell don't want him in my house."

I took the reata from Caleb's hand and turned Rick Bosworth loose. I shoved him toward the workshop door, reached my arm inside, and switched on the overhead fixture. Though it wasn't bright, Bosworth blinked hard as it came on, and I pressed him into a seated position on a rusted metal folding chair. The air inside smelled of damp concrete and machine oil, but Rick Bosworth's odor overcame it. The stench of damp sweat and a funk like mold issued from his skin and his clothing. I threw open a sash window over the workbench and stood in the wash of cold wind.

"What are you doing on my ranch, Rick?"

"I had to bug out. Caught a ride with a log hauler. Guess I hopped out at the wrong spot."

"I don't need the whole travelogue," I said. "I asked what you're doing *here*."

"They're starting to freak out, man. They're gonna kill my ass."

"Who's gonna kill your ass?"

"Who the hell do you think, dude?"

I crossed the room in three steps, drilled my forefinger into the hollow of his throat.

"You will not address me in that manner," I said. "You're lucky my foreman didn't rope-drag you all the way out here and leave you tied up to the snubbing post. Answer my question."

"Vessey. Marcus Vessey."

"I thought you were Detective Wehr and Halloran's informant. That's what I thought because that's what you *told* me."

"I was."

By definition, snitches are untrustworthy and the information that they share is often tainted by their perception of what they think you want to hear. I had believed him when he'd first told me he was their CI; by extension, I had assumed that he was also being run by Lieutenant Morgan, though every one of Morgan's people denied it. Having just now been reminded that every player on the score-card was a liar, I found myself operating on my own again.

"Don't you get it, man?" Bosworth said. His eyes looked like something had popped loose behind their sockets, and his voice put me in mind of a rusted nail being pried out of a board. "If you screw with them, they can make one single phone call and convince people that you are the biggest threat to national security since Lee Harvey Oswald, the Weather Underground, and the SDS combined. You understand that, don't you?"

"You're suggesting that Marcus Vessey has that kind of stroke?" I said. "Hard to believe a man like him has any influence with anyone. I'm not convinced that Vessey could identify a golf ball inside a shoebox."

"It's shadow puppets, dude. Him and Stricklyn are connected way, way up the line."

"You need to start making sense, Rick."

Rick Bosworth startled when the hinges on the workshop door protested and Caleb stepped inside. Bosworth rotated his head slightly to keep Caleb in his peripheral vision.

"Don't look at me," Caleb said. "I ain't even here."

Bosworth complied and turned his eyes on me.

"At first, there were three of us," Bosworth said. "The Countess set us up with jobs, working for Marcus Vessey, but that all turned bad pretty fast."

"Ivy told me there were only two of you."

"She didn't know about Tanner. Me and Buzzy were introduced to him later, at Vessey's restaurant."

"What happened?"

"Buzzy got popped by the narcs; he was moving black tar on the northeast side. One thing led to another, and him and me both ended up working as rats for Detective Wehr."

"Reselling the dope he'd pinch from the dealers you'd snitch off," I added for him. "I've heard all this before."

Boswell shook his head, scratched at the matted hair beneath his wool cap. Even in the low light inside the shop, I could see that his skin was nearly as caked with dirt as his clothing was and that his eyes had a peculiar mien to them. Every word he uttered seemed to require great concentration.

"We didn't start moving police dope until way after that," he said. "That was mostly Halloran's deal anyway. I got the impression that something heavy was going down between them two."

Boswell was right about that.

I made a go-ahead gesture and lit a cigarette.

"Can I have one of those?" he asked.

"Maybe later," I said. "Talk first. What did you think was going on between Wehr and Halloran?"

"They would just say shit in passing. Plus, I know there was some unhappy days between them two and Vessey."

"Like what?"

"I don't know for sure. Those guys don't exactly confide in guys like me."

I turned and exhaled through the open window, the outline of the pines barely visible against the purple sky.

"Did Dan Halloran kill Clark Wehr?" I asked.

"Yeah."

"How do you know?"

"He bragged about it, man. Tried to use it to put the fear in Tanner, Buzz, and me."

"Why?"

"Why did he brag about it?"

I crossed the room and slapped him on the side of the head.

"Stop acting like a sausage," I said. "You came to me, Rick. Start being worth it."

"*Okay*. Shit. What was the question?"

"Why did Halloran kill Wehr?"

"I guess because of whatever was going down between them and Stricklyn and Vessey."

"We're talking in circles," I said.

"Well, I don't know, damnit!"

"Was it about the police dope?"

"Maybe," he said. "Or maybe it was porn, or prostitution, or any of that other shit they all were into."

"What other shit?"

"I don't know, man. Some kind of real estate thing."

There it was again. I squeezed the lit end off my cigarette and dropped the cold butt in a jar.

"You and Tanner are going to have to testify," I said.

"Testify? Like in court? Hell with that noise. They hammered Buzzy's kneecaps off and cut his tongue out. Plus, you heard what they did to Halloran, and *that* dude was police."

"Who's 'they'?"

"Can I have one of those cigarettes yet?"

I shook one from the box and lit it for him. He closed his eyes and inhaled like he had just come up from underwater.

"Who's 'they'?" I asked again.

"C'mon, man."

"You came out here expecting me to help you," I said. "What the hell would I do that for? You're not telling me a thing I hadn't already figured out for myself."

"Okay, shit," he said and blew smoke at the ceiling. "Vessey, okay? I mean, Vessey, Stricklyn, what's the difference? If Dean Stricklyn has a problem, Marcus Vessey makes it go away."

"And Halloran had become that kind of problem for him?"

"From what I heard, Stricklyn told Detective Halloran to clean up the Clark Wehr thing or Halloran was going feet-first in the chipper."

Which explained why Halloran did the murder at the fishing cabin in the first place. Wehr had wandered off the reservation somehow. Their solution had been Cop Suicide in a backwoods county policed by small-town law enforcement. It was supposed to have been simple.

"But you wouldn't play ball with them, Sheriff," Rick Bosworth said. "So Detective Halloran told Stricklyn he could shove the whole deal up his ass. Said he had something on Stricklyn he'd take straight to the state attorney general, and it was like, stalemate or something."

"I need to talk to your buddy Tanner," I said.

"Tanner's long gone, man. He split the minute he heard that Halloran went tits up."

"Where to?"

He shrugged and crushed his cigarette under the sole of a high-top tennis shoe. "Nevada maybe? Vegas?"

"What did Halloran have on Dean Stricklyn?"

"How would I know, man? I am strictly street level, dude."

"Find out."

"No way."

"I'm losing interest in this conversation," I said.

Bosworth looked at me and didn't blink. The expression on his face was so vacant that it seemed like he had suffered some kind of spasm that left his skin dead to the touch.

"Stricklyn meets with Vessey at the steakhouse every Tuesday night," Bosworth said.

"That's why you sent me there the first time."

"That was Halloran's idea, man. But you and the old man didn't stick around there long enough to see what you were supposed to see."

"Which was what?"

"I don't know, but Halloran was pissed."

"Do they know you're here with me right now?" I asked. "Vessey and Stricklyn?"

"Hell no. But they probably noticed by now that I ain't *there*."

"You've got to go back and find out what Halloran had on Dean Stricklyn. If you do, I might be able to help you out."

"No chance, man. I can't go back to the city. They'll skin me alive. Literally. I'm not kidding."

"You've been lying to me from the get-go, Rick," I said. "For all I know, they sent you here to keep jerking my chain. Maybe worse. Come back to me with something I can use and we'll talk about what I can do for you."

I saw Caleb's eyes shift out the window. The string of colored lights Jesse had hung along the eave of the gallery flickered on.

"The missus is awake," Caleb said.

"Looks like we're out of time, pard," I said.

For a moment, it looked like Bosworth was deflating.

"Just let me go, dude," he said. "I hitched down here. I can keep on hitchin' 'till I'm waaay gone."

Caleb was leaning in the doorframe, his arms folded across his chest, wagging his head at me.

"Drag Paul Tucker out of the rack," I said to Caleb. "Have him drive Mr. Bosworth back to the city and drop him off."

"You can't—" Bosworth said. But I cut him off.

"Caleb," I said, "you'd better tell Tucker he should play the radio real loud so he doesn't have to listen to this guy."

Bosworth attempted one final appeal as Caleb took hold of the kid's collar and pulled him up out of the chair.

"What'm I supposed to do?" Bosworth whined.

"The man already told you the answer to that," Caleb said.

"But, how?" Bosworth asked. "They'll kill me."

"That ain't my movie, son. I'm sure you'll figure something out."

CHAPTER THIRTY-SEVEN

LATER THAT MORNING, I was splitting a pile of bucked pine to use for fire-wood when Jesse stepped out on the backdoor landing and waved me inside. I dried the perspiration off my face, buried the blade of the long-handled axe in the stump, and went inside. The kitchen felt warm from the oven and smelled of jam and freshly baked powder biscuits. I took one from the cooling rack, and Jesse pointed at the telephone handset she'd placed on the table.

"It's Chris," Jesse whispered to me. "He sounds . . . off."

When I answered the phone, he asked whether I could meet him somewhere halfway between his office and mine.

"I know a café out on 159 that sells elk and buffalo burgers," I said.

"Little close to Jericho, isn't it?"

"Afraid they might throw something at you, Chris?"

"Not if you aren't."

I pulled off the highway about forty-five minutes later, but I didn't see Rose's unmarked Crown Vic in the pebbled lot. The "n" on the neon sign that was supposed to spell out "diner" had flickered out and seemed as though it should have been seen as an omen to someone.

On the opposite corner, a pair of flat-wheel train cars had been abandoned along a siding that ran parallel to the riverbank, on the edge of a thick stand of hemlock and alder that had rooted between the river and the tracks. One of the cars was an old tanker, streaked with rust along the top fitting and where the rivets had penetrated the shell; the other, a Gunderson box with a Santa Fe logo still visible on a wood frame that had rotted like a wine cork.

I took a seat at a window booth inside the café, ordered coffee from a heavyset woman of indeterminate age, and waited for the arrival of Captain Chris Rose.

"You ever feel like you spend your whole day pushing on strings?" Rose asked as he slid into the booth a few minutes later.

The waitress returned with a refill for my coffee, took one look at Rose's uniform, and studied him as if he was something she'd seen on the floor in a public washroom.

"Have you got chicken salad?" Rose asked her. "On wheat toast."

She turned away without writing anything down, and he touched her on the elbow to stop her.

"Coffee, too, while I wait for the sandwich," he said. "Please."

"What's up, Chris?" I asked when the waitress had gone.

He cast a glance over his shoulder, scanning the room before answering me.

"I didn't want to talk about this at the office," he said.

"Am I supposed to guess what it is?"

Outside the window, I saw Porter Brayfield touch the brakes as he drove by in his green-and-white county squad car. I was about to mention it to Rose, but Brayfield had already passed out of sight.

"I spoke with the Deputy IG this morning, Ty."

"Deputy Inspector General of what?"

"The United States Department of Justice."

"You might want to keep your voice down when you say words like those around here. Emotions are still running high."

Rose rearranged the paper napkin and silverware in front of him and looked as though he was rehearsing his next sentence in his head.

"They asked me not to release KC's autopsy results or the names of the FBI agents involved in the incident. Or *any* photos of the crime scene, particularly Jordan Powell's truck."

"They 'asked' you," I repeated.

"DOJ is filing felony charges against two of the agents for making false statements and obstruction."

"And nobody's identified the sniper?"

"Not yet."

"I think I'm going to throw up," I said. "And what about Oregon State Police? Are you pursuing the shooter?"

"Obstruction of justice carries a sentence up to twenty years, Ty. False statements are another five years on top of that."

"I'm not your priest, Chris. Sell it to somebody else."

Across the street, a low-slung project car pulled up to the pump at the gas island. A young man with a nimbus of curly blond hair got out of the front seat, leaned on his fender, and watched as the service station attendant checked under the hood.

"I asked you a question," I said. "What's your department going to do now?"

"I wanted to tell you about this in person," he said.

"What about Bahle and the federal judge?"

"What about them?"

"Tell me they're not getting off, too."

"Don't be an asshole."

"Those two killed KC for control of his ranch, plain and simple. If they get off, there's going to be hell to pay."

"Nobody's getting off, Ty."

"Lose the tone, Chris. You're looking at me as though that kind of thing never happens."

Outside, I saw Porter Brayfield drive by a second time. This time he pulled in behind the hot rod at the gas pump across the street and climbed out of his car. I watched the sheriff exchange words with the fuzzy-haired kid as they eyeballed Rose and me through the window of the café. Rose followed the direction of my gaze, and we stopped talking long enough to see Brayfield and the kid finish their conversation and drive away in opposite directions.

The waitress came back and delivered Rose the coffee he ordered. He was about to say something when she pushed a small plate of burned wheat toast beside his cup and saucer.

"I ordered a sandwich," Rose said.

"The owner don't want you to stay in here that long, trooper," she said. "The coffee's on the house, but the toast is gonna be a buck. You can pay at the register on your way out the door."

He watched her walk away, then shook his head.

"I'm just the messenger, Ty."

"You insult both of us when you say things like that."

I slid out of the booth, took three dollars from my billfold, and laid them on the glass counter, next to the register. Once outside, I put on my sunglasses and looked up and down the street for any sign of Brayfield or the hot rod, but the street was empty. Farther beyond, the patches of sunlight on the hillsides had faded and moved westward as the wind pushed the clouds toward the coastline.

"I guess the folks around here need a little more time to shake it off," Rose said as he followed me outside.

"Can you blame them?"

MY WRANGLER, Paul Tucker, was washing his truck in my driveway when I returned from my lunch meeting with Rose. I hopped across a stream of soapy water and made my way to the back door.

"Hope you don't mind," Tucker said. "The hose bib at the barn is busted. Miz Jesse said it would be alright if I used yours."

"Tell me what I owe you for gas," I said.

"You don't owe me nothing for that, boss."

"Here's ten bucks anyways."

"Much obliged," he said. "Tell you what, though. I'd like to scrape my ears out with a bottle brush."

"You should've played the radio like I suggested."

I turned to walk inside, but what he said next stopped me cold.

"Is it true what he told me about the mayor and that little girl?"

"What did you just ask me?" I said.

JESSE WAS in the mudroom, weaving a holiday wreath from willow stems she'd cut, when I came in the back door. I kissed her on the forehead and moved toward the kitchen.

"Where are you going?" she asked.

"Out to the office. I need to make a phone call."

"We've got a phone right there on the wall."

I ranged my eyes outside the window, saw Paul Tucker rolling up the garden hose. He was humming a tune I'd heard before but didn't know the name of.

"It's not that kind of call," I said.

I didn't wait to see Jesse's reaction.

"WE'VE GOT a problem," I said.

"I don't like the sound of words like that," Ivy Novack said.

There was a lightness in her tone that offended me at a level I didn't even understand. I could picture her perched on the windowsill in her office as she spoke to me, gazing out across the courtyard garden, tilting her face to the warmth of the sun, enveloped in scents of vanilla and lemongrass, every aspect a fantasy and façade.

"One of my cowboys heard something from Rick Bosworth that I found extremely disturbing."

"Ricky's one of my girls' baby brother," she said. "I told you all about him, remember?"

"I lost a friend to murder a few days ago," I said. "And a deputy of mine is in a traumatic coma and may die too. My friend was a seventy-two-year-old rancher who was shot through the throat while he was minding his own business in an idling vehicle. The deputy just celebrated his twenty-fifth birthday and was engaged to be married soon. He survived two combat tours in Vietnam, only to be taken down by sniper fire right here in south Oregon. I believe the man who pulled the trigger was an agent of our own federal government."

I could tell by Ivy Novack's silence that she didn't know how to respond, that the oblique nature of my statement had confused her.

"The greed and psychopathy that infects the souls of men like Halloran, Stricklyn, and Vessey is contagious. Those men contracted the infection from somebody else. I want to know who it is."

"Honey," Ivy said. "You need to slow down. I don't understand what you're saying to me."

"What do you know about the mayor and a little girl?"

I thought I heard her breath catch. I waited, but nothing else came.

"You told me you'd level with me, Ivy. That was our deal."

"I don't trade in children," she said. "Everything I've told you has been the truth, things that I've seen with my own eyes."

"We're way past that now."

I waited through a very long silence.

"There's a party house down by the river," she said. "Invitation only. I keep the bar stocked, keep the sheets clean, but I don't run my girls out of there anymore."

"Why not?"

"It turned into rough trade," she said. "Then they wanted younger girls. Very young. Dean and Marcus handle the entertainment personally now."

"You told me Marcus Vessey was a rapist and a bagman for Dean Stricklyn. You never said anything about *this* before."

"Marcus Vessey is something you scrape off your shoe. They say he pirates girls off the kiddie stroll. Twelve, thirteen years old. Most of them are never seen again."

"Who does Vessey do this for?"

"I told you, I just handle the housekeeping."

"Who else besides the mayor?"

"I don't know. I've never seen it with my own eyes. I've only heard about it."

"Who's on the guest list, Ivy?"

"You promised you'd get me out of here, Sheriff. You gave me your word."

"And you gave me yours," I said. "Where is this party house, and who's on the goddamned list?"

CHAPTER THIRTY-EIGHT

ANYONE WHO HAS spent much time outdoors will confirm that there are certain noises produced by nature that can incapacitate a human being with paralytic terror. Ask a fireman, a cop, or a veteran of warfare, and they will tell you that among the worst of these is the cry of a human being in the throes of agony. It was this sound that awakened the residents of Creekshale Condominiums at approximately 2:15 the next morning.

About that same time, the snow began to fall, and two armed men dragged a hogtied Rick "Bosco" Bosworth out of the trunk of a 1930s Ford coupe that had been painted in purple metallic and customized as a street rod. Using a passkey in their possession, the pair of armed men manhandled Bosworth past an iron security gate and into the center courtyard of the Creekshale, four stories beneath Ivy Novack's window.

The two men fit a length of plastic surgical tubing onto a stemmed funnel, then force-fed nearly a quart of premium-grade gasoline down Rick Bosworth's throat and dropped a lighted kitchen match into his mouth.

AT 2:19 that same morning, my bedside phone began to ring. I reached out in the dark and knocked it off the nightstand. I groped blindly until I found it on the carpet and sat on the edge of the mattress as Jesse switched on the bedside lamp. Between the bedroom curtains I could see the falling snow.

Ivy Novack was panicked to a point nearing hysterics as she tried to explain to me what was happening in the courtyard of her building.

"Lock your doors and windows and stay inside until I get there," I said. "Don't speak to a soul."

"Jesus Christ," she said, "his clothes are still burning, Ty."

I could clearly hear the screaming in the background on her end, could hear her panting as she moved across the room.

"Stay put," I said again. "I'm on my way. Don't talk to anybody. Not the police, nobody, until I come for you. Tell me you understand."

"I can hear sirens."

"Repeat what I just said to you, Ivy."

Someone on her end began speaking to her and she covered up the mouthpiece, then came back on the line a moment later.

"We've still got a couple customers here," she told me.

"Get them out and lock the door behind them. Do it now, before the fire department and the cops arrive."

"What about my girls?"

"They can do whatever they want," I said. "But they have to do it right now. You've got about three or four minutes before the cops get there, maybe fewer."

"Okay," she said and sounded as though she might have recovered some of her composure.

If I knew who to trust in the PPB, I would have sent them to collect Ivy. As things stood, the only choice left to me was to go get her myself.

"You wait for me there, Ivy. Doors and windows locked. Don't answer for anybody except me. Tell me you understand."

To her credit, she repeated every word I said.

"WHO'S IVY?" Jesse asked as I threw on my clothes.

"The madam of a Portland brothel," I said. "I need you to make up the spare room, Jesse. Ivy's likely to be staying with us for a while."

"Excuse me?"

"I'm taking Caleb and Griffin with me, Jesse. The Winchester's in the mudroom and your pistol's in the nightstand. Keep them close to you until I get back."

CHAPTER THIRTY-NINE

THE DETECTIVES slow-clapped me as I walked through the bullpen at PPB Vice and Narcotics, their special ritual for expressing contempt at my unwillingness to lie to protect Halloran, Wehr, Quentin Bahle, or Judge Bonner, or anyone else in this town. A blue cloud of tobacco smoke floated below a ceiling stained by ancient water leaks and peeling plaster, and the phones rang unabated until I passed through the entire length of the room.

"Well, look who's here," Lieutenant Morgan said as I stepped into his office. "You've been a busy fella."

He had just hung up his telephone, and he cocked his head sideways at me.

"Lean on in real close and get a good peek, Dawson," he said. "Tell me: Do I still have an ear? I only ask because during the past half hour, I've had three different people try to chew that sonofabitch right off my head."

"You'd think the power structure would be pleased to learn that bad actors have been taken off the field."

"You'd think that, wouldn't you?"

I moved further inside his office, tipped the door shut, and heard the latch engage as I forced it all the way into the frame.

"What the hell is that smell?" he asked. "Honest to god, it smells like burnt hair."

"I'm aware that you've been playing me since the day we met," I said. "Pointed me at people and places you didn't want to go to yourself. But I'm not going to dwell on that right now."

The flippancy dropped away from his expression, and he looked at me as if I had just materialized from an alternate dimension.

"What is it that you want, Dawson?"

The metal hinge beneath his chair protested as he leaned forward and leaned his forearms across his desk blotter.

"Let me guess," Morgan said. "This is the part where you say 'jump'?"

"Yep."

I HAD sent Ivy back to the ranch with Caleb and kept Sam Griffin in Portland with me. Sam and I had gone over the setup, and now it was all about the waiting. We were seated in the cab of my pickup, partially hidden by a rubbish enclosure at the far corner of the Stumptown Chophouse parking lot.

"Nobody comes in after I clear the place out, understood?" I said. "Nobody."

"Roger that."

Griffin's voice was monotone as he gazed out through the windshield.

"Get 'em in their cars and get 'em gone," I said.

"Shouldn't take long, Sheriff. There's, like, three cars parked out here."

"I'm just making sure you're clear on this."

"Are you alright, sir? We've gone over it a half dozen times. I got it."

Griffin kicked his hat off of his forehead with a knuckle, turned, and looked at me.

"Due respect," he said, "do I have to get out and take a walk to get you to stop talking about this thing?"

Neither of us spoke for a long while, each of us lost in our own thoughts, double checking radio equipment and firearms, and waiting for dusk to fall. I don't know where Sam Griffin's mind wandered off to, but I know where mine went.

On top of orchestrating the murders of Rick Bosworth and Clark Wehr, and perhaps even KC Sheridan, it turns out that Dean Stricklyn and Marcus Vessey had been jayhawking little girls for the local elite and their guests for years. I knew this because Ivy Novack had been asked by Stricklyn to run the operation for him at first, though she'd drawn the line and refused outright. But there was something else I knew now, too.

As any cop will tell you, every bookie has a book; every escort, call girl, and madam has one, too, as does every shakedown artist, badger operator, and blackmailer in the history of mankind. I now knew that Dean Stricklyn kept *his* book in a vault-quality, dual-key, bolt-down Sentry safe in the upstairs office at the Stumptown Chophouse. It contained the name of every customer and client that Stricklyn had ever pimped for. I now knew this because of Ivy Novack.

"You still good?" I asked Griffin.

"Aces," Sam said.

We had a decent sight angle on both the front and side entrances of the restaurant, but there had been no sign of Marcus Vessey's purple street rod until the night had fallen nearly into full darkness. Snow had been coming down lightly, though constantly, all day long, and Vessey's tires carved dirty scars through the whiteness of the lot.

Thirty minutes later, Dean Stricklyn pulled his Cadillac Eldorado into a spot marked "reserved" nearest the doorway. He angled his chin to catch the shimmering glow of the neon sign on the restaurant and checked his appearance in his rearview.

Sam and I gave the two of them another twenty minutes to settle in before we slid out of the truck. Sam angled off across the lot and took up a position within a few strides of the main entrance. I ducked in through the back door, the one meant for deliveries and restaurant personnel, moved down a narrow hall past an employee break room, and stepped into the kitchen. Six men dressed in a varied assortment of chefs' attire worked at the grills and flattop, stirring the contents of simmering crock pots inside a cramped prep space that easily topped eighty-five degrees.

The head chef's eyes went wide when he saw me standing in the archway, but

I put a forefinger to my lips, peeled open the front of my duster, and displayed the badge clipped to the gunbelt at my waist.

"Everybody out," I said in a tone barely loud enough to be heard over the clatter of the oscillating fans that had been bolted to the ceiling. "I don't want to hear a word. Get in your cars and drive away. Do it now."

It took a moment for the kitchen staff to process what I said, so I began to herd them down the same hall I'd just entered through. The last man hesitated for a brief moment before crossing the threshold, and I shook my head.

"Do not come back here," I said. "Not tonight. Maybe not ever. Do we understand one another?"

The kitchen smelled strongly of sautéing prawns and meat drippings and the metallic odor of superheated cast iron skillets on the flame broiler. I left everything as it was, moved between the push-doors toward the lounge, could hear piano music behind the partition drapes that marked the end of a short corridor.

I shouldered through the opening between the drapes and moved swiftly to the bar. A silver-haired man wearing a shiny suit was playing Ellington at a piano on the riser a short distance from the rail. A bored-looking bartender with a nose that suggested he'd done time in the ring was paring his fingernails with a penknife behind the stick. The place was nearly empty, one couple at a horseshoe booth in the back corner of the bar, and two more tables near the window in the dining room being served by a lone elderly waiter.

The bartender was the first to notice me. He took one look and reached for the counter beneath the register, but halted when I shook my head and showed him the Colt Peacemaker at my side.

"Don't do it," I said.

"What the fu—"

"You're closed," I said. "Get out of here now and take all these people with you."

I kept one hand free, the other resting on the butt of the Colt as I watched the bartender duck beneath the hinged board. He whispered something to the piano player and stepped into the dining room to announce that everyone needed to leave.

I watched him herd all six customers and the geriatric waiter toward the door, the piano player making for the rear entrance instead.

"Use the front like everybody else," I told him.

He froze in his tracks and complied, muttering to himself as he moved away.

The bartender was the last one to leave the building, halfway out the door before he stopped and turned to look at me.

"Where're Stricklyn and Vessey?" I asked before he could say anything.

"Upstairs. In the office. I hope you understand what you've just done to yourself, pal."

I waited for the door to swing shut behind him, noticed the gray smoke that had begun to drift out from the kitchen.

I weaved between the abandoned tables to the front door and locked it from inside, caught a glimpse of Sam Griffin in the parking lot, watching the departure of last of the vehicles.

The air inside the lounge had already grown acrid, stinging my eyes as I made my way back to the bar. I reached behind the counter and groped along the shelf beneath the register, the one the bored bartender had instinctively reached for. My fingers discovered the weapons I suspected would be hidden there, a ball bat tucked up beside a blue-barreled revolver whose butt had been wrapped in duct tape.

The smoke had grown noticeably heavier as I slid the revolver into my coat pocket. I grabbed the ball bat, scanned through the haze to the ceiling, confirmed what I had been led to expect. No fire sprinklers. I glanced at my watch. Fewer than four minutes had passed since I'd first entered the kitchen, but I could feel the heat steadily rising.

In a near corner of the dining room, a pair of security doors marked a restricted stairway that led upstairs to a private banquet space and to the office from which Marcus Vessey oversaw the less savory elements of Dean Stricklyn's businesses. I propped the bat against the wall beside the doors, drew my sidearm, and pushed through, took the stairs two at a time.

I paused when I reached the landing, looked to my left, and saw the office door was shut. I stepped up close and clearly heard two male voices inside, engaged in an animated discussion. I couldn't make out the words, but the tone was unmistakable.

I twisted the handle, shoved the door inward, and leveled the Peacemaker at Vessey's forehead as I advanced on him. Vessey had been standing behind his desk, gesturing broadly as he shouted at Stricklyn, who was seated on a sofa against the adjacent wall.

"What the hell is this now?" Vessey said. "You gotta be goddamn kidding me."

I took one final stride toward his desk.

It had been a while since Vessey had worn a state-issued jumpsuit, but the tale that the yard left on his features was as conspicuous as it was undeniable. He glanced between Stricklyn and me, his profile like a wingnut. I would have recognized that silhouette anywhere.

"You're the cowboy," Vessey said to me.

"That's a fact," I said.

He feinted for the pistol he kept tucked into the small of his back, but he froze when he heard me thumb the Colt's hammer.

"If you think you can air out that weapon before I squeeze this trigger," I said. "I'd like to see you give it a go."

He hesitated, but I could see it in his face.

He went for it, but he never got the chance to draw. I fired a slug that came so close to Vessey's ear that I am sure he felt the slipstream just before it blew a hole in the damask wallpaper beside his head.

Stricklyn uncrossed his legs and raised both of his hands without my having asked, but didn't bother moving from the sofa.

I nodded at Vessey, and he raised his hands, too.

"Are you out of your mind, Dawson?" Stricklyn said. "You're a dead man."

Stricklyn was wearing a peach-colored leisure suit, his hair combed straight back off his forehead. His surgically scarred lip twisted itself into an angry pout for a moment, then forced his expression into one resembling indifference. He leaned himself into the sofa, spread his arms along the back cushions.

"Toss your weapons out that door," I said.

Vessey plucked the automatic from his waistband with two fingers, pitched it out through the office doorway and onto the landing.

"Ankle holster, too," I said to Vessey, and watched him lob that gun out to the landing as well.

I glanced at Stricklyn, who responded by peeling open the lapels of his jacket.

"I don't carry a gun," he said.

Men like Stricklyn expected other men to do their heavy lifting for them.

"Of course you don't," I said, but gave him a quick pat down anyway.

"I smell smoke," Stricklyn said.

"By now, you probably smell fire," I said. "The kitchen staff may have left the burners unattended."

"What the hell?"

"I assumed you guys liked fire," I said. "I saw the work you did on Rick Bosworth. Ugly business."

The safe was exactly where Ivy had told me it would be, though I was surprised to see that the door was swung out on its hinges and had been left partially open. I covered both men with the Peacemaker as I sidestepped toward the box, used my foot to wrest the door out all the way.

I kept the two men at the center of my focus, but in my peripheral vision I could see at least two dozen packets of banded currency stacked up inside, though I could make out little else. It wasn't a large vault, barely bigger than a television set, but it was deep, and I figured there had to be at least a half million in cash inside. I didn't want to take my eyes off either man for long, even if to get a better look.

"Just take the goddamn money and go," Stricklyn said. "You won't live to see breakfast, asshole."

"I don't want your money," I said. "I want your book."

Smoke had begun to drift up through the floor vents, and I could tell that Stricklyn was beginning to worry, saw his chest rise and fall as he glared at me with an expression that now mingled equal parts fear and antipathy.

"Where's the book?" I said.

"Bite me," Stricklyn answered.

I squeezed the Peacemaker's trigger and a copper jacketed round passed beneath his seat cushion and lodged deep inside the sofa frame. It seemed unnaturally quiet during the moment that it took for him to register how close he'd come to taking a round between his legs. Stricklyn broke loose with an involuntary shriek that sounded like a locomotive with its wheels locked up tight, kicking sparks on the downside of a grade.

"First one's free," I said. "The next one's gonna hurt."

I kept the Colt trained on Stricklyn as I dipped my free hand into my coat pocket and withdrew the bartender's revolver, drew a bead on Vessey's crotch.

"I want you to know I'm a dead shot with both hands," I said. "I've got trophies on my shelf to prove it."

Vessey's eyes locked onto my face.

"Your turn," I said. "Where's the book, Vessey?"

He didn't hesitate.

"Top shelf," he answered.

I knelt at the door of the safe, laid the bartender's gun on the floor between my feet, the Peacemaker firmly in my fist. I groped around inside the box until my fingertips felt the spine of a bound volume that felt to be about two inches thick. I took hold of it, stood, and kicked shut the safe door. I spun the combination knob and tested the lever to make sure it was locked and latched.

Stricklyn's face was twitching involuntarily, like a fish left out to die on a dry wharf.

"You look as though you just discovered you're a real boy, Stricklyn," I said.

I glanced at Vessey, but he only glared back at me, the shadow never having left his eyes.

"I understand it takes two keys and the dial combination to open that safe again," I said. "I'm told that each of you carries a key on his person. On a chain around your neck. Take them off and toss them out the door."

I stole a glance at the wall clock while they did as I had instructed. I hadn't been inside the office that long, but I could feel the building beginning to consume itself.

"Do you know who writes history books?" I asked. "Survivors."

I could feel the heat rising, radiating from the walls and the floor joists. It wouldn't be long before it imploded.

"I suspect only one of you knows the safe combination," I said. "That puts the other at a bit of a disadvantage, doesn't it?"

"You're dead, Dawson," Vessey said.

I thumbed the hammer and kept the bead on the tip of Stricklyn's nose.

"We'll see."

The odor of combusting wood, textiles, and plastic was growing thicker, black clouds collecting in the stairwell.

"You two are going to have a choice to make in about a minute," I said. "You can either follow me out of here right goddamned quick, or you can try to collect your keys and clean out that safe before trying to save yourselves. My guess is neither of you is smart enough to leave it behind."

I backed slowly toward the office door, kept Stricklyn squared up in the Colt's sights.

"I'll leave your guns out on the landing," I said. "If that makes your decision any easier for you."

I watched their eyes peel off of me to take measure of one another. I felt something structural give way somewhere beneath my feet and backed more quickly out the door.

True to my word, I left their firearms where they'd landed, expecting the men to turn their guns on each other before they'd have the chance to use them on me. I knew that a half million in cash was too much for them to leave behind.

I felt my way down the smoke-filled stairwell, the surface of the walls having grown hot to the touch. I was moving more by sense now than sight, but clearly heard a scuffle break out above me as I reached the foot of the stairs. I shouldered through the security doors and fell into the restaurant dining room, where the air had begun pulsating with heat.

I blinked against the conflagration, could barely draw breath, reached blindly to where I'd propped the ball bat, and finally got a hand on the grip. I cast a glance over my shoulder, judged the distance to the front door.

I had time enough for one last calculation, one final judgment that had far more to do with the man I was prepared to be from that moment onward than the man that I had been up to now. I hefted that bat and considered sliding it between the U-shaped handles of those security doors, barricading Stricklyn and Vessey inside and leaving them to the agonizing death they both deserved; a singular decision, a private bargain that carried with it the knowledge that I hadn't shied when it had fallen to me to stack the deck.

But I didn't.

I dropped the bat onto the floor, drew my duster up over my nose and mouth, and raced through a cavern of roiling smoke and flame. Seconds later, I reached the entrance, wrapped my hand in a bandanna, threw the bolt, and fell out through the opening and into the cold.

IT WAS at least fifteen minutes later, likely more, before the fire department arrived at the scene, owing to a combination of factors that might have included road conditions. In this part of town, response times could be difficult to predict even in the best of weather.

"You alright, Sheriff?" Griffin asked.

"Aces," I coughed.

I breathed frigid air into my lungs and spat black ash and soot into the snow.

"Do you know how it went with Lieutenant Morgan?" I asked Sam Griffin.

"His teams grabbed all of 'em up. Everybody you told him to pick up, anyway."

"Even Overton?"

Griffin nodded, and I saw the flames reflected in his irises.

We were standing side by side in the empty parking lot, leaning on the grille of my pickup when the Stumptown Chophouse finally caved in on itself. A bloom of glowing embers rose into the night sky, rising past the falling snowflakes as they drifted to earth.

PART SIX

WAKE OF THE FLOOD

CHAPTER FORTY

I SAT IN the passenger seat and read through the ledger I'd liberated from Stricklyn's safe while Sam drove us home that night. He waited until I had finished reading before he filled me in on what he'd learned about the arrests Morgan's team had made.

"What are we supposed to say about it?" Griffin asked me. "To the press, I mean."

"About the mayor and the little girls? Not a goddamned word. That's Morgan's collar to grandstand."

"You know they're gonna call us and ask," Griffin persisted. "The mayor and deputy chief of police taken down on the same night? Damn."

I watched the mileposts tick by in the wash of our headlights.

"He don't know everything, does he?" Griffin asked a few minutes later. "He doesn't know why you told him do it."

"Are you referring to Lieutenant Morgan?" I said. "I'm guessing Morgan would have gladly arrested DC Overton just so he could use his office furniture."

"There's gonna be a crap storm in the paper."

"There'd better be."

Griffin dropped me at the substation, grabbed his own keys off the hook on the wall, and went home to bed. I had declined his offer to spell me at the Xerox machine while I copied Stricklyn's ledger, reading every page again as I went along. Every single entry, every single transaction, every name, and every date, the whole repulsive story laid out line by line.

I BROUGHT the book to Captain Rose's office first thing the next morning, strode past his secretary and straight into his office as he sipped his morning coffee.

"This is where we are now, you and me?" Rose said. "No pretense of manners or decorum whatsoever?"

"You can have this," I said. "But you've got to help me finish something."

I placed the ledger at the center of his desk, moved to his office window, and waited while Rose looked it over.

"Care to tell me what the hell this is?"

I closed his office door before I told him.

"You'll find connections to your case involving the feds, KC, and Jordan Powell," I said. "It won't take you long to see the pattern."

"Where'd you get it?"

"A friend of mine told me where I'd find it."

"Jesus," Rose said, and began to massage his temple.

IN THE days following the arrests of the mayor and Deputy Chief Overton, PPB thought they might finally have purged the last remnants of the scandal and corruption that had plagued the bureau for decades, that maybe the city could finally wash its hands of the public humiliation that had all begun with the Senate hearings a decade before. Better still, they now had a poster boy to carry the banner for them in the form of Lieutenant Benjamin Morgan, head of the Special Investigations Division.

For those reasons, and the fact that Morgan smelled promotion in the air, the atmosphere inside the SID bullpen had improved markedly since the last time I had come to see the lieutenant. This time around, I was largely ignored by the detectives in the squad room, not even a single slow clap. Morgan himself even greeted me with a begrudging kind of gratitude when I stepped into his office, though I could tell he still nursed a wish that he'd left work early on the day we first met.

"Not for nothing," Morgan said, "but I thought you and I had concluded our business."

"I suspect we're almost finished. There're just a couple things nagging at me, though. Burrs under my saddle. You familiar with that expression?"

I saw his eyes wander to the key-clock on his credenza.

"What's on your mind?" he asked.

"Why didn't you ever set up surveillance on the Chophouse?"

"What kind of question is that?"

"I'm curious is all. You staked out the Countess's place for weeks but never Stricklyn's restaurant? It gives me pause."

"It gives you 'pause'?"

"Sure does."

Morgan leaned back in his chair, threaded his fingers behind his head, seeking signs of my personal agenda.

"I wouldn't want to vex you, Dawson," he said finally. "I'll tell you why not: Because walking in and out of a steak restaurant isn't illegal."

"Neither is walking in and out of a condominium building."

"Maybe not," he said. "But you've probably never had anything to lose in your life if you're not acquainted with The Squeeze."

"You're talking about extortion," I said. "You've been shaking down Ivy Novack *and* Stricklyn this whole goddamn time?"

"Now, that's an ugly term," he said. "What I'm talking about is nuance. Insinuation. The fear of revelation and reprisal."

"Do you hear some kind of difference between that and what I said?" I asked. "Do you make eye contact with the mirror when you shave in the morning?"

"Oh, wise the hell up, Dawson. It's The Squeeze, baby. It makes people behave differently than they might otherwise, that's all. Nobody gets hurt. Nobody decent, anyway."

"And Bosco Bosworth? What about him?"

Morgan leaned forward and sized me up again.

"Are you new to this planet?" he said. "That kid was a confidential informant. A snitch. He was dead from the moment he met Clark Wehr."

"It doesn't trouble you, the way he died?"

"They eat their own young out there," he said and gestured vaguely outside the precinct walls. "Far as I'm concerned, it was a public service homicide."

"I used to think I respected you."

"I'll miss that when I'm Deputy Chief."

I watched him smile to himself. I wondered if you could feel the sensation as it was happening, as you sold off your humanity piece by piece.

"Want to step on out in the hall with me for a minute?" I asked.

"What for?"

"A friend of mine would like a private word with you."

Chris Rose and two uniformed state troopers were waiting in the hallway for Morgan, with cuffs and a recitation of Miranda.

"What's this, one of those TV prank deals?" Morgan asked.

I pulled open the front of my shirt, gave Morgan a look between the buttons at the tiny microphone taped to my chest.

"No, Lieutenant," I said. "I don't believe anybody's going to find much amusement in this."

JESSE AND I had dinner with Ivy Novack at the Gold Hotel that night. To my surprise, Ivy and Jesse had developed an unusual sort of friendship during the week or so that the Countess had been staying at our home. Once I'd convinced myself that the physical danger to Ivy had been contained, and that she wouldn't hare-out on me and disappear when it came time for her to testify, I agreed to let her move out of the spare room.

She set up temporary quarters in the penthouse suite at the Gold Hotel, using her free time to read novels, take long walks, and even allowed my ranch hand, Paul Tucker, to teach her how to fly fish. Part of the agreement between us was that she'd use the nest egg she had set aside to get herself out of the city and to get herself out of the life. She promised me she would, and I believed her. Ivy had set her sights on opening a clothing boutique somewhere in southern California, and she'd made arrangements to depart the next morning.

Jesse and Ivy shared a bottle of pinot noir between the two of them that night, and I shared my private introspections with Mr. Jim Beam. There had been no sign of snowfall since the night the Chophouse burned down, the days clear and bright with winter sunshine, and the night skies dusted with stars that seemed so near to hand that you could use them to construct a pathway to the moon.

That night we didn't speak of the people who had delivered such misery and grief to our lives, though we did lift our glasses to the memories of the ones we had known, loved, and lost.

But a part of me still dwelt among other ghosts.

It would take months, perhaps years, to build the cases against the ranks of the accused, and even longer for the trials to begin. I intended to see that every one of them was held accountable.

Firefighters located the charred remains of Dean Stricklyn and Marcus Vessey in the Chophouse rubble. The coroner determined that both men had suffered gunshot wounds before having succumbed to the smoke. The safe itself had been damaged nearly beyond recognition.

When last I heard, Lieutenant Morgan and several of Stricklyn's law practice clients had been tripping over themselves trying to make deals to turn state's evidence with anyone possessing the authority to minimize the time they would inevitably spend in Crossbar College. Turns out that Dean Stricklyn had convinced a number of his deep-pocket clientele—and those of his law partners—that he could help them make some very fast cash. Deal was, if you let him have fifteen or twenty thousand dollars for a couple weeks, Stricklyn would double your money, with Lieutenant Morgan running protection for the entire scheme. Stricklyn's investors claimed that they never asked him how he did it, which was unabashed horseshit, of course, but it was easy to see how the whole racket could mushroom.

In a matter of a few months, Stricklyn had become one of the largest financiers of heroin traffic on the west coast. And mushroom it did, at least until Wehr and Halloran climbed aboard and started ripping off competing dealers to clear the playing field for Stricklyn. The dealers began snitching-off one another, and then the cops took over. Which was great for a while, but Wehr was becoming a liability. Stricklyn and his pals, detectives Halloran and Wehr among them, had set out on a white-collar path, a chance to make millions in a single score, hijacking KC Sheridan's ranch. But Wehr got dollar signs in his eyes and made the mistake of expressing his desire to retire, to move down to Florida with the Countess so they could live happily ever after.

With only so many jailhouse deals to go around, it remains to be seen which one of them turns out to be the biggest rat. What I do know for sure is that they represented only the tip of the iceberg.

The book I had turned over to Chris Rose had led to thirteen additional arrests, so far, of prominent private citizens as well as politicians. Each of them had ties to one another and, most frightening of all, had the willingness to exchange favors that were merely extortion dressed up in nicer clothes.

As for the murder of KC Sheridan, Quentin Bahle fingered Judge Bonner for the setup, Bonner subsequently pointed upstream to a deputy in the AG's office, and the Deputy AG was pointing back at Stricklyn. The most alarming aspect of it: the blithe and cavalier attitudes each one maintained toward the outcome of their actions.

The killing had been arranged with the simplicity of a string of phone calls, in exactly the same manner as when Rose had been ordered to stand down. At Stricklyn's direction, Judge Bonner and Quentin Bahle conspired to tell KC and me that they had reached a deal for KC to turn himself in. As KC was preparing to leave his house, Judge Bonner made a second call, this one to Special Agent Nash, informing him the deal had blown up, and that KC and I were armed and dangerous, with plans to run the blockade and turn KC Sheridan into a martyr for the cause. Suicide by fed. The bonus in the scheme being that I would be sitting in the driver's seat.

But I wasn't in the driver's seat that morning. Powell was.

Judge Bonner remains on suicide watch.

It is my sincere desire that someone on the judge's guard detail falls soundly asleep. Failing that, I will look forward to Bonner's evisceration in the courtroom. The details in the ledger I recovered from the safe should take care of that.

We still don't know what will happen to Special Agent Nash or the men who actually squeezed the triggers on KC and Jordan Powell. The feds will fill us in when they're damn good and ready. But that's not how it works in Meriwether County. I'm still on the case, and I'm not going anywhere.

The mayor and DC Overton have been transferred to protective custody due to the nature of their charges. Pedophiles and child-killers have a short life expectancy inside. In the hierarchy of inmate society, those men had targets on their backs that would never disappear, nor would they ever be completely safe from harm. It is my belief that such matters end up taking care of themselves, and I lose no sleep over either man's fate.

I poured the last of the pinot for Jesse and Ivy, swirled the whisky and ice at the bottom of my glass, and watched the two of them bring a précis to an unlikely acquaintance. Outside the arched dining room window, a deer grazed on the lawn, raised her head to look at me before she moved out of the light.

My mind wandered back to KC Sheridan and the morning I had met him on the rise overlooking his reservoir.

The whole thing had begun as a simple land grab, perpetrated by men who simply wanted to take it from him and who believed they could get away with doing so. Resistance in any form was never really considered to be much of a threat to them.

But resistance did appear, and when it did, avarice, iniquity, and political ambition arrived as coconspirators, and not only cost a good man his life but rippled through the community at large, leaving Hemmings County to bear the twin scars of mistrust and animosity, and ravaging deeply rooted personal allegiances that will likely never be repaired.

"I loved that man," Ivy Novack said. "I really did. I don't know why."

She was speaking about Clark Wehr, and I didn't know how to interpret Jesse's agreement with Ivy's statement.

We said our goodbyes in the lobby, and I watched the madam and my wife embrace for one final time. Ivy stood on tiptoes and kissed me softly on the cheek.

"Be careful, Ty," she whispered. "Distrust can be the greatest loneliness."

We waited as she stepped into the gilded elevator, and I saw her wink at Jesse as the doors sighed closed.

CHAPTER FORTY-ONE

CRICKET CAME HOME for the holidays, Christmas came and went, and we all maintained a respectful distance from acknowledging the unspoken emptiness that lingered in the atmosphere.

One morning, I was on the back porch using a wooden-handled pick to chip ice off a block when I saw an unfamiliar Jeep Cherokee driving up our road. I waited for the wind to carry the dust away before I walked down the stairs to meet it.

The driver was one of Irene Sheridan's newly hired cowboys. He touched two fingers to his hat brim as a way of acknowledging me as I crossed over to the passenger side to open Irene's door.

"Planning a New Year's party?" Irene asked as she got out.

"Chipping ice for the ice cream churner," I said. "Family tradition."

She was dressed in slacks and a freshly pressed print blouse that she left open at the neck to reveal a simple turquoise necklace and a pair of matching post earrings on her ears.

"Looks like you're dressed up for the city," I said. "Come on inside. Jesse and Cricket are making pie. They'd love to see you."

Irene smiled, but in a way that didn't look the same as before, and I was certain she classified her life in that way too, in terms of *before* and *after*.

"Thank you, Ty, but I'm on my way to Salem. I have some documents to record before year's end."

"Buying or selling?" I asked, and regretted the insensitivity of my question the moment it crossed my lips.

She ignored my gaffe in the unaffected and genteel manner that I'd always known in her, showed me her melancholy smile again, and looked off in the direction of the dry creek.

"BLM renewed our grazing lease," she said. "But it has to record before December 31."

"Cutting it a little close."

"Appears to be a pattern in my life."

This time, we both ignored the irony, and I was left to wonder why she had driven so far out of her way to see me.

"I heard the good news about your deputy," she said. "I hear he's gone home from the hospital."

The sniper's bullet had entered beneath the base of Jordan's skull, missed his spine by mere millimeters, and taken a trajectory out through his jawbone. It had cost him some fine motor skills, and he had months of rehab ahead of him, but he'd come out of his coma, and he was alive.

"He's staying with his fiancée while he recovers," I said. "He's a very lucky young man, all in all."

I could see something new in Irene Sheridan, a sense of resolve growing inside the shadows of her grief.

"I owe you an apology, Tyler," she said, "for the way that I behaved before."

"KC was one of the best ones, ma'am. One of the best ones that I've ever known."

I took both of her hands in mine and squeezed gently, felt a new strength in them as she squeezed mine in return.

"I really do wish you'd come inside for a piece of pie," I said. "If only for a minute."

I DROVE home from the substation later that afternoon beneath an uncluttered sky, the hills bathed in plum-colored light. I had more than half-expected some level of guilt to reach out to me, or at least some kind of longing for atonement. But neither of those things ever happened. There is still a chance they might catch up to me later, perhaps when I'm an old man, or as I draw my dying breath, or maybe as I'm branding my cattle in the springtime inside an open pasture marbled by drifting cloud shadows.

Or perhaps it wasn't worth thinking about at all, that some choices are simply made under circumstances and by forces for which there are no explanations. I could live with that.

Beyond the long rise in the road, I could see the light shining inside the recreation room behind the church Jesse and I regularly attended. I pulled into the lot, parked, and went inside. Pastor Dunn, Monsignor Turner, and two others whom I had seen before, but whose names I did not know, were seated at a folding card table they'd set up beside a time-blemished upright piano.

"I saw your light was on," I said. "Thought I'd drop in and say hello."

Pastor Dunn laid his cards face down and stood to shake my hand.

"We've missed you at services, Ty," he said. "When will we see you and Jesse again?"

"Soon."

"Sit down and join us," Monsignor Turner said. "We're just finishing a hand of hearts. We'll deal you in for the next game."

I thanked them both, waved away the offer, and turned for the door. I heard the Monsignor follow me outside.

"Thanks for not ratting me out," I said.

He smiled and his attention grazed the basilica across the street.

"Discretion is my business," he said, turning his eyes back on me. "Are you going to be okay?"

I nodded and tucked my hands into the pockets of my coat. The way he studied me made me uncomfortable, as though he could read my thoughts.

"Why is it that the commission of great evil is so easy," he said, "and the construction of true works of greatness so hard?"

A flock of starlings flew in from an open field, shape shifting in overhead patterns before roosting in the trees. The noise they made sounded like rushing water. I opened the door to my truck and looked back at the Monsignor as I climbed inside the cab.

"The offer still stands," he said. "To hear your confession."

"I'm good for now."

"*Vaya con Dios,*" he said.

"Same to you, Padre."

EARLY THE next morning, I saddled Drambuie and Jesse's favorite horse, a dun-colored mare she'd named Firefly, and strapped saddlebags behind the cantles of both saddles. We rode a trail that wound between the trunks of old growth conifers, and made a picnic where the river forked, in the shadows of laurel and juniper. I watched a dorsal fin score the flat water that pooled behind a deadfall stump that had slid into the river along with a section of the bank.

We talked as I built a fire ringed by lichen covered rocks, listened to the pulse and rhythm of the river as it coursed over the bed of smooth stones, and shaped our idle thoughts into iambic cadences. We spread a blanket across a flat spot in a boulder that had been warmed by the sun, took our time with one another between intimate silences, and didn't return to the ranch until dusk.

EPILOGUE

THE WHEEL

THE NEW YEAR had come and gone, and a week later, I found myself at the train station seeing Cricket off again for her return to Colorado. As always, the parting was bittersweet and left me longing after lost time.

It was late, moonless and dark when I returned home, and I could feel the wistful emptiness of Cricket's absence from the moment I walked in the door. Jesse had already gone to bed, but the remnants of a fire still lingered in the fireplace. I placed an applewood log on the embers and sat down near the hearth with an old favorite book. I turned to the story of Prometheus and began to read, but soon found my mind wandering. It had been a season of loss and heartbreak, and a sense of theft of a part of our collective innocence was suspended over the entire valley that winter.

I tried to return to my book, read a few pages, but soon found myself drifting again.

AS A YOUNG man, after college, I enlisted in the army and graduated from officer candidate school at Fort Benning. I served as a captain in the military police and participated in some of the most hellish battles the modern world had ever conceived. I have never shared the stories from this part of my life with Jesse, though she endures my periodic nightmares with a stoicism that can only be borne out of love. Only men like my deputies Jordan Powell and Sam Griffin, veterans of the heat of battle, can know what it is like, and for the most part, we bear our private knowledge in silence.

It is said that war is made up of long stretches of boredom punctuated by moments of ass-puckering terror. I also found this to be true. When in Indian country, one learns to cherish silence, if and when it ever arrives.

For me, when it did, I took comfort in reading, having developed a life-long fascination with ancient mythology, a subject to which I have returned frequently over the years. Among the stories that intrigued me most was that of Prometheus, a tale of hubris, hauteur, and contempt. It was a tale that turned out to have far more significance in my life than I could ever have anticipated.

THERE IS a coda to the story of Prometheus.

He was punished for his hubris not with death, but with eternal torment, shackled to the ground as vultures tore away his entrails and devoured his organs.

Against the will of Zeus, Prometheus had given man knowledge of fire, though he tried to warn man to handle it with caution, lest it destroy their lives.

But when Zeus looked down from Olympus and saw that man had learned to harness its power to cook meat, to craft torches to light the darkness, and to build great structures, cities and towns and sailing ships, Zeus was infuriated. Prometheus may have given man the forbidden gift of fire, Zeus reasoned, but man himself had proven willful enough to accept it.

Zeus' first inclination was to obliterate mankind, but ultimately decided it would be more entertaining to allow man to bring about his own punishment. To this end, he commissioned the finest artisans to craft a magnificently ornamented box, one more beautiful than had ever been seen before. When it was finished, he gave it to Pandora with the admonition that it must never be opened.

Pandora adored her new treasure, kept it near to her always, where she could admire it and speculate on its contents. Over time, however, curiosity weighed heavily, and before long it was all she could think about, her obsession eventually becoming so great she encircled it in chains and buried it deep in the ground. But even this stratagem proved insufficient, and one night, in a fit of furious compulsion, Pandora dug it out of the hard soil with her bare hands, leaving them abraded and bleeding, fingernails torn out from their beds.

She gazed at the container with an emotion bordering lust. *Surely if the outside of the box is this beautiful,* she told herself, *its contents must be even more so.*

As she opened the lid, she was assailed by a foul odor and the noises of great rustling inside. As she held the box up to the light, horrific creatures with reptilian scales, red eyes, and ratlike claws swarmed out through the opening on fleshy bat wings and circled her head, taunting and jeering before they disappeared into the night.

Pandora sank to her knees, terrified, and tried with all her strength to refasten the lid. When she finally succeeded, Pandora saw that she had trapped only the last one of the beasts; all the rest had escaped and flown free. She thrust the lone creature back into the box and locked it up tightly again, after which she dropped it to the ground and fainted dead away.

When she awakened, it became clear that what she had unleashed from the magnificent container were all the ills and calamities that would beset mankind forever onward; old age and sorrow, famine and insanity, and all the countless ailments and pestilences that would be loosed upon the world, invading every household, affecting every family. The beasts would forever hang down from their rafters, laying in wait.

But the one single creature that Pandora had managed to keep captive would have made the others all the worse, and was perhaps the most insidious of all.

I HEARD Jesse come out from our bedroom, wearing a pair of my flannel pajamas and an Indian blanket draped across her shoulders, her eyes reflecting the dwindling light inside the fireplace.

"The snow stopped," she said softly. "It got so quiet."

I put down my book and crossed over to her, took her in my arms. I buried my face in the crook of her neck and inhaled the lavender scent on her skin.

"Step outside with me," I said. "Just for a minute. I wouldn't mind hearing a little silence before I turn in."

She followed me out onto the gallery, and we settled in close together on the glider. I pulled the Indian blanket tight over the two of us and gazed out across the new-fallen snow. A barn owl called out inside the deep woods, and a soft gust moved among the high limbs and died away.

"So, what now, Ty?" Jesse whispered. "What changes now that it's all over?"

I knew it to be the question that had been heavy on her heart since our daughter had returned to school, but she'd left it unspoken until this moment.

My mind drifted back to the story I had just finished reading and the single calamity that Pandora had managed to keep contained, the one that mankind had been spared.

The name of that lone captive beast was Foreknowledge. And had it been allowed to escape with all the others, humankind would have been made aware of each and every forthcoming adversity, every future misfortune, hardship, and affliction that awaited us, tormenting every waking moment of our lives.

So, having been spared this indignity, we humans have managed to live side by side with uncertainty ever since, learned to adapt to our unknowing fate. Some would say we've even flourished.

I turned to face Jesse, studied the angles of a face that had become the centerpiece of my life for the past two decades. I kissed her gently and answered her as honestly as I knew how.

"I don't know what happens next, Jesse," I said. "But I know that as long as there is uncertainty in this life, hope lives right there alongside of it."

ACKNOWLEDGMENTS

As always, to my family for their endless supply of enthusiasm, love, and rein-forcement: Christina, Allegra, Britton, Christan, Nick, Ashton, Kheler, Liam and Declynn . . . Aloha pau ole.

Grateful thanks to my agent, Peter Riva, who made it happen and helped bring Ty Dawson all the way from my head and into the bookstores. You are not only a true professional, you have become a trusted friend; and to Mara Anastas and all the great professionals at Open Road Media for being in my corner. I couldn't be more fortunate or grateful that you're all on my team.

And to my writer friends for whom I am profoundly grateful for your posi-tivity, energy, humor, and friendship, you truly are my Tribe. You know who you are. A special note of gratitude to Bruce Robert Coffin, Reavis Z. Wortham, and Patrick Milliken for the early reads of the manuscript.

Now, before anyone starts sending me emails busting my chops about elec-tronic "red-dot" LED gun sights, the first ones were commercially marketed by Swedish optics company Aimpoint AB in early 1975. It combined a curved mirror and a light-emitting diode mounted on a telescopic sight, and was based on a design by a Heisenberg engineer. Other manufacturers promptly followed. So, yeah, they existed at the time.

I have, however, taken certain (minor) literary liberties with a couple of loca-tions in downtown Portland, purely for creative reasons.

A note regarding the soundtrack: As usual, the section titles provide the backbone of the soundtrack to the book, and in this case, almost all are by the Grateful Dead. "Transitive nightfall of diamonds" is part of the lyric to "Dark Star" by the Grateful Dead. For soundtrack purposes, the version of that song to which I was referring when I wrote the book was from the album *Live/Dead* (1969); Similarly, "no simple highway" is a lyric from "Ripple" by the Grateful Dead. The rest of the titles should be self-explanatory. Also, as usual, there were a couple more songs that I was listening to as I was writing that didn't make it into the book: "Just Call My Name" by Poco; and "As Falls Wichita So Falls Wichita Falls" by Pat Metheny. I hope you enjoy!

Until next time, "may the four winds blow you safely home . . ."

CODE OF THE WEST

1. Live each day with courage
2. Take pride in your work
3. Always finish what you start
4. Do what has to be done
5. Be tough, but fair
6. When you make a promise, keep it
7. Ride for the brand
8. Talk less and say more
9. Remember that some things aren't for sale
10. Know where to draw the line

—Author Unknown

ABOUT THE AUTHOR

Baron Birtcher spent a number of years as a professional musician, and founded an independent record label and management company. His first two novels, *Roadhouse Blues* and *Ruby Tuesday*, are *Los Angeles Times* and Independent Mystery Booksellers Association bestsellers. Birtcher has been nominated for a number of literary awards, including the Nero Award for his novel *Hard Latitudes*, the Claymore Award for his novel *Rain Dogs*, and the Left Coast Crime "Lefty" Award for his novel *Angels Fall*. He was the 2016 Silver Falchion Award winner for his novel *Hard Latitudes* and the 2018 Winner of the Killer Nashville Reader's Choice Award for his novel *South California Purples*. Birtcher currently divides his time between Portland, Oregon, and Kona, Hawaii.

THE TY DAWSON MYSTERIES

FROM OPEN ROAD MEDIA

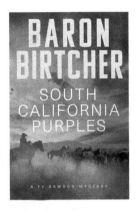 

 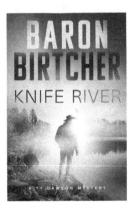

INTEGRATED MEDIA

Find a full list of our authors and
titles at www.openroadmedia.com

FOLLOW US
@OpenRoadMedia